Words
to
Shape
My
Name

Advance praise for
Words to Shape My Name

'Beautifully written and brilliantly controlled, this story of friendship and courage never drops a stitch. *Words to Shape My Name* intrigues from start to finish and has to be among the very best of novels in 2021.' —*Christine Dwyer Hickey*

'An ambitious and vital novel with an epic sweep: a complex, timely story about liberty, equality, identity. With acute intelligence, Laura McKenna has focused on a marginalised figure who is a unique witness to events that make nations. No longer at the margin, Tony Small is now the centre of his own story. This book is an act of salvage, performed with great skill: cleanly written, sharp-eyed, undeceived.' —*Hilary Mantel*

'Laura McKenna's first novel is a deeply intelligent mosaic about the nature of freedom and the lineage of hope. *Words to Shape My Name* unspools a complex story in a daring and ambitious style reminiscent of Joseph O'Connor and Hilary Mantel. By turns demanding, lucid and poignant, it sets out to unravel the mysteries of belonging. McKenna's debut is the song of a writer who is here to stay.' —*Colum McCann*

'A sophisticated novel, abundant with competing voices, bringing the rich, raw revolutionary world of the late 18th century to life. Laura McKenna writes with elegance and wit. *Words to Shape My Name* is as accomplished as Mantel, as humane as Heaney.' —*Mary Morrissy*

'A powerful historical fiction debut.' —*Joseph O'Connor*

'Arresting and absorbing from start to finish, a remarkable debut.' —*Eibhear Walshe*

Words to Shape My Name

LAURA McKENNA

NEW ISLAND

WORDS TO SHAPE MY NAME
First published in 2021 by
New Island Books
Glenshesk House
10 Richview Office Park
Clonskeagh
Dublin D14 V8C4
Republic of Ireland
www.newisland.ie

Print ISBN: 978-1-84840-795-4
eBook ISBN: 978-1-84840-796-1

Edited by Susan McKeever
Proofread by Meg Walker
Typeset by JVR Creative India
Cover design by Kate Gaughran, kategaughranbooks.com
Printed by ScandBook, scandbook.com

New Island received financial assistance from The Arts Council (An Chomhairle Ealaíon), Dublin, Ireland

New Island Books is a member of Publishing Ireland

Novel Fair: an Irish Writers Centre initiative

For Íomhar. Grá agus buíochas.

I

must be given words to shape my name
to the syllables of trees

I

must be given words to refashion futures
like a healer's hand ...

It is not
it is not
it is not enough
to be pause, to be hole
to be void, to be silent
to be semicolon, to be semicolony; ...

—Edward Kamau Brathwaite, *Negus* (1969)

For a people who have endured a long, long history of waiting ... silence is an old familiar companion. Time and silence. Silence and time. The silence attending waiting, waiting through times of enforced silence. Silence the ground upon which wishes are inscribed while the endless waiting continues.

—John Edgar Wideman, *In Praise of Silence* (2003)

I
BEGINNINGS

Miss Wellington, Miss Harriet Pamela Small, Mrs Marquess, Mrs Miss Hattie, Mrs Bloew, Songbird, Black Spur, Hattie, Miss Harriet Pamela Fricker, Hattie Fricker, Sable Songbird, Black Spur, Hattie, Mrs Bloew, Mrs Harriet Pamela Small, Harriet, Miss Harriet Pamela Small, Hattie

May is a month what I hold in particular fondness after the gloom and damp of winter has passed. London offers little cheer during those earlier dark months and I look forward to my journey through the countryside and my visit to Baaba's grave. So last week, I took a Hansom cab outside Euston Station as was my habit. The driver accepted my price once I told him I'd made the journey every year for the past twenty and knew better than he how far and how much and it would serve him ill to talk of half-mile fares and time spent standing, for I could just as easy give my custom to the next man, whose horse looked a deal livelier than his, and would likely do it for less than a pound. He raised both his hands in a gesture of defeat.

We passed straight through Wimbledon and on to St Mary's. I instructed the driver to take himself and his cab some distance hence for I had no wish that he should sit up there, looking down on my comings and goings, he being a cold sort, darkly whiskered and darkly dressed, in the manner of drivers who think they're gentlemen when they are no such thing.

I made for the far boundary wall, to my parents' grave, marked not by any stonemason's handiwork, but a metal cross, fashioned by myself from some ironmongery what came my way. Nothing fancy, only two spiralled bars wrapped tight with string on which I'd once chalked their names. But the rain is no observer of such formalities. I knelt to straighten the cross, and saw a peep of yellow nodding above the grass.

Cowslips. I'm most partial to them, and mayflower. Cowslips for their lowly beauty and the soft fuzz of their necks.

The sun were beginning to warm the ground and I sat there waiting, waiting for a sign. And all the while my fingers worried the grass and delved into the claggy earth beneath. A black crow perched on a broken headstone nearby, stretched out one wing like a widow's fan and reached under it to tidy and trim himself. Never cawed nor made a sound. A shadow crossed my heart. The jackdaw's feathers flared suddenly, and my eye were snagged by it. A breeze, I thought, struggling to my feet, while the bird struggled to take to the air, all aflap and afluster. The sky were overrun by a rabble of clouds. I heard the hedgerows seesaw, branch on branch, thorn on thorn and the weather vane screeched round sharp to the west. And there it was, the scatter of mayflower blossom.

Now you may think it strange for a woman of my years, being almost sixty, to stand atop a grave, with her arms thrown wide and her eyes closed and her head flung back, while the mayflower shakes out her petals but so it was I received again the blessing of those white blossoms, their touch gentle, their smell familiar and dusty. An Sceach Gheal my Ma used to call it, in her Gaelic tongue, though she never cared for it, being superstitious for such things.

The jack-chat calls of the birds scattered my rememberings and I opened my eyes to see them circling above me, three of them, smuts blown about by the breeze. And then that cough, that sound, ahem.

Excuse my impertinence but I wonder if I have the pleasure of addressing the daughter of a Mr Anthony Small.

I turned – sharp mind – to see a scrawny man swamped under the weight of a thick coat, woollen muffler and felt hat, though Lord knows the weather hardly called for such. I took a step back, near stumbled over Baaba's resting place. The man reached for my arm and steadied me.

I must apologise. Miss Small. It is Miss Small, is it not.

His cheeks were pink with what looked like excitement, though perhaps he weren't used to exertion.

What's it to you, I may have said.

Oh. It is you. I'm certain of it. I can hardly believe it. He clapped his hands together. Oh this is too, too good. What a happy occurrence.

I don't mind saying my first thoughts were that my bastard husband, gone near thirty years, had sent someone after me. Looking for a stake in my house in Euston Grove. I started to walk away, heading for the safety of the church.

You leave me alone, I said. Tell him he'll not get a brass farthing out of me.

He had no trouble keeping pace with me. No, no. Please Miss Small. I don't know this man you speak of. I have been sent by another. A Lady Lucy Foley. You may have known her as Lady Lucy Fitzgerald.

That stopped me in my tracks. His face fizzed with delight.

Lady Lucy Fitzgerald. Was she still alive. Perhaps he could tell my thoughts.

She died six years ago.

I turned from him.

Wait, he called after me. She left detailed instructions. A kind of treasure hunt. In reverse. Please allow me to introduce myself. His legs crossed and dipped like a fold-up washstand. It seemed he was attempting to bow. He had my attention then.

I am Mr John Butler. Solicitor. Of Tooley Street, Borough. His voice scooped up at the end as if in a question.

How did you find me ... how did you—

Oh but I've been searching. You seem to shed your name each time you move.

But just now, how did you—

Pardon me, but I guessed you to be the daughter of Mr Anthony Small, he being a black man, and you ... well, also black. And today being the anniversary of his death. Last year the verger mentioned a lady such as you had visited and I alas, too late, too late. I hoped against hope that you might visit on this day again, and that this year I might find you.

He paused, removing his hat, one bone-thin hand appearing from his over-long sleeve. His pale blue eyes swam over me.

Where's the harm, I thought, extending my hand to his.

Ain't it strange how time can be squeezed backwards, to when you was a child, just by the slightest thing – a snatch of a song, the smooth warmth of a wooden toy, the way an apple may tumble from a cart and roll just so. Or the smell of ink on paper. Baaba's ink, on his papers, what he wrote himself. That whiff of pickled walnuts were a potion, pulling me into the past, away from the dark panelled office, and Mr Butler fussing with papers on his hulking desk, and talking of bequests, and land deeds. Instead I were picturing my Baaba, sitting at his table – a half moon it were called, lovely – his quill in hand, waiting for his memories to walk past the window or tap on the pane. My Baaba, for so I called my father and that, not like all the other names he were given, that at least were at his own bidding. Baaba's quill scratching across the paper, each word bringing a bead of sweat to his brow, a tremor to his hand.

A clock doled out the time. Six dongs. Its face was smug and pale behind the glass. I lifted one of the sheets of paper that sat on my lap and pressed my nose to it, breathed in the dusty past of it. That must have been one of the last batches of ink that he made.

A drawer were scraped opened. I looked up. Mr Butler took out an envelope, placed it on the desk in front of him with a fussy flicker of his fingers. I made no remark, just continued to look through some of the pages what he'd given me earlier. My Baaba's papers. Written a half century before. I couldn't take it all in. Them words, his words, inked on the paper.

Tap, tap. He were tapping the bloody envelope now.

Miss Small, I beg your pardon, but if I may …

Well, now you've started, you may as well say what you have to say.

His eyes swirled large behind his spectacles. He offered to read through my Baaba's papers with me. Said he could explain them. Given that the writing might present a challenge to me and ahem, he cleared his throat, that some of the language, being old-fashioned, may need, ahem again, a small amount of simplification and whatnot.

There's no need for your help, I told him, while getting to my feet. I am perfectly capable of reading.

I smiled at him then for really he were not the worst of his kind. Oh, he begged my pardon, regretted his presumption, said as how it

was not on account of my … Then he stopped. Couldn't bring himself
to go on and his pale face fired up.

Don't fuss yourself, Mr Butler, said I. Sure how could you know
anything about me, save what you see of me and hear me say.

He dipped his head, pleaded with me to indulge him in one whim.

Please. Allow me to read aloud Lady Lucy's final letter. She dictated it
to me shortly before she died. Her sight, you know, was almost gone.

He rubbed his eyes at this, then turned to light two of them fancy
gas lamps, and while they hissed and flickered he plucked a letter from
the envelope. I saw it were trimmed in black.

He coughed, adjusted his spectacles and began to read.

> Château de Belle Vue, Marseilles, France
> 1851

Dear Harriet,

I am tempted to call you Ettie as that is how I think of
you, but you have most likely left that childish name behind
and would not recognise it. Over the years, amid much sorrow,
The Lord has always been my guide and I am entrusting
these papers to Him that they may find you. I have sought the
assistance of Mr Butler in this task. He has proved his worth to
me in the past and I know he will do his very best.

I believe apologies should be brief. Anything more is self-
indulgence. I am sorry you and your family were ill-served by
mine, and that your father's loyalty was so carelessly dismissed.
Please accept these papers and accompanying deeds and notes
as an act of heartfelt repentance and reparation.

It gives me ease to think of you reading them. I picture you
as you were, a wide-eyed joyful little girl. I pray that some of that
joy still rests in you.

I will not trespass any longer on your time other than to
assure you of my regard and affection.

May God bless you,

Lady Lucy Foley

He peered over the letter, looking anxious. Well.

Fine enough words as words go, I expect. Mind you, there ain't an awful lot of them.

He seemed encouraged by my remarks and bustled around behind his desk.

Perhaps you would like to know the context of your father's writing. What you are holding in your hands there, is his Narrative. His account of his life as a slave – though perhaps not so much – and after, when he was saved by Lord Edward Fitzgerald during the terrible Independence Wars in America. Of course Lord Edward was a loyal British soldier then.

His voice trailed off and sucked in through his lips. Yes well. Then of course he returned to Ireland and England with Lord Edward for a master. Free of course.

I tried to interrupt, save him the bother of all his speechifying, told him I knew all this already. But once he had the bit between his teeth, it were hard to stop Mr Butler.

Such a man, Lord Edward. You do not know …

He paused to look at me over the top of his spectacles, a gesture what got my hackles up. You may not know that Lady Lucy added a codicil to her will, and explained how she persuaded your father to write about her brother, Lord Edward Fitzgerald, master to your—

My father worked for him. He were a gentleman's servant. Almost a companion.

Indeed, indeed. Mr Butler had turned pink again. He ran his hand over his head.

Poor, tragic Lord Edward. So beloved of all who knew him. Your father too, I expect?

I nodded, thinking of the stories I had heard from Baaba. Why, even Ma spoke fondly of him back then. Mind you …

Ma always said as how my father had saved himself.

Mr Butler settled back in his chair, behind his cluttered desk. He'd kept his muffler about his neck and his hands strayed to it, worrying at the knot.

Yes well. Perhaps you are not aware of the true reason for the endeavour. It was not what it seemed. Not to encourage your father to write of his experience of slavery but rather to present His Lordship ...

His fingers flicked up and down as he struggled to find a word.

I know what it were about, I said. The Family wanted to present Lord Edward in a pretty light, not as a traitor, so they could get all his confiscated money and land back. I know.

Mr Butler shuddered. Don't use that word I beg you, he was never a traitor. That ruling was overturned.

But I'd had my fill of Mr Butler's misty-eyed tales and told him so.

Lord Edward organised a rebellion in Ireland and if that don't make him a traitor, well what does. Not that I care. All I care about is that when my father died, he'd not received one brass farthing of what he were owed by that Family. Not a farthing. And that's in spite of all his years of work, and the effort of writing what cut his life even shorter. And none of the Fitzgerald family, not the old Duchess nor the new Duke neither, saw fit to recompense him.

The blood rose in my chest and my heart squeezed tight but I couldn't stop.

So it's a bit late don't you think for Lady Lucy to come over all a-jitter on her deathbed with her talk of God and send her, her ... you out to find me and do what was right by me.

He shrank back, tut-tutting under his breath.

Don't say that, please, he urged again. She was the fairest of her sex, a true Lady, noble and charitable.

Saintly, said I.

Why yes, that's exactly what—

He caught sight of my expression and pressed his lips in a thin line. Forgive me, perhaps I am a sentimentalist. I was so caught up in the story. Tragic Lord Edward and his Dear Little Wife. Lady Pamela. So beautiful. To be widowed at such an age. And of course your Father. Poor Tony.

I were forced to interrupt.

It's easy to be sentimental about things what got nothing to do with you, said I.

He blinked twice at that but I know his kind who like to claim even a distant connection with titled people long-dead and fancy it enough to bestow a lick of polish on them.

You may think you knows something from reading words, may even think it's the truth but the Truth is altogether different.

My breath were in my fist as I spoke and the gas lamps hissed back at me. But I kept on.

It's like a Queen of Puddings, I said, or a Plum Duff. Words is just some of the ingredients. But then it gets mixed up and cooked, and ends up looking and tasting nothing like what went into it in the first place.

Miss Small, says he, shaking his head from side to side though I could not tell if he were annoyed or amused. Miss Small, he said, I'd quail at the thought of meeting you as an adversary in a court room.

Well, then, I said and stopped, for in truth I were a bit flustered by all this talk about Baaba and Lord Edward, and by talking so sharp and with such feeling and though I wanted to ask questions about the rest of the will, I needed to be gone, to be by myself, to think without Mr Butler's moist gaze upon me. I'll be off, says I, bundling the papers into a box.

He held the door for me, begged me to return as soon as I had completed my perusal of the documents.

Then we can discuss the provisions of the will.

24th May, 1857
A carriage ride to Manchester Square

Lady Lucy wrote she still thought of me as Ettie. That were my first and dearest name. Ettie Small, and I just a young child with love about me. Names matter. The one you go by, what others may call you, and how you sees yourself. Some speak of tenderness, and some serve to bind you. I lost the name Ettie at eighteen when I became Mrs Harriet Fricker. A mistake. Names just give a quick inkling of a person, but still they matter. Perhaps that's why my father had me call him Baaba. Said it was of his people. Never said who they was though nor where they come from. Ma insisted I call her Ma, not being of his people, as anyone with two eyes could see. I've been branded with many names, some mean and cheap and others I were flattered by. Names what showed but a tiny part of me, one that were true perhaps for a moment, but were never the whole of me. One such name was writ on a playbill, stuck up outside the music hall in Camden Town. *The Sable Songbird.* That were a long time ago. Least I only had to sing then.

Since last week, I've been shuffling through Baaba's papers, making fluttery piles of them on the table in my front parlour. I own I'm finding it difficult to make sense of them, not that I'd give Mr Butler the satisfaction of knowing. Some things is best left unsaid. It's also a bit queer, them faded black lines, because I know the page is silent, his writing mute but I swear I can hear his voice when I read. Or someone's voice for it's sometimes familiar and sometimes not. Gives me a squirmy feeling. Unsettled like. So I've started to write my thoughts down, odd gubbins of memory what have come back to me, like the day Baaba was summoned by Lady Lucy. I know my hand ain't up to much. Not like my Baaba's, his being long and smooth and marked by curls and other faldedaddles. My hand is rough and spiky—

Still I make no apology for it. It's served me well over the years.

Air Street in Piccadilly were busy of a morning back then, when the century were but a few years old and I not much older, so I paid no heed to the grumble of the carriage and the snorts of horses drawing up outside, nor ever imagined that the man with the ruffles and buckles who called were a footman, come for my father.

I have a note for Tony Small. His lips hardly moved at all. From Lady Lucy Foley, Lady Fitzgerald that was. She has asked me to wait upon his reply.

Has she now. I expected to see Ma spitting out pins. She snapped the paper from his gloved hand. Told the man she'd take the note to Mr Small herself. Pressed the word *mister* hard and hissy, like she were brandishing the flatiron.

The workshop were choked with steam and vinegar. One of the copper vats were bubbling, and the whole tangle of tubing shook. Baaba frowned when Ma and I entered but she paid no heed, pressing the note on him. He broke the seal and walked to the window, rubbing the pane, the better to read it. Poor Ma were twisting her hands in her apron, all in a fluster. I think Baaba read slow on purpose.

What does she want, is it about the money. Are we finally to receive our due.

Baaba shook his head from side to side, the letter open in his hand. I could see there weren't much writing on it.

She says nothing about any of that. Just that she has a proposal to make to me in person, and has sent the carriage that I may attend upon her immediately.

I tugged at Ma's hand but she folded her arms. So after all this time, and all your letters, she demands you come to her just as soon as she bids.

What would you have me do, Julia. I must go. Hear her out.

You'll take Ettie then, Ma said, spitting on both her palms and rubbing them through my hair, pressing so hard I thought once more of the iron.

Let her see for herself.

The house sat on the corner of a square, tall and white, with two pillars to the front. I skipped up the steps with Baaba following through the door which opened magically before us. After what seemed an age, we was brought up a curving staircase to a room on the next floor. The footman could scarce bring himself to look at Baaba, and didn't trouble himself to look at me at all, just held the door open and called out. Mr Tony Small, Your Ladyship.

I have little account to give of what passed in that room. Lady Lucy talked and so did Baaba but my ears were deaf to their words. My eyes were trapped by my inspection of the Lady. Her dress were of the finest cloth. Green of a kind I'd not seen before, mossy I think and trimmed at the hem and waist in a blue, like a fly's wings. She wore a shawl in the same stuff, just set across her pale arms like it were spun sugar. Her hair were a bit like Ma's in colour, almost red but darker, like the ale Baaba sometimes drank and it were piled in soft ringlets that shook ever so gently whenever her voice rose.

She does stare, does she not, she said, eyeing me calmly.

Baaba touched my arm, murmured. Ettie.

Ettie, said she. I remember you as a little baby. In Kildare. She turned to Baaba. Of course, she can hardly remember Ireland.

He shook his head, No Milady.

She was always a lovely little thing. Come Ettie, let me look at you.

I stood before her and it was her turn to examine me. She took my hand in hers. Should you like to draw or paint, she asked. I shook my head. I wanted only to stay and feast my eyes on her and the room.

Young girls are such gulls for beauty and everything about her seemed beautiful. I see it all the time, how they are drawn to pretty things like mice to sprung traps. Perhaps they hope some might rub off on them, or they can fossick among the crumbs and scents that beauty leaves behind.

She gave me a spinning top, said it belonged to her niece, who most likely wouldn't miss it and I should play with it, in the hall with the maid. It were beautiful, painted with white horses what seemed to run faster and faster as it twirled. When I finished playing I brought it back in and left it on Baaba's lap. Then I explored the room, trailing my fingers along a cold marble table. Staring at a horrible gold clock squatting on top, surrounded by fat babies wearing nothing but little wings. Tripping over to a golden mirror, jumping to catch a glimpse of myself. Only managed see a few curls fly up and down. Baaba called me, told me to sit by him, to take a drink of what the maid had brought for him. I sipped, and squeezed my eyes shut, it were so bitter. The Lady laughed.

Quite a nip to it, she said. It's lemon shrub. She turned back to Baaba. Said something about a proposal. A brilliant idea.

It will help you and … the family.

Baaba placed his glass back on the tray. You mean my family, he asked and the Lady tilted her head to one side.

Yours, she puzzled. Yes, yes. Of course yours. And Edward's.

She got to her feet in a fit of excitement. Asked my Baaba to write an account of his life. I checked to see if he were pleased about this but his forehead were creased and his eyes tight. Lady Lucy went on, words I hadn't heard before. Rebellion. Treason. Attainder. Parliament. Confiscated. Abolitionists. She said as how abolitionists were crying out for such accounts.

Why, you'd be doing your own kind a great service.

All this she says while pacing back and forth on the beautiful damson rug, and her skirts whispering, and her little slippers making hardly a sound at all. I tucked my grubby boots under my chair. She were still waxing on. About Edward. Dear Edward. His good heart. And how he was incapable of treasonous acts, just led by his good heart and by bad men.

What do you say, Tony, she asked and her voice had a little wobble in it, like she might cry. You can tell people how he saved you from the clutches of slavery, how he led you to God and such.

I'll think on it, Baaba said and the Lady smiled at him. I nudged him to smile back but he didn't. Instead he stood and told her we was leaving. He placed the spinning top on his chair. Lady Lucy handed him a bundle. Baaba looked none too pleased at this but he gave a queer little bow. I tried out a curtsey what I'd practised at home, but no one paid me any heed.

I had no inkling then what all the talk were about but I heard so much about it afterwards, listening to Baaba and Ma, Ma all snippy about money, and Baaba all solemn about the Attainder that I feel I've always known these words. I even fancy I remember Lord Edward for I have such a perfect picture of him in my head. But that could be on account of Ma's talk. So much of what she said seems like my own memory. I used to remind her, long after Baaba passed, about Lady Pamela and Lady Lucy sewing their green patriotic emblems on their dresses in Kildare, and she'd look at me, with a queer expression.

Quit your talk, she'd say. You couldn't remember that. You were but a baby.

But when I told her how I remembered her father, and recited how he were shot by a damned redcoat outside the gaol in Naas, and the bastard soldier planting his booted foot atop her poor father's chest, jabbing him again and again with his bayonet, arís agus arís, and his last words uttered as the lifeblood drained from him, Éireann go brágh, Julie, mo stór, my dear, when I said them words, well, Ma looked horrified. Like I were one of them changelings what gets swapped for another woman's child.

That is my story, she cried. Mine. You weren't there. Unborn.

I wasn't there for many happenings yet I can bring them to mind clear as if it were yesterday, and I standing watching. Can't explain it. Maybe I'm a pickpocket for bad memories. Can't tell who owns what story anymore. All of them's mine.

We returned from Lady Lucy's house in a chair. It were nowhere near so exciting as the carriage. The seat were just a hard plank, the window open, the air cold and the two chairmen rough and careless. One of them muttered something about carrying blacks. Baaba were reading a little note and paid no heed. He read it softly, over and over.

My instructions. My instructions. His mouth snagged on the words, like they was stuck in his teeth.

I am to write and she will ensure that any errors of form or memory will be corrected.

I am to write and must not concern myself with too many details or dates for she can refer to her letters and amend the Narrative as necessary.

I am to write. In my own words. As from my own tongue. As I speak them now, *with grave formality*.

Grave formality. In God's name what does she think.

He crunched the piece of paper in his hand and let it fall. He was silent for the rest of the journey. I were glad to clamber out on Air Street again though I made sure to grab the paper from under his seat. I were glad to see Ma in the hallway as I threw off my boots, even if she frowned and asked Baaba what it was he had in his box.

Paper, he replied. Paper and a book.

Are you telling me now she didn't pay you. Ma's eyes were narrow.

Not yet.

Came over all béal bocht, I suppose. Ma peered at him. I said as much. They're as mean as sin.

She brushed down the front of her apron, muttering that something or someone would be the death of her, and she linked her arm under Baaba's where he held the bundle close, and I took his free hand in mine and swishing my stockinged feet across the flagstones, I led them to the warmth of the kitchen.

Ma placed a bowl of broth in front of him and waited for him to talk. Baaba could let silence stretch tight across a whole day if he'd a mind to. But not that day. He showed her the box, the leather-bound sheaf of blank white papers tied with packthread, the clutch of quills. A book.

Ma put her hand on his shoulder. Sure when have you any time for reading? And it's November. What is she thinking, the light so poor, and candles so expensive.

Baaba laughed then. I told her all that, he said. But she insisted I take it. Not to read through exactly, but to *use it as a guide*.

I glanced at the book, opened the cover and saw a black man inside.

Oh, I said. Look Ma, it's like Baaba, but not him.

Ma leaned over me, smelling of onions and lard. Who is it, she asked.

Olaudah Equiano. The greatest of Africans. Baaba were none too excited.

I remember, Ma said. You had the book in Ireland. Mr O'Connor gave it to you. But what's the point of it now.

Lady Lucy imagines I can write as he did. His voice changed, sounded strangely like the Lady's, like he were sucking a sugar comfit. *Think of it as a map, Tony, or signposts. Start at the beginning as he did and*

...follow his tracks. Indeed, you could draw from the wording itself, his way of shaping a sentence.

Ma snatched the empty broth bowl from him. I don't have a notion what you mean. What does she want of you.

To write something like this Narrative. He tapped Equiano's book. A bit about me. Most of it about Edward. She thinks it might help the Family's effort to overturn the Attainder.

Ma flung the bowl and spoon in the tub near the back window, shouting over her shoulder. The Attainder. That word. The English have an official word for everything but 'twere malice alone what caused them to brand Lord Edward a traitor. And him hardly cold in the grave without a means to defend himself or his name. And all so's they could take his land and his children's inheritance like they've been doing to the Irish for three hundred years. But they dress their thievery up in a fancy word and parliament puts a stamp on it. Attainder.

The word were a gob of spit in Ma's mouth. I felt thrilled and scared just to hear her rage on.

They've taken everything from his wife and children. How in God's name could anything you write change that.

Baaba shrugged. Lady Lucy will publish it, and it will change public opinion. She hopes. And she'll pay me for my efforts.

Ma snorted.

Just like they paid you for all your years of service. Like they were supposed to honour Lord Edward's bequest to you.

She were in such a flap, her hair had come loose, and her cheeks were pink. Baaba reached out to her, pulled her into his arms. Their heads were tipped together, and he murmured in his low voice like he were soothing a baby.

What choice do I have, Julia. What choice.

Funny word, choice. The more I turn it over in my head the less I understand it. It's got a plummy sound, like you could almost bite into it. Choice. A word what belongs only to them who's got money. Not my Baaba. He had no choice but to write all that fancy Narrative. Don't sound like him when I read it. Not a smitch like him.

Poor black, Unfortunate black, Poor Tony, Freeman, Mr Tony Small, Wicked Irishman, Retches Citizen, Intruder, Mr Anthony Small, Faithful Tony, Manservant, Tony Small, Mr Tony Small, Wicked Irishman, Retches Citizen

THE TRUE NARRATIVE
of THE MOST
REMARKABLE PARTICULARS of THE LIFE of TONY SMALL,
THE DEVOTED AFRICAN SERVANT
of
LORD EDWARD FITZGERALD

The Author's account of his origins; his terrible enslavement; 1781, the Battle of Eutaw Springs and finding Lieutenant FitzGerald.

This account which I set before you, my indulgent Reader, is written not from any vain hope of literary merit, or for the sympathy of my fellow man, and as such I own it differs from many a history told by men of my hue. Rather, by virtue of its detailing my humble beginnings and enslavement, it will shed light on He who saved me and elevated me to a position of Knowledge and Faith. But I embark upon this venture with trepidation for although fully proficient in English words as they are spoken, and to a degree which often surprises those who are born to it, my hand is less sure, having come later to the Art of the Pen. I must confess I am reluctant to commit any errors of expression or indeed to sully the unrelenting Whiteness of the Page for it casts a very cold light upon me and my attempts to write of my origins. Is it good enough to say I remember only smells of grass, sweet and green; and the smoky comfort of charcoal fires; the warm dung odour of reed baskets, and the meaty tang of a great river? Perhaps not.

In the beginning. In the beginning there was ... What? A land of uncommon riches and fruitfulness, with fertile soil that yielded great abundance. Is this what you expect of me? Ah yes, and that I was born in the year 1760, in a country in Africa. Perhaps of the Igbo people. That's it, isn't it? That's what you'd like. Shall I say my mother was of noble birth, that her father was King of our tribe from the shaded mountains of the North to the lush plains of the South and all along the gleaming rivers to the sea? Shall I tell you how I was raised on the old stories of our people, suckled on the milk of heroic songs? That I ate from the fat of the land, feasted on hunted wild Beasts and the finest most exotic fruits growing in the Forests? Or do you want to hear the tales of gold? Gold plates that we dined on, gold Goblets that we drank from. The many armlets and gold rings with which we decorated our bodies. I shall not tell you these things. You can read them elsewhere, in other Narratives. That is not my beginning.[1]

I must depend upon my Reader's indulgence and trust that when I say my life began some eighteen years or so after my birth, I will be believed. This then is the beginning, the account of a poor ignorant Negro man who had the good fortune to be taken up from the wilderness by a kindly Lord. A Lord in whose heart burned a righteous impulse, a passion for Liberty. Forgive my earlier digressions. They stem from a certain anxiety that I should find myself unable to put before you the Truth artless and unadorned. Bear with me, for this is the account you seek: The True Narrative of the most Remarkable Particulars of the life of Tony Small, the devoted African Servant of Lord Edward FitzGerald.

On the morning of September 8th, 1781, when the earth cracked itself open in loud blasts and crashing trees and, swept on a tide

---

[1] What is this about? Why must you scribble it out? The details of your birth and childhood are expected even if of little consequence. And you really must mention something of the trials of your enslavement. That is the least a sympathetic-minded reader would expect. Lady Lucy Foley.

of blood, I was truly hatched into the world. The occasion was the terrible Battle of Eutaw Springs, one of the last and bloodiest of the Revolutionary War in the Americas. I was a witness to those events and the memory is yet scorched on my mind. From a shelter in scrub, some half a league away, I watched four hours of barbarous fighting. Time itself was shaken as though the hands of the Celestial Clock knew not whether to advance or retreat, such was the power of the explosions and the flashes of gunpowder and fire. Smoke billowed and rose in angry spurts before forming a thick, grey miasma which hung over the entire scene. The sounds were terrible. Men's voices: shouting orders, screaming, loud cries as the wounded fell; horses whinnying in high-pitched terror; trees cracking, branches thudding to earth; the clashing of metal blades; and blast after blast of muskets and rifles.

Once or twice the fighting came near me, horses' hooves beating up the hillside. I heard the slap of leather on flesh, the clink of stirrups, of swords, and the heaving breaths of animal and rider. At some point, the hands of the clock folded together, and the big guns stopped firing. The rifles slowed to occasional cracks. Then ceased. Voices quietened. The sun remained. Hot and suffocating.

Hours passed. The sun began to slip past its peak. Hunger gnawed in my belly. My throat was dry. I ventured down the slope, seeking the cover of the trees as best I could. The gurgle of running water in the creek was birdsong to my ears. Pushing through the dense wattle, thinking only of my thirst, I paid no heed to the other sound, a low humming which set the very leaves of trees to quaking. I dropped to my knees by a fallen branch at the creek's edge, and scooped up handfuls of water to my parched mouth. Too late I noticed the black drape of flies rise in a hellish frenzy. Not a branch beside me but a corpse. The dead man's head, glowing in a snatch of sunlight, was flung back in the creek, his mouth agape, his chin pocked and stubbled, the water swirling around his hair. His bloodied hands were crossed over his jacket as though he died in the act of buttoning it up. The flies descended again, like a black mourning sheet.

I ran, forging on through the scrub that bounded the stream, my face and arms lashed by low-hanging branches, my bare feet scourged by stones and roots until I plunged into the open. There the sun was softening in its afternoon descent. It flickered on the wing tips of the circling vultures, a strange daub of beauty on those auguries of death. Their carrion covered the field, in a tumble of corpses, men and horses, ruined carts. Sunlight polished the blood-rusted edges of fallen bayonets, the grimy buttons of crushed uniforms. All was light and moving shadow. Flies. The field and woods throbbed with their insistent hum as they clustered on open wounds, blasted faces, shattered limbs – rising and descending as one, like a dark spirit. I picked my way among the dead, tried to ignore the flies' gritty drone, reciting an incantation to myself: Rest now O Spirits, thy journey ended.

I could not comprehend how they could leave their dead, piled three or four deep, in undignified disarray, fodder for vultures and crows, feast for flies. Every man deserves a burial, a passage to the other side. But abandoned they were. And some wore boots yet. Boots that they no longer needed, whereas I was barefoot. I set my sights on those belonging to a dead Militia man, who lay atop a heap of bodies. The unfortunate soul was grey as the gunpowder that stained his fingers, but his boots, plain countryman's apparel, would suit my needs. The first boot came without much effort. The second required more force. Sweat rose on my forehead. I braced myself to pull harder, planted my foot on one of the bodies beneath and pulled the boot free. The bootless corpse tumbled from the heap. Two vultures, some distance off, swivelled around at this sudden movement. One fanned out his wings as though about to take flight, then folded them back, hooked his head in and resumed the task that nature had assigned him.

My body chilled despite the heat of the day. This place was not the work of nature or God. It was the evil spirit of men who caused this bloodshed. I turned to leave. The boots would suffice. I would take no more from the dead.

A sound then. Like water on a fire's embers. A hiss of breath. A word.

'Please.'

A cold trembling seized me but some higher Power steadied my fears, strengthened my hands such that I overcame the reek and smears of butchery, and I pulled the dead off, dragged them aside, to deliver the living one beneath.

Buttons and braiding. A soldier. A boy soldier, gulping snatches of air, struggling to raise himself, hand flailing for purchase. I knelt to him, and his hand clawed at me, grabbed a fistful of my shirt. There was strength in his grasp, as he pulled me close, close enough to smell his breath, a sickly sweet taint like apples left to spoil.

'Shush.'

I clicked and shushed at the boy, as I would for any trapped animal, or frightened horse.

Thus, Dear Reader, did my life begin. You may wonder that I say my life and not that of the boy soldier whom I delivered from the arms of the dead. For deliver him I did and he never stinted in his public acknowledgement of this debt. But given all that had gone before, years of enslavement which I cannot describe (I trust that my Reader's wider learning will suffice to fill these gaps), I can only repeat the truth. My life began that day.

I half-carried, half-dragged the young lieutenant back to a burnt hut on the edge of a nearby farm. There was no one left there now, all fled, probably months before, when the war came banging and crashing around them. I laid him down in the shadow of the blackened wall and furnished the charred beams with a crisscrossed shelter of brushwood and willow, to keep out the worst of the sun. He tossed and mumbled but made little sense, adrift on a tide of fever. Dark blood crusted the skin surrounding a long, puckering wound on his thigh. I tore back the cloth of his breeches. Fragments of stone and shot studded the purpling flesh. I looked at his flushed face, his hair wet with sweat, the rapid rise and fall of his chest. He was tainted with the spirits of the dead among whom he had lain. If he could not shake them off soon, they would reclaim him. Though I knew he was beyond the reach of my words, nevertheless I spoke to him, told him I must go, find some medicine for his wound.

There are plants in that part of the world can still a cough, stop a bloody flux or bring on a baby; the leaves of one will banish a purging sickness, the roots of another ease a fever. Then there is the bark of old greybeard, a tree that grows near the water's edge, not the rough, craggy bark but the sappy stuff underneath that can be boiled and pounded into a paste. I have seen this paste used to cool burns from the press of a branding iron or the splatters from indigo vats. Indeed I had occasion to experience its balm myself during my days spent churning that stinking morass of rotting indigo plants and caustic lime. I also knew where to look for it. The sun was spreading low by the time I returned to the hut, with the soggy strips and a leather bladder filled with water. I took the Lieutenant's tinder box, lit a small fire and set the pap to boiling in some water. I tried to rouse him, to force water between his cracked lips; soaked a rag and wiped it over his face and trunk. Then I set to work on the wound, washing it down and picking out fragments of cloth and grit. He called out, but I continued, scooping the cooled brown stringy paste from the tin on the fire, and rubbing it deep into the angry flesh.

I hardly remember how I spoke then; that 'I', that person in the Carolinas. Not as now, that is certain. I took pains to be other than him. How then can I speak for him? He seems so far away, waiting in that ruined hut; a ragged black man, still wearing his stolen boots, waiting for the Lieutenant to recover or die.[2] Perhaps I should write as though of someone else, a distant Tony, so that those who come after me, may read the real account. Two accounts then. One for Lady Lucy, in that formal language she insists upon, that parroting of Equiano. And the other, my own ...

... The dark hours did little to cool the air; the day's savage heat remained, coiled under the brushwood roof. The wounded boy began

---

[2] I must confess to some surprise at how few lapses in grammar and literary style are contained here, though remembering how particular you were in your management of the house in Kildare, perhaps I should have known better. However your version of events differs widely from those reported by my brother. The family often recall his early adventures in America. These tales have passed between us many times and thus the memory of them has been kept alive. You make no mention of the times he risked his life to come to the aid of fellow soldiers and you fail to record his noble ways in dealing with the enemy officers who fell under his protection. LLF.

to shift in the early light. Boy or man, he wore the scarlet uniform of the British. His first question, uttered through tightened lips:

'Who are you?'

Not what are you? Or who's your master? Now, when there was no one to brand a name on him, he found it difficult to think. Who was he after all? Not that name he'd been given. Not anymore. But what then? A voice in his head spoke in a fading whisper. Andoni. Remember you are Andoni.

He must have said the word aloud, for the boy struggled to sit upright.

'Tony? Your name is Tony?' He hissed the words through clenched teeth and flopped back on the dirt floor. 'You saved me. I thought …' He closed his eyes. 'I thought I should have died there. So many men calling out. I couldn't …' His eyes opened again, dark with horror. 'Move. I couldn't move.'

His name was Edward. Edward Fitzgerald. Lieutenant. The words were hissed in ragged snatches. He stared at the wound in his leg, oozing blood-stained paste in a gash of livid flesh. He swallowed hard, and muttered.

'It's nothing. A flesh wound.' He attempted to smile.

Tony then. He became Tony. Was as good as any name.

Three or four days over and over. Forced water in. Pressed the paste into the wound. Cleaned him when he soiled himself. Ignored his bleats of mortification. Brought cedar branches, and meadow grass for fresh bedding. And just when it seemed he'd never recover, his fever dropped away and the boy wanted to take himself out for a piss. By himself. Wanted to eat. Everything. Fast – and looked for more. And talked. Talked between mouthfuls of food. As he fell into sleep. During his sleep. On waking, he took up where he left off. Questions, questions. How did you manage to escape? Where are you going?

Tony searched inside himself but could not pluck words from the empty place within. It did not appear to bother the boy. He was happy to hear the rustle of his own voice around the wooden walls. Talked of his family, of how they would be so grateful for the great service Tony had rendered. Of how his mother, the Duchess, would take him to her and weep with thanks.

Once, in the midst of the boy's offerings about his family, he asked what a Duchess was.

'It is a title.' The boy's face flickered with the effort of finding an explanation. 'Like a queen or prince. In Ireland. Where I come from.' He stopped but not for long. 'Do you have such things in your country? Chieftains perhaps?' He brightened. 'Have you heard of Oroonoko?'

Tony continued to skin the rabbit he had caught, refused to show his ignorance of this boy's world. Ran the animal through with a sapling spit, set it over the fire and shunned the boy's eyes.

'What do you say? I suppose you've no inkling of where Ireland is? What could you know?'

Tony got up slowly, turned the rabbit once and walked away. Did the boy call out? Perhaps. He did not look back. Could go anywhere now. No need to feel guilty about the little English soldier. He'd done his best for him. Paid his debt to the Gods for stealing the boots. He'd recover just fine, go back to his regiment, to his country some place over the sea, and then to his family. That beloved family. All that talking. Words that scraped him raw. He walked with little sense of how far he'd gone, or where, listening to the silence. Silence of breezes, and leaves and wing flutter. Shufflings in the scrub. Ripple-skittle of creek water. Stir of dust at his feet.

It was late afternoon when he returned. Not walking but astride a horse. It had sought him out, while he lay under the shade of a great copper beech. Came up behind him real soft. Put its bristly nose to his ear, and snuffled with hot, moist breath. The thought of this horse, of riding it, gripping its mane in his hands, urging it on to the hut, filled him up with a feeling he could not name. Was brim full of it when the boy hobbled out to meet him, shading his eyes from the slant of the sun. The boy's mouth opened, then closed again. Tony said nothing, did not dismount. Just held the horse there, though it tossed its head and the mane was knotting through his fingers.

'You came back. I wondered whether …' The boy reached out to the horse. 'I mean … you found a horse. How? It's wonderful.'

Tony shook his head. Could not shake off the smile. 'Had to chase him down,' he said. 'Took a jump at him in the end.'

The boy stared for a moment, unsure. Ran his hand over the horse's neck. Looked up again, a half-smile, eyes squinting into the sun. 'Pity you left the saddle behind.'

Travelling at first light, they followed the river, sheltering from the worst of the day's heat, allowing the boy to rest, before setting off again in the early evening. Took two days to encounter a small scout party from the regiment, who brought them back to the camp. Back to the chaos of large guns on wheels, muddied wagons, pitched tents and penned horses; bootless men in filthy uniforms sitting together on the grass, making musket cartridges; a sprawl of wounded men, some lying on litters, most on the open ground, a smell of rot hanging over them. Tony tried not to look at them. They reeked of death.

'Lieutenant Fitzgerald, Lieutenant.' A tired-looking soldier approached them. 'Major Doyle wishes to see you.' He pointed to a tent, set apart from the rest, on a small bluff.

Tony followed several paces behind. Listening. Waiting to be told something. Anything. Neither soldier paid him any attention. At the open flaps of the command tent, just as Lieutenant Fitzgerald was about to enter, Tony finally muttered, 'Sir?'

'Ah, Tony.' Like he was surprised to find him still there. 'Why don't you find some food, the cookhouse perhaps, I'm sure they'll look after you there.' Lieutenant Fitzgerald looked to the other soldier for help, but he just shrugged.

'There are some other blacks, camped beyond the guns and carts. You could try them.' A jerk of his chin was all the direction offered, before he turned into the tent announcing, 'Lieutenant Fitzgerald.'

THE TRUE NARRATIVE

June 1782, and the Author leaves the Carolinas with Lieutenant FitzGerald.

The only ships making their way between the twin forts on Sullivan's Island and James Island were British transports come to evacuate Charleston. Meanwhile jostling queues formed outside a large pillared house where the English soldiers had set up their command. They were mostly Loyalists, demanding that the English Government should honour their sacrifices for the King, should indeed recompense them; demanding to be given free passage to the Indies, to Nova Scotia, back to England, indeed to just about anywhere. Red-coated soldiers set about strengthening the barricades around the town, ordering Negroes to strip empty buildings of roof beams and floor boards and carry them to reinforce the palisades. The town was awash with Negroes; some free, some still enslaved. Charleston was a place of desperation: grubbing for food, squalling fights, rumours of attack. Everyone wanted to be away from that place which sat like a great tinder pile awaiting a taper.

It was suggested that I should join the Charleston Negro Battalion, and in that way I could be of service to the English and thus ensure my future freedom. However Lieutenant FitzGerald said he would guarantee my freedom, that he would not part with me for he had become used to me and had decided that I should wait upon him in the future, both in Charleston, back in England and in his own Dear Ireland. He asked me what I thought of this scheme and I am afraid, Dear Reader, that I was overcome in the face of such Generosity and could only nod my head in reply. He arranged for me to board one of the transports at the earliest opportunity to ensure my safe passage from that place and to put me beyond the reach of 'those damned slave-grabbers'.[3]

It seemed his fortunes were changing. He was relieved to leave the chaos behind. Only one more day and he'd sail to another life. The transport was anchored only a short distance from Charleston, but separate. Small boats made their way to and from the wharves, bringing out the last of the provisions and men. He stood on deck watching the activity, looked down when one of them pulled alongside, a voice barking orders. An officer clambered up the side, red-faced and sweating with effort, his wig askew. He snapped his fingers at the quartermaster and gave orders to gather all negroes.

'Too many, I tell you. You were given orders. All property to be returned to the rightful owners. That includes these slaves.' He cast about, and saw Tony watching from the port quarter. 'You. Get over here now.'

His fists tightened. 'I work for Lieutenant Fitzgerald.'

'Yes, yes. I'm certain every one of you has a similar story. But that's no concern of mine. Just get with the others.' What choice did he have? He joined the small group gathering on deck. One of them then spoke, a tall, lean man, with scars dotted on his cheekbones, who went by the name of Moise.

'Sir. I am no slave. I am free man.' He straightened himself, squaring his shoulders.

The officer rejoined, 'I have been instructed by the Commissioner for Claims for negroes. These slaves belong to Loyalist landowners of

<hr/>

[3] Remember that many who will read this are of a pious inclination, Quakers and such. While Dear Edward was free with his words, it is best not to record it. Better he should be shown as a Man of high moral character. Which he was! He was. Dear Edward. And this chapter is excellent. It shows his kindness and loyalty. How he went to great lengths to save you from slavery. This is exactly what is needed. L.I.F.

repute. Or even if they do not ...' He turned his head away, explained to the quartermaster instead. 'They are to be allocated in lieu of their lost property. As compensation, you might say.' He shifted awkwardly, his boots scuffing the sanded deck. Moise moved slightly, his breath surging, loud as the tide. He did not speak but his presence caused the officer to shuffle his feet, take a step backwards. 'What is it?' he snapped.

Moise looked straight at him. 'General O'Hara promise I go with him to Jamaica. To work for him.'

'I'll see if there's an exception.' He waved a hand toward Moise. 'But for the rest ...' he turned to the quartermaster, 'my orders are to return them. Find Lieutenant Fitzgerald. He is to see that they are sent ashore by evening.'

The officer turned quickly, clambered down to the waiting boat. The two boatmen fixed their oars and pulled away, despite the water sounding thick and resistant. The quartermaster disappeared below deck. No one spoke. The ship shifted lazily like an animal stretching. Overhead two men worked, daubing pitch along the rigging. Moise cursed. Said he would not go back. Turned to Tony and thumped him in the chest. 'You?'

Tony shook his head. No. He would not go back. He sensed the change in the other men too, from bewildered to angry, from individuals to an assemblage. Five men. Now together. Lieutenant Fitzgerald emerged on deck with the quartermaster, buttoning his jacket, his hair tousled from sleep, swearing loudly.

'What in God's name is this about? Who would give such an order?'

His voice was loud but he looked uncertain. Moise shook his head. Shook out his arms. Repeated what he'd said about General O'Hara. The promise to go to Jamaica. The Lieutenant put a hand up when he heard this.

'O'Hara you say? Well now. You Moise, will come with me. We won't wait till evening.' Moise stiffened. Lieutenant Fitzgerald clapped his arm, smiled briefly. 'To see your General O'Hara.' To Tony he said, 'It won't happen, you know. I'll be damned if it does.'

Tony waited on the transport while the two men were rowed to the quays. Waited while hope ebbed and flowed and ebbed.

They returned some hours later. Moise was expansive with relief, but tried not to show it. Lieutenant Fitzgerald was delighted and made no pretence of it. He was a preening cock, so pleased with his idea to take Moise along. The General, it seemed, was busy, dealing with impossible requests; a departing colonist urging him to find passage for his string of racehorses, another seeking private quarters on board for his mistress. He said he had no time for petty orders to remove negroes from their transports. Said they were to weigh anchor by morning.

And so we left the Carolinas, the place of my enslavement. I took with me nothing from that place. Nothing but a small leather pouch worn about my neck, containing what few memories I wished to preserve. I prayed that I could sail beyond the other memories and never more encounter them. Thus I looked forward to our departure.

My excitement was countered by some trepidation for despite my new Master's kindness to me, and his efforts to explain what was to happen next, I had no real understanding what lay in store for me as we sailed for the Indies. If any Readers are interested in the Indies; in its Climate and Geography, the way that people live, what they eat, and yes, the abominations of slavery there, then I suggest they read some of the celebrated travel accounts which would inform the Reader in ways that I never could.[4]

[4] I must confess I am disappointed by your lack of description of Edward's year in the West Indies. This is an opportunity to show the great work he did for the Regiment, to demonstrate his Loyalty; how he engineered the repairs of the island's Fortifications in Antigua; how he played a pivotal part in the negotiations with the French in Martinique − he had such a command of French. And from your own point of view, you could mention the conditions of your countrymen. I believe the slaves in The Indies are far worse off than in the Americas. The Abolitionists would wish for more detail. LLF.

The True Narrative

1782; A year in the Indies and Lieutenant FitzGerald gains Advancement.

Lieutenant FitzGerald made good his desire to serve as an example of the best of British soldiery in Antigua and St Lucia. Despite the difficult conditions he succeeded in repairing the Island's paltry, war-damaged fortifications to the highest standard, winning him a commendation from General O'Hara, and advancement to the rank of Major. His proficiency in French proved useful when he was asked to travel to Martinique to assist in negotiations with the French there.

I was somewhat fortunate to have seen little of the slaves' conditions when I was on those islands: I stayed close to the garrison; rarely travelled alone unless some extreme circumstance dictated it (as when Lord Edward required the services of the apothecary); I kept my papers – those which confirmed my status as a free man in the private employ of Major Edward FitzGerald of the 19th Regiment – stitched into the pocket of my breeches. Even at that, I sought constantly to reassure myself of their presence, tapping the cloth to hear the rustle of paper beneath – a habit I have never quite shed. For the most part, I travelled in the company of my Master. I have vague recollections of men working in the fields. And voices. Perhaps they were singing. That must be right. Though the heat would not lend itself to song. Such heat as would curdle milk in the pan or corrupt a cask of fish as soon as the lid was prised off. The place had a very particular smell that hung over it; as though the trees and vegetation – no, the very island itself – was just beginning to turn; as though the heat brought out a sickly Blight that wormed under one's skin and inside one's skull, dulling all thought and blunting all feeling. Major FitzGerald spoke the truth when he called it a Godforsaken place. I tried not to see then and now I try not to remember.[5]

Antigua. Godforsaken. No God could exist there. Not in the cane fields nor in the army quarters. Soldiers dropped almost as fast as slaves. All manner of fevers carried them off. Typhoid. Dysenteric. Choleric. Putrid. Yellow. Every morning, waking without a fever was like a blessing. Except there were no blessings and he could scarcely believe he'd left the Carolinas for this. Couldn't bear to see men and women under the yoke of slavery while he was free. Freedom brought its own shackles. Fear of becoming one of *them* again; shame at being separate from them. He kept to the quarters. Kept his head down. He became concerned with small things; the temperature of the water that his master would shave with; the necessity to prepare clean clothes three times daily for his master; the mildew blooming on his master's neckcloths that defied scrubbing; the dirt floating in the water jar; the tiny creatures that crawled through his master's letters, his papers. Tiny creatures, some curled and slowly purposeful, others many-legged and scurrying across the pages, consuming the corners, foraging on the ink. He swiped at them, crushed them, leaving stains: brown, black and dull red.

The newly appointed Major Fitzgerald was restless. He paced, sat, lay down. He would send to his mother for some more of the lightest and best Irish poplin, else he would die of sweating.

'If I die of some damned fever here instead of in the field, in battle, I'll curse the British Ministry to hell – from hell. Why, I'd welcome a

---

[5] But you must remember. I find your account somewhat distant; even, at times, cold. I know you to be a man of great reserve, but I had hoped that your portrayal of Dear Edward would reveal more of his Energy, his comical side and his Generosity. Perhaps you can find a way to convey this. LLF.

French attack, doing what a soldier should do, damn it Tony, not argue with our own men, these undisciplined lazy men, those blockheads of engineers who couldn't build a privy without poring over their designs for weeks and arguing and starting again. Christ, Tony, this oppressive climate, and no women of wit or comfort. Only those fat, indolent and stupid Creoles. And as for slavery. It's everywhere, the smell of it hangs over everything. Would take any joy out of any endeavour, if there was any joy. Which there isn't. There's no escaping the misery of the wretched negroes. Nor their vile, corrupt owners – a few worthy exceptions obviously but still …'

Tony listened with one ear to this. It did not require any comment in return.

'You know something, Tony,' Major Fitzgerald said, 'I'm as much trapped here as any of those poor blacks in the fields.'

Tony had just laid out a second change of clothing on the bed. He looked over to where his master sat by the open window, a slight breeze ruffling his new poplin shirt, opening the latest communication from General O'Hara and drinking punch though the hour was not yet midday. He did not respond but pressed his hand to the pocket of his breeches to feel the outline of his papers and made to leave.

'I don't mean it, Tony. It's this hellish place. It's corrupting me. I can feel it.' Major Fitzgerald called after him.

Tony stared at his hands. 'Then you must not allow it to, Sir.'

'Easy for you to say.'

'Why is that?'

'What is there to tempt you, what could turn you? Not even the heat could corrupt you.'

'So I may not be corrupted because I was a slave?'

But Major Fitzgerald was bored with the argument. 'Tony, I'm talking about the heat and you're more accustomed to it, but I … I'm from Ireland. Not used to it. I can't think in this heat. It's like wading through a swamp.'

When they received notice of their leave, leave to go to England, he asked Major Fitzgerald to help him remove the mark.

At first, he refused. 'It is mutilation. I cannot do it. I won't do it.' Looked like a young boy who'd been asked to deliver a hammer blow to a dog's head. 'What does it matter now?' he said. 'We are leaving.'

'Please. I will not take it with me.'

'Show me.'

He pulled his shirt over his head. Four years had passed, and the skin still looked puckered, almost raw, the letter R just about visible in the large scar under his right collar bone.

'What …' Major Fitzgerald's voice was a whisper.

'Runaway.'

'You tried before?' He reached out a hand, as though he might touch it but pulled back, his face pale and set. 'Very well,' he said. 'How shall we do this?'

This is how.

The camp blacksmith leaves the furnace untended. For a half hour. No longer he says. The heat has claws. Both of them sweating even before they begin. Hands shaking.

'Don't stop, even if I cry out.'

A knife then, heated white hot. Cut and burn. Doesn't matter about mess or pain or scars. The smell of singed skin, metallic blood and charred meat. Vomit. Whose? No matter. This scar will be his own doing then. He will leave this place without the mark of another man on his body. That history will not travel with him.

28th May, 1857
A walk to the British Museum

I suppose I knew he were once a slave, but I just never thought about it. He weren't ever a slave to me. An ink maker. A father. Never a slave. And never spoke of such. Not to me. Not so far as my memory serves me, though I'm beginning to doubt my own remembering.

I know now there are two voices speaking out from my father's papers. One is Baaba, and the other ... not someone from my childish memory. He is speaking all fancy but with a dose of meekness, too much for my liking. Perhaps he were just doing as Lady Lucy asked. Writing with 'grave formality'. His hand is different too in these writings, like he conducted the pen across the page with great care. The other passages are Baaba. The hand freer, not so many flourishes weighing it down. Sounds almost as he did when he told his stories to keep me occupied and out of Ma's way. I loved these tales even if he did take a different path in the middle or turn a different corner at the end in spite of my cries to do it proper like the time before. But I sat, almost quiet just to hear him. And glad I am of it. And for learning to read from him and make my letters, for when he passed there were no more words or paper for me, just the needle and the threads and the coarse feel of American cotton between my fingers.

But that sort of maudlin talk don't butter bread, as Ma used to say. She'd a lot to say too about Baaba's Stories. Said he made them up. That he remembered nothing of Africa if ever he'd been there and that he'd never told her nothing of the place and like as not he'd gleaned all he told me from that book by Equiano, the one whose pages he fingered even in his sleep. What's the truth of it. I dunno. But his voice is still in my head all these years on, telling the story of two brothers.

Once there were two brothers. Not sure if they were blood brothers nor if they were stolen from Africa. They arrived at the farm, same cart as brought the cook Odile and a field worker, name of Moses. The master came driving back from Charleston with all four in the cart, the two little boys clinging to Odile's skirts. Moses didn't last a month. Legs swelled up like a water buffalo's stomach, and he just died. Seemed he was not father to the two boys, nor Odile their mother neither. Least that's what she said. Said she never had any children and she was thankful for that, for being spared that misery. But they decided she was the one, and there was little she could do to shake them off no matter how often she beat them and tossed them out of the cookhouse.

Pair of goats, she called them. No use to anyone.

Other times though she'd pass some mushed up yams to them, under the table while they shelled peas into a bowl. For weeks, no one knew what to call them for they had no names and the master hadn't gotten around to calling them anything. Maybe only their mama knew what name she had whispered to them at night, if indeed they had shared the same mama. The names they may have had back then were forgotten, fallen away like leaves floating downstream, their whispering sounds drowned out, dashed against rocks. So their master gave them what names he thought were fitting for two young boys. He hung those names around their necks as hard and fast as a chain, so they would never be swept away. Sort of names he thought would hold them to his land. One he called Jack, said he reminded him of his dead uncle, kind of sly but with a bit of spirit, and the other he called Ben, because, well, because he thought that would be just comical, seeing as how he once had a dog by that name who had that same miserable look, and there was nothing he liked better than to give that dog a kick when he could.

Baaba never finished a story the same day. He'd pick it up the next, like a piece of Ma's sewing and he'd start in a different place but make it seem like he'd just left off there.

Those two brothers were blooded under the African sun. They ran after the hunt, following the men through the long grasses along the glorious river that flowed from the high wooded mountains beyond the golden plains. And there by the water's edge were great herds of antelope, and buffalo and wild birds of every size and hue and lying down to sip the water a whole pack of lions, and they were lying with all of the others, all drinking from the same water given to them by the Gods of the skies and the Earth. And the hunters sent up silent thanks before they sent forth their spears. After it was done, the leader – a man whose name is forgotten in this country but never in his own – he called the boys to him and, giving each a short spear, urged them forward where three antelope lay in their last throes and told them to make the final kill. And one of the brothers who was named for his father, he rushed at the largest animal and raised the spear as high as he could before plunging it deep in its chest. The other brother, perhaps younger and named for his mother's father, stood back as if he was not a part of it, but the urgings of the men and his brother forced him on. He approached the nearest beast, looked into its open eyes and saw the creature was patient in the face of death. He reached a hand down first, felt its last tremors and closing his eyes, his eyes that spilled tears, he speared the animal. After, the men painted the brothers with the blood of their kill and one wore it with fierce pride.

That were how he told stories. He'd thread it back and forth and double back again like he were stitching something that needed to be secured from unravelling. Stitching it into my head. Writing it down in my own hand now brings back to my mind the memory of his voice and his telling. It's only now, on reading his Narrative, I realise just how far he travelled. He talked of great oceans, of ships and sloops and sailing to Canada and the Indies, of carts and carriages, across France and Spain, even travelling along canals. So much travel, so many countries. And all just names. I felt a lack in me, not knowing much of geography and such. I felt I didn't know my father at all.

One of my lodgers, a Miss Crawford, on seeing the great pile of papers in the parlour had engaged me in conversation, something I usually avoid beyond the common courtesies. I had her pegged as a governess, and I weren't wrong. You can tell them by the way they are buttoned up and corseted, their faces stiff. Still it were she who suggested the British Museum as a place to find out about other countries. Told me it was a treasure trove of knowledge. I thanked her for it. Her face opened then in a little smile.

You might be the first black woman to go into the library, she said. What do think of that.

Someone must go first, I said. And likely more will follow.

I could still put on a show of spirit. Men used to like that about me. Leastways they liked it until they was at the receiving end of it and then the names would start, names I refuse to write down. When things get writ they risk becoming true for people are generally stupid, easily led to the trough of gossip, and more easily led to the belief in all things printed. I had other names though, names what made Ma wary when I were young. She kept a close eye on all the dogs who came sniffing round, hoping for a pluck at an exotic bloom, or dark flower, or African beauty, or dusky maiden, or black siren. In the end, Ma thought I'd be better married. Safer. So when Mr Henry Anthony Fricker came calling with his face shining pinkly under his whiskers, she thought he would be perfect for me. See how well he dresses. Such a fine hat. A respectable Englishman – she was fond of that word, like it added some value to him when really he were just a hat-maker's apprentice so the fine hat should have been no surprise. Not to mention the fact that she considered all Englishmen responsible for the murder of her father outside Naas Gaol. But that were Ma. Full of her own contradictions. I were seventeen or thereabouts when she rushed me to the church, first to get baptised and the following week to get married. Such a hurry. Mr Fricker was in a hurry.

Did I want to marry Mr Fricker. I think I did. He shared one thing in common with my father. He could tell a story. And I believed his stories of how he would cherish his exotic bloom and give her light and protect her from the bad weather, and set her up carefully in a beautiful house, and be content to spend his days gazing at her.

A body is only exotic when it's unfamiliar. Once he acquainted himself with mine I suppose he tired of it. They were not good times. Perhaps not for him neither. Every day had an edge to it. An edge of not knowing what were around the corner. My firstborn, a girl child, loosed her hold on me early and slipped grey and lifeless from my body. We had a room then behind the Golden Crown on Faggot's Lane, but she came so quick, there were no time to call the midding woman. No time for nothing. Mr Fricker dropped her in a greasy news sheet and rolled her up like leftover herrings. Told me he'd bury her at the edge of St Mark's churchyard or St James, that I should clean myself up. Disappeared into the night with the tiny package under his arm. Only told me later how he'd gone and tossed it into the river. But perhaps he said that in spite.

He did a lot of disappearing back then. Could be gone for days. And I with no money nor any hope of getting it. And my lad born just the year after. Named him Edward. What else. I were reared on that name. 'Twere like a prayer, or one of them saints' names what Ma used to chant when she had her beads. Ed I called him. For the longest time I loved him, feeling so tender for his little baby ways.

And then Mr Fricker just never came back. He weren't dead or nothing, just living another life, and leaving me to look after my Ed. I needed all the spirit I could muster to get through them years.

I don't mind saying I also had to muster some spirit to get me up the wide steps of that great building, that British Museum, even though I'd taken the trouble to wear my best day dress. I reminded myself, I were too old to worry what people might think, and I were as good as the next person even if he happens to be a lily-white gentleman in a top hat and fine coat. I straightened my back, pinched my cheeks, only a little nip, and I were ready for anything. The young ginger-pated man at the desk looked past me, so I went straight to a gentleman in a black frock coat who were strolling up and down the large hallway. I asked him straight out to be so good as to show me a map, as I were reading about my father and places he mentioned. He rocked back and forth like a penny skittle as he thought about my request, looked almost comical with his tufty white hair and white whiskers. Asked if it were to see where my father came from. Funny but I'd never even thought of that.

No, I said, not where he came from but where he got to.

He showed me to a large globe, the span of both my arms, tucked into a large stand behind the door in the next corridor.

Do you have the names of the countries, he enquired, and his spectacles glinted as I fumbled in my bag for the list. He flicked the globe around at the mention of America. There, he said as though that were that. I kept him busy though, with the reading out of Antigua, St Lucia and Martinique. He had to bend down and press his nose to the pale green ocean to find them, ignoring the passage of people who traipsed in and out past us. After that he flicked the globe round and back as I listed the countries where Baaba had been, and each time his finger came to rest on a yellow or green shape, he repeated the name, whistling it almost. And muttering my, my, under his breath. When he drew his finger down the map of America for a second time, he smiled at me.

Your father was quite the explorer, given the times. That line there, that's the great Mississippi River. I believe, back then, fellow explorers were still tracking its many tributaries. They must have been wild times.

I'm almost sixty years of age, and still people can surprise me. He were not the dry bookish sort I had thought at first. A learned gentleman certainly, but happy to paint a picture for me of how long the Mississippi ran, what the Indies was like, and much more, though all the while insisting he had travelled there only through books.

Haven't left the shores of England in many years, except in my imagination.

I smiled at him and remarked that I wished to travel likewise.

I would be honoured to suggest a book for you, even one written by a woman traveller, he said. Told me about the magnificent new Reading Room, filled with books on every subject. I felt most pleased with myself and his interest in me, but told him I had quite enough to read for the present. I asked him for one last thing, a piece of paper and a pencil so I might draw a rough sketch of Baaba's travels just to remind myself. By the time we parted company, he were calling me Mrs Small.

Did he tell you stories of his time as a slave, he enquired.

No, I said. I'm not sure I ever heard him mention it.

Perhaps he could not bear to.

His words gave me a queer stirring in my stomach. The mention of slave. Like a bucket of eels, all twisting and squirming. But I kept my face straight. Gave no hint of what I felt. Buttoning up my gloves, and folding the sketch into my bag, I thanked him, most politely, even called him Sir.

It's Mr Panizzi, he insisted. You must ask for me when next you visit.

II

MIDDLE: JOURNEY AND ADVENTURE

Harriet, Miss Harriet Pamela Small, F-atie Bloom, Attie, Miss Harriet Pamela Fricker, Hattie Fricker, Sable Songbird, Black Spur, Miss Marquess, Miss Wellington, Miss Harriet Pamela Small

Dearest Eddie, Beloved Eddie, Artful Eddie, Romantic Edward, Impulsive Edward, Lieutenant Fitzgerald, Misguided Edward, Captain Lord, Uncel/Irishman, Tragic Edward, Ill-fated Edward

Poor black, Unfortunate black, Poor Tony, Faithful Tony, Manservant, Tony Small, Mr Tony, Footman, Small, United Irishman, Brother Citizen, Innkeeper, Mr Anthony Small

The True Narrative

May 1783, and Lord Edward voyages back to England after two years in the Americas and the Indies, having been elevated to the rank of Major.

'You'll do very well there, Tony.' According to Major FitzGerald, I would encounter plenty of my kind around the city. I could get work there. Learn to dress hair. Grooming of a sort. Nothing I could not manage. He laughed at his own joke. I sensed his gaze on me but did not look up from my task of polishing boots. Major FitzGerald had trouble finding his sea legs on that voyage and despite his best efforts to overcome it, he spent the first weeks stretched out on his mattress, plucking splinters from the struts of the bunk above him. I had done my best to rid the room of the odour of sickness with the usual concoctions of vinegar and turpentine. Only a bunch of thyme, which I wheedled from the cook and knotted to the side of his bunk, seemed to have helped.

I applied the brush more vigorously to the leather.

'Or you could continue to work for me. Or perhaps my mother. You'll be free to decide for yourself.'

I tried to imagine it – for so long the word 'England' had lit up my mind like a lantern. So much talk, among the slaves and free blacks in Carolina, in the Indies. People said England had no slaves, that it was a place of Freedom. But what did Freedom mean? That I could no longer be bought or sold? That no one should own me but myself? I understood that but not how to live with it. Back in the Carolinas I had listened to men talk of Freedom and the word seemed to lift, to take flight but I could never imagine where it landed. And now, now that I was free, I felt no change. I was the same person still, though I was now Tony. No wings, but bound to the earth, bound to this boat and, it seemed, to Major FitzGerald. Not by way of a deed or title but from circumstance. Or so I thought then, being confused and unable to see beyond what life unravelled in front of me.

Now my Master was more concerned with throwing off the shackles of sea sickness. 'Toss me the boots,' he said. 'I'll dine with the other officers tonight even if the effort kills me.'

But it was not to be. As he stood, the ship heaved and plunged downward, before lunging again. My Master gripped the sides of the bunk. 'How is it you are thriving on this voyage and I am suffering almost as much as I've seen even my sisters do on the packet to Dublin? To think I used to tease them so ...'

I managed to place the bowl in front of him just in time to save his boots.[6]

Humour. Bodily functions. If there was a paucity of the former, then the latter more than made up for it. From shaving and dumping the spiky-haired water, to emptying the vomit bowl, the ablutions jar, and the necessary tub. Life aboard ship was all about bodily functions and smells. And smells to hide smells. Tony sought out the familiar comfortable smells of the horses, and chose to bed down with them: straw, horse sweat and manure, leather and rope were preferable to any place else on the ship. Better than the hold and the soldiers who lay about their hammocks and benches, playing cards, drinking grog, hiding grog; ill-tempered and foul-mouthed in equal portion; unable to tolerate the gap

---

[6] Amusing perhaps but at my brother's expense? No. Readers do not wish to hear of common illnesses or bodily functions. And humour is not something they expect from one who was once a slave. LLF.

between going home and being home. And the stench of that hold; as though all the air had been replaced by the foul odours of human bodies. For reasons beyond understanding, he could not pass that open hatch without a churning in his bowels. His dreams were troubled by the shape of the hatch, appearing as a block of light above his head.

As the voyage progressed and conditions on board worsened the way they usually do, he avoided not just the hatch but the men too. Some of them sensed his unease, feral creatures picking up the scent of an injured prey.

One evening he took the vomit-filled bowl to the gunwales as usual. There was little light, only that thrown by the poop lanterns. The wind was brisk but steady and the ship propelled along in full sail. When the stern dipped, he emptied the bowl, and stared down into the blackness. What lay beneath? Or ahead? He saw nothing but darkness. A voice slithered through the night. A hissing, singsong voice, familiar and unwelcome.

'It's Little Lord Neddy's black.' Corporal Smithwick, a slack-jawed soldier who often sought him out to hiss spittle-filled words, was standing silhouetted in the chequered shadow of the masts. 'Servicing His Lordship again, were you?'

A dash of sea spray shocked Tony into alertness. He knew the corporal's kind. Stupid and all the more dangerous for it. Don't speak, he told himself. Give him no cause to …

'Come see, T… Tony.' The man stepped into his path, into a dull wash of light from the overhanging lantern that clattered against the mast with every surge and dip of the waves. Each of them was briefly illuminated then eclipsed by darkness. 'See this.' He tugged at his breeches. 'I need somewhere to put it. Just give me what you give your master. A bit of what Lord Neddy fancies.' In the half light, he was a shadowy form, a flickering creature all shuttered eyes and unshuttered cock. 'Come closer – happen you'll see better. I've heard you Negurs like the windward passage and I'll take any port tonight.' His voice was a curdle of wheedling and sour humour.

Tony clenched his fists, straightened up.

'I'm a free man, Corporal Smithwick, same as you.' His breath was coiled in his chest. 'Don't have to give anything to anyone.'

'Is that what you think?'

A dirty gob of spit landed at his feet.

'Indeed,' he said, holding his ground as the corporal moved closer. He looked directly at him in the half light. Saw his life etched into his skin, a life of soldiering and hard travel, of fighting and sparse comforts. The man thrust his face close, so close, Tony could smell the sweat of him, the salt of him, and effluvium from his teeth.

'Indeed, you say. Mimicking how your master speaks? You'll fool no one. And you're only fooling yourself if you think you're a free man. There's none of us free Blackie, saving the likes of your Lord Ned. You'll see soon enough.'

Portsmouth gave no special quarter. The city had no time for one more ship among the many that sailed in and out of the harbour, day in, day out. One more ship that disgorged its cargo, human and otherwise, onto the quays amid the roaring and clanging of humans and cranes and rigging and guns.

Major Fitzgerald and Tony disembarked first along with a party of officers. Tony waited with his master's boxes and bags, while the Major went to pay his respects to the commander-in-chief of Portsmouth and, with any luck, secure a carriage. After weeks at sea, the noise of the place, the circling gulls, the push of dockers and draymen, the bustle of warehousemen checking off inventories and the jostle of hawkers and porters weaving in and out with handcarts was dizzying. Or maybe he had yet to find his land legs. He watched the soldiers totter down the ramps, ragged and unsteady as young children. They assembled, heads hanging, waiting for orders to march. Much of the fight had gone out of them over the voyage, the rum having run out long since and their last week at sea spent in silence or in sleep. For the first time, he felt a sense of kinship. They didn't know what was ahead any more than he. They were just waiting to be told what to do, where to go. Waiting for orders. He knew the landscape of waiting and it was bleak. There was no horizon, no clock, no sound. Only silence. Still, these men would walk to the barracks but he, the poor black, would travel in a carriage. Perhaps his position was not so precarious.

Unlike the horses. One dangled high above the deck from a sling before being swung down to the quayside. Two had already been delivered safely, but this beast was wild with panic, flailing against this unnatural and enforced flight. His high-pitched neighs sounded almost human. Someone shouted: 'Back. He's slipping. Send him back.'

The horse kicked hard, struggling to escape his bindings. Those aboard ship exchanged curses with those on land. But it seemed inevitable, the animal's fall determined before it happened. The sling would give way. It crashed against the gunwale and toppled into the narrow heaving space between ship and quay, entering the water in a shrieking jumble of thrashing limbs. A shocked crowd pushed forward to witness the beast's final struggles, in a roiling frenzy of foul green harbour water.

To have got so close, within sight of freedom – Tony shuddered and turned away. Gathered some of the bags and hoisted the larger crate, and went in search of his master.

The True Narrative

July 1783, and Lord Edward visits his family in London;
He returns to Ireland without the Author and is elected to the Irish
Parliament in August.

A footman came to fetch me, and I followed him through the stables across the straw-strewn yard, along a long low-ceilinged corridor, guarded first by a row of wine casks, and then butter casks. We turned up a narrow stairwell, a spiral of limestone flags, up and up until the footman pushed open a door onto a pale-pink hallway. He paused by a small door, placed a finger on his lips and knocked three times with his gloved hand. Then he pushed the door with no further trace of hesitation and proceeded into the room, beckoning me with his other hand, secreted behind his back like a trapped dove, and announced me as Mr Tony Small.

I had never heard those words spoken aloud before.

The room glowed. Everything – the walls, the rugs, the chairs – everything the colour of corn. And in the middle, on a gilded upright sopha, the Duchess sat, hand in hand with Lord Edward, whose face was alight with laughter. I did not know what to do.

So, Tony.

In contrast to her stiff, ornately gowned figure, her voice was a snap of fresh air. I glanced up briefly, enough to see that they looked alike, mother and son. She thanked me for returning her Darling Eddie to her. Said how they'd thought him dead, after that terrible battle, when word had come that he was missing. And then some six weeks later, the wonderful news ...

Lord Edward interrupted, endeavouring to sound penitent, protesting that he had written as soon as he could, urging me to vouch for the fever that prevented him from writing sooner.

When I confirmed that he had suffered with fever, Lord Edward leaned into the sopha, with his arms spread along the back and smiled, first at his mother and then at me. She patted his arm, and asked that I tell her the full story, all of the parts that her Dear Edward could not remember.

His Lordship rose at this, laughing that while we may talk about him, he did not need to listen. Besides, he said, he wished to find Mr Ogilvie.

Throughout the voyage, he had spoken with eager anticipation of his reunion with his stepfather, Mr Ogilvie. Of how at last he should have proved himself. Of how they would at last look each other in the eye, and see each other as equals.

But his mother apologised on her husband's behalf. He had gone to Dublin to see to repairs at one of the family's homes, Frescati. My Master was crestfallen on hearing this, and wondered if perhaps Mr Ogilvie had not received word of his homecoming. The words 'but of course he did' were the blows the Duchess dealt to her son, seemingly insensible to his distress, though he rose to his feet in some agitation. She went on in a calm voice, as though she were ordering tea, to remind Lord Edward that Mr Ogilvie liked to avoid fuss and considered there would be plenty of time to hear of his adventures.

'Adventures?' Lord Edward repeated the word. He twisted his gloves in his hands.

The Duchess patted the seat beside her, but he was not to be placated, protesting how he had expected him to be there. Two years he'd been away. Two years and he thought Ogilvie should have been pleased, proud even ...[7]

[7] Oh, poor Edward, he felt that keenly. I hadn't realised. Still, it's probably best not to include Family disagreements. LLF.

The gloves crumpled. He excused himself, gave the Duchess a brief kiss. She touched his face and urged him to return in the evening, telling him just how much she had missed their talks. He bowed, looked in my direction, and left the room.

In the corner, a long wooden clock hammered out three dull blows. Since Lord Edward's departure, the Duchess had not spoken, had not moved. The sun, however, had moved and was warm on his back. He was aware of the smells he carried with him. Of the outside, of horses and dust. And the smell of the sea still. Seemed it was not yet prepared to release him. From the corner of his eye, he sensed his dark outline in the gilded mirror which hung to the side of the fireplace. He looked down, at his dusty boots, planted in the rug, and at the rug like a garden of curling branches and vines. Large clusters of fruit; grapes, apples, peaches and odd figures, with little ribbed horns in their curled hair. Fat hands strumming—

'Edward says you will need some employment?'

The rug left him dizzy. He looked, as far as the pale blue of her skirts, could just make out the tips of two shoes nudging under the hem. He nodded. 'Yes, Mistress.'

'Mistress?' There was a smile in her voice. 'Well that's different.' Her hands swept over the shiny surface of her skirts in a whispery movement. 'What can you do?'

Horses.

'Ah, you're a groom? Or a farrier?'

He shook his head. 'No. But I have done those things.'

'What else? What did you do in the Carolinas? You were a slave there, were you not?'

Everything. Worked the fields. The vats. Did some carpentry. Before all that worked the kitchens, fetched round the house, till his age caught up with him and then it was outdoor work, same as every other child there. Did he say any of this aloud?

Her skirts remained still but for the occasional shush as her hand brushed against the fabric. He too remained upright, unmoving. He was not invited to sit, nor would he have done so, being so travel-worn and dusty. He was reluctant to speak of life before. To present it as a thrilling entertainment. Why would she wish to know of it? They would just be words to her, words that would not reach beyond her stiff dress. It seemed the clock spoke more than he, until she asked him about her son, and then his voice found a way out. She questioned him about Edward's fever, his wounds, what he ate.

'You know about remedies? How?'

He said he knew some about plants, healing plants. She told him how she had planted a garden in Frescati in Dublin. How she missed her flowers, not having visited for some time.

'Thank you Tony. For saving Dear Edward. You've no inkling of how precious he is to me.' Her words had tears in them. She paused. The clock sounded out four dongs. 'Lord Edward feels you may want to make your own way. With the Family's assistance of course in finding you a suitable position. He told me that London will afford you more opportunities to meet with fellow Africans than Ireland and it's certainly true. You know of course Lord Edward must return to Ireland to take up the management of his estates, and he hopes to stand for the Dublin parliament.

He felt the ground shifting. Yes he would like to make his own way. So why this sudden unease? He said nothing.

The Duchess rang a bell. 'You'll do very well here.'

He remained in London perhaps a month, working in the stables. Long enough to be introduced to countless members of Lord Edward's family as they visited. To take his place again on that vine-tangled rug. Always he was Poor Tony who saved Our Dear Edward. Always there were questions. Demands for answers. The younger ones wanted stories. About Africa. Especially Lady Lucy who was still a child then, a wild child her mother said, and brimming with interest and energy. But they were disappointed. He had no stories for them, no answers. He kept them to himself. They were not for sharing. Perhaps they were as relieved as he when Lord Edward sent for him. He'd written to the Duchess. She waved the letter, saying he had asked for his black to be sent back to him; said he could not do without him.

The True Narrative

Autumn 1783, and some account of Carton House in Kildare; The Author encounters Mr Ogilvie for the first time.

The Duchess herself arranged my travel to Ireland. Indeed she kindly asked her gardener, Mr Doyle, to accompany me – he having travelled from Ireland that very week to present her with specimens from her beloved gardens at Frescati Villa in Dublin. He was familiar with the particulars of travel along that route from London to Parkgate and thence on the packet across the sea to Dublin – and for this I was most grateful. I was to make my way to Carton House, the magnificent seat of the Duke of Leinster, eldest brother of my Lord Edward. Mr Doyle remarked on my good fortune at working for such a fine gentleman. Once he stepped on his native soil, he became increasingly garrulous and filled my ears with tales of His Lordship's adventuresome childhood; as like to be found grubbing for mushrooms and berries in the woods as learning Latin or French from his tutor. I warmed to these tales of youthful exuberance and was filled with even more gratitude on once more entering into his service. Though I was still at a loss to conjecture my destiny in this new country, Lord Edward greeted my arrival with all the kindness of the most benevolent Master, thus gladdening my poor heart exceedingly.[8]

Mr Doyle began drinking in the inn at Parkgate where they waited for news of the packet to Dublin. Fortunately the wind and tide were in their favour and the voyage took no more than thirty-six hours. For most of it, Mr Doyle continued to drink. And talk.

[8] This passage is excellent. Exactly as Mr Equiano might have written. LLF.

'It's the only way to deal with it, the waves, the fear and the sickness is something terrible. I've never yet made the crossing without the help of a drop or two.' He patted his pocket to ensure he had not lost his flask. ''Tis the most fearful thing is it not? Being at the mercy of the sea. A man the likes of yourself must have done a lot of travelling, or voyaging, should I say? I'm thinking you've seen many a queer sight. Sea monsters, eh? May the Lord preserve us from such frights. Though I haven't heard of any in these waters.'

He seemed compelled to speak. An outpouring of yarns, and familiar asides – most of them concerning Lord Edward, for whom he expressed a particular fondness.

'A fine cuddy cub. An exceptional boy, aye.'

He also professed great devotion to Lord Edward's mother, the Duchess. 'Strictly speaking you understand, she's the Dowager Duchess. There's not a finer Lady in all of Ireland. Wanted her children to be proud Irishmen, though she herself is English.' He drifted off, momentarily. 'I knew the first Duke well, bless him. Wouldn't hold a candle to Her Ladyship, not at all.' Another slug from his bottle. 'Bit of a dullard, some said. And it seems the new Duke, your master's brother, is cut from the same cloth as the old.' The boat groaned and he took another drink, wiped his mouth with his sleeve. 'But Lord Edward takes after his mother, no doubting it.' He laughed. 'He ran rings around his tutor, forever running off, hiding in the woods to avoid lessons. Had him tearing his hair out.' Another laugh. 'What little he'd left of it.'

The boat swayed gently, and Mr Doyle swayed in harmony with it.

'Have you met him yet?'

This was the first time that an answer was required. 'Your pardon?' he said, confused.

Mr Doyle winked. 'The Tutor. Sure you know well who that was now, don't you.'

He shook his head.

Mr Doyle leaned in, face alight. 'Mr Ogilvie. You'll have heard of him I suppose.'

Some surprise must have shown on his face, for Mr Doyle leaned back again, and smacked his thigh. 'Sure it was the most terrible scandal at the time. Couldn't she have had her pick when the Duke passed. Still a fine-looking lady. Any man would have been happy to warm her bed ...' he coughed, '... but the tutor?'

His attention drifted again before a drink restored him. And he continued, never seeming to reach the point of drunkenness or somnolence. Never taking enough to silence him. Just kept tipping away and talking away until Tony placed his pack under his head and informed him of his intention to sleep.

They arrived at Carton, the home of the Duke of Leinster – or so Mr Doyle announced.

'Brother to your Lord Edward. Not the cutest fox in the henhouse neither. No more than his father before him.' He scratched his head. 'I think I'm repeating myself. Sure that's how it is with all this travelling. Now, I'm off here,' he instructed the cart driver as they pulled up to a gate lodge. 'I'm to take some peonies from his garden to plant up in Frescati.'

He winked at Tony then. 'You may as well get out too and walk up there to the house. They should be expecting you.'

He looked in the direction that Mr Doyle indicated. No sign of any house, just a rutted road, curving gently past some woodland and disappearing over a small hill. His relief at Mr Doyle's departure was countered by unease. A feeling of exposure. All was strange and he a stranger. Where to go? Should he follow Mr Doyle? Probably not. He was supposed to find the steward up at the main house. He set off, clutching the strap of his knapsack. All of his possessions contained in this. As he walked, he listed them under his breath. Odd items of clothing, a pair of breeches, a smock shirt. A knife, gifted by Lord Edward when the sheath clasp wore out. His leather amulet. A flute, though he hadn't played it since leaving the Americas. Why bring it? It wasn't even one of his best, being made from mere cane. What else? His papers. Still had those, though the ink had faded and he worried sometimes that his freedom was not stated clearly enough. He'd checked that document so often. Knew the shape of freedom. Had traced the long slope of the first letter, the backward curve at the foot of it, which put him in mind of a rocking chair. The sight of it, the line of it, gave him ease. No one had asked for it since leaving the Indies.

He'd unpicked it from his pocket shortly after the packet had docked at Dublin, telling himself he'd have no need of it in this country. He reached into the sack to check. The parchment crinkled, and he restored it to the pocket in his breeches, where it belonged. Yes. He did need it still.

The road led to a densely wooded area and divided in two, one half sweeping around it and the other forging on through. Where was the house? Neither road proclaimed its destination either by signage, which he couldn't have read anyway, nor by usage.

Couldn't even tell where he was going.

He should not have come to this place and even if it was the right place, it was too empty. Trees and grass. And cloudy sky. And sheep in the distance by the sound of it. He kicked the ground. A stone flew into the undergrowth, dislodging a few pheasants who emerged with indignant squawks and ruffled feathers then circled back into the scrub a few short paces from him.

Trees, grass, sheep and pheasants. And heat. The day was warm and sunny, a surprise given that Lord Edward had spoken only of rain – and snow, though that was difficult to imagine. He removed his coat, threw it on the ground and sat down, aware of the shift of his papers against his thigh. He didn't have to account for himself to anyone. Not yet anyway. No one knew he was here. He went through his possessions until his hand found the amulet. The leather felt warm against his skin once it was safely knotted about his neck. A familiar warmth. Steadying. He took out the flute, frowned at his workmanship. It looked like nothing more than what it was – a length of cane. Nothing remarkable. And yet it had hidden purpose. It was more than it appeared. Still, he made a promise. At the first opportunity he would make a perfect flute, not cane but wood. He looked about, eyeing the trees, assessing them. Yes, the finest flute. Some day. He turned the cane over, circled the tiny holes with his fingertips.

Felt like yesterday. Sitting at the edge of the huts in the evening, beyond the gaze of the big house, of the master. Putting the finishing touches to the flute he'd made earlier in the workshop, when he'd used the auger to bore holes along the length of the shaft. Thing is, for every completed one he'd ever produced, there were four or five tossed aside, cracked along their length. It's a question of pressure and timing with the auger. Too much and a thing can snap or crack. Steady, steady and the cane will yield, allowing the point to bore through cleanly. Six holes down one side, blowing away the dust. And the one behind to fit the thumb. Always do that one first. No point doing the six only to find you slip up at the last. Slow and careful.

He selected a stone and used it to smooth the top of the shaft. Back and forth, feeling his way around the flute in the dimming light. Marvelling again at the way something so ordinary could be transformed.

A voice interrupted his thoughts. Minda. She is urging him to try it out, to let her be the first to hear it. And he's not shy about it. He can make anything sing: cast-off cane, a discarded animal bone, a broken branch. He puts his lips to the top and begins to blow. The notes flutter through the night air, across the fire's giddy flicker to where she sits. He keeps on playing, his mind filled with her smile. And even though his brother hunkers beside her, he senses her attention is still on him for a time at least or perhaps his music, the music that flows through him, that his breath releases to his fingers. He closes his eyes, the better to keep the moment in.

'Tony, I presume?'

The notes plummeted to the ground. He looked up, confused for a moment, and saw a figure that was all lines and angles, limbs and elbows. Even his head, haloed in wisps of grey hair, seemed long and pale, and shadowed. A stork bedecked in black, leaning on a dark stick.

'Your playing is excellent.' He pointed to the flute which now lay by Tony's side. 'May I?' The man straightened up. 'Very nice,' he declared as he ran a hand along the length of the shaft. Very nice indeed. Your own work?'

'Yes, Sir.'

'I've seen primitive work like this before, at the Royal Society Exhibitions. Fascinating thing, the instinct for music, being so universal.' The man shifted awkwardly, as he handed back the flute. Long, thin hands, bony fingers, hardly covered in skin at all. 'I'm Ogilvie. You've heard of me.'

He suppressed a smile, dropped his head. 'Yes, Sir.'

The man was leaning over him. 'All good, I presume?'

He presumed a lot.

'Lord Edward has been looking forward to your arrival. And I may say that I am not without curiosity myself.'

It felt as though the man was trying to see inside his head as he leaned in further but Tony knew better than to meet his gaze. A sigh of exasperation and the man juddered to an erect position once more.

'Come with me. I'll show you where you need to go.'

They walked together. Mr Ogilvie talked. No, not right. He stated things. He was not so much interested in replies. Except when he asked of him where he came from.

'Near Charleston, Sir. Place called Jackson's Creek.'

'But you are African. You were not born in the Carolinas.'

'Can't say.'

Mr Ogilvie could not accept this answer. 'But you must know. You must remember. You travelled by ship. I've read accounts.' He walked quickly for such an awkward man, head thrust forward and legs following. Neither the sunshine nor the pace had much effect on his rate of speech. 'You were a child then, I must surmise. Even so you must have some memory.'

He shook his head. 'No, Sir.'

'What of your slavery?'

He made no response. It sounded like a question but not one he had any intention of answering.

A sharp hiss of frustration from Mr Ogilvie.

'I would like to hear of the conditions, to determine for myself. The abolitionists' descriptions are horrendous, beyond what a rational man could contemplate ...'

He made no acknowledgement. The man could ask whatsoever he wished but it didn't mean ...

The house interrupted his thoughts. They had just crested a small hill and there it was. He stopped.

'Carton.' Mr Ogilvie declared. 'Quite something, eh?'

Something? It was a vast building, at least the length of the King Street in Charleston. Longer. Set in gardens that looked like an exotic

Turkey carpet. Like the one he saw in the Duchess's drawing room in London. Everything matching, dark green hedges on one side, perfectly aligned with hedges on the other. What looked like bright green swirls, four of them, in front of the house (or perhaps it was the back) and in the centre of each, a tree, dark and tapering. From his vantage, he could see window after window, martialled in three rows, set into walls of pale grey stone. The sun gleamed silver in the glass. And four pillars standing guard in the centre.

'This ... was Lord Edward's home?'

'For a time,' Mr Ogilvie said. 'Though when I taught him, he had moved from here. To Frescati, near Dublin. And later in France at Aubigny. You know I was first his tutor.' One ragged grey eyebrow lifted with the question.

He nodded, thinking of what he'd heard of Frescati. Lord Edward talking of it like it was some haven, a mythic place; the way, back in Carolina, people had spoken of their distant homeland.

The thrum of hooves on stones announced a horseman. He looked over his shoulder to see Lord Edward dismount, in a flurry of coat tails. He was suddenly unaccountably relieved. At seeing the one person in this entire country who knew him.

'Ogilvie. You are keeping my poor Tony from me.' He clapped Tony on the shoulder. 'Has he been teaching you? Quizzing you?' He looked from him to Mr Ogilvie, receiving a scowl from the latter.

'I wished only to inform myself,' he protested. 'To have a slave's perspective on the conditions of slavery.'

'You asked him this on your first meeting? Could you not wait? And he is not a slave.' Lord Edward looked at Tony. 'Besides Tony does not perform that role. He will not be used to entertain or thrill anyone in that respect.'

Mr Ogilvie swished at the grass with his stick.

'Don't worry about him, Tony. He does this to everyone, can never resist the challenge of what he calls the unformed mind. And even after ten or so years of tuition he will still say that *my* mind is the "rawest and most resistant" of any he has ever beheld.' He smiled at Mr Ogilvie. 'Is that not so?'

Mr Ogilvie managed a grimace in return. 'If you say it, then it must be so. I think you need to work on your black's English. I'm not sure if he'll be able to manage over here.'

'Don't you worry about him, Dear Ogilvie. He will not be another of your projects. I suspect he knows as much English as you or I. He just doesn't waste it, or give too much away. Am I right, Tony?'

'If you say it, then it must be so.'

Mr Ogilvie's eyebrows pulled together. 'Hm.'

'Oh, that is too good.' Lord Edward was delighted with the riposte. 'We'll leave Mr Ogilvie to contemplate your rapid advancement in speaking in tongues. Come on Tony. You take Prudente.' He tossed the reins. 'And tell me all about your time with my mother. And London. How did you find it?'

The True Narrative

1783, Kildare, and the Author encounters some Irish servants.

In the servants' quarters at Carton, the steward, by way of introduction, declared me to be Lord Edward's servant. Nonetheless I was greeted with no small measure of curiosity tempered by a pinch of bemusement. This, I would find, was not an uncommon response to my presence. Several faces turned in my direction. Two maids, in aprons and caps, peered in from the kitchen. Two young men dressed in gleaming blue livery and white stockings sat at a long table and conducted a sly sideways examination. Another man, dressed plainly in breeches and a jacket, glanced over his shoulder, acknowledged me with a slight upward tilt of the chin.

'You may as well sit yourself here.' He sipped from his tankard, and called for one of the maids to fetch me a drink. The maid, a pale, round girl, fetched a pitcher and a cup and poured me a drink. Though the beer was good and I thirsty, I drank carefully, aware of the collective gaze.

The maid whispered loudly to my companion, without any care that I might hear. 'Where's he supposed to go? With the upper servants? Or with us? I've never before seen a fargurum.'

One of the liveried men interjected with a story of a visitor to the house who had brought with her a servant, a young black boy. 'Lady Aldeburgh it was, came one Christmas and the young lad kitted in gold and scarlet breeches, with a collar round his neck.'

I must confess to some distress on hearing this, for I had not realised that such practices occurred in this country. But the footman dismissed the maid's fascinated enquiry as to whether the boy could talk. 'Máire, this is why you won't get beyond the kitchen. Sure wasn't he just a boy, like anyone else, just got up by Her Ladyship to look like a plaything.'

Did they think I couldn't hear as they carried on their conversation? What was a fargurum?[9] I stared into my cup. My companion must have noted my distraction, for he reminded the maid of what the steward had said, that I was Lord Edward's man.

'So he'll go where all visiting servants go. Same as myself. Besides it's not your business but Mrs Dineen's. Let her attend to it.'

The jounce and bounce of voices from the kitchen mixed with sounds of pots clanging, dishes scraping and water bubbling. His companion banged his mug on the table.

'I'm guessing you're thinking about that word.' He slid a platter of bread across to him. 'Fear Gorm. Means blue man in Gaelic.'

Tony turned his hand over in amazement. 'Blue?'

His companion shrugged. 'Sure who knows how it came about. Anyone can tell you're not blue.' He turned to look directly at him, framing his head in his cupped hand. 'So what are you then?'

'I'm a free man.'

The man smirked. 'Not what I meant. Are you a groom, a stable boy, a valet? If you're a valet you'll eat with the upper servants. If you're a groom, you'll eat next door.'

'Ah, thank you.'

The man stuck out his hand in a considered way, his eyes staring directly, strange grey eyes. 'Name's Jerry. Jerry O'Leary. Valet to one Arthur O'Connor, a gentleman just released from Trinity College and seeking

[9] This is very funny Tony. I know what it is! A Blue Man. So comical to think the Irish referred thus to black men. I remember this word from my time in Ireland, when we lived in the Lodge in Kildare. Such days, happy days. But you should check the spelling of the word. I have little Gaelic beyond 'Erin go Bragh' so I am no help. Ask Julia. Or perhaps not. Can she read and write? LLF.

a few days' diversion here.' He inclined his head. 'And yourself? What manner of exotic name have you? Don't tell me you're a Caesar or—'

'Tony.'

'Tony? So ordinary.' Jerry's narrow mouth curved at one corner as if at a secret joke. 'Ah well.'

There was no hiding in that country, that life, that place. Place. Another word with hidden meanings. Everyone was supposed to know their place. But he was on swampy ground. Not knowing. Always thinking he'd put a foot wrong. Place and Fear Gorm. He imagined putting words such as those in the amulet around his neck. To be examined later. Along with so many others, all manner of shapes and textures, lying in the leather pouch, and stitched shut. He kept them until familiar with them, until their value became clear. No point taking one out at the wrong time or in the wrong company. He'd picked up scores of words from Lord Edward. Imagined them as seeds, to be planted, one after another in straight rows, that one day would grow and stand up straight in any field, any company. When he did this, he would leave the other self behind. Remove those traces as surely as he'd had the brand removed from his chest.

Until then, he held back, made himself still. Though no amount of dropping his eyes would prevent others from inspecting him. This was not the Carolinas nor the Indies and the scrutiny was less about assessing his worth or where he belonged but rather his difference. And the people here did not bother to hide their curiosity. But such interest was short-lived. Servants had jobs to do. Life continued for them. And for him.

THE TRUE NARRATIVE

The years 1784–1787; Some account of the ways of this country and the Perils of Politicking; Lord Edward takes up his Commission again; The Author travels with him and sees many wondrous places; He comes within sight of Africa.

I stayed in many of the great houses in Ireland and in spite of my hue, I was always met with the highest degree of civility on my Master's account. In addition to Carton, Lord Edward was a frequent visitor to the neighbouring Castletown House, home to his aunt, Lady Louisa Conolly. It was here that His Lordship met and mingled with many important people at the various balls, hunting parties and Grandes Fêtes Champêtres that were held there. In those days I worked in the main as Lord Edward's groom, and my treatment by my fellow servants was determined by this. My Reader may not be aware that just as in the best society, there is a system of ranking within the servant class which determines where a person shall sit at table, and with whom he may speak. Within the two houses mentioned, being a groom meant I was placed just above the stable boys and garden boys but not high enough to allow me sit at the table occupied by the coachmen or footmen. But do not think this was any hardship. Apart from a few tricks and jests (and these were to be expected), I rubbed along well enough with all of them.

Frescati House was Lord Edward's favourite – this was where he had received his schooling. Edward's mother, the Duchess, considered it her own special place too, and though she never visited in all my time there, the signs of her influence were many, especially in the garden. There was less formality in that house, and all the servants sat together in a small servants' dining hall. Of course I had regular encounters with Mr Doyle there, but he never once mentioned our journey from London to Dublin and I never saw him the worse for drink again.

The house lies south of Dublin, situated on a slight rise overlooking the coast. Sea breezes lapped at the windows, chickens wandered freely through the undergrowth, and it seems to me that flowers bloomed in the gardens all year round. It was in that place that I saw my Master at his greatest ease, whether that meant working in the garden, planting seedlings and chopping logs or dining with his brother after a day spent in the Parliament in Dublin. He kept abreast of all matters political, reading newspapers both Whig and Pittite, and engaged in a lively correspondence with his cousin, Sir Charles Fox, at a time when that great man was active in the London Parliament. I admired Lord Edward's ability to scan a letter or pamphlet, and take in the meaning, and strengthen his own opinions. It was my secret wish at the time that I too should be able to decipher the markings on the page, that I might hear the inky words. But there was no one to teach me for my Master was always busy.[10]

He applied himself to the business of politicking with admirable zeal, and supported the Opposition in their bid for greater freedoms for Irish trades and taxes.[11] Inevitably this brought him into conflict with his brother, the Duke, a man of more conservative leanings. Lord Edward struggled to support the Duke when it went against his principles of fairness.[12]

---

[10] This could be construed as a criticism. Remember the tone of humility as used by Mr Equiano. LLF.

[11] Though I remain proud of Dear Edward's outspoken views, it is best not to mention the Opposition when you consider where such disputes with Pitt's Government led. Violence, Oppression and the Act of Union. Hopefully, the Catholics will have their day, but this Narrative is about Edward. LLF.

[12] I beg you Tony, to refrain from commenting on Lord Edward's relationship with his brother and indeed other members of the Family. Readers would consider it unlikely he should have discussed his political and personal views with a servant. My two brothers were prodigiously fond of each other. You must show how Lord Edward did everything to support the Duke's political position (apart from that Militia Bill). LLF.

Lord Edward moved between Dublin and Kildare. Attended the Parliament in Dublin. Attended Balls, Theatres, Assemblies. Was a house guest of this Lord and that Great Family. He travelled to London, to Bath, to Malvern. He took a great tour across France, into Portugal and on through Spain. He was so familiar with the French tongue that while we were in that country he talked with me as though I could understand it. The Reader may be surprised, as I was myself, how readily I acquired the rudimentaries of the language, enough to negotiate the details of my Master's travels. Lord Edward kindly pointed out that since my grasp of English was so remarkable, it was no surprise to him.

The tour terminated in the resort of Barèges, high in the Pyrenees, where Lord Edward passed several weeks in the company of his mother and sisters who were taking the waters there. Wheresoever he went, so went I. His Lordship's facility for friendship was prodigious. He was as easeful with the common peasant in Cadiz as with the Governor of Gibraltar or Madame de Levis in Paris.[13] He returned to Ireland and his duties in the Parliament, later taking up his commission in the army once more, near Woolwich. (Though perhaps he was at Woolwich before he went to France and Spain, I am not quite certain of those years, though I remember Gibraltar quite well.)[14]

Lord Edward's past did not appear to trouble him. The future, however, as set out by his position as one of the younger, 'younger' sons, was a different matter. There was no money in politics, he was patently unsuited to the church and he couldn't possibly join others of his class in seeking a life in the Indies. 'Oh no,' he said. 'Once bitten, twice shy. No amount of money would induce me to return to that place. That climate. The debauching effects of slavery. Not ever.' All of this was said plainly to Tony, and more besides.

When Lord Edward went to Woolwich to take up his commission once more, Tony accompanied him. At first they found rooms in the

[13] Why do you mention Mme de Levis? Admittedly Edward was not always discreet in his affairs but you must be, especially in your Narrative. LLF.
[14] I'll refer to Mr Ogilvie regarding dates, so don't concern yourself. Mr Ogilvie is a hoarder of dates and names. LLF.

town of Woolwich, a rough place, filled with noise and stinks and the press of people. Later, when they moved to the Officers' apartments in the Royal Artillery Barracks, Tony wished himself back among the stinking press of Woolwich. Uniforms, braiding, epaulettes, this hat, that feather. His place, in that place, was uncertain. While Lord Edward was gaining instruction in the manufacture of explosives, fuse filling, the preparation of saltpetre, Tony took himself back down the narrow, leaning streets of Woolwich. He watched the two hulks that were docked off-shore and their daily disgorgement of their convict inmates into smaller boats, to be rowed upriver, downriver or out to one of the dredgers. He saw one or two black men among the sorry prisoners, wondered what misfortune had led them there. Told himself to be thankful, grateful. He wandered about the shipbuilding dockyards. A group of men clambered from the skeleton of a hull, downing their saws and drills to warn him off. 'There's no work here,' they said. 'Only them what belong to the guild. And we've not seen you before, not here nor in Deptford.' He protested, said he had work already, but their suspicion would not allow them to make an exception. He walked out instead through the woods on the fringes of the military grounds – when they were not practising with cannon or explosions. Or up on the common, among grazing sheep and the occasional cow, to pick up wood or furze for the fire in the barracks apartment.

Back at the barracks, he did what little was needed to be done for his master. Small matters of clothing, shaving, boot polishing or waking him. Lord Edward took his meals in the officers' mess, so Tony made his own basic dinner in any one of the eight flag-stoned kitchens near the men's quarters. Still, Lord Edward professed great relief on seeing Tony, morning and evening.

'There's no one else but you who will listen to me.' It was true. This posting was a disappointment just as politics in Ireland had proven to be a disappointment. 'Nothing happens there. It's all about keeping things the same. To think the Riot Bill was passed, despite opposition from people like myself. And for my uncle, Mr Conolly, to support it. Such a shabby act. To impose more restrictions on the people of Ireland. It looks as though there'll be no concessions to the Catholics, because that will threaten all those who depend on them for rents. Myself included. Not that the income from Kilrush is much to talk about. And my army pay, not much better. I'm stuck with begging for handouts from brother William. And he's in a state of permanent apprehension over the debts accrued by Carton and Leinster House. I think brother Henry would have made a better Duke than William. But such is the lottery of birth.'

There were times Tony thought of himself as an ear. An attentive, silent ear. Present, morning and evening, that his master might have some place to whisper his thoughts. Like those sacred trees he'd heard of, where a man could confess his secrets, or his desires. And be certain they would be held, safe in the bark. Lord Edward's secrets were safe within the bark of Tony. There was no one for him to tell.

Luckily when he got his first dose of the pox from a bawdy house in Woolwich, it so happened Lord Edward was similarly afflicted following a two-day trip to London. And so they both shared Mr Mann's powders, His Lordship delighted by the coincidence.

'Well Tony, two sorry dogs are we!'

Shortly after he suggested that Tony should have more occupation. 'This is no life for you. I'll set you up with someone in London, you could learn to dress hair. That way you would have a skill if ever you wanted to work elsewhere.' A position with a gentleman barber and some lodgings in London were secured. As to what Tony thought of this? He'd no wish to dress hair. Had no interest in wigs or powders. But it was a chance to do something. That might lead to something else. So he would take the chance to learn a trade, one that might earn him money. More than he was being paid then. But it came to nothing.

'What would I do without you Tony? If you leave, I'll be stuck in this miserable, stinking hole with not a soul to talk to. You'll have to stay.'

He stayed. But thought more and more beyond the small things, the small necessities.

It was morning, summer. The windows of the apartment were open. In the distance the regular sounds of ordnance. Training continued winter and summer. He had finished shaving Lord Edward. As he folded the blade into the heavy canvas roll, he asked, without any great display of feeling, if he might learn to read.

'I might prove useful to you.' His voice was steady.

'Of course. It's about time you should.' Lord Edward fixed his neckcloth. 'I'll ask one of the tutors at the academy to teach you. They sometimes take on servants and young boys for classes.'

His first lesson took place, seated at a desk, in the front row, along with a motley group of some eight or nine boys and men. Each held a chalk and slate. The tutor was a small man of middle years, who seemed immensely weary at the challenge he faced in teaching these ignorant blank minds the art of reading. He talked of his years of teaching. Of Mathematics and ancient languages. Of Greek and Roman. Of Rhetoric.

'Nevertheless, for these hours, I will dispense with great learning, in order to drag each one of you rude and uncultured men into the world of letters. Take out your slates, your chalk and let us begin.'

He began. Forming the letters A to Z. Laid out in rows.

That evening when he left the classroom, the sky was resolutely blue. He skirted the training grounds, the courtyards, crossed the kitchen gardens as usual and up to the second-floor apartment, in the Officers' Quarters. He stood back to let one of the ensigns pass on the steps and the man greeted him by name. 'Good evening Tony,' he said, and Tony nodded and said 'Sir' in response. When he entered the apartment, Lord Edward was already there, randomly slinging some clothing in a bag.

'My apologies,' he began, about to explain about the class, the slate.

'Don't worry Tony, I'm back early. We need to pack up. I'm to accompany my uncle, the Duke of Richmond, to the Channel Islands, on an inspection of the fortifications. Thank God we'll get out of this place for a while. And,' he looked at Tony for the first time, smiling like a small boy, 'I'll likely get to visit my cousin, Lady Georgiana at Stoke House at some point. You know how much I long to see her.'

His lessons would end. That was the fact of it.

'I don't care about anyone else,' his master was saying. 'Not Kate, not anyone. I love only Georgiana.'

He'd been so close. He still had the slate, and the chalk. Perhaps he could continue. Perhaps Lord Edward himself …

'I know her father's view,' he was saying. 'Uncle Lennox is nothing if not disagreeable. But if I show him my dedication to the army, he may overlook my income, don't you think?'

For a moment he seemed to see Tony. 'I'm sorry,' he said. 'About the classes. I'll take care of it myself when we are settled again.'

The trip to France, and Spain and Gibraltar. What year was that? No matter. It was shortly after Lord Edward first fell for his cousin and some time before he was rejected by her. And denounced by her father, Lord Lennox, for proposing without *his* consent, for the *audacity* of his suit. And berated by his stepfather, Mr Ogilvie, for the *futility* of his suit and the embarrassment to the family. Gibraltar was before that.

They were staying in the house assigned to the Major General of Gibraltar, at General O'Hara's insistence. He would not suffer his young friend to stay in one of the many inns that clung to the Rock, and urged Lord Edward to abandon the rooms they had already booked. Tony set out from the inn an hour later, carrying the baggage, around circuitous lanes, dusty gold in sunlight, up stone steps, past donkeys that leaned over gates, and mules pulling carts. The sea air was tinged with dust, smelt of donkey pelts. He stopped in an empty square, under a tree, heavy with lemons, and placed the bags at his feet. There was a low well, set in a grotto. Tony bent to scoop out some water.

'Not a good idea.' A low voice. Tony turned. Moise. Five years since they last saw each other on St Lucia. Tony knew him immediately and would have even without the scars along his high cheekbones, and his height and bearing. That voice. Something cavernous about it. Low and echoic. Tony shook the water from his hand and stood.

'Moise.'

'Tony. The General sent me. Your master thought you might be lost.' His directness of gaze was disconcerting. 'That water, not for drinking.' He pointed to a small chapel across the square. 'It's a holy well.'

Tony began to feel irritated. Caught out. Ignorant. 'Thank you,' he muttered.

'If you got sore eyes, or pox, well then …'

Tony laughed. Moise grinned. It changed him completely.

The General had a small house. It was loud and busy. Windows open to the sea, doors open to the trail of people who called and petitioned and paid their respects. Lord Edward and General O'Hara dined together, a noisy wine-fuelled dinner, with fellow officers and other guests, other visitors. Tony and Moise both served at table, assisted the guests, and then the serving girl with clearing away. After the visitors and fellow officers departed, the General called loudly for Moise.

'Where's that blackguard black of mine?'

What was wrong? What could he want? Tony felt a stab of uncertainty. Moise, on the other hand, told Tony to fetch a tray and four fresh glasses. Without hurrying himself, he went outside to the stores, returned with two bottles of wine.

'Thank God,' the General said. 'Let's have some of the good stuff. The really good stuff.' The wine was poured. 'No taxes paid on this shipment,' he added.

'To those we lost in the Indies.' He raised his glass. 'Sit, sit,' he said, irritably, waving at Tony and Moise. Lord Edward looked delighted. In the narrow dining room, the four men sat together. They talked of St Lucia, Jamaica. Of campaigns, of the state of the Empire. Of that time in Charleston when the young Lieutenant Fitzgerald brought Moise to his office. 'Sly dog,' the General said. 'I could hardly send your man back to a life of slavery and keep my own.'

Tony was silent for the most part, not altogether at ease, speaking only when addressed directly. Moise was different. He spoke, not to argue so much as to clarify. How was he so confident in his voice, in his words? After half an hour, they were dismissed. 'Moise, sort Tony out for the night. Back here before sun-up.'

It was dark when Moise led Tony to a low cottage a short distance from the General's house. 'I have my own quarters,' he said. 'Married quarters.' Tony heard the smile in the man's voice. He knocked and a small, dark-haired woman – Spanish perhaps, or Creole – opened the door, holding a lantern. 'My wife, Maria.' Such emphasis on the word *wife*. Possession, achievement, devotion. Tony was struck. Like the door had been slammed in his face while in fact Maria held it wide, and her smile was wide, as she said, 'Bendito sea Dios, Moise.' She grabbed Tony by the arm, pulling him into the tiny low-ceilinged room, placed the lantern on a hook, and turned to her husband.

'Es este tu hermano?'

'Sí,' said Moise. 'Él es mi hermano. My brother.' She leaned up to kiss Moise, then took Tony's face in both her hands and kissed him. 'Tú eres mi hermano, ahora.'

'She says you are her brother now.'

They spent a week in Gibraltar. Lord Edward continued to dine at the General's house, apart from two occasions spent at the Governor's residence where he met the Governor's nephew who was also his aide de camp.

Lord Edward reported back to Tony. 'The most silent meal I have ever partaken of. The Governor hardly touched his food, and took no wine. His nephew, Lieutenant Sirr, appeared to match his restraint, mouthful for mouthful. Even paused with a spoon halfway to his lips just as the Governor did. He'll go far, by the way. But seriously, it was painfully restrained. There was nothing else for it but to call for more wine though I swear it was watered down. Thank God for the General and his hospitality.' Edward walked daily with O'Hara, toured the fortifications, the barracks, the battlements, the ordnance, the quays, and then just walked for the sake of it. On their final day, at the outside kitchen of the General's house, Lord Edward asked Tony to help carry a picnic lunch to the highest point on the island. 'The General wants to explain some plans he has for a watch tower. Unfortunately the Governor's nephew is to join us. Maybe you could engage him.'

'I doubt if I could,' Tony said, as he hefted two bags, over each shoulder. He was about to sling a blanket over as well.

'Enough.' Edward did not like fuss. 'There are no women in the party. We can sit on rocks. There appears to be no shortage,' he laughed gazing upward. Lord Edward was dressed in a simple white shirt, breeches and boots. General O'Hara had dispensed with his wig and regimental coat. 'Too warm,' he said. 'And besides, it's Sunday. Moise, since you're escaping this expedition, you can direct any and all visitors to Governor Elliott. After all we are to mind his nephew.'

The Governor's nephew arrived in full regimental uniform, polished jack boots and a cocked hat. He gave a stiff bow.

'Looking very correct there, Lieutenant Sirr,' the General remarked, as they began their uphill walk. 'You're welcome to leave some of the uniform behind. The coat perhaps, or the sword?'

'I'm sure Tony wouldn't mind returning to the General's house with it, if you'd like.' Lord Edward said. 'The Fahrenheit thermometer read 92 degrees, just a half hour ago.' But Lieutenant Sirr pulled his chin back, and refused the offer.

'I'd prefer to remain as I am.' His face and neck flushed red.

No more was said on the matter. Some time later O'Hara called to Tony. 'You should be able to see Africa from the peak, if the mist holds off.'

Africa. Could he be so close? That he might see it? He tried to imagine it, sensed there was something inside him, some memory stored in a deep cave. He tried to dig for it. The rhythm of walking and digging. Tracking the phantasm. No good. Nothing. The path got very narrow higher up, and the surface was dusty and strewn with small stones. The picnic bags were heavy and sweat trickled down Tony's forehead. Ahead, Lieutenant Sirr walked in silence, sweeping his sword from side to side, through dried grasses, while he scuffed his boots on the pebbles, sending up eddies of dust that descended on Tony, four paces behind.

'Excuse me Sir,' Tony coughed. 'If you please.'

The Lieutenant looked over his shoulder, before continuing on as before. At the peak, after General O'Hara had outlined his ideas for the tower, all three men sat about, while Tony distributed bread and cheese and a bottle of ale apiece. He then took himself off from them to look out, across the sea. Such a height. He felt close to the sun up here. And the ships below, playthings bobbing on water that was too blue to be real. There was no cloud, just a vague mistiness, and there, the outline of land. Africa. It looked like … nothing much. There was no jolt. No recognition.

What did he think he'd see? Dark, lush green? Fool. At this distance it looked the same as where he stood. He eased out his neck. And yet. Who could say what might be there, somewhere far to the south? He'd seen maps. Knew the shape of the continent, its vastness. Hard to hold that vastness in his head. Still, somewhere out there, if he followed the coast … but no. Hope would be swallowed by that enormity.

'You there. Another bottle of ale, and be quick with it.' Sirr had removed his hat and was mopping his forehead. 'Quickly, now.'

Lord Edward looked at the Lieutenant. 'Feeling the heat, Sirr? At least you didn't wear your bearskin hat.' General O'Hara laughed shortly.

Tony looked in the bag. The ale was gone apart from his own bottle, from which he'd taken just a mouthful. 'You are welcome to mine,' he said proffering the bottle.

'Good God, I can't take that. You've drunk from it.'

'It doesn't matter, I can wait until we return.' Tony continued to hold out the bottle. And then realised what Sirr had meant. As did Lord Edward.

'Tony, don't bother the Lieutenant,' he remarked. 'Clearly he is not thirsty. See, he looks quite refreshed.'

Lieutenant Sirr's face was a fury of brick-red skin and sweat. Tony withdrew the bottle. 'Yes. I see that,' he said.

Sirr sucked in his lips until he appeared to have no mouth at all, just a thin slash in his long, raw face.

General O'Hara intervened, in a voice that was tight. 'Not as abstemious perhaps, as when you are in your uncle's company.' He reached into his pocket, and took out a small canteen. 'I have some brandy here. Medicinal you understand.' He held it up, pulled it back. 'Still if you are not *thirsty*, and do not care to share …' He drank from it, passed it to Lord Edward.

The Lieutenant scrambled to his feet.

'Sit, Lieutenant. Stay,' General O'Hara smirked at him. Tony refused the canteen offered by Lord Edward, turned away and sat with his back to the group and finished his ale. All the while, his skin prickled, and his neck tightened. He knew the Lieutenant was staring at him.

General O'Hara took the lead again, taking the cliff path down, conversing with Lord Edward. Once again Lieutenant Sirr trailed behind them; once more wielding his sword, slicing the air.

The sun was just dipping past its peak, and glaring directly into their faces, glinting off the edge of the blade. Tony heard mutterings ahead of him; Sirr hardly bothering to conceal his rage as he continued to thrust and jab. The path dipped suddenly at a bend, and Sirr lost his footing. The sword flew from his grasp, out into the void of air and sea below. Sirr turned sharply, reached out for it, and his body angled awkwardly. His boots danced on the stony path, scrabbled for purchase. Spitting stones. Dust. Air. He dropped, that long mouth open now, screaming. Tony flung his body forward at full stretch. His hand reached out. Caught the other man's chest, his shirt. Handful of linen, loose cloth. He tried to get his other arm over but it was tangled in the strapping of the bag. Damn it. Sirr's body began to slip out of his own clothing. He was dangling, flailing, his feet kicking out. Now Tony shifted, freed his hand from the strap, reached out, and grabbed at the man's neckcloth. His fingernails dug in. Impaled him. They were as one. One sliding mass, shifting stones and dust, grating over the edge, pulled on by Sirr's thrashing, his wheeling legs. Dust filled Tony's mouth, his ears.

Behind, scuffles, shouts, someone gripping his legs, someone else outstretched beside him. And an urgent voice. 'Hang on!'

Who? The Lieutenant? Him? What choice? He couldn't move his hand from the man's neck even if he wanted. All his life force was poured into that arm, that hand, that man's neck. All that lay between the now and the vastness below.

Now Lord Edward was shouting. 'Give me your hand Sirr! Your hand.' Then heaving him, dragging him up the rock face, until they all lay, gasping and coughing in a sprawl of bodies and dust.

'Let him go, Tony, let him go.'

Tony's hand was not his own. It still held to the man's neck until Lord Edward took each finger, dug them out, while Sirr grappled uselessly, his breath sawing the air.

Sirr insisted on returning to the Governor's House, gesturing with a mix of fury and exhaustion. The army surgeon attended him, spending an hour or more, closeted with him and his uncle. Later he rode over to attend Tony, sitting in General O'Hara's cramped study. His left shoulder was dislocated. That explained the pain, the useless arm. He'd thought perhaps he was imagining it. The surgeon removed his own jacket, rolled up his sleeves. What now?

'Now you'll see why we surgeons are men of bulk,' he laughed and told Lord Edward, 'Restrain your man.' He pulled on the arm, steady, steady, turning it sharply back in place in a startling flash of agony.

'No avoiding the pain of it. But it's done now,' he said, while Lord Edward patted Tony gingerly on his good shoulder. The surgeon prescribed brandy. 'A hefty shot of it and you'll be fine. Can't say the same for that mess of a scar you've got there,' he said, gesturing towards the mangled flesh below his shoulder. Tony laid his good hand across it, to check. Just the usual ribbed skin, no letter. No R. He looked up, caught Lord Edward's momentary wince.

Moise brought brandy, and gave Tony a glass before setting one in front of the officers. Tony listened dimly as they discussed the Lieutenant.

'I thought at first it was Moise who saved him.' The surgeon swirled the brandy. 'He kept whispering about the *damned black*. And whispering is all he'll manage for the next week or so. That's some grip your man has, Major Fitzgerald. To hold on to someone of Sirr's bulk. I told him he was fortunate. That any scars would be easily hidden by a neckcloth. He's a lucky man.'

His final advice was not for Tony, but for the General. Not advice exactly, he just mentioned that the men, some of the men, were unhappy that General O'Hara's man had received preferential treatment in being granted his own private quarters. It was not, he said, a question of Moise's hue. Just the fact of the preference.

'My business. My money. My man. He's not a soldier. Not bound by army rules. They can go to hell.'

Those years of travel. A man cannot travel the world and be left untouched by it. He comes to know, to hold in his head a picture of hundreds, thousands of other lives, each lived within its own confines, each full of its own meaning. But a man can come to know these things and still not understand his own passage to the place he is at, and may still feel his past, like a scar. One that cannot be scratched. Or rubbed. Or relieved.

That's a story, ain't it. My father rescuing that man. Not sure I'd have
held on to him, he being so rude and above himself, but maybe, in
the moment, I'd have done the same. Reading about Baaba, and his
injury, reminds me how he were already ill when he took on Lady
Lucy's Narrative. How he no longer had the strength to lug them
sacks of alum and gum arabic and whatnot. How he coughed and
coughed when he poured the vinegar over the copperas in the vat,
and a cloud of vapour exploded forth, a smell I hated too but at least
I never coughed up great clots of blood. How he told Ma he'd not
order any more ingredients until spring, just use what he had to make
the best inks ever, the finest, blackest ink from the finest Aleppo galls,
enough to tide them over the winter. And how I never thought he were
particularly bad, because there was days when he seemed not ill at all,
but suddenly full of energy, out in his workshop, mixing and heating
and decanting. And his fine face were full of vigour, and I fancied
I were helping him, spending long afternoons watching him, as he
measured and stirred and poured, or I'd puddle around, taking care
not to go near anything hot or bubbling, searching among his bottles,
and quart jars, and flagons, hoping to find an egg laid by one of our
hens, the one I hated, what Baaba called the contrariest of hens, and
Ma called Lulu.

Lulu had the run of the back yard and Baaba's workshop. She
were a fearsome hag of a bird; half plucked and scabby with one good

eye – the other pale blue as a milky posset – and a beak so sharp it could strip the skin from my legs. Ma liked to take the broom to her, chase her round the yard, hissing Lulu, Lulu, while the two other hens squawked and raged. She were a poor layer, offering up an egg once a week at most, and always doing her best to hide it where we were least likely to look. Except I knew she liked to hide them in Baaba's workshop. And I found one, lying snug on an empty sack behind the door, picked it up and put it to my ear to listen to what was inside. Next thing that Lulu came out of nowhere, and launched herself at my stockinged feet. Peck peck. I dropped the egg in my fright and ran into the yard.

Why must Ma keep her, I cried.

Baaba stooped to pick me up, laughing so much he ended in a splutter.

And why does she call her Lulu, I cried.

Your Ma, he said, gasping for breath, Your Ma is a wicked woman, she is a mistress of Juju. She has named that hen after L—

Mind your talk and the child listening. Ma had come out to see what were going on. Sure it's just a name, doesn't mean anything.

Baaba put me down again and fixed Ma's hair, tucking it behind her ear. He were always doing that for her. They smiled at each other.

Ma caught his hand. Besides, said she, we Irish have our piseogs more powerful than your Juju. I'll cast one on you, to make you better. And she wrapped her arms around him, pressing her face into his shoulder. I tried to copy her, holding tight to Baaba's legs. Rain started to fall in a grey drizzle, spotting the dirty yard, darkening the earth and staining Ma's skirts. Baaba turned his face up to the narrow patch of sky. Even Lulu were quiet for a time.

The next day though Baaba had a chill. Ma said he'd caught it by standing in the yard with scarcely a shirt on his back. She told him to stay in bed, to eat porridge, broth, warm possets. But he didn't like to stay in bed. Instead he sat on the settle in the kitchen watching as Ma and I kneaded a batch of dough. He dozed off while the bread was set to rise. While he were sleeping a footman called with a packet from Lady Lucy. Ma tugged the string a little, then laid it on the table. She set me to polishing spoons, while she went out to feed the hens, shoo-shooing them, making clucking sounds, shooing and calling them to her. She came back inside, closing the door behind her, hair tossed, the basin tucked in the crook of her elbow.

The cold air woke Baaba. Why do you insist on Ettie polishing that tin cutlery.

You know well. Ma busied herself tidying away some spoons. It's good practice for Ettie should she need to go into service. It doesn't look like she'll make a seamstress and she'll need something, some trade, some money if your scheme with Lady Lucy doesn't come through, if that Family don't pay up what's owing, if that Surgeon Heavisides doesn't find the right cure for you, and you don't get better—

Ma clamped her hand over her mouth sank into a chair.

I fetched the packet from the table and placed it in Baaba's lap. He pulled the string free and I saw the sheets, his own writing, but lines and lines crossed through and scribbles down the sides and at the bottom.

Surgeon Heavisides. The name begat the man. Eating and drinking off the dying. As the flesh fell off Baaba's bones, the doctor's fat palm were slipping the last of his money into the pocket of his bulging waistcoat. Used to waddle into our house, a scented gander, fatted for the feast. Don't know what the smell were, but I never could bear to have violets anywhere near me after that. Poor Ma used to welcome him like he were the Messiah, and plead with my father to listen to him, to let him use the leeches but after the first time Baaba just smiled and said no more. The Surgeon puffed out his chest and said he'd still need to be paid, and Ma cried, so he let the surgeon cup him, drawing up an ugly blister behind his ear. But nothing seemed to draw out whatever it were that ate up my father's insides.

THE TRUE NARRATIVE

June 1788, and Lord Edward travels to Halifax, Nova Scotia; The Author discourses with a fellow free man of Africa.

Though a rich man has the Freedom to choose whither he comes or goes, and the money and position to indulge his whims, there is still one part of his life over which he has but little control. In affairs of the heart, a rich man is almost on an equal footing with a poor man, or even a slave. He may choose to give his heart, but nothing can force love from the object of his affections. A slave owner may force himself upon a woman, and take his pleasure, but he will never take her love. Even a fine, handsome, titled man like Lord Edward had no guarantee of success in his pursuit of love. That it was his cousin who stole his heart, made little difference to the Lady's father. Lady Georgiana was expected to make a better match than a younger son, with only a minor estate in Ireland, and an unimpressive commission. For months, he refused to accept the impossibility. He was like a bull trapped in a shed. Banging against the door. Throwing himself against the walls. Peering through the slats for a glimpse of what lay beyond. But he was never to be allowed enter that field. Letters were written, words exchanged, urgent, whispered meetings held. Lord Edward was persuaded by Mr Ogilvie to take a far-off, two-year posting. Time to cool his ardour and focus instead on his army career. But always he held the hope that when he had distinguished himself in the field, and was given his deserved majority, his suit would be warmly received by his Uncle, Lord George Lennox.[15]

Having departed Bristol at the beginning of June, the Coliston, bearing my Lord Edward and the 54th Regiment, anchored off the town of Halifax a mere three weeks later. That time at sea was uneventful, a rise and fall of hammocked sleep, of waiting upon my Master – though in truth he required little – and of watching the men tend to the sails and rigging, all ascurry and aclamber. There was something of a dream about it, that very absence of incident, marking it out as unusual. In those days, everything uncommon made a singular impression on my Mind. Perhaps that is why I can recall my first encounter with the town of Halifax with such clarity. So many ships cluttering the bay that we were denied a mooring alongside the quay, being forced instead to take the longboats to shore.

We pulled up to the quayside steps in the shadow of the Fort, with its hulking grey walls and batteries and great thrusting guns challenging all who dared approach. Major FitzGerald was first to disembark, taking the steps two at a time. I followed, struggling to keep apace but was soon overtaken by the sights which I beheld. The Quays and nearby dock, the roads which led to the town, were thronged with men, unloading barrels and hogsheads, casks and tubs, heaving them onto waiting carts, shouting instructions, swearing; others hauling in ropes, tossing sacks down to waiting arms. All was busy. Voices spoke what I took to be Irish, and English. And other languages then unknown to me. But these served merely as noise against which I heard, as if from one of my oft-repeated dreams, the voices of my own people.

My attention now was completely taken with the sight of not one, but what seemed an entire crew of Negroes. So accustomed were they to working together that they paid no heed to me. I attempted to engage one fellow in conversation but he was brusque in his responses

[15] My dear Tony, whatever were you thinking of? This cannot be included. Besides it was just a mere flirtation – over as soon as begun. Lord Edward took up his posting as a loyal member of His Majesty's Army and with the aim of further advancement, nothing more. LLF.

and I took this as a sign that he was under the yoke of a slave master. Later when I joined Major FitzGerald at his lodgings, I enquired of the Innkeeper, whether indeed this place allowed the practice of slavery. He informed me that most of the men I had seen on the quays and working as draymen, were in fact Free men, though in the outlying settlements there many farmers, Loyalists who had fled the War, who yet maintained a parcel of slaves brought with them from the old country.

Lord Edward was flushed and in high spirits, engaging the innkeeper in heated discussion on the merits of granting land to negroes. The innkeeper had no doubts and no hesitation in speaking out in front of a black servant.

'I'll say it now, they haven't a notion of what it takes to grow food, nor even how to survive. Many of those stupid devils perished in the first snows. They have no comprehension of the necessary clothing or footwear.'

Tony remained silent.

'Perhaps …' His Lordship toyed with a knife, tapping it on the table. 'Perhaps it is the case that they have no means of procuring such essentials. I take it they arrived here with nothing. Difficult for anyone to make something from nothing.'

The innkeeper scowled. 'You visitors always think you have the answers. You should try living here. Hard enough for honest white men to find decent employment when the negroes will work for the price of a ship's biscuit.'

Lord Edward turned, eyebrows raised. 'So, Tony. What say you to my friend's comments?'

'I have not yet had a chance to observe this place, having only come ashore this past hour. It will take me time to form an opinion.'

The landlord gaped, his wet mouth hanging open.

'Ha.' Lord Edward laughed. 'Let that be a lesson to us all. A wise man withholds his judgement. Something I have yet to learn myself.'

Tony left the inn, taking the opportunity to walk the streets and quays of Halifax, to see for himself the free negroes who worked and visited there. He wanted to listen, discover if any of those voices, familiar and unsettling – with their slow, round sounds and shortened sentences – belonged to someone he knew. But all he saw were strangers.

'You there!'

A man shouted, struggling with an edgy draught horse, who reared and shrieked. The cart behind lurched with every skitter the animal made, and the load, a precarious cargo of bales and casks, began to spill over onto the road. Sprawled against a rope-heaped mooring post, two white men looked on and did nothing but puff slowly on their pipes. Tony stepped past them towards the drayman, his irritation held in with his breath.

'Think you can help me some?' The man's face was bathed in sweat, his dark eyes bloodshot, shirt stained under the arms. He tugged at the animal's bridle, ducking back at the same time.

'Let me,' Tony said, taking the rope from him. 'You look after your load.'

He eased one hand up along the harness, laying his palm open in front of the horse's nostrils. The animal whinnied and blew out in short, gusty breaths while his hooves lifted and kicked up dust, but more easy now. Tony leaned in close, touching his forehead off the horse's coat, shushing, clicking. He ran his hand in long stokes across its back and shoulders. Everything slowed.

The drayman thanked him, his face still set from the strain but his eyes smiling. Together they replaced the spilled load, heaving the last cask on to the cart.

'You new here?'

He suggested a place of work, where they took on negroes, for half the wage of a white man right enough, but still, better than no money.

Tony shook his head. 'I'm with the Regiment.'

Ah. His eyes ran over Tony, making a private inventory. Boots – old but good nonetheless – Lord Edward's cast-offs; breeches, cut from good worsted, not the rough nankeen that this man was wearing; and his shirt of clean white cotton, such a contrast to the drayman's sacking tunic.

The man took his leave, blowing his cheeks out as he clambered up onto the cart.

'Wait,' Tony called, taking hold of the bridle. The words had their own shape, their own will. 'Where are you from?'

'Birchtown.' The drayman nodded his head to his right.

'No … before. Before this place.' The horse snuffled. Overhead two gulls circled and called.

The drayman eased back in his seat, shifting the reins to one hand. 'I'm from Savannah, came out 1782. With my boy. Name's Samuel Forbes.'

He extended his right hand. Tony seized it, shaking it more vigorously than necessary. It brought a smile to the man's face. Broke the grim shell of him.

For the next while they ran back and forth over names; family names, masters' names, slaves' names. Samuel just shook his head as easy as the horse shook off flies. He was sorry for him, but he knew none of them. Finally Tony took out a name, as though it did not trouble him to roll it into the conversation like a dice, see what came of it. Minda?

'Yes, there's a Minda.' He smiled broadly and his grizzled face opened up. 'If it's the same one … up Digby way. Came here with last of the ships, from Charleston. Name writ in that book, that *Book of Negroes*.' He blew out his cheeks again. 'But things better for her here. She got herself fixed up now. A good man.'

'But is she free?'

'Oh yes. Just like me.' He laughed. 'Though nothing ties a woman so much as her own babies.'

He must have seen something in his inquisitor's face. 'May not be the Minda you're looking for.'

Tony was not deterred. Where was Digby? How long would it take to get there? Could he walk?

'Listen.' The man leaned down from the cart and up close, his face was run through with lines like a dry river bed. 'Why would you go cause trouble for someone like that. Like as not it's a different girl. Not the one you looking for. When you see her last?'

An empty field. A place where she was not. 'Seven years,' he said.

'What's she to you anyhow?'

What was she indeed? Everything. Say something. 'My sister.'

The words were stones in his mouth.

The True Narrative

Summer 1788, Digby, Nova Scotia, and the Author's reflections on a meeting with his Sister.

Before setting out for New Brunswick, where my Master was to take command of the Fort at Fredericton, he kindly indulged my whim to ride out to the township of Digby, on the Bay of Fundy. I had received a notice that my sister, or someone of the same name, was living there. Oh, the Reader may imagine as well as I, the heady mixture of Joy and Trepidation that filled my heart as I took to the trail. The promise of finding one who had been so close to me in my younger years, was as much of a temptation to me as the apple was once to Adam in the Garden of Eden. The day was golden; a soft, melting sun in the sky; the leaves were young, bright green and oozing their sticky juices, while out on the bay the sea was feathered with light. I felt blessed with all the possibilities of God's Benevolence, as ripe as shining cherries. I fancied I could see fish leap in sunlit arcs from the water. The road by the sea dipped and soared with visions of great pastoral beauty and for the first time I held in my heart a real sense of the hand of God on all of my life's Trials and Twists, and especially in my good fortune in having as my master, Lord Edward FitzGerald. It was he who had urged me to take his horse, to give no further thought to the matter but to travel immediately to meet my sister. Such a heart, so given to the first impulse of Kindness toward his fellow. I cannot think of another of his ilk.

It pains me to write of this happiness. To think of that journey, of the sea, and sun, and nature's bounty. To set the scene. Did it happen?

Exactly as I imagined.

A tidy wooden house, shingle-roofed in a clearing on the edge of the village. Fenced off, with a newly built shed to the side. All green grass and trees in the background. A handful of chickens, wandering freely, and a vegetable patch, neat rows of shoots pushing up, and beans pegged on stakes. It was a picture of simple country living and a balm to my Soul. I hesitated before putting my hand to the door. How would she greet me, my Sister, my Brother's wife whom I had last seen in the Carolinas? She whom I also had loved. I can scarce describe the scene. She met me with outstretched arms, showered me with kisses and it was she who begged forgiveness for having run, and run without me. And on seeing her face, so straight and true, I felt all my past shame and guilt fall from me. Her three young children clung to her skirts, fine, healthy young ones, and she talked to them in tones of pride and love. The eldest, a girl, she had named Ruth. I looked across the child's head at Minda, and her smile told me all. This was the baby I had seen come into the world. Oh the difference in the passage of years. While we spoke she cupped the back of her head to urge her forward. You can see the likeness can you not? And in truth she was a fine girl, brim full of Vigour, with calm eyes that had never been cast down in fear and dread. What else could she have done? she asked. She had thought only of her, she said, back there in Carolina. Nothing else in her head when she walked away, just the feeling she should keep moving. Away, away. Her child must know a better place. Keep moving.

She laid a place at table for me. A jar of nodding poppies sat on a neat cloth in the centre. She poured me cool water from the stream. Placed fresh bread in front of me. Her husband, she said, was out working a Fishery up river. No one I knew, a good man, she said. She was happy. Was I? she asked. I told her of my good Master, that my life was filled with Adventure and Travel and was more than I had ever imagined. Did I have a woman? No, not yet. It was a small rent in the tapestry of my happiness, but one I assured her would soon be mended. We parted in joy and the ease of mind that comes from knowing, from knowing, from knowing ...

When I recall this memory, I see it as though through one of those great stained-glass windows, that distinguish those magnificent Cathedrals I have visited in Lisbon, Westminster and Hamburg. Her face shifts in colours of blushed pink and sea blue. Her children play in a pool of green light. And when I glance back as I set off on my horse, I see the family wave me off in a glow of sunny yellow. And the glow warms my heart, as each recollection betters the last.

At times like these I feel the presence of our great God.[16]

Imagination burns more brightly than any happy rememberings. The image lasts because you have made it yourself, peopled it, weathered it, spoken everything you have ever wanted to say: Even years later you can embellish it yet more, with additional kisses, rosy light, sunshine and flowers. Imagining is so much better than not knowing. Not knowing is an icy landscape of snow and black tree trunks reaching to a grey sky and no end, no end.

Only bad memories stay. Burn like a brand in your very soul. So deep, there's no words for them. They just are. As they were. And no tricks of imagination can do anything to change them.

[16] My dear Tony. To think you never mentioned your sister before. I wept when I read of your joyful reunion. This is a most affecting scene. And it shows Edward's generous spirit in lending you his horse. LLF.

The True Narrative

September 1788, and the journey to Fredericton; Winter and some account of life at the Fort of Fredericton; New Brunswick, under the command of my master, Major FitzGerald; The Author finally becomes acquainted with Books, and the Art of Writing.

We travelled all along the Bay of Fundy on the way to my Master's new command, passing farms and settlements that were strung out by the water's edge like flags. Scots and Irish, they were hospitable settlers, their wooden houses clean, their farms shipshape. There was so much to admire, and Major FitzGerald spent much time meeting with the farmers and enquiring about their histories and methods. In most cases, they had arrived in the country with little more than a handful of shillings and now they could point proudly to their neat, productive farms, where everything was achieved by hard work. Major FitzGerald was excited by the experience. 'See them, every man is exactly what he makes himself. No rents to pay landowners. No tithes. No titles. A simple equitable life,' he said. 'And one I should like to live.' [17]

We passed the autumn and early winter months in Fredericton where Major FitzGerald had charge of the Garrison. He proved to be an excellent commander, encouraging the men while keeping discipline at the same time. Despite the heavy snows that year, he insisted on

---

[17] I wonder if this youthful exuberance might be misconstrued as the beginnings of a more radical turn of mind and therefore best omitted?

the usual Drills and Parades, to maintain morale. The routine suited him though he would have denied such, and the harsh, cold weather appeared to suit his Temperament. I have often noted how those of a hot-blooded disposition do best in a cooler climate. Here at Fredericton, the chill appeared to sharpen my Lord's fine nature, and the absence of other diversions meant that his energies were spent on outdoor pursuits such as Fishing and Exploration.[18]

During those harsh months in New Brunswick, a Miracle came to pass. I had long wished to be able to read and write and though I took every opportunity to gain instruction, I had made little progress. Major Edward FitzGerald, having realised my great yearning to know the contents of Books, to have written Words speak for me and to me, took upon himself the task of bringing me into the world of Ink and Letters.[19] Perhaps my educated Readers take such a thing for granted but for a poor man like myself who once was Slave, it was akin to sight being granted to a blind man. I was admitted to a rarefied group of God's humans who could communicate across oceans and speak to those whom they never met in person. My slave self, diminished.

'Here I am, Major Edward Fitzgerald, Commander of the garrison, of the 54th Regiment, my highest appointment yet, and I'm stuck here in this Godforsaken place. Another Godforsaken place.'

As was Tony. At least Major Fitzgerald could find things to do, determine his own activities. For his servant, one day opened onto the next as blankly as the snow that covered the surrounding hills and bogs. Instead of looking out on bleak acres of hacked tree stumps and scorched bush – which had so jarred his senses on their arrival some four months earlier – all was now uniformly white and smooth. Torn out of the surrounding forest, the fort was a monument of wood, layered and stacked, knuckled around the cluster of rough buildings

[18] Yes. I remember his letters. He was so open to adventure. And he made sure, always, to include you, that you might share in all the novel experiences. Few men are so fortunate, and women like myself, not at all. LLF.
[19] Dear Edward! So like him. LLF.

within. Everywhere there was wood. In the apartments of the Officer-in-Charge, sawdust found every uncovered jug, every ablutions jar; dulled every surface, every window; slurred every footstep. Resin oozed from tables, chairs and doors, sticking to hands, so that the smell of pitch became a part of every man there. Better pitch though than the reek of the mouldering deer hide which graced the floor in front of the fireplace – those soldiers had not mastered the art of drying out pelts.

A miasma of boredom hung over the place. And snow. There appeared to be no end to it, not as far as the eye could see nor as far as he could imagine. Down in the cluster of houses and streets that made up this township it was said the snows would last another two months. Beyond occasional trips to the merchant stores, or a tavern, there was little to do, and Tony found this almost more of a shackle than having his days filled with tasks. Edward rose early, and he a little earlier, in time to set the kettle boiling and break the ice on his basin of water. After his master had supped his coffee and breakfasted, and if he could be persuaded, Tony shaved him. 'But Sir,' he would say, 'it is important that you of all people should look presentable and above reproach. If you should let your standards slip, think how the men may receive it.' And Edward would nod in agreement and offer himself up to the blade.

Now, Edward turned to Tony. 'Faithful Tony. I'd be a miserable dog if I did not have you.'

Tony hoped he would not mention his cousin, Lady Georgiana. That kind of talk could last hours, starting with his great love for her, despite, in spite of, even with all … and then he would lurch from his uncle to his stepfather to his need to make his mark in this wilderness. To *show* all of them. But no. No mention of his cousin. A relief.

'I'm thinking of mapping a new route, from Fredericton to Quebec. It hasn't been done before. Apart from the natives. It would be a first, something to show for my time here. Something to write home about.' He paused. But the look of excitement faded. 'You're my one familiar face. My connection with home. Mother still asks after you, you know.'

Yes, Tony knew that the Duchess mentioned him in her letters so that he would continue to look after her son. She had made a point of asking to see him before they embarked, had bade him sit, while she spoke about her dearest son. Told how he was still upset over the affair with his cousin, but that it would pass, of course.

'He is given to impulses of the heart, and I should hate to see him becoming too forlorn.' He'd tried to extract the real meaning from the froth of words she was uttering. He found it difficult – to be seated so close to her; to hear each tiny shift and whisper of fabric as she moved, as she breathed; to catch the hint of rosewater; to see how she twisted her rings on her fingers, one with a deep red stone, the size of grape, turning it round and round—

'Tony, please look at me when I address you. How can I know if you understand me?'

How indeed? He was forced to look at her, and to realise how creased and worn she appeared, how reddened her eyes were. It came as a shock. He understood then what she was asking of him; not just to serve her son but to look after him, to look out for him. He understood her love and her fears.

'And please, Tony, ensure that he writes often. He can be careless but if you should prompt him, then perhaps …'

Every day he laid out a sheaf of notepapers to encourage Edward to make good his reply. He checked the ink bottle and mixed up a new batch if necessary, then spent some time trimming the quill, shaving the ends on the diagonal, leaving a narrow blunt tip just as he desired. This part gave some satisfaction, reminding him of making flutes, of fashioning some child's trinket out of a rough end of wood, before he dismissed his own stupidity. It was a nib, nothing more, and one he could not use.

Boredom. Restlessness. These feelings dogged him. He saw how Edward responded to each letter. How he savoured each word on the page as though it were a tasty morsel. How sometimes he took the words apart, cut into them to find their message. And all the while Tony was excluded from this; relying on his master to read aloud. The other officers were the same. The post bag contained all the promise of a world away from this one. The men took to the quiet of their bunks, preferring to read by the dull glow of a reed lamp than in company.

The words within those pages belonged to them alone, taking them away from the now of the snowbound fort back to their homes in England, and their wives or mothers, their daily doings and illnesses. Tony's only escape was imagination or memory and that was not a place he wanted to be.

If only ... If only those inked words could bring him somewhere else. He tried to match words to what Edward read out. He knew most of his letters but that led to confusion, adding to his frustration. He teetered on the edge of knowledge, grappling with the suspense of being able to recognise the Duchess's even hand, or Mr Ogilvie's, spiky and peremptory, but unable to tease out the details of the words. He held the map but had not the compass.

There were days he wanted to do something just to produce an effect. To make something happen. Like the morning when he threw some scraps to the dogs who skulked around the fort. One of them, a shaggy misery, failing to get his share, whinged and turned its dark eyes on him. He couldn't help himself. He put his foot to the dog, kicked it, and watched it scuttle off, bony legs puncturing the snow. A moment of pure relief filled him, then a string of curses bubbled up, against the dog, against this place, this town of wood and snow and huddled people.

The following night, his sleep was disturbed by the sound of distant howling – dogs or wolves, he could not be certain. A beat of fear started in his chest and sweat broke from him so that he kicked off the blankets, stumbled to the door and flung it open. It took a moment to unsee swamp and wattle, to unsmell rotting indigo and the taint of heat, and sense instead that the lash he felt on his face and arms was an icy rain driven across the snow-packed yard. He sank to his knees, welcomed the crunching cold on his hands and legs and gave thanks to a God whom he neither knew nor yet believed in.

'Milord, you must write. Your mother ...'

But he did not wish to write. He was too busy, he said, his legs sprawled in front of him, his fingers toying with the pages of a book, *Gil Blas* – again – alternating with his tumbler of wine. The officers still maintained certain standards when it came to drinking. Not for them the rough local grog or rum. There'd been enough traffic of boats on the river, at least until the recent freeze, to ensure a steady supply of wine; though the cost according to the quartermaster was some four times what you'd pay in Halifax or St John's. But some things you cannot put a price on, or so said Major Fitzgerald.

'My last letter from home, Tony.' It was not the book he had been toying with, but rather a letter, kept within its pages. 'From my Uncle Richmond. Seems he is having difficulty securing my promotion to something useful.' He crumpled the letter into a ball and tossed it towards the fire. It fell short.

'But he has tried?'

Edward shifted in his seat and gestured to Tony to sit down. 'Actually I think not. He does not like to use up all his favours at once. He must feel that my case will not bring a good enough return.'

'He would be so …?' Tony searched for a word. Failed, as always when trying to interpret the motives of that family. They addressed each other with extravagant outpourings of affection. They used so many words to convey something simple. They argued over small matters at length and described, in great detail, petty trifles of illness or slights given or received; failure to respond to letters, failure to return a visit and so many others that were read aloud but he'd forgotten. Yet for matters of importance, such as promotion or his commission or whatever it was, they slipped around it as smoothly as fish past a rock. Neither would Lord Edward ever convey to his uncle, in anything other than words of polite courtesy, just how much he wanted a real appointment; command of a body of men engaged in active duty; planning a campaign, making strategic decisions; leading an advance party from Gibraltar, or the Indies or wherever there was something happening.

'So calculating?' Edward smiled, then shrugged. 'My uncle does what's best for himself. The trick would be to align my request with his own interests. Or think of another way. Perhaps my cousin Fox. At least I can be plain with him.' He sighed. 'I won't apply to my brother no matter what. He has sided with the government for the first time. Where are his principles? Besides I'm not so ambitious. If I am found fit for command I shall get it. It's too soul-destroying to beg or pay one's way. To deserve a reward is far more pleasant than the reward itself.'

'Huzzah,' Tony murmured.

'Even Faithful Tony mocks me,' he laughed. 'The world has turned upside-down.'

'But we are here for the duration?'

'Seems that way.' He poured himself another glass of wine. 'Have one yourself.'

If the three other officers had been present, Tony would have refused. Since Gibraltar, he took more care in the presence of others.

'What would I do without you?' Lord Edward had drunk to excess, and was tearful. 'If only you could do my writing for me. I could sit here and dictate to you. You could be my amanuensis.'

Amanuensis. Not a word he knew. He tapped the amulet beneath his shirt. One to keep.

'Why do you do that?' Edward pointed. 'Why do you tap that thing, that leather pouch you keep?'

How to explain it? It would mean unpacking all those words and setting them out. He wasn't sure he could do it. A log shifted in the fire setting off a trail of sparks and falling ash. He made a move for the poker.

'Leave it Tony. Just tell me, I want to know.' He leaned forward resting his elbows on his knees and giving the full force of his attention, of his grey eyes.

'It helps me remember words. Words that may be useful. I ...' Tony paused. How to make him understand? 'I imagine this pouch is like a money purse, only I don't collect money, just words.'

'Words? Why?'

'Imagine if I used that word, amanuensis, with certain people? Or any amount of your words. If I spoke like you. It would confound them. If I could read and write.'

A wind funnelled through a gap in the wooden wall, stirring a tiny eddy of sawdust.

'Dear God, how often have I promised you, started and not seen it through.' Edward slammed his glass on the floor in a pool of wine.

Got up, pacing. 'I who have been taught by Ogilvie, raised on the milk of Rousseau himself.'

Tony put his glass down carefully, unable to control a slight tremor. A tiny splash of wine dribbled down the edge.

'To hell with collecting words, Tony. By the time the snows melt, you will read and write them.'

He could not speak. How often had he stood at this door, gripped this handle, even glimpsed through the crack, fields of swaying grass, pages fluttering. Too often. No. He would not get his hopes raised. He moved his hand along the base of his chair, felt the grooves and knots of the wood and the warmth of the grain. Deal. Like the floors.

'It'll be a real test too.' Once more the glass was filled, knocked back. 'Not of you, Tony. Don't misunderstand me. I mean of my abilities to teach. You know me, I'm not always patient.'

'That's true.'

'Ah, so you haven't been struck dumb.'

'No.' He wanted to get started, now. To stop the talking, the jesting. To learn now, to catch up.

'I mean it's only so you can be useful. Give you something to do instead of making coffee.' Edward laughed to underscore the jest, swung away again to the table behind. 'You could keep the ledgers. You're better with money and calculations than I am.' He searched through a small stack of papers at the end of the table, pulled out a sheet, containing numbers and lines and took up a pen, waving impatiently. 'Get another candle, Tony. Two more or you shall go blind before we ever begin.'

Two tallow stubs alongside the ink pot. A chair drawn up.

Tony did not speak, as Edward scraped the nib across the page, forming the letters TONY. He did not say that this was the one word he'd taught himself already, for he knew somehow, that this time *would* be the time he'd learn fully.

'Now you. Take the pen. Copy what I have done.'

He dipped the nib in the small pot. It beaded darkly, like old blood. His hand was steady, mid-flight, hovering over the page.

'Don't worry about the paper. Just start at the bottom under my writing.' Edward's voice was quiet.

So he did. Began with the curve of the T, and was off, scratching and sliding on the paper like a hen on ice. The Y lurched drunkenly off the page. His heart swelled, as though it might burst. He threw the pen on the page, laughing, and Lord Edward was shouting, 'Bravo, a toast, we need a toast, get the bottle.'

Their glasses clashed and spilt on the page, red wine splatters running through the inked letters.

He held him to his promise, though never had to remind him of it. Not exactly. Just enquired if this was a suitable time, or if later would suit. Just left out sheets and two pots of ink. If Edward ran his hand through his hair, or sighed and or cast about for a drink, he just said to him, very well, the morning would be a good time, when both of them would be more refreshed. In between he busied himself, copying out words from inventories, words he knew. He tried *Gil Blas*, sounding out words when no one was around, muttering them under his breath as he went.

A month after that and he could record his thoughts on paper. His hand was crude, and there was no one to whom he could send these writings. Still he consoled himself that writing linked this present to a future yet unknown. It did not then occur to him how that was the same as creating a past.

The True Narrative

Spring 1789, and Major FitzGerald undertakes a dramatic trek to Quebec; He makes contact with some Indians; The Author experiences unexpected Benevolence from a young Warrior.

In the early part of that year, Lord Edward determined to journey to Quebec. There was already an established route, by way of the river, some three hundred miles long, but as yet no one had sought out a direct path across the mountains except, perhaps, some of the Native people. This, then, became my Master's ambition. He gathered up a small party, two experienced woodsmen, two officers and a handful of men who expressed a desire to join the expedition. Toboggans were loaded with provisions, dogs set in harness, and clothed in our blanket coats and fur gloves to the elbow, we embarked on our journey. My Master, being filled with the spirit of adventure which so characterised all of his activities, kept the men in good cheer. When we encountered difficulties and hardship, he was able to rally their drooping spirits, and urge them on. Despite the conditions, I never saw my Master struck low. Even at a point when we appeared to have lost our path, there was never a time when he doubted himself or the purpose of his expedition. In our third week of travel, when we were beginning to experience some hardship for want of fresh game, we encountered a band of Indians, a family group dressed in the Native way in skins and furs. They were much taken with us, and Lord Edward offered to share some of our provisions. In return, the Indians demonstrated some of their hunting methods.[20]

Scuff and creak. Scuff and creak. Snow shoes. Scuff—

A blinking daze of black and white. The dark and light of tree against snow that went on forever. Dark trunks rising upward, from snow to cloud. Flickers of movement interrupting the pattern, distant figures, five or six, and a dog pack, moving steadily among the trees. Impossible to distinguish one from another, for all were hooded or hatted, and their garments – a motley array of ragged greatcoats and filthy blankets – over-slung with axes and rifles. All shifting across the snow. Scuff and creak. The sound of snow shoes.

Tony lagging behind, dressed in similar fashion, just one more in the shuffling line, listening to the sound of the snowshoes, the rhythm beating like his lifeblood, coursing through his limbs, his chest, his neck. His extremities were a different matter, for those he could not feel at all. Neither his hands, encased in fur mittens, nor his feet strapped in those wondrous constructions of ash and deer hide that allowed him and his companions to move across the soft snow, as light as twigs on water. Silent while walking; each man discovered for himself that talking broke the rhythm and that this place, this endless forest should be undisturbed. Except, that is, when hunger dictated otherwise. And then all thoughts of quietude exploded.

Scuff and creak. Scuff—

'Damnation.'

Edward stopped suddenly, reaching under his greatcoat. Fumbled uselessly. He pulled his glove with his teeth. A crunching sound as he bit against the icy fur. Once again he searched for the compass. The men stood and waited with frozen eyes, except for Ezra, the old

---

[20] Could you not elaborate? I understand you are not naturally given to storytelling but nonetheless I find your account to be overly staid and dry. Write more of the Indians. How they looked upon Dear Edward with such respect that they granted him the highest honour of making him a chieftain. I cannot recall the name of the tribe. Perhaps it was not this particular one but I do not suppose it matters too much. The honour is what matters. LLF.

woodsman, who darted forward to snatch it from his hand. Ezra was like a wild creature as he turned his fur-skinned head upward, searching for the sun, almost sniffing for it. But there was no sun; nor had there been any for three days. All heads turned upward, following the black, grainy trunks, rising towards a hard, grey sky, which offered no quarter. Nor did the endless untouched snow spread at their feet.

One of the men muttered, 'Anyone any idea where …'

Ezra sniffed against the muffler that covered half his face. Edward looked at the compass lying in the man's hand.

'We're still headed north west. I'm certain of it.'

Ezra merely shrugged. The dogs whined, loud and mournful. They did not like these pauses. They liked to be on the move, given their lead. They seemed to sense indecision, becoming peevish and snappy. It was contagious. The men felt it too, and hunger.

For the first week of the trek, the men were lulled by the steady routine. Rise early, breakfast, walk for three hours, eat some hard biscuits or berries, walk again, then prepare a camp before nightfall. Everyone worked together; gathering wood for a fire, trapping or shooting wild birds and animals, cutting and stacking branches for shelter, and laying spruce on the ground as bedding. If they failed to trap anything, it was of little matter. They had their rations, salt pork, three-quarters of a pound per man. And they used it, sometimes taking more than allotted – and why not when the woods had been filled with squirrels, turkeys and any number of deer? But not now. Not here. Just the lure of shadowed punctures in the snow: moose tracks. But no sign of the moose despite two days' tracking. The short-lived camaraderie among the men had worn thin.

The man who'd complained earlier, kicked the snow. 'So what are we following? The compass or the damn moose?'

Another officer, Lieutenant Brisbane, interrupted. 'You'd better watch yourself, MacKenzie. Remember who you're addressing.'

MacKenzie kicked the snow again.

Edward replaced the compass in his pocket and put his glove on again. 'We'll take the ridge over there. Get beyond the tree line. Then we may have a view of what lies ahead. Get our bearings.'

The moose kill mollified dogs and men for a time. But the memory of a full belly does not last. Hunger becomes a presence. And cold. Tony felt a sharp pain in his teeth and throat with each breath. He concentrated on walking in the tracks of the man in front, on the snow shoes, watched as they slid across the surface, dropping clumps in their wake.

The men took turns at the lead, stomping down the fresh snow to smooth a path for the toboggans. Even still, there were times he needed to heave the load from behind. Better to push than deal with the dogs.

In the distance, the dogs yipped and yauled.

Two days later and the provisions were all but gone. Nothing but trees and snow in the line of vision as they trekked uphill, the toboggans a hindrance, snow shoes an encumbrance. On with them, off with them.

Camp was a snowy enclosure under a rocky outcrop. Above the rock, more trees stacked, up and up. Though not yet nightfall, there was little light and the fire was a paltry affair of hissing branches and acrid smoke. Tony placed a pan of cornmeal, and a kettle filled with snow, in the centre.

'Is that it?' MacKenzie spat. 'Fucking cornmeal?'

He looked at Tony and off into the blackness, where Edward and Ezra could be heard arguing.

'Right,' MacKenzie said. He stamped to the toboggan, rummaging through it.

'What are you doing?' Tony called.

'Biscuits. I know there are some left. We should have our share.'

Tony pushed him off the toboggan but MacKenzie swung his fist at him, catching him under the chin, knocking him flat. Ezra darted forward. Holding a knife? It was difficult to be certain. In the firelight, a shadowed scuffle ensued.

'Stop!' Edward shouted. But the scuffling and cursing continued. The dogs barked noisily, unused to such commotion. There was a brief flare of light and the air erupted with the sound of gunshot. A branch cracked, and snow fell to the ground in muffled thumps.

'I gave you an order. I said stop.' Edward's voice was hard.

The snow around the fire was littered with biscuits. Edward was still pointing his pistol at MacKenzie.

'Now pick them up and give them to the men before they're completely sodden. They'll be no use to anyone after this.'

Edward addressed the group huddled around the fire. The gunshot had left them subdued and even the unexpected food did little to lift anyone's spirits.

'Ezra will accompany you men back to Fredericton. You'll be back beyond the forest line by tomorrow evening. Probably pick up some tracks, get some trapping done. I will proceed to Quebec with Lieutenant Brisbane. And Tony.'

'You won't make it on your own.' Ezra spat on the ground, staining the snow. 'You'll need me.'

'Perhaps you're right, Ezra. But these men need you more. You're the only one who can manage the dogs and they're little use on these mountains.'

The following morning, a bright, hard-edged sun sliced through the trees as the other group departed. Their dark outlines crisscrossed the distance, until they merged with the trunks and disappeared. Had Brisbane been asked, Tony wondered. He had not appeared surprised at the announcement. What of him? Was he just like one of the dogs, or a toboggan, to be taken or not taken as suited? As suited Edward. He kept behind the other two. Kept his thoughts to himself. Without the other men, and the dogs and the toboggans, they moved more quickly up the slopes. By midday, the trees were far behind. There was only snow, and the blade of sun suspended overhead.

Edward fell into step beside him, his greatcoat sweeping the snow behind him. 'You don't mind coming, do you?'

Tony let a pause open, cool and wide. 'I'd prefer to be asked,' he said. 'You may as well have said I'll proceed with the toboggans.'

'No!' Edward sounded horrified.

The moment of silence grew, apart from their boots creaking through piled up snow. Tony shifted the bag behind his shoulder.

'Forget it. If you had asked, the outcome would have been the same. I'd no wish to travel any further with those men, especially MacKenzie.'

Two more days and the thaw started. Everywhere the sound of water: wet snow shifting and slipping to the ground; drip, drip from the ends of branches, trickling through tiny gaps; and the splat and suck as though the earth was gorging on each footstep. All was physical: wet, cold, hunger. Each man nursed his ailments privately; Tony no longer attempted to remove his boots for fear the skin on his swollen, oozing feet would slough off entirely; Brisbane coughed into his muffler, clutching at his chest with each stumble; Edward pissed blood on the snow, though he could not resist some utterance, some fuck or Christ.

They followed an ice-frilled stream to where it turned at a shallow dog-leg. Brisbane was the first to enter the water, plunging to his knees, swinging a small net through the water. From the bank, seeing the hop and jump of fish, it seemed impossible that he could miss them. That he should only have to hold out his hands and they would jump into them. But each time he raised the net, it came up empty. He thrashed about, soaked and shaking.

'Get out, you fool!' Edward shouted.

By the time they had dragged him to some trees, he was almost rigid. They rolled him over and over in his hastily cast-off blanket. When Tony tugged off his boots, it was like removing the boots of a day-old corpse. A sudden flash to another time, a pile of corpses and pulling ...

He got a fire going, a poor, stuttering fire but enough to heat some water, something for Brisbane to drink. Then he left the two men, took the net back to the stream. He moved slowly, watching the flow of the water, the place where it rippled over the stones. He walked back to the fire, and sat with the net and one of his snowshoes. He unpicked the base of the shoe, taking care to save the lengths of hide. He used it to weave the net to the frame, leaving some loose at the top. His hands worked without active thought, just some memory of reed or hemp beneath his skin. He stopped to consider it. He took the remaining hide and bound the loose end of net into a tight ring. Not rigid enough, but still. Edward made no remark but watched with weary interest as Tony returned to the stream with his snowshoe net. He placed it in the water, where the ripples gave way to a steady flow inside the curve of the bank. He weighed the front down with stones, watched the small net balloon and tug with the current.

Edward joined him, the two men standing together, huddled in their coats.

'How is the Lieutenant?' Tony asked.

'Like a felled log. If we can warm him up, he'll recover. And if we're near to Quebec. Or the river at least.'

He leaned forward, looking in the water. Tony had seen it too. The sudden jerking movement in the little net.

'Dear God. Tony, you've got one.' Edward hunkered down, reaching for the net.

'No,' Tony said. 'Wait.'

They waited. Watched as more fish pushed and butted the base of the net, one or two small ones managing to escape the crude hide ring. Tony lay along the bank. Not hurrying. Grasped the frame, and pulled it from the water. Edward took it from him as he clambered to his feet.

They tossed the fish in a pan and set them cooking. The smell woke Brisbane. Edward showed him the net.

'Where did you learn how to do that? From your people?'

Tony coughed. His people? He thought it just made sense. A question of looking, seeing. Knowing what the problem was, what it required. And yet. Some part of him, his hands, had worked almost without thinking.

'I don't know. It seemed right. Your people's method wasn't working. Blundering in and splashing about, succumbing to the cold.'

Brisbane laughed. Then coughed. His face was pale and sweating despite the cold.

'You should eat, Lieutenant,' Tony said. He piled a plate with charred fish and handed it to him, enjoyed watching the two men greedily stuffing it into their mouths.

'Thank you, Tony.' Edward said, passing him a bottle. 'Rum.' Each of them had a share. A warm stomach, a warm, rummy throat. It felt good.

The first sign of the Indians was two days later. Scuffed snow, footprints, a doused fire, and a neat pile of picked bird carcasses under some stones. Tony boiled them in a kettle of meltwater, and the two officers each cradled a cupful, sipping carefully.

'Bone broth.' Edward looked at Brisbane. 'That will fill your belly, put fire in your blood.'

Brisbane managed a smile in return.

A cup of imagination, Tony thought, though he drifted into dreamless sleep. He woke to the sound of voices. A low chittering sound. Birds? A face bent over his. Dark eyes staring, curious. He jolted back, his actions mirrored by the other. A man. And there were more, at least twelve people, dressed in furs and skins, arrayed as coats and cloaks, hats and boots. He reached a hand out to the body sleeping next to him. 'Milord, wake up. Visitors.'

He never broke eye contact with the man who stared back. Neither friendly nor threatening. Nonetheless he felt threatened.

Lord Edward was awake in an instant. 'Ah,' he said. 'Ah.' He stayed on the ground. Smiling as best he could.

Still the group stared, though some looked away, chattering among themselves. 'We are pleased to meet you.' Edward said loudly, bowing his head.

A child came forward, proffered a bowl.

'What's in it?' Brisbane's hunger was overcoming caution.

'Some sort of cake. Corn perhaps.' Tony said.

Edward continued smiling and bowing, speaking from the side of his mouth. 'What can we offer in return? Tony?'

Tony reached for his pack. Slowly. One of the men cocked his head to the side. Tony took out a spoon.

'Good. Yes. A spoon.' Edward muttered. 'Brisbane?' Again he spoke quietly, without looking over at Brisbane. 'Have you your gun?'

'No Sir. Sorry.'

Tony held out the spoon.

The child took it, turning it over in his hand, before retreating to the back of the group. An old woman in a gleaming beaver coat pointed to the bones in the kettle, and then the bowl, gesturing at Edward with her fingers up and down to her lips.

They were Mi'kmaq people. They spoke some French. Edward negotiated, ingratiated. The mention of Quebec brought a brief nod. One of the men drew some patterns in the snow which Edward took to be a map. They would show them the way, he declared. At first it was a struggle to keep up with them. They moved swiftly, even the children, who swarmed over rocks and fallen tree stumps, lithe and full of courage. They shared their food but at night made their own fire and slept apart. The old woman slathered foul grease on Tony's feet – having first examined him, pulling his sleeve up his arm and turning his hands over – then boiled a foul drink for Brisbane, and another, the foulest of all, for Edward.

Brisbane said little to them but Edward hunkered beside the women while they prepared food. Some of the young men pointed and laughed. Later Edward joined them, gestured at their bows, their knives. Tony sat apart, watching. Such ease Edward had, an assumption that his interest would be welcome. Returned even. And it was. By the men, and a woman, whose eyes followed him, though her expression never changed. Still, he knew, knew that Edward would probably entice her somehow. Bed her.

The group had turned their attention to him. One of the men, a small, thin youth, took up his bow and loaded an arrow, so quickly, that Tony wasn't sure. And yet, he was raising the bow, looking to where Tony was sitting. What was—?

He scrambled to his feet, skidding in the slushy snow. The air parted by his left ear. A slight ripple. A whoosh. The arrow twanged in the tree beside him.

'What the hell—?' He waved his hands at them. Edward was laughing along with the young warrior. Careless bastard. Brisbane too was laughing. Bastard as well.

The next morning, as they moved off again, the young Indian who had shot the arrow fell into step with Tony. Tapped him on the arm. Tapped his own chest. Mabou. Tony found it hard to let his anger go, moved away. Mabou followed him. He was wound tight. Hopped from one foot to the other. There was no escaping him.

He showed him how to use a spear – a strange three-pronged thing like a fork. Showed him how to stand in a river pool and wait. Wait until his feet were beyond feeling. Until the fish nibbled his numb toes and it was only a matter then of which fish to impale. He was glad to be away from the others. To see the abundance about him. Was it the thaw that awakened them or had they been there all the time: fish, beavers, porcupines and birds? Countless birds. The forest was alive with the sounds of them. Cawing, croaking, chirruping, quacking. This place, which had felt harsh and threatening, seemed filled with possibilities.

The great river revealed itself long before he saw it. Tony felt it first. A low, deep hum, something growling in his bones. And then the smell, different from the forest, the snow. Rich with life. He breathed in deeply.

'It's the most wondrous sight in all the world.' So said Brisbane who dropped to his knees at the water's edge. 'How long to Quebec?' he asked.

Too soon.

Together with two of the Mi'kmaq they dismantled a pile of spruce branches. Underneath, canoes – three large birch canoes. On the water, Tony found his arms held a memory of paddling, knew how to slice the water and pull back. He fell into a natural rhythm, his mind drifting with the current, following a different river, brown and slow-moving. An overhang of trees, giant dark palms that lean out from the shore. A flash of green and red swooping in front of the boat, three birds, calling, a sound that echoes and rises. He paddles. There's heat coiling around him. Breathing heat. And words spoken. He tries to listen. Familiar voices, but deep, down in the caves of his mind. Distantly echoing. Was this memory or imagination? He struggled to get back into that place, find that mind cave.

A splash of freezing water washed away the memory. For it was a memory. He was certain. There was Mabou turning around, shouting at him. Pointing at Edward, who was in the nearside canoe. Edward who stabbed and thrashed at the river, and cursed.

The night had closed round them when the canoes scraped into a small, stony inlet. The Indians wouldn't go any closer, said something about the foul stench of the place. A smell of burning, blew downwind of the town. Edward and Brisbane stood in the lick of icy water, shouldering their guns, their packs. Edward gave his watch to the old woman.

'Perhaps I can get another in the town,' he murmured as she slipped it into a leather bag. She reached for Edward's head and laid her hands on him, muttering something into his ear. Tony turned to remove his pack from the canoe just as Mabou reached for his bow, plucked the string, releasing a hum, the sound of a swarm of bees flying into the distance. The canoe rocked gently in the water. Another gift for Edward, Tony thought. But it was not. Mabou placed it in Tony's hands. He held it to his chest, still standing in the icy shallows. Edward and Brisbane clambered to the shore.

'Tony,' Edward called. 'We should go.'

Mabou gestured to him, then pointed to the canoe. And Tony heard the arrow again, the thwack of release, the parting of air. Was that how freedom sounded? Mabou waited. The old woman regarded him gravely from under her fur-lined hood. Tony looked at the two men on the shore; Brisbane already moving off, hunched under his blanket and pack; Edward turning.

'Tony?'

Was that concern or irritation in his voice?

'Tony? Are you coming?'

The True Narrative

March 1789, and Major FitzGerald visits Quebec and Montreal.

Lord Edward was greeted warmly in Quebec and later in Montreal. He made some short expeditions and tours, meeting different Indians who were unanimous in their approval of him. He was also much sought after by all the best families of the two towns, and rarely had a quiet evening during his stay there, being much taken up with dances and musical entertainments, including one or two concerts at the Barracks.[21]

Quebec, a stinking, teeming cesspit of a town. He understood why the Mi'kmaq avoided it. The odours of man's presence hung about the place: tar from the caulkers by the quays; rank blood from the slaughterhouse; congealed fat – a slaughterhouse or a tallow maker, who could say? And all mixed with the stench of daily living in the cramped lower quarters, where the wooden houses, some three storeys high, leaned towards each other as if to share in some sordid gossip or shameful secrets. He too was stinking, following in the wake of the two officers, who in turn trailed all manner of odours. Edward led them along the river front, up the narrow lanes behind the wharves, past the barracks and into the busy Rue Martin.

[21] Why not describe Quebec? And show Edward's comical side? I remember Edward's tale about an innkeeper and how she refused him admittance. The Family were much diverted by this and I am certain a reader would find it amusing also. LLF.

Following once more. Back in what Brisbane called 'civilisation' and he was following behind them again. His stomach knotted.

Up a slushy street, lit by lanterns hanging from brash establishments, announcing themselves variously as Madame Belle's, Madame Carlier and Chez Victoire. Brisbane was alert with interest, his head swivelling in all directions. He moved towards a doorway, lured by the sound of an accordion, the smell of beer or perhaps the sound of voices inside. Laughter. A woman's laugh. Edward pulled him back.

'Not now, Lieutenant. You're still an officer. You need to clean up.'

Easier said than done. Three inns later – each time turned away by owners repelled by their smell or appearance or both – they arrived at a stone building in the upper town, its windows framed with curtains, and a smell of roast meat wafting from the doorway. Edward tried his best with the elderly landlady.

'You have been highly recommended to us.' The woman's face froze in disbelief. 'By General Carleton,' he offered.

There was an audible sniff.

Edward pushed his hood back from his face, attempted a smile. 'You see Madame, that we are gentlemen.'

At this the woman lifted her lantern a little higher and let the light fall slowly across Edward before moving on to Brisbane and finally Tony. She let it drop to her side. Another sniff.

'There's a room out the back. No stove mind. Nor beds neither.' Once more she swung the lamp. 'I'd say it's just about good enough for bedfellows such as yourselves.'

Brisbane moved forward but Edward put a hand on his arm. 'We'll find somewhere better than this.'

The woman was unmoved. 'You think so? This town is full to the rafters. Seems to me beggars can't afford to be choosers. Or should I say *gentlemen*?'

By the time they were finally admitted to a respectable establishment, and each had finished a large bowl of fish coddle and hunks of stale bread, Tony did not care about anything. Brisbane slept as soon as he lay down. As he snuffed out the lamp, Edward brought up the matter of the Mi'kmaq, and Tony's reluctance to leave.

'I might have gone with them, had I been you,' he said. 'Nothing to bind you, no family.' He sounded envious for a moment as though Tony had greater possibilities and choices than he.

'Perhaps I do not regard such ties as a hindrance,' he answered.

'But you were tempted?'

'Yes. There was something about them. I felt, I don't know—' So difficult to put shape on ideas. Words on feelings. He wanted to crush something. He turned over on the mattress, turned his face to the wall.

'Can I presume to suggest you felt—'

'No,' Tony cut in, turning again in the darkness to where Edward lay on the other side of Brisbane. 'Please don't. I do not think you can speak for me. That's just what made me consider it. With those people, I was a person as much as you or the Lieutenant. On equal footing. A man in my own right. Not just Lord Edward's man.'

The dark was silent. Had he gone to sleep? Was there to be no response? Time passed, he'd almost slipped into sleep himself when he heard Edward's voice, as though they'd just left off speaking.

'Yes, I think I understand. Thank you. And I'm sorry that an explanation was necessary. Goodnight, Tony.'

Edward slipped back into civilised life with all the ease of a man slipping into a bath. Which is what he did, for an hour, wallowing in the warm water, while Tony shaved him and attempted to pick out the ticks which hid under his matted hair. Edward avoided any further talk of leaving.

'I'll pay a visit to Lord Dorchester after I've cleaned up. Since I owe him for the change of clothing.'

Tony squeezed hard on a tick that had burrowed deep in the back of his neck. Edward slapped his hand. 'Damn it Tony. Must you? And where did the damn things come from? In the snow? How is it possible?'

Tony shrugged. 'How about I cut your hair short? It might suit you. You could purchase a wig if the occasion demanded.'

'Purchase a wig if the occasion demanded?' Edward laughed, and the bath water churned. 'Trust me Tony, you can safely dispose of that word pouch now. You're fit to attend on Lord Dorchester himself.' He turned around, sending a splash of water over the edge of the tub. 'You do know he, Lord Dorchester, is actually Sir Guy Carleton, the one who refused to give up the loyalist negroes in New York, after the surrender.'

'No. I did not know. Will I crop your hair?'

'Do.'

Minutes passed. He cut the hair away, some falling to the floor, some into the water. Edward continued talking. 'Carleton had all the names written in that *Book of Negroes* and arranged their passage to Nova Scotia and other places besides.' He laughed. 'Said he'd make sure the British government compensated their owners for their loss. They've yet to receive a penny.'

Why this account now? Why the show of interest?

'Tony?'

'Yes?'

Edward was out, drying himself off. 'You're thinking of the Indians again?'

'No, I'm not,' he replied. He looked at Edward, at his hair. 'I'm thinking you should have sent me to London that time. To learn to dress hair.'

'No matter. I'll do.' Edward struggled into his new boots. 'Use my bath, Tony. You can't go anywhere looking like that. You're a disgrace.'

Tony smiled and Edward was delighted.

'You'd never have gone with them, would you? Think what you'd have missed. I know how you love conversation.'

The bath looked less than inviting: hair and ticks floating on murky water. But the only alternative was the public baths near the quayside. At least only one foul body had been washed in this water. Once he lowered himself in, he forgot all about dirt and relished the still-warm bath. He looked up, counting the beams that traversed the wooden ceiling, then reached for the soap on the table beside him. Such an improbable luxury after the last four weeks of travel. Or was it five? He'd lost count. His feet were not as bad as he had feared. That grease potion was good – those Mi'kmaq really knew their plants and cures.

A rap on the door.

'Are you finished yet?' Edward put his head in. 'I've had an idea.'

'I've just got in,' he protested, splashing the water to make his point.

'Yes, well, finish up and for God's sake don't forget to shave.' He tossed a bundle on the table. 'Some clothing for you. All of our belongings are feeding the brazier in the yard below.' He opened the window, and cold air rushed in, bringing with it the smell of burning wool.

Brisbane was standing by the fire in the small sitting room downstairs. He had kept his long hair, and tied it back with a small ribbon. Otherwise he was unrecognisable as the feral man of yesterday. He smiled at Tony's approach.

'Good to be human again.'

'Yes, Sir, it is.'

'What is the Major planning? I thought we were to dine with Lord Dorchester.'

'You are, but he wishes to pay a visit first. He refuses to say where.'

Brisbane sighed and smiled again, warming his hands to the flames. 'As long as I don't have to get cold or wet.'

They were back at the stone house in the upper town, where the woman had refused them the day before.

'This will be funny. Like a scene from *Gil Blas*.' Edward straightened his neckcloth, rapped on the door. Brisbane coughed discreetly as the landlady's stony face appeared in the doorway.

'Ah, gentlemen,' she exclaimed, sweeping the lantern back into the hallway. 'You are looking for rooms? Please follow me.'

She led the way. Edward turned to Brisbane with a smirk while Tony tried not to laugh. They were shown into a sitting room, decked in lace and cushions and needlepoint pictures on the canvas-covered walls.

'Lovely.' Edward said and the woman gave a little bow of satisfaction. 'It would have been perfect. Yesterday.'

She looked confused.

'Remember what you said about beggars.' He couldn't contain his glee. 'Yes it's I. Us.' He was laughing outright. So was Brisbane. 'There's another saying about not judging a book by its cover ...'

The woman looked horrified. Her hands flapped like market-day chickens.

'I must beg your pardon. Sir, Captain.'

'Major actually.'

'Major. It's just you looked so ... and the negro man... I assumed you were all of the same ilk, of the same standing, I see now he's your servant of course but ...'

Brisbane coughed.

Edward stopped laughing. 'What of it?'

Tony felt suddenly weary. Shouldn't have come. Didn't want to witness a confrontation. He wanted to go back to the rooms, by himself, let the two gentlemen go off to the Governor's House, let them talk, chew over their adventures. Perhaps Edward would have news of the family. Maybe his post would have arrived in Quebec by boat. Perhaps the Governor would finally have word of Edward's anticipated promotion —Lieutenant Colonelcy in the 44th Regiment. Edward, Edward.

He would like one evening, just one, to himself.

The woman's hands flapped once more. Edward was waiting for a response. Tony filled the gap.

'By your leave, Milord. I must attend to matters back at the lodgings.'

Edward was surprised but Brisbane seized the moment. 'Indeed. We are expected this very minute at the Governor's dinner. We should leave.'

Edward blew out his cheeks in exasperation but followed Brisbane outside. Tony bowed briefly, wishing them both a good evening.

It was snowing again. Great flakes seesawing downward, golden in the light of the street lanterns.

'Wait, Tony. You have no money.' Edward plunged his hand into his coat pocket, pulling out some coins. 'Just in case you can be persuaded to part with some of it – some of what I owe you.'

The snow softened everything, covered up the melting morass of muck and dirt. Even in the shadowy lamplight, the edges were smoothed out as snow swept against walls and doorways, and settled on overhanging eaves. And all of yesterday's sounds – drips from overhangs, splatters of falling snow, hooves and feet sputtering through sludge – all of them silenced by this return of snow. He took the long way back to the lodgings, down the alleys and narrow steps to the lower town, leaving a trail of prints. Seeing how far he had come, where he could go.

The docks were stilled, the water a mere suggestion; the few ships, ghostly apparitions of masts and folded sheets. A fire glowed in small brazier by a lean-to on the dockside, shadowing the figure of a hunched man. He looked up at the sound of footsteps.

'Night, Sir.' The cadence was familiar, the voice not.

'You're the watchman?'

The man waved his hand towards the ships and then to the darkened warehouses as if to say, all this is mine. Tony held his hands to the fire. They settled into a slow, back-and-forth exchange of how they came to be there, just the bare morsels. Carolina, Virginia. Not the before that. Just the how of his arrival in this place. The watchman came up from New York, made it to Canada with his wife.

'She died, soon as we got to St John's. That place was no good for me.'

'And this place?'

'There's no memories here.'

Always talk of memories. He wondered which was worse; to be somewhere that reminded you always of before or to live in a place so absent of memory that you had no connections, no past.

'You got to England and come back?' The watchman spread his palms wide, cupping his amazement in the fire's glow. 'You staying here then?'

He shivered, reached out to the heat again. 'No. My master will soon get leave to return.'

'Lucky man. England.' The watchman shook his head, jabbed at the charcoals and a shower of sparks illuminated the darkness. 'Lucky man.'

A different conversation.

There was to be no promotion. Lieutenant Colonel Bruce had died unexpectedly, without giving Edward the nod.

'He looked to be in the full of his health at that dinner I attended with Brisbane.'

As though someone had deliberately played a joke on him.

'If he could just have signed the damned thing. A final gesture before he went to meet his Maker and I should be so much the better for it.' Edward was pacing again. The floorboards rattled under his boots. 'I'll be damned if I go back to Fredericton. I'll not spend another summer sowing vegetables, and stewing in that garrison, surrounded by bored men, getting lazier and duller with each passing day.' He paused, and pointed a finger at Tony. 'The men I mean, not me.'

A small pile of belongings lay on the bed. He had just begun to ready things for Montreal.

'What now? Do we go?'

Edward resumed pacing. 'I'm thinking ... Why don't you order some food? It might help.'

'As you wish, Milord.'

'Oh dear. I know I've said or done something wrong when you say that. Nonetheless I still think food might help.'

'Here's the nub of it. I have no chance of getting a promotion here in Canada, where nothing, absolutely nothing happens, therefore there's little point in staying.'

Tony tried to suppress his relief but asked, 'What of the Duke? Or your cousin Mr Fox? Will they not ...?'

'My brother has no intention of helping me out. And as for Cousin Charles, I think his influence is not what it once was.' He drained his glass, swung the empty bottle in Tony's direction. 'No, I am on my own. Ogilvie will be vindicated by my failures.'

Another bottle. This time Tony joined him. Montreal would wait until tomorrow.

'Dear Faithful Tony. What would I do without you? You're the only one, the only one who …' Edward reached out to grip his arm. 'Next to my own family, there's you …' The hand was gripping tightly. He tried not to pull away. 'You never … what I mean is … you never disappoint me.'

Good, though he might wish for better.

'No, that's not right. I do you a disservice.' Edward's eyes were on him. This outpouring of sincerity was uncomfortable. 'You are my dear companion. We do well together.'

'Thank you, Milord.' He made a move to clear away the remnants of the meal.

'Sit, sit.' His gesture impatient. 'I've been thinking. What you said the other night. Your words put shape on something I've been feeling. About things that I thought I believed in but I see now they were just ideas. Christ, how difficult it is to put words on ideas. Ogilvie was forever quoting Rousseau at me, but I'm not sure how much he believed it. Rousseau questioned something, about whether strength of mind, and wisdom or virtue, are always found in individuals in proportion to power or wealth. You are proof to me that they are not. I've been thinking this over, this proof. And you, you then said it. Equal footing. In this place, we should be on an equal footing. Not Milord and his servant. We should be as the settler people in St John's. You remember them?'

'Of course.'

Now he said, 'No more mention of Lord Edward in this place.'

Tony, thinking he spoke from the glass, on a whim asked, 'If not Lord Edward, then what?'

He frowned. 'Sir?' A pause. 'But you say that anyway. I'll think some more about it.'

He closed his eyes and Tony stood once more, made for the door.

'Edward,' he shouted after him. 'Of course you'll call me Edward.'

'It might be awkward in company.'

'Well then in our own company. Say you agree.'

'As you wish …' It was only a name, a word. But it sat heavy and awkward in his mouth. 'Edward.'

'Tony! I want you to see this.'

Dust breathed from the ceiling timbers in sighing puffs. Edward was pacing overhead again. Tony brushed some from his sleeve, climbed the stairs.

Edward stood in the doorway. 'Good, good, come in.' His shirt was loosened, and he ran a hand through his dishevelled hair, looking about him for something. 'Damn it, where did I leave it.' He grabbed a map that lay on the bench.

'Remember how I said we would travel as far as Detroit, taking in the Falls on the way.'

'Yes, Sir. But that's not happening now.'

Edward shook the map open and pointed. 'I propose we go north from Detroit, to Michilimackinac and on perhaps to Lac-Supérieur. I have a mind to follow the trails of the coureurs des bois as far as …'

His finger tracked over the map following a snaking black line down the page, where he paused, clearly absorbed.

'I'm sorry, Sir. I don't understand.'

'I'm determined not to go back to Fredericton. And now that fate has made it difficult for me, I shall not return to England in a hurry. After all I've seen and done, England and Ireland seem much too small for me. Instead we will track that Great River, The Mississippi.' His finger stayed on the map, gently tapping at a large space. 'See, there are no markings. No one has been there.' There was nothing: none of the drawings, writings, and inky trails that marked the right side of the map.

'Except, presumably the native peoples, Sir?'

'Edward, please, you must call me Edward.' Once again he pointed at the space on the map. 'Yes, possibly natives. Think of it.' His voice was urgent. 'We will travel by river, through native country, to the Spanish territories. I've heard stories of the silver mines there. There is no one of my acquaintance or even knowledge who has done this. I shall be the first.'

He was no longer addressing Tony. This speech was for Ogilvie. The pity of it was that he was an ocean away.

'But Milord ... Edward, what of the Duchess who will be expecting you? And there's the question of money. How will you fund this?'

Once more, he found himself clasped about the arm.

'So cautious, Tony. And so right.' His voice sounded mournful. 'But when will I ever be twenty-five again and in this place? With this adventure ahead of me. Of us.' He poured a glass and handed it to Tony, took up his own. 'To adventure.'

Wine spilled from his glass and down his shirt. He swiped at it carelessly.

'Actually Tony, I've thought it through and I shall propose a kind of survey of the Spanish territories to Lord Dorchester. Cast an eye over their forts, their defences and prepare a report. He'll have to give me their blessing and supplies. Everyone knows there's trouble coming with Spain. And seriously, if I can give a well-observed report back in London – my uncle will be sure to get me an interview with Pitt, then I think my chances of promotion would be vastly improved.'

'And who's to join this expedition?'

'Lieutenant Brisbane will come with us to Niagara and Fort Erie, perhaps even as far as Detroit. But we're bound to pick up guides. Indian or French.'

'Will we pass through American territory? Slave territory?'

'Unlikely.' He ran his fingers against his mouth. 'You'll be fine, Tony. You'll be with me. No one can touch you.'

Baaba were wary of them slaveholding territories. I expect he feared he might wind up back where he started. I don't care to think of him that way. Reminds me of them old black men, the ones what used to have occasional work on the docks, but in their dotage spent their days near the station at Euston, begging and retelling old tales of misery. They seemed to think I'd have some special interest in them, just because I shared the same colour skin. Pressing their warm palms on my arm, forcing me to see into the wretched darkness of their eyes, to see a memory of my Baaba in their brown faces and salted hair. I told myself that sharing the same skin weren't worth nothing. I had nothing in common with these men. Nothing. Over the years I'd learned to avoid those of my own kind. You could be swallowed up by all that misery so I tried not to listen, not to see.

I know now why Ma pressed Mr Fricker's suit on me, saying I'd be better off in the long run with a white man, even though she had been ever so content with my father. Those men don't know how to let go of them shackles, she said. They just go round in circles, smaller and smaller circles till they can't go anywhere. I'd have a better chance in life and so would my children if I stayed away from all that misery.

Ma were mistaken in thinking misfortune were specially attached to black people. These days it's more common to see Irish beggars by the station, ones that have crawled away from the famine in that desperate country. I must admit my sympathies come no easier at the sight of their wretchedness than they did with the poor black men. Such misery lays a chill hand on my soul and I am forced to turn away.

What did Ma know about it. She were only trying her best. I see that now. Like I see a lot now. But only looking back. The pity of it is there's none of us able to look forward and so most of us end up going round in circles. Most of us are no different to those beggarly old men who once was slaves.

So Lady Lucy didn't know everything, didn't remember everything. She got it wrong about that Indian Tribe what gave Lord Edward his great Honour. Making him a Chief. I remember the name because Baaba told me. It were the Bear Tribe and he told me that story the day I came home from the market filled with fear and terror on account of a dancing bear. He were trying to make me feel better but it never worked for that bear is still roaring somewhere in my memory, still giving off its stink, its misery.

It were at a market near Piccadilly, and Ma and I were making our way through the stalls when I saw the bear. He were roped about the neck and muzzle. I stopped to gawp. A dancing bear I'd say he was but perhaps he didn't have a fancy for the horn player's music or the crowd that day, for he would not dance. Stayed on all fours no matter how the rope man shouted and prodded him. The crowd became jaded by his tired shuffling, and they too set about provoking him, jeering, jabbing him with sticks. I heard Ma's voice calling to me just as he reared up, but I could no more have moved than I could have stuck him with a knife. Terrifying he were, all matted fur and huge leathered paws, with long, long curved claws. The crowd seemed to drop back from me. I heard Ma again, shouting Ettie, run, and the bear man cursing as he grappled with the rope. I were standing right in the dark shadow of the beast. Couldn't help but stare up at him, at his jaw working against the rope in a froth of spittle. I could smell the suffering pelt of him, feel his muffled roar judder along my bones, the blast of his raging breath. Then it was over, the trance broken by Ma hugging and half-slapping me. Berating me and then comforting me with her Irish words. Why don't you listen to me. A mhuirín, a stór. And the bear was backing away, the rope man beating him with a stumpy whip. The crowd spread like spilt milk, draining away into cracks and gaps. It was over.

Some memories never leave you. Seems they're carved into your body. That bear. That smell. That look. Saw it years later in my own son when I got my last glimpse of him – got close enough to touch him though he pulled away – as he tramped up the gangplank of the *Augusta Jessie*. He turned round though, when he reached the top, and the look in his eyes set my bones shuddering just as that bear did.

THE TRUE NARRATIVE

August 1789, and Lord Edward interrupts his great expedition down the Mississippi at St Louis.

Before reaching the town of St Louis, Lord Edward visited many of the Indian tribes to the North, some forty Leagues above the Falls of St Anthony. He held conference with the Indians there and made enquiries about the state of the Spanish defences. He was, as always, an attentive listener, and received some important communications regarding the business dealings of a merchant in St Louis, who, it seemed, was not above going beyond the confines of the Spanish Territories to deal with enemy Nations.

We stopped at St Louis to take on provisions and for Lord Edward to meet with a representative of the Spanish Governor, to seek permission for continuing south through Spanish territory. Not yet twenty-five years since the first posts were driven into the ground high on a limestone bluff on the west bank of the river, and yet by the time of our arrival, it had all the hallmarks, good and bad, of a town long established. At the heart of the place were two men, Pierre Chouteau, and Jacques Clamorgan, fur traders and land grabbers. The latter claimed an acquaintance with Lord Edward from his time in the Indies. He swore he remembered him, though my Master rejected such prior knowledge and indeed I could not imagine that he had ever before any reason to cross paths with him. Jacques **Clamorgan** was low bred, rough and a callous slaver.[22]

The river had offered no respite from the day's heat. Tony had looked forward to reaching the frontier outpost of St Louis and the shade and comforts of an inn. Their guide, a man of mixed French-Indian heritage who'd been with them since leaving the French territories, asked Edward for payment as soon as the settlement appeared in view, high on the bluff at the bend of the river. This was as far as he would go. Edward settled on him what had been agreed three weeks before. A gun, Edward's old musket. The guide accepted it silently, then punted the small flat boat toward the wooden pier and moorings. He squeezed it between two larger vessels, piled high with sacks and what looked like deer skins, rotting under the unyielding sun.

'Any drink will do, grog, piss, wine, whatever. And who knows Tony, we may be lucky in other ways. A chance to cool the blood. If you can bring yourself to be a little less particular.'

A shadow loomed over the boat.

'Greetings, Lord Fitzgerald.'

They looked up. A large, bearded man stood on the landing stage above, booted feet planted apart, wearing a white shirt, a leather jerkin, and a strange red cap angled over a wild head of hair, carelessly tied back. He grinned broadly. Edward looked at the man and then at Tony, his shoulders raised in bemusement.

'C'est une surprise, n'est-ce pas? I was told you were coming.' He laughed. 'Monsieur Clamorgan's Indians are everywhere. They are the eagle's eyes, the otter's nose; they tell me everything.'

The guide hopped onto the quay, the musket slung over his shoulder, and ignored the man, his laughing speech, and the two black men who stood behind him. He walked off without a backward glance.

---

[22] A slave trader? I cannot imagine this. Edward's principles would never have allowed him to befriend such a man. He was raised on Rousseau, a devotee of Mr Paine, a Democrat to the core. He even considered women's suffrage. How could he have associated with a slaver? No. There's something about the tone of this piece that is disagreeable. **LLF.**

Did the guide know this man? Tony wondered. Was this man implying he was one of his Indians, one of Clamorgan's Indians? Did Edward know him? He was reaching a hand down to Edward.

'Come.' He laughed again. After a moment's hesitation, Edward accepted and was sprung up onto the pier to be greeted with, 'Bonjour. You remember me. Jacques Clamorgan. Old friend. It is good we meet again.' He turned to the two black men, ordered them loudly to 'prenez soin de bateau,' before turning his attention back to Edward.

'Now Milord Edward, you will of course do me the honour of staying with me?'

'Have we met before?'

A short bark of laughter greeted this question.

'We have plenty of time to reminisce about Martinique. You'll need refreshments first, yes? Come.'

Edward looked uncertain, young, beside the bulk of Clamorgan. Tony waited where he was, watching as one of the black men jumped into the boat without any acknowledgement and began throwing their goods up onto the pier.

'One moment.' Edward turned back to the boat, reached his hand down to Tony. Clamorgan watched Edward pull him up. He shrugged and shouted out. 'Baptiste. Ramène les bagages à la maison. Immédiatement.'

Clamorgan ran a large establishment aided in no small measure by his housekeeper, Miss Esther. His house was one of the largest in the settlement. It imposed deliberately over its wood-built neighbours, with its rough-cut stone and pillared frontage. A row of warehouses and sheds occupied a large plot behind the house. The front was fenced, planted with a row of trees but with little other attempt to prettify it. Inside, the house was raw, the floorboards still oozing sap, a smell of lime wash and something else – grease or perhaps blood. Something unaccountable. Later, when Clamorgan mentioned his great store of furs and skins, the source of the stink became clearer. Clamorgan too trailed some of that smell after him in a way that none of the Indian hunters ever did. But it was not just the smell which was unsettling. It was the six or seven slaves he kept.

'I cannot recall the man.' Edward was insistent when they spoke later.

They'd met in a whorehouse in Martinique. Or so Monsieur Clamorgan insisted. Yes, yes. During the Treaty negotiations, in '83.

'Truly. I don't believe I have met him before.'

Clamorgan had been quite certain. Said he'd been waiting for a safe departure, nice little cargo of slaves. Dangerous times. Hard to tell which way the wind would blow. Whether t'would be a French wind or British.

'Besides, it is of little consequence now. I have accepted his hospitality.'

Clamorgan had ordered that Tony should have a change of clothing. If he is to wait on his master, he should at least look the part. Edward had laughed at Clamorgan, telling him not to trouble himself as it would not do for the servant to be better dressed than his master. Tony silently thanked his master.

'Truth is Tony, I did attend a friendly establishment in St Pierre during one of my visits. I only remember the beauties there, not a Monsieur Clamorgan – if he even used that name.' Edward had just finished bathing. Tony held a razor to his chin, slowly working around his jaw.

'Dusky beauties, most accommodating, one in particular ...'

Strange the way the light bends on the blade. How a face may become distorted when it is angled just so. Almost human but not. Shadows really.

'Tony?'

'My apologies.' He withdrew the blade for a moment. 'Nearly done.'

Edward said no more on the subject until he was clean shaven again.

'I'm sorry we've ended up here,' he said.

Tony tidied away the razor in its roll, folded a pair of breeches, then shook them out again. 'Why? Monsieur Clamorgan could hardly be more hospitable to you.'

'I know. And yet ... I did not know this would be a slave-holding territory. Nor that Clamorgan would offer me money for you. I was shocked. I won't tell you the sum he offered, and with such a calculating look. He was testing me. I'd never thought of you as a ...' He searched for a word.

'Commodity?'

Edward closed his eyes. 'No that's not what I mean, of course you're not but it's just that he sees you as such. It confused me.'

Tony's jaw tightened. He looked at his hands. 'You mean because I came free to you?'

Silence again. Edward pulled a shirt over his head, then sat down on the edge of the bed. He studied his fingernails. 'Tony, please. Forgive me. So stupid, careless.'

When there was no response, he continued.

'You are my Ogilvie in this wild country. My troubling conscience.'

The True Narrative

September 1789, and Lord Edward holds conference with the Indians of the region.

We passed some days in the region of St Louis. Lord Edward used his time there to seek out several of the Indian tribes with the aid of a guide provided by our host Monsieur Clamorgan. He held conference with the Shawnees, the Delawares and though word came that he would be welcome to visit the American side east of the Mississippi and in particular the region known as Kaskaskia, he did not embrace the invitation. He carefully recorded the Spanish fortifications and their mercantile interests. His Lordship maintained a detailed account of these encounters, and sometimes called upon me to write his words into the journal on his behalf. He also made sketches of the villages that we visited, as he had done ever since we left Michilimackinac, the last British Garrison on our journey. I often looked at the maps he had devised of our travels and remarked how well he could render the river, forts and villages we encountered on our way. He was adept at conferring with the Native people, seeming to adapt his ways to theirs with remarkable ease. They in turn were content to accept him among them.[23]

[23] This is Edward as I remember him. This is how he was with the Irish people too, and the reason he was so beloved of them. Remembering Mr Equiano's Narrative, I think you would do well to introduce a version of your Christian beliefs to your own account. It may not be necessary to include a long section on Religious Instruction. A short section demonstrating your Faith and Gratitude to the Lord would be sufficient. And expected. LLF.

Miss Esther ran Clamorgan's house with her daughter Siley, a silent, watchful girl. Miss Esther was a tall woman, and attired with great formality – a dress of dark silk, lightened by a touch of lace at the neck, and a cream calico band about her head. Was she a free woman? Tony could not tell. Everything about her spoke of control and purpose. She was a ship with a deliberate course. Her English was poor but she made no apology, merely spat out orders to the rest of the household. And most impressive of all, she was resolutely even-handed in her contempt. This she directed equally at the slaves who worked in the warehouses; the visiting traders who appeared at the wooden office adjoining the house, caked in the dirt and sweat of months spent upriver; the Spanish representative on his weekly visit, dressed in formal garb, all epaulettes and Brandenburg cuffs, as though for a state occasion; the arrival of an unknown British Lord – who claimed to be indulging his sense of adventure – and his servant, a man of little consequence.

Miss Esther was as dismissive of Clamorgan's offer of purchase as she was of Tony himself. She pointed to a stool outside the lean-to kitchen and planted a dish of stewed meat in his hands. He felt wrong-footed by everything. Baptiste and the other man whom he'd seen at the landing stage, with a distinctive scarred face, sat apart from him, talking to each other in low voices. The previous day he had tried to engage them in conversation but only Baptiste had answered, and only with a yes or no.

Now Esther was speaking, but only on her terms. She had no interest in his questions, his attempts to discover more about her. She talked of Clamorgan, her words harsh as grapeshot.

'He buy everything. What he cannot take, he buy. Ne se soucie pas. You …' She pointed at him, 'you nothing. Rien. Il aime seulement l'argent.' She made a gesture with her hands as though counting out coins onto the table. 'And …' she paused and cast a sly sideways glance at him.

'Yes?'

Now her hands moved from counting imaginary money to something much cruder and he stared in shocked fascination as one hand pumped back and forth over the other.

'Ha.' She got up and moved back inside and he knew she was aware of his eyes on her retreating figure, that she swayed her hips with a contemptuous determination.

'You keep your eyes off her.' A voice behind him. Baptiste. He had finished his food, and was sprawled under the shade of a dogwood tree. 'She'd kill you 'fore the master ever did.'

His companion added, 'If they don't kill each other first.'

In the night, he came to understand what they meant. He was lying on a narrow ticking mattress under the window in Edward's room, and grateful for the comfort. If Miss Esther had had her way he'd have been lying on the floor outside. 'Comme un esclave,' she had said, her lip curling over the word. But Edward had insisted otherwise, despite Clamorgan's assurance that Esther dealt with all domestic arrangements.

'I'm sorry but I will not have him sleeping outside my door like a dog. Let him share my room. I'd be grateful if you could furnish him with a mattress.'

Clamorgan had turned to Esther with his hands raised as though in defeat and Esther turned a look of contempt on all three of them, and marched away.

But despite the comfort of the mattress, he could not sleep. At first he thought it was just sounds of vigorous lovemaking, but Clamorgan's guttural utterances sounded more sinister than warranted and the cries from Esther – he presumed it was her – suggested pain. He covered his ears, but could not escape it. He walked to the door, turned the handle and stopped. What could he do? Wake Edward? Edward whose sleep had been eased by the wine shared earlier with the Spanish representative. Edward who was oblivious to the grubby, sickening transaction next door. Disgust filled his throat. This place made a coward of men, of him. A loud cracking sound. An open hand across the face? A fist? Not a whip? Please not that. Crack. He would not stay, would seek sleep elsewhere.

Outside the night was thick and warm and it settled around him like a familiar blanket as he lay down outside the kitchen, under the trees. He breathed in deeply, the smell of charcoal thankfully masking the stink from the sheds. He turned his mind from the room upstairs and leaned into the night sounds of cicadas, the rustle of night creatures, bent on their foraging, and the distant craw croak of toads. He drifted off, dimly conscious of another sound in the background, a low hum, a song of sorrow from another time, another place.

A hand touched him gently. Oh, how long since he had felt such a touch. A whisper in his ear. A name spoken in a soft voice. A rich voice that curled around the name, pulling it out slowly, making it sound other. Tony. He stayed in sleep, allowing himself the comfort of the dream. Tony. The hand on his arm squeezed gently. Wake up. He opened his eyes and looked into the smooth, unblinking face of Siley, Esther's daughter. Her eyes were thick-lashed, almond shaped, and regarded him with calm interest. A simple tignon was knotted on her head but a few curls strayed around her cheekbones. She held out a cup of water. He struggled to sit up, accepted the drink. She hunkered on the grass beside him, her gaze unwavering.

'Votre maître? Il a …' Her voice was soft. She raised her hand, brought it down hard on her chest, once, twice, again. 'He beat …?' She pointed to him.

He puzzled over this for a moment, remembered what he'd heard the night before and shook his head.

'No. Never. He's never raised a hand to me.' The idea was shocking. He wanted to cut off the suggestion. He wanted to ask about her mother, but the girl's face had closed down again. How old was she? She hugged her knees like a child but he had already noticed the curve of her breasts above the neckline of her dress. He turned his face away. Sunlight caught the two of them, as it pushed up from the side of the house. He sensed its heat already in the warmed soil, and the faint drifts of smells from the warehouses nearby. The girl beside him. Her skin was glowing, something aromatic about her. He should go inside, see if Edward needs anything. He should …

'Your mother?' The question was out before he realised.

The girl did not respond. Her finger trailed through the dirt, tracing circles or spirals. Round and round. She tilted her head sideways, a vague smile.

'Elle est forte.' Unexpectedly she raised her hands, clawed them towards him, made a growling sound. 'Comme un ours.'

He backed away, laughing. 'A bear?'

She nodded, looking pleased.

'Ah.'

They sat for a few minutes more, listening to sounds of early morning: the chickens jerking through the bushes, halting abruptly at the sight of the pair idling under the tree; flutterings in the trees above; the sound of hammering in the distance, shouts, the muffled thud of hooves on the dirt road beyond and beneath it all the low hum of the Mississippi.

He gulped back the water, got to his feet and reached a hand down to help the girl up. They walked back to the house. In the unaccustomed shade of the back corridor, he was slow to make out the presence of Esther, hovering in the doorway. Siley was slow too, and unable to avoid the blow dealt by her mother, or escape the scorch of her words.

'Stop.' He tried to get between them. 'What is—'

Esther drove her seething face into his. 'You, away.'

She reached for her daughter, pulled her close, one arm tight about her waist. 'Elle n'est pas pour vous.' She jabbed his chest. 'Not you.'

'Siley?' He asked. The girl's eyes slid away from him.

Esther jerked her head toward the ceiling. 'Monsieur Fitzgerald.'

She wants me to go, he thought, to attend to Edward. One last glance at Siley revealed nothing, her face closed, tight as a sealed cask.

THE TRUE NARRATIVE

*September 1789, and Lord Edward remains in St Louis and
the Author is aware of the providential hand of God.*

During my time in St Louis I discovered a long wooden building marked
outside by a rough cross. It was a house of God, belonging to those of
the Catholic Faith. Despite this I felt the urge to enter, in the hope
of finding God there, for I believed in my heart that the same God
oversaw all of the Christian Religions. I pulled open the door and looked
inside. It was cooler than on the street, darker. A couple of planks
tacked together on the ground marked the walkway between the few
scattered benches. At the top, a single stand, on narrow legs, and a
small set of steps, three in all behind it. There was no one there. No
sense that God was present. I tried to call to mind some lines from the
Bible that had served as my reading primer in Fredericton, during the
long, snowy winter months. I had learned the words by heart in order
to help me trace the letters, make the words real. But the meaning had
never come to me. The God in those pages had always remained distant
and unconcerned with a man such as me. Now in this dark empty place
smelling of dust and tallow, and wood, always wood, my mind threw up
a prayer that I couldn't even remember learning.

The Lord is thy keeper: the Lord is thy shade upon thy right
hand.

The sun shall not smite thee by day, nor the moon by night.

The Lord shall preserve thee from ...

The rest refused to come but I was happy with what I had. I repeated the words, pictured the sun and the moon and the shade cast over me. I lowered my head, turned the word 'smite' over, not fully understanding it, yet content with it. My fingers sought out the amulet around my neck.

The Lord is thy keeper ...

The Lord is thy keeper.

Thus Dear Reader, with the sense of God's mercies so great on my mind, Christ was revealed to my soul. And the word of God was sweet to my taste, yea sweeter than honey and the honeycomb.[24]

Sunday. They would depart south on Sunday. South to New Orleans and a ship to take them east to Ireland or England. Away from there. Two more days. Thinking of Siley gave way to an expansive regret. Best not to think of it. Of her. Instead he focused on the list in his hand. Edward's instructions: more gunpowder (and see if you can get my rifle repaired), two new kettles (in case we need to buy our way out of trouble), soap (try to get Marseilles – anything but that vile woodash and lye), one or two casks (and the usual foodstuffs), and a formal jacket (I've declined one of Clamorgan's – his taste is a bit rough even for me – I wish you luck in finding one here, but if anyone can find such a thing, I know it's you). The last item, he did not write down – Edward's suggestion that he purchase some ribbon or a kerchief for that girl (and you never know what may happen). That girl. What could happen and for whom? He crumpled the paper in his fist.

Clamorgan had directed him to his trading store, but instead Tony attended on his rival's business, a long wooden building, belonging to the Chouteau brothers. It occupied a wide plot at the foot of La Rue de la Tour, overlooking the traffic on the Mississippi and was fronted by wide steps leading up to a covered porch in the manner of several of

[24] This is perfect. It might very well have been written by Mr Equiano himself! I think it would be prudent to include more of these Reflections as I believe readers may expect such sentiments in Slave accounts. LLF.

the best houses in St Louis. Inside it was dark, the only light coming from the row of small windows overlooking the dirt street, windows which were largely blocked by stacks of boxes filled with yams and melons. A whirl of smells greeted him before his eyes adjusted enough to the dim interior; tobacco or snuff, the iron reek of blades and saws, the oil of guns and their companion smell of nitrates, a hempy odour from ropes and baskets hanging from wooden beams.

The jacket that he managed to purchase was not new. It was overly long, the tails reaching to the knees and the fabric a dusty claret silk. Edward suggested it might have been the property of an adventurer Vicomte who had vanished while exploring the Cahokia Mounds over fifty years before. Or, Tony suggested, more likely traded upriver from a merchant in New Orleans, the property of an unsuccessful French clerk.

But Edward preferred his own story. 'See the tailoring. And look at the braiding. Pity the original buttons are gone, though hardly surprising.'

He tried it on, straightened his shoulders. His months in the wilderness had changed him. He was leaner, but broad across the shoulders now. As was Tony.

'I haven't seen the like of this since we lived in Aubigny and played with the old clothing belonging to my grandfather.' He ran a hand over the sleeve. 'By the way, Clamorgan knows you went to the Chouteau Brothers for the supplies. Asked me if it was usual for a servant to disobey an order.'

'And?'

'I told him it was your habit to find the best price. That you were careful with money – mine and yours.' He was trying hard for a sincere expression but failed to suppress his delight in his own words. His delight was infectious.

'It's good to see you smile, Tony. You've been out of sorts in this place. Clamorgan?'

'He's dangerous. For me at least.'

'Actually, I think you may misread him. He holds most people in a kind of callous indifference but I don't believe he differentiates between negroes and white people, or Indians for that matter. The only thing of importance to him is money. There's more than a touch of the pirate about him.'

'He's a slave trader.'

'Yes, but his chief clerk at the warehouses is black and a free man.'

'Who?'

'You've met him, I'm certain of it. Couldn't miss him. Scars on his face, and not like your friend Moise had. This man's face looks like it was engraved. I think Clamorgan calls him Antoine.' Edward checked himself in the mirror. 'Huh.'

Tony stared at him. This place was all wrong. Too confusing. Baser than the wilderness. 'Do you need anything else, Milord?'

'Edward. Remember? And I'm fine. I'll wait for Clamorgan.' He checked his watch and lay down on the bed, stuffing a pillow under his head. The shutters were closed against the early afternoon sun, but strips of light laddered the floor still. 'God,' he muttered, 'I hope that Spanish representative does not lay on a full feast. I'm in no mood for eating in this heat.'

Tony replaced the soap in its woven cradle, gathered up the wash basin and ewer, but Edward had not finished talking.

'How are you getting along with that girl, Esther's daughter? Smitten?'

'You're mistaken.'

'Give me some credit Tony. I've seen how you look at her.'

'I think, Milord, you should be careful in that jacket. In this heat. The silk is likely to stain if you should sweat.'

'Thanks,' Edward muttered mildly, without opening an eye.

He met Siley a short distance from Clamorgan's. She was walking home, balancing a basket on her head, her arm curved up to hold it while her body swayed gently. He watched for a few moments before catching up with her.

'Let me,' he insisted and she laughed as he struggled to hold the basket in front of him. 'What is in it?'

She pulled back the lid to reveal four rabbits, and one, ears flattened, squeezed his head through the gap and attempted to clamber out.

'Oh … vite!' Siley pressed the rabbit firmly back in the basket and he secured the lid.

She smiled up at him, eyes flecked with dark gold. Her skin shone. He wanted to touch her, to lay a hand on her smooth arm, to brush his fingers on the gap between her neck and the sweep of her bodice, to—

She was speaking. 'Je regrette …' she ran her tongue over her bottom lip. 'You leaving.' She looked about her as if expecting to be watched, then stretched up to kiss him. Her mouth was warm, a hint of dust on her lips. He pulled back to rid himself of the basket, the stupid rabbits, to pull her to him, but she shook her head.

She held out her hands for the basket.

'No,' he said. 'Come here.' He held out his free hand and she took it. Her hand was warm and dry in his, as he led her into an empty allotment. Better than nothing, off the road at least. 'Here,' he said, reaching into his pocket for the length of ribbon he had folded there. He held it out, as a question, and the sun caught the green silk so it shimmered. She turned her back to him, standing perfectly still, so he could reach around her neck, feel her breath on his skin, loop the ribbon behind and tie it in a bow, letting the ends trail where his fingers longed to go. Where they went. Fleetingly. Touching. She leaned back into him, pressed against him.

'Come with me.' He had no other words. Wanted to pull her down, behind the trees. Lay her down. Lay himself down on her. He felt her want of him too. Heard the sound she made as she pulled away from him. She picked up the basket and ran.

Esther and Siley were flapping around the house. Brushes, cloths, linen. Everything swept out, shaken out, hung out. Esther pegging out sheets on a line, her body strong and determined, the sun gleaming on her bare forearms. Her hair was oiled and tightly knotted above her long neck. She whipped her head around to catch his gaze.

'Votre maître. Il part demain?'

'Non. Dimanche.' One more day and they'd be gone.

Esther flung the linen in the basket at her feet and turned abruptly, shouting for Siley as she stalked away. He heard raised voices from within; Esther's a steady axe blow and Siley's like a tree cracking at the final fall.

One day more. Don't think of Siley.

He went to check on the provisions for the passage to New Orleans. Most were stacked in a hand cart near one of the sheds at the back of the property. He crossed the stretch of scrubby ground, aware of the gathering smell of the furs and skins within. He wondered now about them. About the heat. Shouldn't they have been dispatched south before the summer? Were they not rotting in there? Perhaps that explained why the smell had worsened these two days past. He reached the door just as the man with the scarred face came out. Antoine. The scars were not accidental, but the marks of his people, long, repeating lines carved down his cheeks. This man was not of this place, must have come from Africa.

His greeting met with no response. Antoine ignored him, checked the locks and began to move away from the shed.

Tony wanted to ask what every black man wanted to ask of another. Where do you come from? How are you free?

Before the words could form on his tongue, the stink filled his mouth. And he saw the smell, its fearful shape, knew its awful bodily intimacy, thought in that moment that he had always known, but held to the image of dead animals, of pelts stacked up, when all along it was the smell of fear. The smell of rage. Coward. He had carried stones on his eyes and mud in his ears.

'Show me,' he said to Antoine. 'Ouvrez la porte.'

Antoine shrugged, took out his keys and opened the door.

In the rectangle of light, revealed in the gap of the door, ten or twelve people were just about visible. Some seemed to be chained to the wall; others, women perhaps – he could not see clearly – lying on the ground; one cradled a young child. A woman sprang up, naked except for a covering about her hips, and ran at them along the block of light cast by the open door, shouting, her fist raised, her eyes wide and startling.

Antoine slammed the door, drove the bolts across, and secured the locks.

'Where did they come from? Où …' He faltered.

'These slaves?' Antoine shrugged his shoulders. Who knows? 'Perhaps Africa. Perhaps all over. They been travelling months, some of them. Oceans, land, rivers. They couldn't tell you where they from nor where they been.' He brushed dust from his breeches in wide sweeping motions, ignoring the cries from the building. 'Won't do you no good, ask too many questions. You going soon.'

'But you … you could work somewhere else. Why do you stay with Clamorgan?'

'Il me traite bien. Bien. Well as anyone.' He hunkered to the ground, toying with the earth. 'Where else I find work? Sur la rivière? The poor farmers? What they pay?' He straightened up, opened his hand slowly over the ground, letting dirt run through his fingers. 'Nothing. May as well be slave again.'

It was quiet. No sound of human voices. The silence was familiar somehow. It must be hot inside. Still holding the midday sun within its windowless walls, though outside it was sliding towards sunset. Do they have water? Sweat trickled down his back. He watched as Antoine emptied a large pail into a pit around the side of the shed. The stench of excrement turned his bowels.

'No point you staring at me.' The man shouted over his shoulder. 'Vous êtes pareil. Same.'

He tried to ease out his fists. A question that had been hovering at the edge of his mind for days pressed against him.

'Siley? She's free? And Miss Esther?'

Antoine straightened up. His laugh was the sound of raked coals. 'Esther been saving, begging to buy Siley. Before Clamorgan gets a taste for her. Peut-être, too late.' He must have noticed Tony's expression.

The marks on his cheeks were raised, and thickened. Three lines running over his cheekbones, flaring at him, proclaiming his past.

'They're slaves, comme j'étais.'

THE TRUE NARRATIVE

September 1789, and Lord Edward still in St Louis when the true horror of slavery is revealed; The Author is involved in an altercation with the Slave-Trader, Clamorgan.

~~The Lord Edward who sought out these Indians was a different man from the one who accepted the hospitality of Monsieur Clamorgan. I could not help but feel disappointed by the manner in which His Lordship conducted himself in the presence of that coarse man, though I place the blame at the feet of Clamorgan and no other. Yet His Lordship willingly took what he had to offer. He even went so far as to bed ...~~[25]

He stayed away from the house, spent a second night outside, this time under a clump of black willow above the muddy shores of the river, thinking he would find some peace there, in the open.

The water throbbed distantly, frogs or toads croaked and shifted urgently, insects grated in the trees, the grass, the bushes. The sky was pricked with stars pointing harshly where he lay. Sleep stayed away. He pressed his face to the earth, trying to resist what he had witnessed. Instead he was visited by a host of faces in the dark, known and unknown; each one stirred his blood thick with shame. Shame. Bound to him and he enslaved to it. His thoughts lurched, struggled with—

[25] Tony, is this some sort of madness? This will do neither of our causes any good. Who are you writing for? Not for me, and certainly this is unsuitable for any civilised reader. I simply cannot read any more. LLF.

It was a puzzle of memory, that slotted together in his mind. Unwashed bodies sweating fever and fear, bloody flux, iron manacles with their raw meat smell. The sound of dry tears, rage hissed in the dark. The fading song of a mother to her young child, as he fingers the beads and leather pouch about her neck, the feel of cooling skin against his, her cradling grip stiffening now, beginning to hurt, and her eyes shut, not looking, not seeing, her voice, her sad voice not singing.

But he cannot leave her for she is cold and there is only him to comfort her in this place, this dark place, which sways and heaves, while slop seeps across the wet, stinky floor, this place where light comes only now and then through a small door in the darkness above him, and the beasts come, and they come and they come for her, dragging her roughly from him, snatching him roughly from her, beads scattering as his hand holds tight to her necklace, his own screams filling his muddy ears, his tired mud-filled ears, his stony eyes watching as they bring her up to the doorway of light, and she does not fight, her head drops and almost seems to gaze back at him, but her eyes too are stones and stones cannot see.

Dawn brought a new light. He was tired of his thoughts and memories – he'd keep busy instead. Sharpen the knives and blades before they left, clean the guns. He found a cloth and some vinegar in the pantry, and by the time he'd finished the job the cockerel had wakened the chickens with his self-important call. The cook house was cool and quiet as he waited for the water to boil, but he took his coffee outside again, into the shadow of the imposing stone house. They should make an early start. The vision of the river filled his mind, the bow wave pushing through the water and the rough outline of St Louis disappearing behind him. He gulped the coffee back, savouring the harsh gritty slap of it on his tongue, the jolt to his wandering mind. Edward. Coffee. Leave.

He tossed the remainder on the dirt and, filled with urgent purpose, poured another cup to take upstairs to his master. Inside it was quiet, no one stirring, not even Esther. Most likely Clamorgan had her in his bed. He eased open the bedroom door, stepped over the discarded clothing on the floor, pulled back the shutters.

The early morning sun was gentle, pooling lightly on the wooden floor, lapping at the edges of the bed, at its white coverlet, and glimmering on the faces of the pair in the bed. His first thought. How peaceful they seemed; Edward's face buried in the dark coils of Siley's hair, his arm thrown over her shoulder, the green ribbon gleaming around her neck. His second thought, not a thought, an explosion of memory and feeling, a feeling of his body gripped by, inhabited by, rage. Memory of sounds.

a girl crying, Minda
shouting, grating of feet dragged across stony ground
whack of an open hand on a girl's cheek
slam of a rough door, scrape, creak
cursing
a long lonely cry,
ends, no screams, no wailing
curses
silence, a gap, not knowing
silence is the gap between fear and doing
between fear and doing nothing
blood surging in his ears, thump, thump
a hundred horses' hooves
he moves to do, to do what
something
he moves, his brother grips his arm, hisses not now
not now

Now with the thump, drub of his heart surging in his ears, he walked towards the bed. Still they did not wake, but Edward began to stir, in his messy, boyish muttering way, and he wanted to hurt them, both of them, the steaming cup still in his hand, as he stood by the bedside, the light from the window on their faces. His chest was tight, his blood squeezing through, so tight. He wanted Edward to see him. See me, see what you've done. Bastard. Bastard. The words were out. Hissing. The shock in those spoilt, sleepy eyes. See it. Bastard.

He emptied the coffee on the clothing on the floor. Dropped the cup on top. Edward scrabbling upright in the bed, Siley waking now. He walked out, his body coiled tight as a trapped snake. Willing Edward to speak, so he might turn, uncoil, and strike him. Kept walking downstairs and out to the cookhouse to where the knives lay, blades sharpened and gleaming, and the guns stood erect and waiting, cleaned and primed against the wall.

The household erupted. Esther reached the kitchen first, her hair wild, her wrap hastily tied across her. 'You, what you do? What you do?' Other raised voices, approaching. She grabbed his arm, hissed into his face. 'Your master, he buy her now. Pay Clamorgan. Take her.' He tried to shake her off, but her fingers gripped into his flesh.

'He made you free.'

Now he shoved her away. 'I made myself free. Not him, not anyone else.'

His voice was loud, shouting, just as Clamorgan shoved through the door, followed by a dishevelled, alarmed-looking Edward, and Siley, who crept along by the wall and pressed herself against the dresser.

'What's this? Esther? What's happening?'

'That Lord. Il achètera Siley.'

Clamorgan laughed. 'Whoremongering bitch mother! What did you do?' He looked at the others in the room. Tony said nothing. Esther turned now to Edward.

'Please. Siley. You pay.' She took his hand, shouted for Siley, to come. 'Viens maintenant!'

Siley shook her head. Edward looked from mother to daughter and his face was a turmoil of confusion. 'I don't see, I'm not sure ...'

Tony hated that look. The contrived bewilderment.

'You stupid, stupid ...' Searching for a word. 'You don't see because you don't look. You don't see slaves, or misery, or that bastard slave-trader for what he his. You should look out back in his sheds. See what he keeps there. Then you'll see.' He slammed his hand on the table. One of the knives dropped to the floor. The pistol hopped, its walnut stock gleaming darkly. 'Then you'll feel.'

Clamorgan jabbed his finger toward him, told him to shut up. Turned to Edward. 'You make him shut up or he'll be sorry.'

Siley sank to the floor, her hands in her lap, crying. Clamorgan strode over to her, pulled her by her hair. 'Get up. Did you do this?'

Edward moved forward but Esther was faster, lifting a kettle and swinging it towards Clamorgan; his hand, his bear-like hand grasped hers, and the kettle clattered onto the flagstones, spilling water. Clamorgan whacked Esther's face with his open hand, the sound sharp, definitive. Siley scrambled to her feet, screaming, trying to reach her mother as Edward grappled with Clamorgan.

The pistol handle was warm and smooth, a comforting heft to it. Dependable. His heart was not thumping. He rotated the cock. Heard the click. His hand was steady as he raised it, looked along the twelve-inch barrel and fired.

Clamorgan was shouting, cursing. 'Fuck, fuck, fuck.' Clutching a bloodied ear as the sparks and smoke cleared. He kicked at shattered plates that were scattered across the flagstones. Edward signalled to Tony to put the gun down. He did not, could not. He thought of the bag under the table, containing the powder flask, the small paper twists of lead balls.

Edward was talking, hissing at Esther to get a cloth. Standing directly in front of the bloodied Clamorgan, still talking. 'My servant does not even know how to fire a pistol,' he insisted. 'He must have primed it accidentally when cleaning it earlier.'

Once again he stared at Tony, his eyes an urgent signal. But the pistol remained in his hand. Pity it was only a single shot.

Clamorgan spoke through gritted teeth. 'My bloody ear and these,' he kicked again at the shards of plates, 'suggest otherwise and he,' he pointed wildly, 'is still holding the pistol. I will not suffer to be shot at by anyone in my own house.' He dug his finger into Edward's chest and spat. 'You will give me the right of punishment. That fucking negro is mine to punish, in my house.'

Edward moved away from him, placed his hand over Tony's, removed the pistol. He let it go, backed up. Watched the thing play out. 'You should not make too hasty a judgement.' Still Edward talked. 'Esther, see to your master. Siley, get up. Help her.'

Clamorgan remained bullish. 'Antoine, Baptiste.' He roared. 'Get in here now. Bring my gun.' Spittle flew from his mouth, hung from his beard. Edward kicked at the bag under the table. Tony placed it on the table, watched as Edward slowly reloaded the pistol, and listened to Clamorgan.

'You will recompense me for this injury, this insult received in my own home.' Clamorgan stamped over and spat a gob in Tony's face. He did not flinch. Stared back, cold blood flowing through his veins, a hard heart pumping it.

Clamorgan stepped back. 'Antoine,' he shouted once more. 'Siley – go get him.' But Siley stayed on the ground, gave no sign of hearing.

Neither Baptiste nor Antoine nor the guns materialised.

'I'll take that negro from you. Even give you a fair price for him.' He spread his bloodied palms wide to show he was fair in his dealings.

'I don't think so.' Edward sounded relaxed, but his fingers tapped against the pistol handle that jutted from the front of his shirt. 'Why, that was a mere flesh wound,' he said. 'Ears bleed like the devil with only the tiniest nick. Even a child knows that.'

Clamorgan let forth a string of curses, in French, in English. His bloodied hair hung loose around his face. Esther pressed forward with a piece of torn cloth, attempting to dab at Clamorgan's head, but he was having none of it. With one hand clamped to his bloodied ear, the other striking off Esther's arm, he ploughed from the room, Esther trailing in his wake. Edward helped the weeping Siley up from the floor and urged Tony to take her outside, declaring that he had a pressing matter to attend to, and walked out across the back yard in the direction of the sheds.

There was so much he wanted to say to Siley, to ask her. She sat against the back wall of the cook house, her arms wrapped tight around her knees, her face smooth. Only her mouth betrayed her, twitching slightly at the edges.

'I thought,' he began. He laid his hand on her shoulder. She shrugged him off.

'Do not.' Her eyes were wide and fearless. 'Do not. You come, you go. You know nothing.'

'I do. I was a slave. I know—'

'See. You do not know. Tu *étais* un esclave. Étais. You do not have my life. You do not know.'

A sour taste filled his mouth.

There was nothing to say.

Edward walked towards them, through the scrubby grass, coming from the direction of the sheds. Everything about him was tight, as though he were resisting something. He clenched and released his fists, gestured toward Siley.

'Is she alright?' he asked.

The girl answered for herself by standing up and walking back into the house.

'We need to leave. Soon. Where is Clamorgan?'

Tony stood by the open door, while Edward crossed the floor of the dark, shuttered office to where Clamorgan sat, behind a table, scribbling furiously, jabbing at the ink pot. A small poultice was strapped over his ear. Antoine stood behind him, staring at the doorway, at Tony.

'This will ensure your negro cannot leave St Louis.' Clamorgan jabbed at the sheet of paper with his finger. 'I have applied to the Governor.'

Edward was tightly coiled but his voice sounded genial. 'I can take that with me. I'm just on my way there. I shall do my best not to mention your private trade arrangements with the British at Prairie du Chien nor your tentative forays into the Kaskaskia territories.'

Clamorgan replaced his pen. The feather twirled in the pot. 'You pampered bastard. What do you know of my business?'

'I know you overplay your hand. The British, the Americans. I believe your Spanish masters would not be happy to hear of it. Or perhaps they would?'

'English bastard.' Clamorgan claimed again with a short guttural laugh.

'Merci, Monsieur.' Edward bowed. 'Perhaps a bastard, but an Irish bastard. Now I think we will leave here – with your blessing. And I will be certain to convey your loyalty to Governor Miró in New Orleans.'

'Vous avez parlé avec les Shawnee.' Clamorgan's voice betrayed no emotion. He was not the first to underestimate Edward, to take at face value his claims that he was an idle nobleman indulging his desire for adventure. To not consider what purpose lay behind his easy congeniality.

'Oui. And others. But let's not speak of it. Who you choose to do business with is of little consequence to me. We are returning to England, bringing nothing with us, only fond memories of our meeting with an old friend from our days in the Indies.' Edward's smile was broad as he extended his hand to Clamorgan.

He merely stared at it with an expression of contempt and swung around to Antoine.

'See that they leave. À midi.'

The True Narrative

Autumn 1789, and the journey from St Louis to New Orleans takes almost two months as Lord Edward chooses to travel without any guide for much of the time the better to determine his own course. Aside from the changing weather, it passes without incident.

After St Louis, he had time and silence and the river itself in which to let feeling run wild. It gripped him, filled up and possessed his body. He let it run loose. Take over his thoughts. I … I …

I … hate that I'm indebted to Edward, that Edward saved me from Clamorgan, that he expects me to be grateful, that he saved me at all, that I ever saved Edward, hate that Edward bedded Siley, that he fucked Siley, that she gave herself to Edward, hate that I did nothing for Siley, or Esther, or the slaves in the shed, hate Clamorgan, hate Edward, hate myself, hate Edward, hate myself, hate that I'm indebted to Edward, that my only choice was to leave with Edward, hate that there was no choice, never a choice, couldn't even choose love, even hate not a choice.

Something crackled through his body like lightning. It gathered more and more onto itself. New hate sought out old, long-forgotten hate. Took him back to dark places. People stepped into his dreams, his daytime thoughts. Unnamed faces corrupted with hate of their own, looking down at him, booted feet against his ribs; a man, his brother, on a pallet, stripped to the waist, his back laddered with torn and bloodied flesh; Minda pulled from her hut. Edward lying next to Minda. No. Siley.

    hate Edward   hate Clamorgan   hate myself

The words had their own rhythm and he let his arms go with it, plunging the paddle into the river, driving it back, finding satisfaction in the churn of water, and the eddies he created. His strokes were ill-timed, unpredictable, especially at the beginning of the journey. Edward thrashed about to balance the canoe.

'You'll sink us,' he muttered and Tony smiled, dug in more forcefully. The canoe turned hard against the current, pitching from side to side.

'What the hell are you doing?' Edward spat out the words as he attempted to compensate for the fury of those strokes. Edward's anger and the sudden changes in direction, like a compass searching wildly for north, gave Tony a savage pleasure. No need to speak then. Feel the sweat run between his shoulder blades, the burn of his muscles. Watch and listen. Rest his arms on the paddle. See the other's petulant face burn with frustration and the attentions of the last of the autumn mosquitoes. They swarmed over him like a pelt, brown and crusty. His master pockmarked with bites. The pleasure of that, of watching him apply the foul-smelling grease, and to no avail. On they went. Seesawing between silence and anger.

The river had a low, irregular rhythm like the dying heart of a trapped bear. It flexed and strained within the confines of its shores. Its sinewy mass grappled at the base of the canoe. The days grew shorter and cooler, and the south wind worked its way upriver, unpredictable and at times savage. And rain with it. They camped, hunted, and fished in different languages. They had few words in common. Tony spoke only the merest civilities of yes and no and as you wish, knowing that the latter in particular was bound to rankle Edward. Weeks drifted by with barely a word passed between them. The silence was an extra passenger, one who must be deferred to. Edward eventually settled in its company, seeming almost content; or making a good show of it.

The pleasure of rage and hate also settled, leaving Tony with cold thoughts on where it came from. So much time, so much silence in which to search the past. There were no answers there, just sudden feelings as likely to pitch him backward or capsize him as the sudden currents around the canoe might. He came to understand the shape of light, a block of light above him in the darkness. The swaying and heaving of fear. How a cool, stiffening body means unbearable loneliness. How hate is seeded at a young age. And how it grows from fear.

At a landing, one week south of Natchez, Edward swapped the canoe for another flat boat, another guide. This one, unlike the usual sort, was garrulous and filled the gaps in the long tedious days with stories told in guttural French, punctuated by harsh laughter. Edward engaged with him. Laughed with him. Fished with him. Tony cooked what they caught, ate apart from them. They managed to reach New Orleans some two months after departing St Louis. It felt twice that. Once they left the river, and Edward said his farewells to the guide, something shifted. Edward gathered his own bags, his own guns. Tony made no effort to assist him, was neither dismissed nor encouraged, and so followed him. What else could he do? He had no money. Would not have money until Edward could secure a sum in New Orleans. Edward found lodgings for two but the distance between them was vast. Tony couldn't even see across it and Edward made no attempt at conciliation, though occasionally Tony saw him looking at him. After his failed meeting with Governor Miró – the Spanish having no wish to allow an Englishman, even a well-connected one, to travel deeper into Mexican territory, on a so-called whim, to see the famed or non-existent silver mines – Edward was short-tempered, keen to quit the place. Even the city felt tense and withholding, a smell of destruction ever constant. Everywhere he looked, Tony saw signs of the great fire of the previous year, from blackened ruins to raw building sites. Everything seemed insubstantial, temporary. Three weeks they spent in those rooms, with hardly a word between them. Edward went out daily, Tony knew not where. At first it was to secure a passage home. But the city was torn by high winds that rattled and ripped at the shingles of their lodgings, and rains that battered the windows. There would be no ships back to England until the New Year. All were tied up, battened down.

Just before Christmas, the dam burst. Edward was playing chess by himself. He had offered no invitation to Tony, just made a show of turning the board around after each move. There was a part of Tony that wanted to take him on, to rout him as he knew he could,

Edward being too impatient to plan more than two moves ahead while *he* could keep several strategies in his head at any one time. But he wouldn't give him the pleasure of asking to join. Instead he went to the window where the shutters were tugging for release, and he flung them open, letting the outside in. The sky was ragged with dark clouds. A damp charcoal smell seeped into the room, and a hint of the sea, briny and rank. Craning his neck he could just make out the masts of the taller ships and sloops beyond the rooftops. They were restless in their random dipping up and down, sawing at their ropes. The sails were rolled up tight but even so there were odd flutters, here, there along the cross beams, as a determined breeze gnawed and worried the stays.

'Tony.'

He glanced over his shoulder.

'You should go your own way from here. I'll pay you what's owing. I have the monies.' Edward's voice was flat. He turned a chess piece over and back in his hand.

There was no surprise at his words but no relief either.

'Still nothing to say? So be it. It's clear you no longer wish to work for me.' He drained the coffee that Tony had placed, wordlessly, beside him earlier. 'I'm sorry about it, you know. But I think it's your fault.'

His fault? He turned to stare.

'If you'd wanted to, and had a bit of gumption, you could have bedded her. But you're afraid to seize your chances. Always so damned careful.' He was still toying with one of the chess pieces, twirling a pawn round and round. 'And just so you know, I wasn't the first. She was no child.'

Words surged in his throat like bile. He looked at the ground, not at Edward, afraid that the urge to hit him would be too great. But Edward, seemingly taken by a similar impulse, rose quickly, overturning the chair as he grabbed hold of Tony's shirt and pulled him close.

'You know what you need, Tony? You need to go and find a generous whore, and plead with her to allow you a year's worth of fucking for the price of a day's. Might rid you of some that rage. In fact, get her to send me the bill.'

Tony looked back at him. Right at him. Saw only the spoilt twist of his mouth, the bluish-grey of those insincere eyes.

'You think everything can be solved by satisfying your cock. A hangover, a loss at cards, idle curiosity, boredom. Everything.'

Edward gave a short laugh. 'So you can speak. And say what you think. It's refreshing but probably just as well you held your tongue for so long.' He pulled back. 'You're wrong. I don't think it solves everything, but in your case it may help.'

'You used her like a whore.'

'Her mother did that for her. She put her in my bed. She knew what she wanted and so, by the way, did your Siley.'

Siley. He had a flash of her sitting on the step, gutting fish with practised ease, glancing at him with a shy sideways smile, the movement of her body. He lunged blindly at Edward and they hit the floor, rolling over, arms flailing, hitting out, missing their aim, legs kicking, words spitting out in harsh, staccato bursts.

'Bastard. How could she want you?' He held a fistful of Edward's shirt.

'You stupid coward. She didn't want me! Money. She wanted money. Her mother wanted it. Wanted me to pay her.' Edward's eyes slid from his. 'So she could buy her, her own daughter, from …'

His grip slackened. The truth, the realisation, was ice water in his veins. Of course. That's what Edward had. Money. And what had he to offer her? Nothing. No money. It was a simple transaction, but one that made him feel worse. Edward shoved him to one side, clambered up from the floor.

'I wanted to say to you, about that shed, Clamorgan's slaves, all the while we were on that blasted river, that …' His voice trailed off. The shutters rattled. 'I tried to—'

'Don't say anything. I don't want to hear you. What could you have to say?'

Edward looked down at his clenched his fists, opened them slowly. 'As you wish.'

THE TRUE NARRATIVE

December 1789, and the Author parts company with his Master;
Some account of his time in New Orleans.

He was a free man in New Orleans. A free black man with money, more
than he was owed. If nothing else, Edward was generous. Or careless.
A man who trod lightly through life. Who shirked off unpleasantness
like a soiled coat, and dropped a few coins to have it tended.

It was Edward who thought to sign his papers before he left. At first
he refused to accept. 'I don't need your name to say that I'm a free man.'

'For God's sake Tony, don't be a fool. You know it's necessary. Not
by my doing, but in this place you'll just have to accept it.

He watched him write it out. That piece of paper with his name
and Edward's signature seemed to undermine all those past years of
freedom more than anything he had experienced on the journey down
the Mississippi. He was free as long as someone else said so. Free to do
what? To go where?

He found a wretched inn in the old part of the city, untouched
by the fire. Something about it suited his mood. He drank without
thought, wandered slowly as though troubled by a limp. He had no
purpose, watched idly as men continued to battle the storms, to rebuild
the city's houses and churches, replacing wood with brick, and thought
them only fools. No one could stop destruction if it sought them out.
God, if he existed at all, was vengeful, prepared to destroy cities and
cast out sinners.

Rain fell for days, making rivers of streets, sputtering down shingles and tiles and almost obscuring the gaudy gold-painted sign above the entrance. He squinted up at it, holding a hand to his forehead. Madame Claudine's Parlour House. A bewigged gentleman, in a velvet dress coat and matching slouch hat, ambled out the doorway, catching him by surprise. He was about to move on, assuming the establishment was not for the likes of him, when the man called out in a low rumble.

'You'll get relief for your coin in there. Just make sure you don't get nothing else.' He tipped his hat, with the silver top of his stick. 'Good evening to you.'

Splatter, splash. He woke to the sound of water. The woman was crouching over a basin. He watched her from the tangle of filthy sheets under the unwavering morning sunlight. He was forced to see the room's mean furnishings, the hangings of stained scarlet on the walls, the painting over the washstand of a woman in white robes, kneeling before a man's engorged member. What had seemed darkly seductive last night, now appeared dirty and worn out. A cheap conjuror's trick. His mouth was dry. An empty flagon of wine lay overturned on the floor in a sticky, bruised pool. He looked again at the woman, as she sluiced her nethers with grim ferocity.

Unexpectedly he felt a stirring again. He reached down, stroked his erection. A bit bruised but what of it. Pulling back the sheets, he encountered a medley of rancid smells, mostly his own, but he patted the mattress just the same. The woman stood, let the rag drop into the water with a dull splash, and paid no heed as her robe opened to the waist, exposing her breasts. Her expression was one of perfect blankness as though her spirit no longer inhabited her body. His stomach heaved. He knew that look.

'Can you get some food. Coffee?' His voice was harsh as he pulled the sheet over again.

She nodded and folded the robe around her, without a flicker of emotion. He closed his eyes and sank back into the mire of the bed, listening to the chafing of her bare feet on the stairs, shutting out the sounds of the morning outside.

'Mercy.' She said her name as she might have said yes or no. As if it had nothing to do with her. As if she were being paid to provide a name.

'Did you tell me that last night?' The coffee burned in his throat, burrowed through his guts.

'You did not want a woman with a name.' She tore a piece of bread from the batch on the tray and fed it to herself in tiny pieces, sipping from her cup with such delicacy, that he thought himself a clumsy beast. Her cropped head dipped and rose like a bird's.

Mercy. He turned the name over on his tongue. His body was restored somewhat – more awake, more alive.

'Where are you from?'

She placed her cup back on the tray, wiped her mouth with the back of her hand. Rising slowly to her feet, she looked at him. 'You finish your food and go. Your time over.'

'I can pay more.'

She shook her head.

A wagon rumbled by outside, setting the window rattling. A river breeze flustered the limp curtains. Her gaze shifted to the view below and she spoke in a low voice.

'All night you pour your sadness, your anger into me. You make me like a slop jar. I have nothing to give you.'

She glided towards the door, a dark swan.

THE TRUE NARRATIVE

December 1789, and the Author meets Doctor James Durham, a celebrated Black Doctor; He is educated on the meaning of Freedom.

She did give him something. A few nights later, he leaned against the exposed chimney breast of a burnt-out house and cursed himself for a fool as he pissed barbs through a fiery member. A charred smell filled his nostrils. He looked down, almost expecting to see smoke rising from the earth as the tortured drops hit the ground. But the ground was wet from the heavy storm of the night before. He should have known this might happen. Hadn't he been warned? And last night he'd been feverish, listening to the storm whipping about, above the loud breathing of his three bedfellows. Why here, in this town and everyone a stranger? He fixed his breeches carefully, checked his pockets instinctively; money and papers. Papers stating that he, Tony Small, was a free man. Libro. Libre. What had he done with this freedom for the past week? He had no work and was staying in a pestilent hostelry, inhabited by people like him, who were stuck with their new freedom, lonely men with no women, who could not talk of family or pasts and who had no maps and no directions to the future.

His furtive enquiries led him to a Doctor Durham off Conti Street, where a small, neat woman, wearing an elaborate headwrap, led him into a dark parlour at the rear of the house. A pungent blast of aromatic herbs and oils assailed him, mixed with a harsh, burning odour almost like gunpowder. His eyes watered and it took a few moments to adjust to the surroundings: to the cabinets crammed with jars and bottles, each one labelled with a careful hand; the small hessian sacks stacked behind the door; the rough bookcase, with sloping shelves filled with a chaotic heap of books, folders, and loose manuscript papers. At a desk overlooking a small, well-stocked garden, a man dressed in a black coat and long wig in the old style, sat with his back to him, spooning powder onto a scales. He instructed him to sit, without turning around to greet him, and tapped an additional scoop of powder onto the brass dish, all the while muttering under his breath.

Time passed and he was distracted by the sudden appearance of bright sunlight at the four-paned window and the way it picked out a rusty shade on the collar and shoulders of the man's coat and how the wig, greasy and yellowing, must, he thought, be very old indeed – so much so, that there was less hair, horse hair he guessed, and more of the caul, a filthy cotton mesh by the look of it, visible on the crown, along with other areas of—

'… ails you?'

The doctor had spoken at last, looking at him with a long, measuring look.

He stared back.

'Ah, you are surprised to see a man of Africa, in such a place.' He waved his hand expansively, taking in the cabinets, the shelves, the table, the general disarray. He laughed. 'I am Doctor James Durham, medical practitioner and apothecary. And I can tell without laying a hand on you, indeed without you opening your mouth to speak, that you, Sir, you has the pox.' He settled himself back in his chair, cocked his head to one side and narrowed his eyes. 'Am I not the best physic you ever seen? Supposing you've ever seen one before.'

'I—'

He held his hand up, and continued. 'Seems I got just one problem. I got no idea if you has the French Pox, the Spanish Pox or maybe you got the Great Mississippi Pox. Now that,' he shook his head, looked sorrowfully at Tony's crotch, 'would be a holy shame.'

Tony was up out of the chair in a noisy clatter, breathless with anger and perhaps fear.

'I'm sorry, sit, sit.' The doctor laughed, waving him back toward his seat. 'That Madame Claudine. I should thank her some day for all that business she sends me.'

'It was you I saw leaving?'

'Think nothing of it. My powers of observation are matched only by my medical acumen. Now you tell me what ails you, and I will fashion you a cure. I got something for everything here, much of which I grows out there in that very garden. What I cannot grow myself, I send for.' He paused for a moment. 'I send to Doctor Rush in Philadelphia. You heard of him?'

'No,' he muttered, sorry he'd come here, sorry, very sorry he had the pox, sorry about that girl Mercy, and Siley. Sorry even about Edward.

The doctor reached out and patted his knee. 'There's no shame in it. Every man gets it at least once. Shows there's life in you yet. It's hardly your first time?' He eyed him curiously. 'Where you from? Way you speak, it's not from here?'

'And neither are you.' The man's speech was a ragbag of accents; part African, part Patriot, some like an Englishman. He wondered then how he sounded to others, given how careful he was in his speech. 'How do I sound? Where do you think I am from?'

'Your voice, your whole demeanour, it's strange to me. Slave maybe, but not for a long time. Not much Africa left in you anyhow. My supposition is that you been away from this place for many years. Or maybe never of this place. You been to England?'

'Yes,' he answered, surprised. 'And the Indies and Ireland ...'

'Go on. Tell me. I love to hear of travels.'

Each country he mentioned drew an appreciative gesture from the doctor. He clapped his hands at the mention of Spain and Portugal; leaned back, eyes closed, at the mention of England again.

'Ah England! It is my great wish to present a paper, on Putrid throat or the Yellow Fever, at London or Edinburgh. But,' he sighed, 'my place is with my patients and my family. A man can only have so many lives. African, slave and now doctor. Would be greedy to ask for more. But I travel up here.' He tapped his temple. 'I read, I correspond with many esteemed men of this country. And you? You read?'

'Only lately and slowly. The Bible and *Gil Blas*.'

'They as good as any guide from what I know,' he laughed. 'Perhaps you are Gil Blas himself. See how you travel so far, see so much.'

There was more to their conversation, the doctor's path from slave to doctor, Tony's years with Edward. He told him he should read. Not to waste his precious learning when so many of their fellows had none. 'Stop picking over your irritations, your past shames. They nothing. Not special. Just mean you're alive. And free. Being a slave, you not allowed to feel such things. Being free, just means you got to get on with living.' He paused, looking about his room, his eye falling on his heaving shelves, the spill of pamphlets and tracts. 'Living and reading. It's your duty, once you got the gift.' He stood, walked with a tilting gait to remove a paper from the shelf.

'This was sent to me some years ago by Doctor Rush. He has been most interested in my progress in the profession.'

A knock at the door interrupted him, and he opened it to the woman who had earlier shown Tony in. A brief discussion took place with the doctor shaking his head, hands held apart. The woman looked past the doctor, to Tony, before giving a smile of defeat. 'I'll tell them to come back tonight then.'

'That would be excellent.'

He settled back in his chair again. 'My eager patients. My dear wife is concerned for them. Now what was I saying. Oh yes, the pamphlet. I am going to lend this to you, on condition you have it back here tomorrow.'

He embarked on a lengthy explanation regarding Doctor Rush and his friends in the anti-slavery movement. 'Though he did not write this paper. It is by a French man, I believe. A Monsieur Benezet. You will weep to read it. But read it you must.' He rubbed his leg. 'Now before we starve, let me send for my wife. I have had a busy morning seeing to the sick and desperate of New Orleans.' He rang a little bell on his desk, and almost immediately opened the door, shouting out into the dark hall beyond. 'Sheba. It's past midday. Your husband and his new friend are in need of refreshments. A jug of julep and a dish of pecans to start with.'

He moved out of the cramped, pestilent room that he shared with three others, asked for a single room, with a table and chair ... and candles, 'at least two'. The landlady, a dull grey woman, with unblinking eyes, stared at him until he produced some money. No table. Instead, an upended shipping cask. No candles, just two copper cups, filled with stinking fish oil, and a smoking stump for a wick. No matter. The room was his own, and the two lamps gave sufficient light. He had not one, but three pamphlets to read.

The pox was dealt with by a cinnabar fumigation, and unguent of sarsaparilla to be applied over two weeks. His other instructions were to commence his reading with the pamphlet by Monsieur Benezet. 'Promise you will return it to me when you have read it.'

Some Historical Account of Guinea, Its Situation, Produce and the General Disposition of its Inhabitants: An Inquiry into the Rise and Progress of the Slave Trade, Its Nature and Lamentable Effects.

Parts were so creased, the ink faded along the folds, that some of the words defied his attempts to decipher them. Many were unknown to him, his eye and his understanding being not yet fully matched. But he understood the essence of it. He knew what lay at the marrow of the writing. What exactly was writ there?

Something about a ship and seven hundred slaves on board. He read about men snared in irons, two by two, of many who tried to drown themselves or starve themselves to death rather than face that separation from home. Rather than submit.

Submit. Was that what he had done? In every life he'd had. Before in the unremembered place. And in the Carolinas. And even after, this strange life with Edward?

Dreams became memory. The darkness swaying and heaving, the dull clang of manacles or chains, his arms clinging tight to a cooling body that was soon to be wrenched from his grasp and carried up to the doorway of light and, at the last, her head falling back, lifeless eyes falling on all who remained behind in the hold, and on him, scrambling on hands and knees for a tiny bead that rolled between the boards, if only he could reach it ...

'Did you read Locke? What of his words, "*Every man has a property in his own person. This nobody has a right to but himself. The labour of his body, and the work of his hands are his own …*"'

The doctor plucked long passages from his head without reference to any of his papers. Tony begged for more time to study his pamphlets that he too could commit some lines to memory.

'Of course you may. You must. Remember it's the duty of those who can read to do so. To learn. Always.'

It was there, in that cluttered office in the evenings, that he began to see the world not just as it stood in relation to his life but the lives of all those who toiled within it. The doctor was a magpie for ideas, foraging in books and letters and interrogating his patients – 'Tell me of your time in the Indies; were there Mahometans in Spain? Did they look like me, I believe I am of those people; what is the advantage of a sextant over an octant?' – until he found some answers to his queries. He was a hoarder too, committing to memory facts and phrases, repeating exactly, something Tony had earlier told him. Though he had the perpetually furrowed brow of one troubled by inner demons, his manner gave lie to his appearance. For despite all his early travails, and his daily contact with the miseries and inequities of life, he maintained a bright eye, and receptive ear. And an uncanny knowing.

'Take your name now. Tony. Where you get that?'

A voice in his head. A woman's voice. Swaying and heaving. 'Perhaps my mother? I've had other names but I have a memory … of her, or a voice saying, you are Andoni.'

'Ah,' the doctor was gleeful, rubbing his hands together. 'I had a suspicion, same way as I can tell something about a person's body that they have no inkling of. Tony just didn't seem right to me.' He leaned forward until he was practically nose to nose with his patient. 'I consider myself something of an expert in the physiognomy of Africans as it relates to their particular tribe. Or at least I can tell those of the North from those of the West. Or thereabouts.' He finished his speech on a vague note.

The doctor relished his confusion a little too much but eventually put his supposition before Tony. 'I believe your people are Andoni.

Wherever you heard that word, on a ship or back in Africa, it was not your name. Someone wanted you to know your people. Remember them. I have heard the name of Andoni before. From somewhere near Bonny, somewhere on the coast.'

The doctor's face was filled with expectation. 'Now what do you think of that – am I not clever? Could what I say be true?'

It could. But then what? If this was not his name ... Perhaps better than that. His people. He had people. But it was not something he would discuss there, with Doctor Durham. He took it home, along with his reading, and the tiny flames that were flickering in the hidden rooms of his mind.

How long did the good doctor continue to treat him? A week, ten days. Such a short time and so much achieved. That doctor's room, with its attendant smells of powders and potions, herbs and unguents, was itself both balm and tonic, calming and stimulating.

'Problem with you Tony,' the doctor said, 'you expect something will happen to convince you that you're free. That you find someone from your past. Like your Minda. Someone to absolve you. Won't happen. I assure you. Now being a slave, well no one should be so, but even that don't mean we should behave better than other men. That's just a shackle of your own making. You and I, we just poor men, doing our best. That's all.'

All. Best. His mind opened up like one of the doctor's books; there were pages there, unknown to him, already written with his experience, but now he understood their meaning. And these forged other connections. Things Edward had said and read aloud to him now had truth in them. Truth that he could not see before, for it was hidden behind ignorance. *Man is free at the instant he wants to be. L'homme est libre au moment qu'il veut l'être.* His beloved Voltaire. His favourite Rousseau. His talk of independence, and equality, that he'd thought was just puff. Words. Not real.

The doctor was travelling to Philadelphia once the seas had settled. 'My second time to visit that place and at the invitation of Doctor Benjamin Rush himself.' His mind had moved on from Tony to planning for his journey, and his voice had changed, being more formal. 'Papers to write. My treatment of last year's cholera outbreak. And *A Repudiation of the Use of Cupping and Leeches for Relapsing Fever* which I have already circulated. Sadly our pleasant discussions must end. I must turn my thoughts to the mysteries of the body and the science of medicine.' He sipped his whiskey, adjusted his wig. 'Though Doctor Rush also has interesting ideas on disorders of the mind with which I must acquaint myself.'

Tony rose to leave, not wishing to take up more time but the doctor forestalled him once more. 'Sheba, Sheba.' He rang his bell with great vigour. 'Sheba,' he called.

She appeared in the doorway, calm and smiling, apron clean and smooth, and handed him a newspaper. 'I thought you'd ask for it,' she said before looking directly at Tony. 'Will be of interest to you. Though he won't let you read it for yourself. Always reads his chosen passages aloud. Likes an audience.' She touched her husband's shoulder gently to soften her words, and he patted her hand.

'*Le Courrier de l'Europe*. Came in on the *Dauphine*. She docked yesterday.' He laughed into his hand. 'I think you'll understand the irony of that soon enough. Seems France has had its own Revolution. You'll indulge me one last time if I read a piece?' Tony's assent was assumed. '"The King and Queen deposed. Spies, informers and bloodshed, the Bastille stormed." Ah, but Europe is the place to be now for a man such as yourself. No ties. This country has had its Revolution but Madame Liberty has been slow to tend to our fellows. She's been led astray by Mammon.'

No ties. The doctor was right. But not just in the way he meant. He was altered; by what exactly he could not say. Not the pox nor its treatment, which mercifully had eased his misery. By the warm discourse with another man of his ilk? Perhaps. Or the banquet of words and books and ideas from which he had supped. Perhaps the doctor had cut out a festering growth without his knowledge. Or a fetter. That was it.

He straightened up as he walked out of that house off Conti Street for the last time, inhabited his body, his arms and legs and back. Felt how it did its breathing for him, and yet he could make it breathe deeper, more slowly. His heart ceased to hammer, but slowed in harmony. He turned the corner onto the main square and watched as a tapestry of life played out. All was busy: Sounds of hammering, sawing, seabirds squawking; dogs sniffing around a row of stalls; smells of sawdust, turpentine, roasting meat, and still the hint of charred wood. A large wooden scaffold surrounded the emerging structure that would be the new cathedral. Workers swarmed around it, more black men than white. A pallet of blocks was lifted, suspended from a pulley, and hauled in by three men stripped to the waist. Elsewhere, men worked in pairs, in a rhythmic action, a slap of mortar before the block was hefted and hammered into place. Only three weeks in the city, and yet he could see the changes, the brickwork higher, windows taking shape, new beams traversing the structure. He watched their movements, fascinated by the way each small unit was multiplied all over the scaffold, like those ant hills out in Kaskaskia country.

A group of gentlemen descended the steps of the nearby Cabildo, and paused at the bottom, their heads bent in conversation. Even from his distant vantage point, he recognised the animated movements of Edward, his figure slight among the bulky, elaborately dressed group. He waited until the men parted, and only Edward remained, surveying the activity of the square, till his attention was snagged. He raised his hand and plunged through the crowds.

'Tony. Have you heard the news?' He was almost breathless. 'France. Those rumours were true. There is Revolution. The old is thrown out.' He shoved a newspaper into his hands. 'To think all of this was happening a world away while we were just …' He gestured with his arms, mimicking the action of a paddle.

Tony glanced at the paper. 'I heard. The King and Queen. The Bastille. The convention. What of your brother? Was he not posted there within the last year?'

'By God, you're right.' He snatched the paper back. 'I can only imagine what he would make of Revolution. Dear dry Robert must be in the horrors.' He seemed to notice Tony properly for the first time. 'How did you learn of it?'

'A friend, Doctor James Durham, told me this morning.'

'Is that so?' He kicked up some dirt with his boot.

'It is so. I'm thinking of going back to Europe, perhaps France.'

'Is that so?' He said again, looking hard at Tony. 'You look different.'

'Have you booked a passage?'

'Yes, early January. Another week.' Edward smiled, open as a child. 'I wondered when our paths would cross again. What have you been doing?'

'Reading. Talking. Thinking. And ...' He let the sentence hang.

'Ah. Perhaps that's why you look different. I booked a passage for two, by the way.'

'Is that so?'

They fell into step, their silence filled by the noise of the cathedral works. Another brick slid into place. A young child darted between them, chasing after a scraggy shipwreck of a cat. She wove among the hawkers, merchants, servants and slaves, her glossy hair flying out behind her. The cat upended a basket of hens, releasing a cacophony of flapping and shouting and the girl's high-pitched laughter. The hens were rounded up, returned to their cage, the girl was duly collected, and the cat vanished. Still no words between them. Tony straightened his shoulders, turned his face to the sky, and drew cool air deep into his chest. Edward hummed tunelessly.

After the last two weeks of storms, the December sunlight was gentle and quite unlike the harsh glare that had accompanied their Mississippi descent.

For days I had the sense that some of that slave word what Baaba mentions were still in me. It caused a sickening for something. I were as restless as an old hen before its neck were wrung. It were the need to know, about the word, about what Baaba once were. I couldn't face seeking out those old men, who once was slaves, for I were ashamed (am still ashamed) of my previous withering thoughts about them. Ignorance breeds more than fear, it stirs a kind of thoughtless scorn. Caused me to wonder too how come I'd no women like myself to talk with about such things. I used to know a few when I were younger but with all my moving I seemed to have forgotten them, left them behind. There was no one I could ask about that word.

But to borrow from that Doctor Durham, there's nothing to be gained by picking at old scabs. I put aside Baaba's papers for a time and decided to go back to the Museum. I checked myself in the glass on the hall stand, and found I were pleased with my appearance. Nothing fancy about me, but respectable, like my surroundings. I were glad for the comfort of my small home in Euston Grove, despite all the noise and clatter of the trains, and the stink and mess of the horses nearby. I were glad for the comfort of the key I held, knowing it were mine, and the small nest of money I keep in the bank. I don't mind saying neither that I were glad for my looks that had survived some considerable privations, though none so bad as what my Baaba endured, at least as I imagine.

So it was I swept up the steps of that overbearing Museum building, between them grey old pillars, and marched past the front desk and the prissy young man who hovered there. I could feel his eyes on me and out of badness or just a wish to make my mark, I went and set the great big globe to spinning, knowing he would follow me to see what I were at. My heart raced a little as countries merged into continents and all the land whirred into the sea in a blur, the colour of dirty piss. He whined desperately at me. Oh, oh you mustn't. Miss, madam. Please stop. Please return to the entrance. Waving them sweaty hands, he were in such a state. As if I were going to linger like an idle child and keep on twirling it. Besides, I had business to conduct in the Reading Room. I asked him to direct me. Oh but he smirked then, saying it was impossible to enter without a Reading Ticket. So says I, well then I should like one. Turns out there's a whole palaver about forms and recommendations and waiting periods and it's absolutely impossible to just waltz into the most singular establishment of learning in the City of London without due procedure. Due procedure he said. In that case says I, could you please send for Mr Panizzi. What business could you have with him, the young pup enquired and his voice rose so that it echoed and caused some gentlemen to turn and look in my direction. He's an acquaintance of mine, says I, and he will assist me even if you will not. One of his eyebrows twitched upward. You mean Mr Panizzi the Principal Librarian he said. Is there another Mr Panizzi I asked.

After much clicking and whistling noises, and sucking in his lips like a cat's arse, he handed a slip of paper to a young lad and pointed to a chair.

You may wait there, says he. So I waited.

Seems Mr Panizzi is a bigwig in the Library, but he were most kind and gentlemanly to me again. Approached me with a welcome back Mrs Small, and I saw the young man's head duck down like he were pecking grains from his desk. Mr Panizzi said it was his firmest belief that even the poorest in the country should have the same means to pursue their curiosity for learning as the richest men, but not everyone agreed. The young man's face fired up, red as a coxcomb, on hearing this and I felt a little jab of satisfaction as we turned away from him. I'm not sure how much learning I can do at my age, says I, but I would like to read the books my father mentions in his papers, I want to know how his life was when he were a slave and what it's like there still. For I knew that in parts of America, black men and women was still the property of white men. It seemed hard to believe though. Mr Panizzi murmured under his breath about justice, or no justice and lip service to liberty. I gave him the names of the writers, Anthony Benezet, Abbé Raynal, Voltaire and some others. Mr Panizzi considered my request and his eyes held a look of deep thought, brown eyes like my own I might mention. If I may, Mrs Small, those books are somewhat old now, and much has been written on the subject since that time. Fine books by men such as your father. Frederick Douglass and Solomon Northup to name but two. I take an interest in these texts. The idea of Freedom is something close to my own heart.

All the while he's talking we was walking, his shoes squeaking softly on the marbled floor while mine made rude clonking noises. He took no notice, talked on about how as a young man, he too had been forced to flee his home country in Italy under pain of death. So I have an appreciation of the suffering of your people, he said with crinkle-faced sincerity as he pushed hard on a great door. The Reading Room Mrs Small.

Room.

Why must people use the wrong words. A room is my neat parlour, two chairs by the fire, and the only decoration apart from the drapes being a dull painting of a waterfall and, on a side table, a bowl of oranges which I like to have about me, one studded with cloves for the scent. This so-called room were bigger even than the commodious new offices by Euston Station. I were agape, at the whole of the room curved as a temple, the great dome above me, pale blue as my Wedgwood jug and sugar bowl (a small luxury, from a pawn shop, for which I make no apology) and it lit by so many windows that light danced off the brass railings and iron walkways that circled the walls, layered up higher and higher and shelves stacked upon shelves with all manner of books. And below, rows of tables and chairs filled with men. Men bent over books in silence, a lamp set by each, the only sounds being the hiss of gas, and that of pages whispering as they was turned over. By white men. Only. Oh I hears myself say, feeling small inside, as though the air had leaked out of me, and my head became light, most likely for craning up to see all the wonders above me.

Come Mrs Small. A lady such as you shall not be intimidated though I must admit it is quite something. Just opened this very year. A great project of mine. He walked across the floor between the desks, with an air of ownership. If I may suggest a book for you, one that you may find both informative and sympathetic, written only recently … he paused, changed direction to track along the shelves, his hand waving like a conjuror's over the books. And by a woman … his hand stopped, plucked a volume from the shelf … there, take this. See. He pointed to a name on the book. H. B. Stowe. Your namesake. I looked at him, not knowing what he meant by this. The H is for Harriet. That's her name. He removed another book. There are two parts. Bring them back when you are done but take your time. It's a long book, and … you'll see.

I saw. Like someone had lit a lamp in a dark room that I didn't know existed. Such a dark room. And yet.

And yet, it seems there's two kinds of knowing. The knowing in your head where you've seen for yourself and the deep knowing for something, that rests silent somewhere inside you, waiting for a candle to flicker over it. What was Baaba's word. Marrow. I realised I had always felt it in the marrow of my bones. Still do. Had to stop reading several times else I should be drove quite teary over it. Not that I hold with all that religious talk Mrs Stowe uses, quoting the Bible at every turn. I think such matters are best kept private. And I know, most likely, it means she's one of them pious pinched sorts, like them pale bombazined women what attend daily services at St Pancras, but still, the words she has writ down, in that book, *Uncle Tom's Cabin*, I won't never forget what were in it. I can see it behind my eyes like I were there myself, right from the start, when the little cabin filled my heart with such hopes, what with its garden patch of fruit and flowers, and the snug interior and Aunt Chloe, proud as you like in her fresh checked turban busy with her pan and kettle, and greasing a griddle. How I wanted to eat one of her corn-cakes, watch her little boys tumble and play, feel all the comforts of the cabin, and see for myself the fine handsome man that was Uncle Tom. The account of his features, set out with such considerable esteem, detailing his glossy black face, his broad chest, his grave expression set something alight in me that has long been ashes. But that were just a cruel trick to lure me into the book. All that happiness set to spoil. Turns out the story is one hardship and cruel turn after another. Children separated from mothers. Fathers sold away from their loving families. Such love as would make you cry. I read on and on through the night, setting wick to dying wick, being afraid to put it down. The not knowing, couldn't sleep – couldn't shut my eyes for the not knowing.

But it were Cassy who gave me especial grief. Cassy with her proud face of bitter endurance. Bitter endurance. Those words scraped my mind and what she did to her own baby, lest he too should suffer the awful privations same as her other children. And the burden of such an act. My heart were wrung tight like it were put through a mangle. The very breath left my body. I dropped the book to the floor beside my bed. Could not read on. Left a lamp burning to keep the darkness away.

I loved my little boy baby. My Ed.

But it's hard to keep love going when you must work and you're forced to leave your boy with other women who don't need to do work, least not my kind of work, and who can sit in their greasy kitchens, pushing out one infant after another with no thought of how they was going to feed them except that they might take in the child of another woman who cannot sit home suckling her own youngster, who has no man to go out and bring home some coins. I hated those women who'd look after another's child. Hated especially the first one who took him in. She were a large, soft-looking woman, named Hannah. Seemed to have no edges, just soft pink flesh. Never without a child at her breast. I remember how the place smelt of yeasty bread and sour damp napkins.

And milk, her milk. First time I saw her suckling my child I vomited. But a body can get used to anything and I hardened myself to it. Did that cause my own milk to dry up. I don't know nor why it seemed he never stopped crying when he were with me.

I did love him in my way, though as he grew, it got more difficult.

Cassy loved her baby. In the book. And see what she did.

Killed him. For love, though. To save him.

Strange love.

This reading is stirring up thoughts from my muddy mind, dreams of my girl child, the one what come early. I see her in the water, the newspaper gradually unravelling from her little body; sometimes the sun reaches down to her and she turns over so the light touches her face. Most times though the greasy paper parcel sinks back, down and down to the dark muddy bottom.

Perhaps Ma thought that Mr Fricker – with his professions of love and his way with words, and his fancy hat – would look after us. Take us in. She were taken in alright. On no account would he have Ma come live with us. Said he'd only married me. She could go elsewhere. All of us was angry. Perhaps Ma realised he were a mistake for she put her hands to my face and begged me, dear Ettie, to do my best with him. And I tried. What I said earlier about him is not entirely true. Not all of it. Sometimes, back then, I made things up to cast myself in a better light. Not so much for other people but for myself. And some of these stories are so set in my head that I can no longer tell if they're true, in spite of my wish now to put things down as they happened. Even the story of my girl child in the river.

So I tried and he left. And after? I don't mind saying that I did whatever I could to make money to keep myself and my lad. But it ain't easy for a woman on her own. I worked in the White Bear Inn at first, and attracted a great deal of attention, most of it unwelcome, but not all. I met a Mr Nelson there. Not the famous one, but with money enough to look after me, and young enough to be tolerable. Never mentioned I had a son. Left Ed with my mother in the rooms she rented in Rotherhithe. It were easy enough. Respectable too. Almost. I never minded pleasuring him. Like I said he weren't old. When he were finished with me, after a year or two, he said as how he still had enough regard for me to see I should be placed with a friend of his. As if I were a piece of furniture to be passed on. I suppose you're thinking why wouldn't she. What else can a woman like that do?

Were there other gentleman friends after that. What if there were, ain't no one's business, now so much time has passed and I don't hold with dipping in such dirty water all over again. What's the point. Ain't nothing ever changed by such wallowing. Enough to say I shut the door on that life after a time, tried my hand at other ventures. Taking in misplaced goods, finding them a new home, bit like Mr Nelson wanted to do for me. I were good with money. Always kept some back for myself. And money begets more money in my experience. Got a small house, on Park Street, Camden Town. Swapped goods for people. Lodgers is what I mean. Respectable people.

Ed came back to live with me after Ma passed away. That were a sorry time. I missed her and her snippy ways but I determined to care for Ed as best I could. To love him and have him love me. But he seemed to take against me. Probably spent too long away, first with them wet nurses, and then Ma. She'd trained him up in sewing, apprenticed him to a tailor off Bond Street but I think he took Ma's passing hard. It weren't long before he were getting into bad habits, small matters at first, sneaking a length of linen, or some gentleman's gloves. Perhaps he got too cocky. Or maybe he were pressed into nicking to order, and just weren't that good at it. Sixteen years old, the first time he stood in the Old Bailey, and all for a parcel of leather off-cuts. Spent three months in a Hulk at Dartford. Weren't ever the same after. I tried to keep him closer. Truly. I tried. But he were set against me, against everything. He became a wilder and rougher lad so that I hardly recognised him as my own flesh and blood. My lodgers were none too keen on him neither, nor his outbursts.

There were bad feeling between us. He kept up his thieving, but had not the wit to keep quiet about it. Put me in a position, at a time when I were becoming respectable, having my own house, paid for by myself and not some protector who could snatch it all back from me at a time of his choosing. But Ed, my own son, cleared out two of my rooms, and he were caught trying to pawn two bedsteads, two tables, a wash stand and a looking glass. What a sorry list that makes. He even took a palliasse, tried to pawn it. Told the broker I'd asked him to take the furniture. Dropped me right in it. Said I'd given him the goods. I were arrested. Locked up for five days with a shifting, snuffling, stinking press of miserable women. And I in my best clothes. And not even a bloody palliasse to lie upon.

Did I give testimony against my own son? I never. Never said I'd have him transported. Never said as how I wanted rid of him. But I were obliged to answer the questions of the court. So they said when they made me put my hand on the Bible. I took fright then. And the words just tumbled from my lips like I were possessed of an evil spirit. Except my evil spirit told the truth. For the most part. Ed looked so small in the dock. Never had much pickings on him but two weeks in Coldbath Jug were enough to reduce him to a kippered herring. He shouted at me as I spoke my bit. Said No Ma. You tell 'em the truth. And his eyes were wild. But see, I also feared my own son for he had hit me and threatened me and despite him looking so thin, he had such strength in him. Such fierceness. I feared and loved him. In the end, weren't my words what done him in but the broker's and his own. Couldn't stop shouting from the dock. Caused all the motley horde of spectators to ooh and aah. The old beak in the wig weren't going to take that. There were nothing I could do.

When the old beak said them terrible words, *transported to Van D—'s Land for a term of seven years*, my heart squeezed tighter than a mangled shirt. I shouted out then. Begged his honour not to take my only son from me. Ed struggled against the guards as they hauled him away.

Called out to me.

Don't let them take me Ma.

Ma. Ma.

I cursed the judge. Was flung out onto the steps of the Bailey for my trouble.

They had names for me then. Black Ettie. Black widow. They said I'd eat my own offspring. You can tire of such wit after a time. I struggled to leave them names behind when I moved. When the new Birmingham railway tore up my house, I took the paltry compensation and moved to Euston Grove. Out of the frying pan and into the fire you might say. But this time I put the trains to my own use and turned my small house into a proper lodgings. Right outside the spanking new station. A lodgings for travelling ladies what couldn't afford the Euston hotel – respectable house servants, governesses, shop ladies and the like, the Victoria being for working men only – I fancied I saw an opportunity and I seized it. Turned out in my favour. Here I've only ever been known as Mrs Small, the almost-respectable proprietress of modest, clean accommodation. Can take six guests at a time. Three in each bedroom. More if they're willing to share a bed. I keep a girl about me, Irish too, goes by the name of Brigid Lordan. She were but a scrawny orphan when I took her on three years ago, and she refused to believe I were Irish-born. Sure how could that be, she said, and you so exotic. I think she may have been frightened of me at first.

Lately though, I been warming to the girl. She works hard, does the scrubbing, the beds, the fires and the like, though I prefer to look after the breakfast myself – simple fare, nothing fancy. But enough for my guests. Respectable.

I say that word. Respectable. Yet still that nasty ditty comes back to me, at times. And that name. Hattie Fricker.

> Oh hark the tale of Hattie Fricker
> She raised her son a darkling dipper
> But when he nicked her stash of swag
> She turned nark and he were lagged.

Don't know who came up with it, but I heard it chanted so often around Camden Town that it wedged deep in the cracks of my mind. Still catches me unawares, seeping to the top like greasy scum on a pot of simmering marrowbones.

III

WALKING INTO REBELLION

Dearest Eddie, Beloved Eddie, Angelic Eddie, Romantic Edward, Impulsive Edward, Lieutenant Fitzgerald, Disgraced, Misguided Edward, Captain Lord, United Irishman, Tragic Edward, Ill-fated Edward

28th July, 1857
Going nowhere

There's pages missing. Years missing. I've been sat in my parlour all morning, sorting papers, rearranging them, but it's no good. They don't make no sense in them middle years. I'd such high hopes of reading about Baaba and Ma when they was young, when first they met. But there's nary a word, least none that's set in its proper order. No mention of when I were born and I don't mind saying I felt a pinch in my heart at that. Like I were of no matter to him. But I know different, so I tells myself that perhaps it were something private for him that he didn't want to put in them pages for others to read. Though perhaps it were Lady Lucy who, tired of scratching out Baaba's words, scrunched it up in her little white fist and cast it into the fire. Maybe he were feverish, his head in a muddle, and forgot what he wrote and when. Or perhaps he never wrote about it at all. Kept it to himself. Maybe even tucked the memory into the little pouch he kept round his neck and there it stayed. Some passages are so short, writ not on one of them big pages but on scraps, torn fragments and merchandise receipts, without dates or clues. And keepsakes, and printed songs and such.

I wonder if this letter from Lady Lucy made him rush on ahead. It's filled with all manner of do this, don't do that, so maybe Baaba were just following her instructions. Who knows? You can read anything into empty spaces, could make up all manner of stories to fill those gaps.

Boyle Farm, Surrey
5th February, 1804

Dear Tony,

I trust this letter finds you in improved health. I believe
Surgeon Heavisides's reputation to be excellent. While your
most recent chapters were of considerable interest to me,
as they shed light on a period of my brother's life of which
I remained largely ignorant, there were certain passages,
which being quite contrary to my brother's character have
led me to doubt wonder about your version memory of this
time. As you may see from the address, I am visiting with my
brother Henry and Mr Ogilvie at Boyle Farm. Naturally they
enquired about your most recent work. They too expressed
reservations on reading it. But you are not to worry unduly
as it is unlikely we will use that section about Canada and
America, except to mention how Dear Edward was honoured
by the Indians and made a Chief of their tribe. Mr Ogilvie
expressed the view that the rest is largely irrelevant (and
you know how his opinions prevail). I will summarise the
important details myself; a page or two should suffice.

　　Mr Ogilvie also considers it best that you avoid mention
of Lord Edward's friendship with the ill-fated Mrs Sheridan
and his visit to Paris in 1791, though I pointed out that it
would then be difficult to explain how he met his future wife,
Lady Pamela. Where else would he have met the supposed
daughter of the duc d'Orléans?

　　'Everyone knows who that Lady is and where she came
from. There is no need for him to elaborate or to make things
any worse than they were.' So says Mr Ogilvie. In fact he became
quite lively on the subject. I must confess I had forgotten the
depth of his hostility towards Lady Pamela. 'Remember how she
was under suspicion from the beginning of their marriage, being
tainted by Republican associations, by the common knowledge
that she was, is the daughter of Orléans. What kind of man
could send his own cousin, King Louis, and the poor Queen to

the guillotine? What kind of man could give up his title, duc
d'Orléans, to take the name Philippe Égalité? An ugly, bestial
man. That he might have been father to Dear Edward's wife. At
least he got the end he deserved.'

Poor Mr Ogilvie. I thought him at risk of an apoplexy. So I
forbore to mention that our own Edward had also renounced his
title. How often did we hear him declare himself to be Citoyen
Edward? (But enough of that and no mention of it either in
your account or it will send Mr Ogilvie to an early grave.) We
discussed how best to proceed from here. It must be said that
Henry has his doubts about the project. He worries it may
prove a drain on your health but I have assured him that you
are as committed as the Family. Mr Ogilvie is of the opinion
that for it to have any value, it 'must get to the point and reveal
how his associates duped him into aligning his good name
with theirs, how his principles never equated with actual armed
rebellion – how could they when he had been such a loyal soldier
in the service of King and Country – and how indeed he was
scapegoated by the cowardly Irish administration.'

I understand my stepfather's argument though I find his
dismissal of Edward's principles quite hurtful. I remain an
Irishwoman in my heart though it's not something I may speak
of freely, either with Mr Ogilvie or my own Dear Husband,
Sir Thomas. But in the case of our project, I must recognise
the need to balance my heart, my conscience even, with my
duty towards my dead brother and his good name. Thus I
assured Mr Ogilvie you would endeavour to set out your
account showing how others took advantage of his loyalty,
his generosity and his lively interest in all matters to do with
Ireland. It may require the omission of certain events or a small
measure of obfuscation but there is no dishonour in that.

Who among us does not wish to present our past selves
in a more agreeable way? To brush over mistakes or poor
judgements and pose in the best light for posterity's portrait?

Trusting as always to your loyalty,
Lady Lucy FitzGerald Foley

I remember times when Baaba wrote furiously through day and night. Ma said he were feverish, and she worried about him and pestered him, often sitting on the kitchen settle, running them beads through her fingers and muttering prayers under her breath. On one of them spells, I asked him why he were writing so fast, and he stopped his hand for a moment and turned to me.

Ettie, my dear Ettie, he said, smiled and put his stained hand on my cheek. And he spoke in a soft, smiling voice.

I have the urge to write, you see. To spill the inky contents of myself onto this very page.

And for a moment I imagined that it were his very blood draining down his arm and into that pen and all over the page and I were frightened, and told him so. He laughed, said his blood were red not black like the ink, so how could that be.

He picked me up, brought me out to the yard, with Ma following and telling him I were too big for him to be carrying, but he said as how he'd hold his daughter if he chose to, that he were burning with vigour, and perhaps Surgeon Heavisides's powders was working after all. So he held me in his arms, in naught but his shirt, looking at the sky, smiling, with the hens clucking around him and Ma clucking at him in turn, throwing a blanket over his shoulders. Then he put me down and took Ma by the hand and dragged her back inside, and danced with her on the flagstones, a strange hopping dance, and Ma gathered her skirts and twirled and hopped with him, laughing and crying at the same time. Brazen Lulu, that wretched hen, darted about under their feet, squawking and beating her wings, and I banged a wooden spoon off a pot. It were a proper madhouse.

THE TRUE NARRATIVE

1790–1792, and the Author gives a short account of the years following Lord Edward's return from New Orleans.

On his return from his travels, His Lordship made straight for London and his Mother and Family. Their reunion was most affecting. It was noted that although his spirits were charming as ever, there was a reserve, a considered manner in his conversation, that reflected his new philosophies. The Duchess sought to interview me on the matter to enquire whether there was any reason for this, any occurrence over and above those he described to her, such as his time with the settlers, and his appreciation of the Native way of life. I told her I could not account for another man's conscience nor know what matters might strike a chord in another's heart.

What the family said, however, was true. Lord Edward became ever more interested in matters Political. He kept abreast of events in Paris, to do with the Revolution. He was stirred by Mr Thomas Paine's words on natural rights and political rights based on equality in his book, The Rights of Man. He became one of Mr Paine's circle in London, finding solace in the company of working men such as Mr Horne Tooke and Mr Hardy, while maintaining the sympathetic friendship of his cousin Charles Fox, Sir Francis Burdett, that great supporter of lost causes, and of course, the playwright Mr Brinsley Sheridan. He spoke at length to just about anyone who would listen about 'The Levelling Principle'.

He remonstrated with his sister, Lady Lucy who expressed concerns about the mob. 'You must call them "the People",' he chided. Some of his new zeal may have been spurred by his disappointments, not just in the matter of his cousin, but also regarding the manner in which his account of Spanish military and trade interests along the Mississippi were received – with gratitude and compliments on his perspicacity. But no reward, no promotion. This was no mere blow to his pride; it was kindling to the sparks of his radical ideas. Why should not a man be promoted on account of what he has to offer and what he has earned rather than his connections, or his money?

I watched him move from radical coffee-houses to the houses of his well-connected friends. In Devonshire House, within a few months of his return from America, he met the famous Mrs Sheridan, wife of his friend Brinsley Sheridan. Met her and ... Perhaps theirs was a love born of frustration with their social position – of the disappointments, and limits placed upon them. But for the rest of that year and into the next, their devotion and passion for one other was marked. Such a terrible pity that the birth of their little daughter Mary, in spring, should herald that sweet lady's decline, and cause such anguish for my Master, who wanted to keep the child for himself.[26] His Family naturally urged him to leave the child in the care of Mr Sheridan. But it was a double blow for my tender-hearted Master. That is what drove him to Paris. And there he found himself caught up in the excitement of free-thinking men, of Mr Paine's circle, advocates of change, of Revolution.

Paris in 1792. It was a different Paris from the one I had visited only six years before. That November, the blood on the streets was hardly dry, the Royal Family were imprisoned in the Marais and the National Convention declared as Government. The city was a rabid den, always alert, never resting, sleep impossible no matter how full the belly or soft the palliasse. Lord Edward took rooms in White's Hotel, alongside Mr Paine's, and worked on the French translation

[26] Tony. I asked you not to mention Mrs Sheridan. That was a private matter. LLF.

of Mr Paine's book every morning. He took up the pace that the city dictated, while I found himself wary of the clamour of people, especially those who crowded into the hotel. Especially on that day when the newly formed Society of the Friends of the Rights of Man met with members of the National Convention. That day which stretched into evening and on through the night. The crowds in the small hotel, far greater than anticipated, spilling out from the dining room to the adjoining sitting rooms, to the upper bedrooms. I found myself pressganged into helping out the owner, Mr White, at Lord Edward's request.

All noise and clatter, whispers and laughter and a veritable Babel of foreign tongues. A hotbed of ideas and enthusiasms, the whole building fogged with smoke and greasy steam. In the main dining room, a vast wood-burning fire spat ash and glowing embers beyond the stone hearth onto the floorboards, where they smouldered and blackened. Pipes were lit and relit, tapped and tamped, men calling for a servant to bring an ember on a tongs. The first course was served at three o'clock – the gathering launched themselves upon the food with astonishing fervour – and hours later, after the final course was cleared, the tables were replenished with yet more bottles of wine and pitchers of punch. The mood was excitable and Mr Paine himself was in the thick of it. For one so unassuming in manner and appearance, he was a veritable honeypot for the discontented and all manner of liberals, bluestockings and radicals. Well-known men such as John Hurford Stone, and the unknown Irish Sheares brothers. And still flushed from his routing of the Prussians at Verdun, was the famed General of the French, Count Arthur Dillon, who offered that very evening to perform the same service in his ancestral country of Ireland. Lord Edward raised his glass to that as the horns of the military band clamoured out 'Ça Ira'.

I listened from the doorway as an Englishman proposed the abolition of hereditary titles in England, whereupon he flung his glass at the fireplace and Lord Edward did the same.

Lord Edward FitzGerald, Major in the 54th Regiment and member of the Dublin Parliament, in White's Hotel, in the company

of Thomas Paine and a host of Radicals, toasting Revolution, and
the abolition of hereditary titles. That toast was the beginning as
surely as Eve plucking the apple from the tree. How he embraced
it, his jacket thrown off, neckcloth discarded, shirt sleeves rolled to
the elbow, standing on a chair, revelling in the clamour of cheers.
Huzzah, huzzah. Scraping of chairlegs, spoons rapped on tables, feet
stamping, great logs spitting in the enormous fireplace. I must confess
to feeling a stir of excitement at that moment as I stood shoulder to
shoulder with men of courage and belief. Such words, such fervour.
And Lord Edward raising his glass. 'Henceforth I am "Citoyen
Edouard".' Ah the cheers. As alive as ever he had been and filled with
conviction. Lord Edward FitzGerald no longer. Remade. Renamed.
Citizen Edward.[27]

I did not see Lord Edward the next day, nor that night though I
knew he had a box at the theatre to see a performance of an opera.
The following morning however, it was my Master who woke me and
pressed a note into my hand, urging me to go at once and deliver his
card to Madame de Genlis.

'Find out where she is staying. I saw her daughter, Pamela, last
night at the opera. Sitting across from me. She is the incarnation of
my dear Betsy Sheridan. Her hair, her eyes, her beauty. Pamela. I
have begged Madame de Genlis for an introduction.'[28]

Five weeks later they were married.

---

[27] You have gone against everything I detailed in my letter. Is this deliberate?
Perhaps you are unable to decide what to include and what to leave out. You must
not mention Paris. It is a red rag to a bull. LLF.
[28] And to mention the circumstances of dear Edward's meeting with Pamela? Is
this really how it happened? No. No. You cannot, must not, mention this again.
Perhaps this Narrative is not working. If you cannot write what has been agreed,
I fear our endeavour must end. LLF.

The True Narrative

The Author gives an account of the Character of Lord Edward.

Lord Edward was a man unlike all others. I have been remiss in my presentation of him here. Perhaps I assume too much of the Reader's knowledge of him, for he was a man who seemed to me, to know everyone and be known by everyone. Most people live small lives. Planted in the soil of their birth, they grow, scatter some seeds nearby, wither and descend into the earth from whence they came. Lord Edward was a giant tree. Not to start with, but he became such, sending out roots into all kinds of soil, rich and poor, Native and foreign. And countless people were privileged by shelter and comfort under the bounteous branches of his vast good nature. He could not enter a room without lifting the spirits of those within, whether by a mollifying jest, a well-placed enquiry or merely the benevolence of his attention. Possessed of a boundless curiosity and the energy to match it, he drank deep from the cup of life. But what marked him out above all his fellows was his faculty for championing the underdog. And loyalty as fierce and sharp as a finely honed sabre. Once committed to a cause, he was unable to back away but must see the thing through.

Now that these words have taken shape, I know them to be true. He was all these things.[29]

---

[29] This little sketch is perfect. I'm happy you have left off the inflammatory stories about Paris. Now perhaps you should inform the readers about the State of Ireland at the time. You cannot expect educated people to have any understanding of it. You know how they close their ears to such things. But no Politics. Please. LLF.

The True Narrative

The Author attempts to give some account of Ireland during those difficult times.

I confess it is not a little hazardous for an obscure individual, and one so far from being a Native of Ireland, to presume to inform the Public about the affairs of that country. I hope Censure will be suspended, when it is considered that it was written by one who greeted all new circumstances with great interest and curiosity and who was fortunate enough to have a Master who suffered my enquiries with the utmost Patience and Indulgence. It was he who encouraged my practice of close observation of people and events and who gave meaning to them that I might become wiser.

Consequently I propose to detail some observations gleaned from my travels about this country and to accompany them with explanations, many provided by Lord Edward himself, that they may prove more interesting to the Reader.

When I first came to Ireland I was much surprised to see the desperate conditions of the poor. So many poor people; in the city of Dublin, vermin-ridden houses swarmed with a ragged and squalid tenantry in parts of the city marked by ordure and filth and, not uncommonly, by the run-off from the many slaughterhouses that operated there. I had hoped that life in the countryside would present a different scene but alas I was sorely mistaken. Ruinous hovels were to be found, these composed of mud and straw with a single opening, acting as both doorway and window. And inside, there could be any number of inhabitants, a family of twelve or more.

I would like to disabuse the Reader who dismisses such inhabitants as being of some lower order and therefore not having the same feelings as those in lofty positions of money, education and entitlement. They are the same, as human as any Lord or Bishop. Or indeed as the Black Man. The Irish have a long and much-resented history of injustice, especially those of the Catholic persuasion, who form the majority on that Isle, whose religion has been suppressed, whose rights of advancement and ownership of property have been all but taken from them and who are yet expected to pay tithes to the Established Church and rent to absent Masters. Even their Native language is subject to persecution, being trampled and looked down upon, with many people forced to accept the bitter taste of another's language on their tongue.[30]

Just as the enslaved Black Man in the Indies and America chafes against his shackles, so does the Native Irishman resist the impositions of the foreign Government of Britain. But there is another kind of Irishman, one whose forebears may well have come from France or England, and who finds himself not only in possession of great swathes of land but also of conscience and enlightened views and is thus predisposed to see the injustice in this inequality. Such a man was my Master, Lord Edward FitzGerald. Other men, informed perhaps by their desire to secure their own finances rather than the Rights of Man, also resisted the English Government's interference with matters of trade and commerce, resenting the taxes which went to England for the benefit of the people there. Import and export tariffs served to embitter many who would not otherwise have considered throwing over the Government.[31]

[30] This, I suspect, is a little excessive Tony! I know how the Irish love their Gaelic language – I too have a fondness for it – but is it not the case that English is the true language of enlightenment and advancement? Think how well you have done because of it! L.L.F.
[31] I find myself agreeing with all you have written. In fact it rekindles my old Irish passions. Nonetheless I wonder if it benefits us to stir up such old tensions. Surely conditions have improved for tenants. Is not their lot happier now? L.L.F.

Thus concludes my disquisition on the state of the people of Ireland in those years. There are other matters which I found confusing especially those relating to the different divisions in Ireland. I use the word 'division' as my Lord Edward did, aware of how the word may be construed. The organisation of the United Irishmen did its best to call all men under the one banner, be they Protestant landowners or Presbyterian men of business or poor Catholic peasants. It did its best.

And those who remained loyal to His Majesty's Government, they too banded together, forming voluntary local Militias when the regular army was deemed too sparse to deal with the threat of French Invasion. Later Dublin Castle, the seat of British authority in Ireland, organised a paid volunteer Yeomanry, whose name has since been tainted with sordid tales of bloodshed and torture.[32] But I am getting ahead of my Narrative.

[32] Please, do not dwell on the bloody history. LLF.

The True Narrative

*July 1796, and Lord Edward travels to Hamburg for a wedding;
Mr O'Connor joins him for a tour of Switzerland;
The Author learns the Science of Inkmaking.*

Lady Pamela's cousin, Henriette de Sercey, was to marry a rich banker, Mr Matthiessen, in Hamburg. The entire household packed up. Lord Edward, Lady Pamela and her lady's maid, little baby Eddy and his nursemaid. Trunks, travelling cases, valises. Carriage to Dublin, packet to Parkgate, coach through Wales, a visit to Lord Edward's mother and Mr Ogilvie at their summer residence in Ealing, where Eddy and his nursemaid remained. Then on to Hamburg, a difficult passage despite the season, and one that necessitated two overnights in a Dutch port, before we finally sailed up the Elbe on a fair wind, with only a day to spare before the nuptials; and a chance for Lady Pamela to reacquaint herself with her mother, Madame de Genlis; she, a writer of great repute, once known as Comtesse, was by then something of a peripatetic exile following the execution of her amour, Philippe Égalité – once known as the duc d'Orléans. Sometimes a name change is not sufficient to save your neck.[33]

Only days after the wedding, Lady Edward was brought to bed with a baby girl, much to my Master's delight. There were some

[33] How true! But perhaps too sharp an observation and not what readers would expect. LLF.

who, before our departure for Hamburg, were quick to express
their censure at the idea of her travelling so near her time but
they would happily have reversed their opinions had they seen how
quickly she recovered her full health during and after her lying-in.
It was a busy time for the Edwards. Her cousin's door was open to
all manner of visitors. His Lordship was obliged to pay a courtesy
call to the French Minister, but this caused idle gossip among
visitors. He laughed off these slurs, saying he hardly knew what
to wear those days for fear of being called out for his rebel green,
republican blue or royalist red. 'I shall stick to black from now
on Tony,' he declared. 'It's safer.'

I think he was relieved by the arrival in the city of his good
friend Mr Arthur O'Connor. The French Minister suggested that the
two men might like to take a tour, perhaps meet with like-minded
men along the way. With Lady Pamela's blessing the pair embarked
on their impromptu travels, absenting themselves for over two months,
taking in many of the sights of Brunswick before establishing a
temporary residence in Basel. I did not journey with them, the better
for them to move about with ease, and without fuss. It was August
before His Lordship returned, alone, Mr O'Connor having decided to
pursue other friendships recently established, and by October we were
back in Ireland once more.[34]

Tony watched the two men walk ahead of him, as he wheeled their
luggage on a handcart as far as the Exchange to await the stagecoach.
Where had they first met, Edward and O'Connor? Perhaps at one
of the coffee-houses in Dublin, drawn by the dark fug of smoke and
intrigue, or perhaps the Dublin parliament. They were two sides of
the one coin. O'Connor was a physical presence, all height and bulk
and dark passions that seemed to exert a force on him, while Edward,
lighter in mood and stature, walked with a springy step, swept along by
his enthusiasms and convictions.

[34] This is quite excellent Tony. You have detailed the domestic nature of the
visit, and the impulse for the tour as a matter of friendship. LLF.

The coach was delayed. An hour at most. Tony secured a table at the nearby Swan, thankful to escape the summer heat and sweet, viscous air. He ordered food for the two men. Räucheraal. O'Connor's face darkened with distaste. He pushed the dish aside. 'I cannot abide eel.'

'It was that or some pickled cabbage dish.'

O'Connor smirked and took the bowl back, spooned it in without further remark. Voices – high French and guttural German – scuttled and rumbled beneath the dark-beamed ceiling and its coils of vinegar smoke.

Edward rapped his spoon on the table, eager to be off. 'Look after Lady Pamela while I'm away.'

'Of course,' he said.

O'Connor looked at him then at Edward. 'What else is there for him to do? You should have left him in London along with his nursemaid wife, and your little boy.'

His nursemaid wife. Not how he thought of her. Always 'my Julia'. He looked across at O'Connor's hands. There was something oddly muscular about them, not a gentleman's hands really, certainly not a lawyer's hands. Difficult to imagine him holding a quill. He could almost see the nib bend, hear the snap.

'… always try to get a rise out of him?' Edward was talking. 'It won't work you know, he has more self-control than you.' Covering both O'Connor and Tony with his words. Humour to amuse one and disarm the other.

'Still Edward, you must acknowledge he's not so good at disguise.'

Tony laughed at this. O'Connor looked satisfied.

They talked on, about their contact in Switzerland, and how it was that Wolfe Tone happened to be in Paris just as they were in Hamburg, O'Connor hissing what the hell was he up to, and Edward answering that Tone was most likely sitting in a dark Parisian café asking the very same question about them. For most of the conversation they kept their voices low for the tables were packed tightly, and people pressed close as they passed, so close they could well have been listening. Tony was aware of the man seated with his back to O'Connor, nondescript in his long workaday waistcoat and battered tricorn, bent over his cup, for the best part of the hour. Not one sip had passed his lips. At times O'Connor's attempts to lower his voice only served to deepen it. The name 'Reinhard' rumbled beyond the confines of their two huddled heads. The man in the tricorn shifted slightly, tilting his shoulder so his profile was almost visible. Tony touched Edward's shoe and murmured in Irish, 'Spiaire.'

Edward showed no sign of having heard anything. Laughed loudly as though at a great joke, punched O'Connor on the arm. 'Never again,' he said, 'will I listen to you. You are full of puff and tall tales.'

O'Connor was quick to catch on. 'So, you say, my friend but—'

They lapsed into some nonsense for a few minutes until a bell rang loudly. People stood to gather their things. The coach had arrived.

Tony missed Julia. Even she could not have resisted the beauty of Hamburg, though she would try. She dismissed all new sights and fresh experience. Like Leinster House in Dublin on her first visit, 'a cold prison' or the packet from Dublin to Parkgate, the endless sea 'horrible and grey'. It had taken him some time to understand her, to see how such things made her anxious, afraid to grasp them, fearful she might want more than was possible. But he was used to her ways, missed her sharp tongue by day, her fierce body by night.

If only she'd been permitted to travel with him to Hamburg. But no. The Duchess had insisted that the nursemaid must stay with little Eddy in London. Was most insistent. It would help him to settle in. She prevailed, despite Edward's concerns for his wife, giving birth in a strange city, with neither her young son nor her nursemaid to hand. But the Duchess had such a way of asking the right questions. Was not Dublin equally strange when Lady Pamela went there for her lying-in? And see how well the dear girl managed during her confinement with little Eddy. Had she not her lady's maid to help out as needs be in Hamburg. The nursemaid was not needed. And think of the savings. One less passage to procure. The Duchess had a point. Lots of them, though Tony suspected the one about savings was Mr Ogilvie's.

He missed Edward. Their conversations. His quick questions. His interest. Time lay heavy on his idle hands. Lady Pamela had no use for him in Hamburg. She had her new baby, Pammie, to occupy her and her mother, Madame de Genlis, to tend to her, along with her lady's maid.

He refused to waste his time loitering in the hallways or kitchens of the Matthiessens' home with the other servants who had food to prepare, laundry to tend, rooms to clean, gardens to keep; they were not interested in his offers of help. *Every man is what he makes himself.* Edward's words. And what had Doctor Durham said in New Orleans? *If we could only bleed ourselves of our past as easy as we can apply leeches to extract bad humours.* He was done with bad humours.

He presented himself to Lady Pamela in the small sitting room on the third floor. She lay, stretched out along a pale yellow chaise, stitching on a tiny piece of cloth. Something for the baby no doubt, who was tucked in a basket on the floor beside her, sleeping.

He gave his excuses to the other two ladies. Madame de Genlis, seated by one of the three long windows, was writing, with steady concentration, a pair of spectacles on the end of her nose. Lady Pamela's cousin, Henriette, greeted him with a curious glance.

'Monsieur Small.'

This room was quite different from the heavy wood-panelled rooms throughout the rest of the house. No hanging tapestries of hunting scenes here. Delicate furniture, effusions of cut flowers spilling from a pair of marbled tables, a cluster of silhouettes and watercolours on the freshly painted panels. Lady Pamela's cousin had wasted no time in marking out her own territory in this large banker's house.

Such lightness made him feel awkward, heavy. He explained that he wished for some occupation. Could Lady Pamela recommend anything? He would give his time freely, but would like to learn something, a skill perhaps.

'Je comprends, Monsieur Small.' She looked pale, weary.

He pressed on. 'Perhaps your cousin would know of someone?'

Henriette shrugged. Her dark curls bobbed for a few moments. 'My husband is a banker. It's unlikely he could find work for you. Perhaps the Pehmöllers. They have dozens of refineries. Sugar. Perhaps you have worked with sugar before?' Her eyes were so clear, showing only mild interest.

He looked down. Said nothing. Felt the muscles in his neck tightening.

Lady Pamela cut in. 'Henriette. You must not assume … besides we are most particular about sugar in our household. Tony will not have any from the West Indies.'

'Really?' Madame de Genlis put her pen down, removed her spectacles.

Pamela started to respond. 'Yes, the campaign in Ireland has seen great success … tell them Tony.'

'We buy East Indian sugar if we can but it's more expensive.'

'East Indies, West Indies.' Henriette interrupted. 'I know nothing about that.'

'Slavery, Madame,' he said. 'In the West Indies the plantations are worked entirely by slaves.'

The room was quiet for a moment. Quiet and hot. The open windows admitted no cooling breeze.

'I beg your pardon,' he began.

'I did not mean that you were a slave,' Henriette plucked her book from the cushion, turned the pages. 'Just that I know nothing—'

'This city is awash with sugar,' said Madame de Genlis. 'Your husband's bank is thriving on it. Hundreds of refineries. Thousands of workers. You smell it, especially in the present summer heat.' She directed this at Tony.

'Yes, Madame. It is a foul smell.'

Henriette looked doubtful. 'Really? I only ever smell syrup. It is not unpleasant.'

Lady Pamela sat up. 'Enough. Monsieur Small is in need of occupation. What can you suggest Henriette? Newspapers? There are advertisements?'

Henriette shook her curls once more. 'Non. This I do know. The guilds in the city prevent such occasional work. Besides Lord Edward will not be gone so long?'

No one answered. The baby snuffled in the basket. Lady Pamela reached her hand down to pat the swaddled form.

'Peut-être Monsieur Höcker? Kirchhof Strasse?' Madame de Genlis interceded again. Henriette looked perplexed.

'Monsieur Höcker.' Madame de Genlis held up a bottle of ink. 'My favourite shade of violet, only to be had in Hamburg. The ink maker has had an accident, a coach overturned or something. And I am running out of ink,' she said with a half-smile. Madame was a writer and publisher of noted profligacy; books, tracts, pamphlets and a daily output of letters to put the British consulate to shame.

Henriette protested. 'Mais Tante Stéphanie. There are several other ink sellers.'

Lady Pamela clapped her hands. 'C'est parfait. Tony has time and Monsieur Höcker has need. They may help each other. Maman?'

Madame de Genlis waved a hand. 'Yes, yes.'

Ernst Höcker insisted he was no ink maker but an alchemist. Ein Meisterchemiker.

'I make inks for cartographers, so they make maps of great beauty, for manufacturers so they may wrap their tawdry produce in beautiful printed paper,' he said. 'And more recently for ladies' magazines, so that the latest fashions may lift directly from the page, to the eye and thence to the purse.'

He was a man of many talents, a talker who mixed German with French and English. Tony was relieved at how readily he could understand him. Mr Höcker was built like one of his many barrels, with clipped grey hair and a neat beard. He was not a man to give in to something like broken bones. He may have had to drag his injured leg after him, his right hand may have been almost useless at that time, but he spent an hour each afternoon behind the counter, massaging it with his left hand, and plunging it into alternating bowls of hot and cold water. If he was surprised by the visit of the celebrated writer, Madame de Genlis and her black companion, he did not show it. Not even when the unusual arrangement was put to him. He merely nodded, murmured, '... At least he won't have to worry about the inks staining,' before wiping his own stained left hand on his long apron, and extending it. Tony paused a moment, then shook on it. Madame de Genlis coughed. Herr Höcker jutted out his chin. Six weeks, he agreed. Perhaps eight, Tony said.

The morning walk, from the Matthiessens' to Herr Höcker's, took him along the main thoroughfares, busy with carriages and carts, and gentlemen hurrying to work. Down smaller cobbled streets, busier streets, with vendors pushing carts, each announcing his own produce. Vats of milk, crated bread, barrelled fish. Further out from the centre, the stragglers, late for work, hurried on to the calico factories, the button factories, the cigar plants. Who could say? The city was busy, busy. Men, women, boys all on the way to their place of work. Just like him. Only he granted himself extra time, left early in fact to ensure he could walk the longer route by the canal. See the early morning sun spill over the water like a pale billowing sheet. Watch ducks glide from their overnight cover of reeds to lead their ducklings out with solemn purpose. His stride lengthened as he crossed the bridge to Herr Höcker's shop, one of a row of gabled buildings, four storeys high, that seemed to lean outward to catch a glimpse of the water below.

Depending on who presented at the shop, the owner was Herr Höcker, Monsieur Höcker or Mijnheer Höcker. He stayed behind the counter, keeping his palsied hand tucked in his pocket, was polite and efficient, calling for the nervous shop boy to bring ink samples to the customer. In the workrooms behind the shop, he was a frenzy of blunted energy and irritation. Tony watched as he tried to measure out a quantity of deep red powder. Cochineal. But his left hand was not accurate. Flecks like pollen scattered over the table. 'Verdammt!' The spoon dropped in a clatter.

'If you please.' He sat on the bench next to the Meisterchemiker. 'Tell me how much.'

He was careful. Listened. Asked the names for all of the instruments, the containers, the tubing. Began to learn a very particular kind of German, one which would have no use outside of that workshop. Apart from a few choice swear words. This was Herr Höcker's special workshop, his first, established over twenty years ago and the one he still ran himself; while on the outskirts of Hamburg, a bigger factory produced his printing and packaging inks. Herr Höcker watched Tony's every move at first; eyes assessing, measuring, appraising. Gradually he remained seated for longer periods, directing Tony to tend to the boilers, the distillers, the intricate measurements, while he found some satisfaction in pounding out the galls, the beetles, the fish bladders or whatever was required. The pestle and mortar served to release the man's bridled frustration. The shop boy began to unbend a little. The empty bottles were refilled, the shelves restocked. Colour was martialled into order. Blackest black – blacker even than you, Herr Small – through dusk and slate, to winter spruce and mule brown. And see: your Madame de Genlis will have her violet once more.

Six weeks. Once, on his way back in the late afternoon, he stopped at the great church of St Lorenz, drawn by the sound of a choir. He sat inside, felt the evening light coming through the stained-glass windows, warming his skin, turning it through shades of autumn. Imagined God was present. Usually, in the evenings, he went to a coffee shop near the Matthiessens' house, chose a seat near the window. Watched the comings and goings. Listened to the rustle of newspapers, the muffle of voices. All conducted under a pleasant hammock of pipe smoke. Saw shades of colour he'd never before detected. Took his time. His own free time. After all, this was Hamburg, a free city.

It was near the end of July and there had been no word from Edward since he had reached Basel though perhaps none was expected given the way letters were intercepted, in that spy capital, that hotbed of underhand politics, that emporium of disgruntled émigrés. Tony attended on Lady Pamela to find out if she'd heard anything.

'Nothing.' She was listless, her bare arm over her eyes. It struck him how she was lacking her usual brightness, had been for some time.

'Have you been outside, Milady? Taken the air?'

'Non. Je suis si fatigué.'

She appeared exhausted, lying along her chaise, the baby nowhere to be seen, a box of sewing overturned on the floor beside her. The air in the room was stifling, the windows unshuttered against the evening sun. He wondered if she had moved all day, glanced at a tray lying on a nearby table. Most likely untouched. And Edward had asked him to look after her. He had let him down. Both of them. What would Edward do if he were here?

'There's to be a concert outside das Rathaus tonight. For the townspeople,' he announced. 'I may go.'

She made no response.

'It's a pity Lord Edward is not here. He'd enjoy it. Being among the people. Away from drawing rooms and polite suppers.' Lady Pamela showed no interest.

He rose and threw open the windows. Almost immediately the air stirred. He drew the shutters across again. Lady Pamela removed her arm and looked at him. Her eyes were two different colours, one a shade of sugar brittle, the other darker.

'… Et la danse?'

She was sitting upright, looking interested.

'Peut-être,' he said hopefully.

Her expression shifted to indifference.

'Oui.' He was certain. There would be dancing too.

Henriette came too, grumbling as she put on a light coat. 'But why, Pamela? It's just the townspeople, the workers and servants who attend. Why couldn't you wait until the Civic Ball on Saturday?'

'I want to have something to tell Edward. Not just talk of babies or dresses. Hurry.'

Pamela was already dressed for the trip. She had found a yellow bonnet and tied the ribbons under her chin. 'Hurry,' she repeated. 'We are keeping Tony back. He is most anxious to attend.'

Henriette tucked her hand under her cousin's arm. 'Well in that case let's proceed. It wouldn't do to delay Monsieur Small.' She smiled at him. He followed on behind them. Lady Pamela did not want the carriage. 'We will walk,' she said, her bonnet lighting her face like a sunflower.

Herr Höcker's leg was better. He had recovered some of his strut. Though he still insisted on testing his hand, making a fist, rippling his fingers as though across a piano, it too had almost recovered – enough to do the necessary calibrations, and fine adjustments of his ingredients. The shop boy could just about manage the heavier work of rolling barrels from the yard, dragging in sacks of alum and galls. He was still fearful of the steaming linseed oil in the copper vats, but his fear of Herr Höcker's barbed tongue was greater so somehow the work got done. It was August. Edward was due back any day. He decided to clean out the copper vats, the distiller and condensers. He polished the instruments, examined them closely, listening to Herr Höcker's gleeful outbursts. Der Meisterchemiker ist zurückgekehrt. He was back.

He made an inventory for the Meisterchemiker – 'but mind you do not write down any of my secret recipes' – and walked around the workshop checking off everything from the gleaming vats, to the glass vials, and the stoneware ink jars. In the stores at the back yard he counted the casks of vinegar and green vitriol. Herr Höcker joined him. 'Don't forget the gum arabic. It's in the wooden crate inside to keep it dry.' He nodded. 'You would make a good apprentice. You would stay? Vielleicht?'

'No. My wife, I think she would not …'

'Pity,' he said taking the inventory. 'Our arrangement was for six weeks. I offered only six shillings. I did not know what I was getting.' He cleared his throat with a low staccato sound, drew himself up. 'A Meisterchemiker never orders a shipment of galls without testing it first. He may end up with inferior English galls.'

Tony waited.

Herr Höcker explained. 'They make for inferior ink.'

'Ah.'

'You are like Aleppo galls.' Herr Höcker smiled at his own joke.

'Aleppo galls. I've never been called that before.'

'Only in a city like this, Herr Small. Hamburg, a free city. Free trade, free movement and free ideas.'

Before he left, Herr Höcker handed him a twist of paper. He felt the coins within, the weight of them, raised an eyebrow in question.

'One must pay more for Aleppo galls. They are superior.'

Whatever went on in Switzerland and France, it had implications for the Matthiessens. On the evening after his return, Edward asked permission to dismiss the Matthiessens' servants from the dining room. 'Tony may stay,' he added.

When the footman and serving girl left, he spoke directly to Herr Matthiessen. Thanked him. Asked for a favour.

'It's simply a matter of having somewhere safe to direct correspondence, and where better than Pamela's cousin, Henriette, in Hamburg. She need only forward it with her own.'

'As long as it's only letters.' Herr Matthiessen was only prepared to go so far.

'It's agreed. Letters only.'

See what I've found here. I've decided to paste it on this sheet else I'm bound to lose it in all the rickle of papers. Makes me proper proud of my Baaba to see this notice. To think of him when he went back to Hamburg the second time, after what Ma used to refer to as *Everything That Happened*. As good as transported they were, along with Lady Pamela. But Baaba went to work for that ink man again, became quite the expert at it himself, and ended up making his business in London. Them was happy times.

Mr Anthony Small, Ink Maker

lately arrived from Hamburg,
where he studied the Science of fine Ink production under the
Meisterchemiker, Herr Höcker, wishes it be known that he has
established a
Workshop at 10, Air Street, Piccadilly
where he will sell Inks of the finest quality to a discerning
Public. He specialises in the production of *bespoke Colours*
according to the particular needs of his most discriminating
Customers. Additional Stationery items are also retained including
the *finest wove Paper*, and all manner of *Quills and Pounce*.

The True Narrative

Autumn 1796, and an Account of the Author's domestic happiness;
Lord Edward takes a house in Kildare and
Mr Arthur O'Connor visits often.

It was good to return to the house in Kildare after the months in Hamburg. Such a cosy place at that time despite the autumn mists and rain. I must acknowledge my great good fortune in having become a father myself around that time. I have not written before of my marriage, feeling self-conscious about putting such private matters down on paper. But the Reader may wish to know of it. The previous year, Julia, nursemaid to Lord and Lady FitzGerald's son, had accepted me as her husband. My Master and Lady Pamela gave their blessing to our union. In truth I felt blessed. Doubly so with the arrival of my child. The house in Kildare was a sanctuary against all the evil doings of the times; the evictions and burning, arrests and interrogations, spies and informers turning on their old friends, houses searched and destroyed. Fear stalked the land, day and night. Within the ancient castle bawn, my Master created a safe and happy home, a white house, in the town of Kildare.

They tried to keep rumours at bay behind the sylvan screen of their newly planted garden; rumours that had flourished in the hothouse of Dublin all the preceding year as the Edwards walked about the streets, declining a carriage, visiting all manner of radicals. Rumours that Lady Pamela was a French spy, and Lord

Edward a French agent; that both had thrown off their aristocratic upbringings to consort with peasants and disport themselves like commoners at best and revolutionaries at worst. Dublin had been an unhappy place for His Lordship's young wife. Arriving just before King Louis was executed and with the War with France expected daily, she was ill received by the ladies of the city, with the exception of Lady Moira.[35] That good Lady took her to her heart and Lord Edward often commented how the pair could be tucked away for hours in the Moira House library, talking about all manner of Science and Literature, fiddling with microscopes and other apparatus. Most of the elegant Ladies of Dublin refused to entertain her, though the gentlemen conceded she was a great Beauty. No wonder then that she should have loved the peace of her small Kildare house. She was happy there, free to speak in her own language with her French lady's maid without causing alarm. Her lady's maid, on the other hand, was less happy, having little English and therefore uneasy about venturing out for fear of being taken for a spy. That poor lady's nervous disposition worsened, she kept apart from her fellow servants and when faced with the prospect of a trip to Dublin with Lady Pamela, she became so ill that she was forced to remain behind.

The Edwards did not venture out into society as much as might have been expected of them, limiting themselves to the occasional ball at Carton or Castletown. Lord Edward tried to avoid causing offence on account of his democratic views, especially within his wider family. His brother the Duke in particular was angered by Lord Edward's outspoken rejection of the Militia Bill in the House and his association with known radicals. At the same time it was difficult for Lord Edward to reject his brother. His income had dropped considerably; Lady Pamela was no longer in receipt of a pension, following Égalité's demise on the guillotine and his own

[35] Not so! My Aunt Louisa was quite disposed to dote on her at first. And Aunt Sarah too. And later she and I were the firmest of friends. Part of the Beloved Quatuor, along with Dear Edward and Mr O'Connor. LLF.

army pension had been withheld since his marriage – though it may have been due to his assumption of the Republican appellation of Citizen at the dinner in White's Hotel in Paris.[36] Even so, Readers may have difficulty believing that a son of the Duke of Leinster should have so little money to keep his family.

His friend, Arthur O'Connor, visited often, so much so, it seemed he would become part of the household too. I was not alone in thinking that Lady Lucy, Lord Edward's younger sister, was much taken with him.[37]

Tony heard the increased clip of horses on the lane, horses who knew they were almost home. Carrying a lantern, he headed out to the slap of cold in the yard, to await their arrival. They'd been gone for three days. O'Connor and Edward. To recruit for the Militia, Edward had told Mr Ogilvie who had enquired when he paid them an impromptu visit from Castletown, just prior to their departure. 'Do not joke with me,' the older man had said, stern and humourless as a clergyman without a congregation. 'Then do not ask me my business,' was Edward's mild reply. Of course he relented in the face of his stepfather's agitation, his finger and thumb rolling round and round. 'Don't worry on my behalf. I'm careful, but also set. There's nothing to be done about it.' Ogilvie shook his head, dismissing Edward's pledges of love for his mother, and stalked past O'Connor as though he wasn't there watching the proceedings, arms folded, with his dark-eyed stare.

It was Tony's turn to observe O'Connor, as the pair passed under the gate arch. A hard November moon identified each man. O'Connor's bigger frame and the way he pulled the horse's head in tight; Edward, giving his mount a long rein. They entered the tiny courtyard and Edward swung out of the saddle shouting. 'Ah Tony. See to Arthur's horse. I'll stable Prudente.'

---

[36] This is exactly what you must not mention; it suggests he entertained Republican views before he met Lady Pamela. (I know this to be true Tony, but it does not fit with the Family's account.) LLF.
[37] No. It was not so. Do not write of it. LLF.

Tony held the bridle while O'Connor dismounted, a bristling badger. Light from the raised lantern caught the steam from the animal's back, the clouds of air puffing from his nostrils, and fell across O'Connor's unshaven face, his tightened mouth. 'Where's Jerry?' he asked. Jerry O'Leary, the manservant Tony had met on his very first visit to Carton.

'He's in the village, he wasn't expecting you back tonight.'

'Pssh. I pay him too well.' He handed over his whip, turned towards the house, instructing over his shoulder. 'See if you can talk some sense into your master. He won't listen to me.'

In the stable Edward had flung the saddle over a post, but without the lamp, was fumbling in near darkness for the tack hooks.

'Ah, the bringer of light. Just what I need.'

Tony hung up the lantern, and led O'Connor's horse to the next stall. Feed and water were already in place.

He began to brush down the horse: slow, wide strokes. The tension eased from the animal's muscles with each sweep.

'Have you a spare brush?' Edward was still standing with Prudente. She lifted her hooves gently on hay-strewn ground. Click, shift.

'Lady Pamela has waited up for you,' Tony remarked as he tossed him a rough bristle.

'Thank you. I need a bit of time. Did O'Connor tell you about our little fracas with the Militia?'

'No. He suggested something else.'

'Ah yes. He's more upset about our meeting with the Leinster Directorate than with the Militia though I don't think the Directorate represent any real difficulty. Arthur feels I've too much faith in the capacity of the people to support a Rising. That I'm "double-counting the committed", the first count representing reality and the second misplaced optimism. What do you think?'

Prudente tossed her head and shifted her hooves. Edward was being a little vigorous in his attentions.

'I think perhaps you should ease off a bit. Just go smooth. Like this.'

He ran the brush over the horse's flanks, following with the flat palm of his free hand.

'I was brushing horses when you were still picking indigo or rice or whatever it was you did over there in the Carolinas.'

'I never did such a thing, Milord. Horses, I groomed horses. Only that. It was an easy life.'

'You change your story all the time Tony. Did you know that?'

Five minutes passed, maybe ten, in the sweet smell of straw and sweat and leather; the animal warmth; and the knowledge of the cold November outside.

He ducked his head, closed off the stall, and held the door for Edward who lingered in the dull lantern light, looking exhausted.

'Three days of training and drilling men with sticks and a few pikes. It doesn't feel real. Like playing soldiers. They need weapons – rifles, or they'll be slaughtered. O'Connor says the men are the problem, not enough and of too poor a calibre. But I think he's wrong, we'll have enough men. Once the French come, and word spreads down from the North, the West, so will those who take up the call to arms. I know what people are like.'

'And Mr O'Connor? He does not share your faith in people.'

'Not really. He thinks we should leave the whole affair to the French. Thinks the common man will run for the hills or hand over all pikes and guns at the first sight of a redcoat.'

He laid his brush atop the stall wall, and this time followed Tony.

'Speaking of redcoats …?' Tony led the way out of the courtyard holding the lantern high. Shadows puddled at their feet. The ground was hard, and cold.

'Ah yes, the Militia. We had a difference of opinion with a troop of them this afternoon. Seems they objected to the colour of my cloth. My neckcloth. Asked me to remove it.'

They reached the small overhang at the back of the house. The windows glowed behind their shutters. A smell of peat softened the edge of cold. He peered at the cloth around Edward's neck. No doubt. The green one.

'What would any gentleman do? Told him he could try to take it from me. Arthur was spewing some twaddle about the law, and accosting gentlemen. I knew what would come next.' He laughed at the thought. 'One of the soldiers, a pox-faced pup, spouted that no gentleman would wear the traitors' green.'

Tony groaned.

Edward laughed again. 'That's exactly what Arthur did. Groaned. Grumbled. Muttered. Please God – not a duel.'

'And?'

'Disappointing really. Over before it began. The officer-in-charge, I think he's Cloncurry's agent, put a stop to it. Apologised. Nearly spitting teeth with the effort to be polite.'

The kitchen was warm, everything neat, just where it should be. Coppers shining. A pot of peeled potatoes on the table. Two pans of bread dough resting under cloths beside the stove, adding a tang of yeast to the peaty air. It was strangely expectant. The cook and the kitchen girl wouldn't be back until midday; no room in this house for extra servants. Tony would get the fires started in the morning, put the bread on to bake first thing. Edward dropped onto a bench with a sigh. 'I think I'll bid the ladies good night and go to my bed.' He stuck out his foot. 'Would you mind, Tony?'

He dragged off the boots for him.

'Sorry Tony, they have the dirt and mud of four counties on them.'

He padded across the warm kitchen flagstones in his grubby stockinged feet, out onto to the cool tiles of the hall and into the front sitting room.

The boots took more of his time than usual. By the time he entered the sitting room with the turf basket, Lady Pamela and Lady Lucy had arranged themselves as if at some minor theatricals, watching the two men. Lady Pamela was dressed in an old morning coat, lying along the settle, resting her feet on Lucy's lap. Lady Lucy too had dispensed with her shoes, and she sat, elbow propped on the arm rest, toying with her loose hair. The same hair as Edward. A dark copper in the candlelight. Thomas Paine gazed down benignly on the foursome from his frame on the wall above the mantle. The shutters were drawn, only the wall sconces lit, giving an intimate glow. Edward jumped to his feet, and grabbed the basket from his hands.

'Ah Tony, Tony. My dear little wife has only just murmured about the cold, and here you are with the turf.'

He tossed a few lumps on the fire, which puffed in sullen protest.

'Damn it Edward, must you persist with this?' O'Connor waved towards the basket. 'You've made your point, your gesture to the peasants, but the damn stuff gives no heat. Think of your wife and little Pam, if not me.' He rubbed his hands together.

Pamela laughed. The sound was water trickling on stones. 'But Arthur, I have my coat. And the baby is warm upstairs. Julia has tucked her in.'

Edward crossed to her side, kissing her loudly on the mouth. 'See there, Arthur. How's that for a wife?'

O'Connor smiled in an offhand way as he puffed on his cigar. He was too big for the chair he occupied, his body sloping out of it, legs crossed at the ankles. The wolfhound, Bran, lay alongside, mirroring his posture.

Pamela wrapped her arms round Edward's neck, kissed his face, stroked his cheek. He turned to O'Connor again. 'You should get yourself one.'

O'Connor disclaimed the possibility of finding a treasure such as Pamela. 'Besides, I have elected to do without that comfort. Not in these times.'

Lucy stopped twirling her hair. 'Too much of a distraction Arthur?'

'Perhaps.' He smiled at her, teeth gleaming, wolf-like, in the firelight.

'So single-minded. So self-sacrificing.' Lucy's voice rose.

'It would be like having two mistresses. I can only serve one. You'd understand that, Tony, wouldn't you?'

He disliked this kind of jest, drawing him in like one of those pawns on the chess board. He made no reply, taking a taper to the candles in front of the window.

'No, no,' Lucy protested. 'It's much cosier as it is.'

'And cold,' O'Connor repeated.

'The only cold thing is you, Arthur.' Lucy pushed Pamela's feet from her lap and leaned forward.

'Thing is Lucy, I'm a shallow man. I'm not like your brother. There's not enough of me to devote to politics and a wife. If I do something I commit with my whole heart, shallow though it may be.'

'That's just fiddle-faddle,' said Lucy, 'a tale you tell to soften crusty old women.'

Edward yawned. 'I'm for bed. Little wife? Shall you love a saddle-sore, travel-stained husband?'

Pamela reached for him. 'Pour toujours.'

Before they left, Edward pressed Lucy's shoulder. 'Don't waste your affections on this man Lucy. He is a lost cause. And Arthur, don't play games.'

Lucy reached out to the wolfhound who was following his master to the door, claws clicking across the wooden floor. She pulled him to her, showering him with hugs, though he tried to pull away. 'Have no fear. This dog is far more worthy of my attentions than your self-interested friend.'

Arthur collapsed back in his chair, clutching at his chest in a cloud of cigar smoke and ash.

'Oh save me, please. I am mortally wounded. Though another drink might save me yet. Tony?'

Edward sighed. 'Just make sure you don't leave the bottle with him.'

Julia was sewing by the kitchen fire, her hair glowing red in its light. Three candles, wedged in a candlestick on the oak bench alongside her, threw up pale smoky flames.

'Ettie asleep?'

She nodded. 'Thanks be to God. I thought she'd never give up feeding.'

He loved to watch how she jabbed the needle into the silk, pulled it through with a short jerking movement, then bent her head to nip the thread with her sharp teeth. She looked up, aware of his regard. 'Pass me the scissors.'

He stroked her hand, placed the scissors in her palm.

'I know what's in your mind. But it'll have to wait.' She lifted a tangle of braids and trimmings from the basket by her side. 'That

Lady Lucy wishes to make a statement at Castletown House at the weekend, with her green ribbons and stitching.'

'They won't thank her for it. I hear Lord Castlereagh is to attend,' he said, thinking of Edward's aunt, Lady Louisa Conolly, and how she would squirm at such a confrontation. Castlereagh was related to Lady Louisa's husband and consequently a regular visitor to their house at Castletown. A well-connected man, an ambitious Government appointee, his star was on the rise. 'It's all about connections,' Edward said, 'having the right connections.' And Castlereagh's grandfather, Lord Camden, was none other than the Lord Lieutenant of Ireland. Tony had often heard Edward bemoaning Castlereagh's politics. Why should the man waste his intellect championing Government measures to limit freedoms to Ireland? It was becoming difficult for the pair to meet with civility.

He lay along the wooden settle, and continued to watch Julia through half-closed lids. How could she do such fine work with so little light? Perhaps he should find some more candles. But the silk whispering through Julia's fingers, interrupted every now and then by the snip of scissors, the spit of the fire, was lulling him to sleep.

THE TRUE NARRATIVE

Winter 1796, and Mr O'Connor gives the Author a book by Mr Olaudah Equiano; Lord Edward misses his son.

Tony woke early, certain he was aboard ship, feeling the ground shifting beneath him. That dream again. The block of light. His fingers sought the amulet around his neck, but it was not there. Then his eyes opened onto sloping eaves, and a flickering half-light instead. Not on a ship but in their attic apartment at the top of the house in Kildare. And he no longer needed that amulet. Not here. Not since Julia.

There was the sheet that Julia had hung across the middle of the room to divide it up; on this side their bed and the cradle, on the other, odds and ends of furniture, a shelf and hook rack that he'd made. No window on this side but a hint of dawn light seeping in from the small four-paned window beyond the divide.

Now Julia turned over, pulled the blanket close to her and muttered at him to be easy. But he got up anyway, padded down through the silent house, stoked up the fires, set the bread to baking. He headed outside into the November dawn. The freezing ground steadied him but he could not shake off the shadows. Beyond the back gate, a low whey-coloured mist hung over the cold-hardened bog, a hint of lemon and pewter suggesting that somewhere the sun might be attempting to rise. It was hard to tell where mist began and frost ended. He sniffed the air, enjoying the sharp sting of it. Listening now. Nothing. The hens were silent, tucked up in their shed. Bran, who earlier had picked his way around the yard, had escaped the cold by slipping back into the house again. Even the grass was frozen to stillness. The only thing moving was the occasional puff of peaty smoke from the chimney.

He returned to the house, picking up some bundles of sticks from the courtyard. O'Connor was right about one thing. On a morning like this, coal was needed. He left his greatcoat on as he headed inside. Back in the kitchen, Mr Arthur O'Connor was already up and at the table. Jerry, his valet, nodded at Tony as he set a cup in front of his master.

'Some people have trouble sleeping,' he remarked, eyes slanting at the seated figure. Jerry's eyes were like pilchards, all quicksilver darts and flashes. 'And he was up till all hours. Talking with your master Edward's sister.'

O'Connor didn't bother looking up from his breakfast – last night's leftovers of cold lamb shank.

'There's too much thinking to be done to waste it on sleep. Besides' – he wiped his mouth – 'I've business to get to today. Jerry, you'll come with me.' He tossed his napkin on the plate. 'Not much of a breakfast. Just the smell of half-cooked bread to tempt me. Perhaps Cummins will serve us better.'

Tony said nothing. Jerry smirked and muttered in passing. 'He wants to get back early for another evening of high jinks with the Lady Lucy.'

'I heard that, Jerry. That loose tongue of yours could see you in trouble yet.' But O'Connor's voice was unruffled. 'It's good to have some diversion from all the politicking.' The wolfhound rose from his fireside mat, and loped over to O'Connor, placing his large head on his knee.

'Is he just begging or have I made another conquest?' He stared into the dog's eyes, rubbed his head, and handed him some meat from the plate. Bran returned to the fire to chew on it.

O'Connor turned his attention to Tony. 'I hear you've attended some meetings in Ballitore. With the Quakers. Will you soon be addressing us as thee and thou?' Jerry looked almost apologetic. He must have told O'Connor.

'No. I went to hear their discussions on Abolition. But there's little happening apart from the sugar boycott.'

'And of course Edward must uphold the cause here. Your influence, I'm certain. What I wouldn't give for a sliver of sugar now.'

'Human flesh,' Tony muttered. Jerry looked startled.

'That's the cost.' Tony said. 'Every pound of sugar consumes two ounces of human flesh.'

'He's quoting from a pamphlet,' O'Connor told Jerry. 'And he's right of course. But it seems this household must take on every cause, from burning damp turf, to boycotting sugar – not to mention the Ladies wearing naught but Irish cloth. Next it will be women's suffrage if Lucy has her way.'

Jerry applauded. 'Hasn't my master a fine way with words?'

'Speaking of words, Jerry, do you have that book I told you to bring? For Mr Small here.'

Jerry disappeared for a few moments and in his absence, O'Connor regarded Tony with some interest. 'I wondered if you had read it. I was fortunate enough to meet him in Belfast.' His eyebrows lifted with the unasked question.

'If I knew to whom you referred …' He found his own eyebrows lifting in response, feeling vaguely uneasy now with O'Connor's attention. The back of his neck bristled.

'Why, Olaudah Equiano, of course.' He resumed picking at his plate, gnawing at an unfinished cold mutton chop. 'He impressed me. A man of Africa and more eloquent than many whose company I keep.' He smiled. 'Present household excepted. So you know of him?'

'Yes.' How could he have failed to do so? The most famous African of the times, a great writer and a voice for abolition. And it was Tony's ill luck to travel in his wake, always to miss him. Equiano had toured Ireland for six months, during which time Tony had been in London with Edward. When Equiano returned to London, Tony was in Paris. With Edward. And this man, Arthur O'Connor had heard him and—

'Did you speak with him?'

'Yes. He was staying with Samuel Neilson, some years ago. It's a pity for you not to have heard him.'

Jerry ambled in and tossed the book at him. 'Something to remind you of home,' he said, smirking.

Tony opened the first pages and saw the face on the frontispiece, closed it again, his breath tight within him. He nodded thanks and placed it on the shelf above the fire. 'I am grateful that you should think of me.'

'I'm curious to know how his account might fit with yours.'

'My account?'

'The one you never give. Tales of slavery and the like.' He began to brush his hands over his clothing in sweeping movements. 'Christ,' he muttered, picking out hairs from his dark coat.

'Have you a clothes brush, Tony?' He held out his sleeve. 'This place is worse than a tavern. Sometimes Ed takes his democratic ideals too far. You don't have to live like a peasant to do the right thing by them.'

He considered. 'No, Sir, I don't believe we have such a thing.'

O'Connor was unconcerned. 'You'll have to remember to bring one the next time Jerry. I suspect Tony here is hiding it somewhere.'

O'Connor's suspicions were correct. There was something about the man that made him want to keep his distance but keep him in sight at the same time. He occupied too much space, took up too much attention.

For a week O'Connor and Edward had travelled the county and beyond, visiting sympathetic landowners, sounding out the local people, either alone or in small groups. Edward, who continued to learn the language of the Irish, tried it out at these meetings, sometimes turning to Tony for help with words. How had Tony managed to acquire so much Irish, he asked him once. 'A lifetime time spent attending and listening,' Tony had replied. 'I even understand the chatter of birds and the whisper of grasses.' Edward had laughed at that before remarking he'd no doubt Julia had forced the language down his throat. 'No force required, I love the sound of it on her tongue.' Edward had turned serious then, squeezed Tony's arm, and murmured something about being glad for his happiness. That was Edward. He had hidden depth beneath his easy grace. Unlike O'Connor who held himself apart even in the midst of a group of peasants, Edward knew instinctively how to be at one with them. He joined the men by their fires, took turns at wielding a great stick to whack a hard leather ball – badly – knowing it would cause laughter, put the men at their ease. These were rough men, living in rough houses, mostly humble cabins. Some were more meagre, dark and damp without window or chimney, haunted by small faces that brought to mind those on the plantations in the Carolinas and seemed, if anything, worse.

But Tony could no longer accompany Edward on those nocturnal excursions. 'I'm sorry Tony, but you are marked and where you are, then I too am marked. It makes it too easy for those weasel spies to track me and account for me.'

Now with O'Connor gone for the day, Tony was once more a valet and a groomsman, accompanying his master on a social call to a gentleman at Kilkea Castle. The mist had been replaced by cloud and rain. Steady grey. The horses picked their way over sodden tussocks and around surly pools of dark water.

The best way was straight over the bog, Edward had said. 'Meeting others on the road will only delay us.' Others meaning Militia.

Edward was quiet as he stared across the sodden mane of his mount at the landscape ahead. It was slow going. The ground was uneven and the horses stepped carefully to avoid the black holes and the seep of water.

'I miss him you know.'

'Yes.' He knew it was his son he spoke of. Eddy, whom he'd left with his mother in London, when they'd returned from Hamburg some months before. His mother, the Duchess, wrote long accounts of her little grandson's adventures. But the news did little to lift Edward's spirits.

'I'm not sure I have done the right thing. How can I know? And it's so hard on Pamela.'

'Yes.' Tony had heard her crying over those letters when Edward was not at home. Her hand sought out the lock of her little boy's hair, which she kept about her neck. But she never complained to Edward. Kept this sadness to herself while he was about the County. 'That poor lady,' Julia said. 'She cannot bear to look at other boys of his age. She cries, and kisses that husband of hers and he pats her head, like she's a puppy. He is careless of both.' 'No,' he'd told her. 'His heart is sore for his son too. He just cannot show it, cannot show weakness now.' And Julia had nodded, looking tearful herself.

Out on the bog, rain fell on Edward's ruminations. 'It's Eddy's birthday. Two years old today.'

Tony pictured the last time he'd seen the little boy, in the summer, calling for his Papa's attention as he stroked a miniature pony. On impulse he asked. 'Can't you reconsider? Send for him?'

'I'd have a job to prise him back from my mother. And it's not just for his safe-keeping. I promised him to her, in case anything should happen to me.'

'You mean, as a comfort? But what of Lady Pamela? Would she not need him more than ever?'

Rain dripped off the brim of Edward's hat and over the shoulders of his greatcoat. He dug his heels in and the horse started suddenly. 'Fuck.' He wrestled with the reins, trying to settle him.

Tony persisted, trying to understand Edward's reasoning. 'I don't know what to think about that. It seems it's for everyone's sake except Lady Pamela's.'

'Stop Tony, for pity's sake. It's the price we must pay. For all this. For Revolution. Pamela understands better than most. There'd be little sympathy for her and her child. There are some in Dublin who cannot wait to point the finger at her. My dear *Popish* wife. My dangerous *Republican* wife.'

It was impossible to tell if it was just rain on his face.

'Eddy is so dear to my heart. After losing Mary, I never wanted to face such loss again. But Eddy is alive and well. He is safe with my mother. And if everything, all this' – he lifted his hand from the saddle, gestured vaguely at the grim drizzle, the endless bog. 'If all this works out ...' he took up the reins again. 'Well, I hope to God it'll have been worth it.' They walked on, swaying in the saddles, lulled by the steady thrip of rain and the sucking sound of the horses' hooves in the wet ground.

'Pamela should go over to London too. Take baby Pammie with her. I keep telling her that by the time the French come, it may be too late.'

Tony had long appreciated the risks involved in inviting an enemy force to land in Ireland; knew it would be considered an act of high treason in Dublin and in England; he'd been present in the room as O'Connor and Edward looked over maps, argued as they scrawled marks on them; he'd traced his finger around the coast of Ireland when they left the room, paused on the inky crosses that blotted the towns of Cork, Waterford and Belfast. And Galway to the west. He knew what was coming. Knew what all those night time visits were about; recruiting men, arming them, organising them. Preparing for an uprising, supported by a French invasion. Preparing for a new Republic.

'My Lord, is there no way – can you not see the child before?' Tony persisted.

'Go to England now?' Edward's laugh was rough as gravel. 'I'd scarce have a moment alone. I'd be followed from the Pigeon House in Dublin to Harley Street. No, my place is here. It'll all boil down to timing after the French reach Galway. The wave will spread across from the West and down from the North. They are organised there.' He looked over at Tony. 'Here too, I hope. Keen at least. So there it is, I'm stuck here. Must see it through. Though sometimes I'm afraid of it. Am I a coward to say that?'

Tony shook his head, pulled back on the reins. 'Never that. There's something else, isn't there?'

The wind had stopped. The grasses stood upright, sharp and alert. Prudente was restless, dipping her head towards the grass, then wresting it away again. Edward gave her free rein.

'I've taken the Oath. The Oath of the United Irishmen. And Arthur too.'

'Why now? You've always held off. You promised your brother. Said it would make things difficult for him, for you, having to lie.' Tony swore under his breath. Just when he thought he understood what was going on, the politics, the risks, where everyone stood, who was for and who was against a rebellion and why. 'You've been training men anyway, planning, why must you take the Oath? And those recent arrests in Belfast, isn't it more dangerous now than ever?'

'It's a sign though, isn't it? Those arrests in Belfast, they've unsettled people. We could lose momentum. Something was needed, to show that we won't waver. Complete commitment.'

Yes. It was more than just another sworn-in United Irishman. It was Lord Edward Fitzgerald and despite his rejection of it, it was the lofty title that convinced the people of the possibility of change. He was the reason they would commit to an uprising. He had become more than his name.

'There will be a rising soon, and not a disorganised band of peasants. They will be armed and ready. Perhaps next year. And everything will change. You'll be here though, won't you?'

What was the alternative? But he told him there was no other place for him to be.

At Kilkea, Mr Thomas Reynolds Esq, descended the steps of the castle in a dark green jacket, wearing a formal wig and a wide smile. His arms were spread in elaborate welcome. He was a young man but acted like one of middle years, one known to have patriotic leanings. Was the jacket a sign of this? Would Edward take him on or was he just tasting the fare? Difficult to know. Edward had managed to persuade many reluctant men to become ardent supporters. But this man? He acknowledged Tony with cheerful fluster.

'Of course, of course, your black. As expected. Most welcome.'

The True Narrative

Winter 1796, and the Author's reflections on life at the Lodge in Kildare; Dances, music and meetings with local people.

Days passed with the unnerving pulse of a relapsing fever. Long spells of indolence as the men went abroad about their business and the two Ladies reached for one distraction, then another; Lucy on the harp practising Irish songs and Lady Pamela singing along in her tumble of French and English, laughing at the chaotic results; sewing little emblems and cockades on their jackets and hats. Both were highly entertained by their own efforts.

Julia entered the kitchen, baby Pam asleep over her shoulder, to be greeted by her own child, Ettie. Tony had placed her on the opened settle on a blanket. She was waving something in her hand.

'Oh,' said Julia.

'It's a gift, Julia. For you.' He smiled at her wonder.

She laid the baby in the cradle near the fire, tucked her in briskly and crouched down to her daughter, hand open to receive the gift. Ettie placed it down carefully, her little face made solemn with the task. It was a small wooden mouse, with a length of string for a tail. Julia kissed it, and then planted one on Ettie's curly head. 'Tá sé go hálainn.'

He had enough Gaelic in him to understand. It's beautiful. Even the fact of her speaking in Irish pleased him – she only did so when she was upset or lost for words in English.

'May I give it back to Ettie?'

He nodded. She lifted her from the settle box, sat beside the table, briefly wiping a cloth over her face, before settling the child on her lap to feed.

'You should see them,' she said. 'Draped on the sopha. Yards and yards of green thread and ribbon spilling about them. And the pair sighing and sewing, holding up little trifles for praise.'

Julia never thought much of the needlework of others. Especially Ladies. 'He who's never had to work for money, will never work well.' Neither did she think much of their attempts at speaking Irish. Apart from Edward; she could forgive him anything.

Her eyes closed. Ettie had finished feeding, the little mouse lying in her hands, but she stayed so still, so focused on her mother's face as though any movement would waken her and spoil the moment. He turned away from that contentment, too afraid of what might spoil it.

Another evening, one like many that played out there. The sopha pushed back against the wall, the Turkey carpet rolled up to one side. The butcher's daughters, Ellen and Mary, were pink-faced; whether with excitement, wine, or exertion it was difficult to tell. Lady Lucy and O'Connor had just finished dancing a set with them. The floor was scuffed from their energetic footwork. The girls attempted to detain O'Connor but he declined with ease.

'Ask Tony,' he suggested. 'And I'm certain Lady Pamela would oblige, in place of Lucy.'

They glanced over at him, where he stood by the window, wrapping his flute back in a strip of linen. His finest work yet, carved from yew. It offered a rich melodious sound. Pamela threw him a smile. 'Il nous provoque sans cesse.'

In fact Tony enjoyed dancing, just not here, in this room. He'd had many occasions to join in Irish jigs when he'd accompanied Edward to villages around the county, which more often than not – after Edward had finished his talking and persuading – ended up in one of the larger cabins or a barn, or if the weather was good, outside by a bonfire. Those Irish could not be without their music and dancing. And Edward always joined in, so what choice had he? Julia heard about his dancing from another maid in Kildare, who'd spoken to a man delivering turf, who'd met a woman on the road bringing chickens to market, who'd spoken to an old fellow who'd been there at the fireside near Rathbeg and had witnessed with his very own eyes, a man of Africa, black as the night itself, leaping around like a hare in spring, and quite neat about the ankle in the jig. Julia recounted the tale to him with such merriment that he'd obliged her with a little demonstration on the kitchen flagstones, in his stockinged feet. She looked him up and down like he was a horse at the mart, hands on hips, her shawl slipping from one shoulder, circling round him. 'By God I married a man of Africa and he can dance a jig with the best of them. And you've kept it a secret from me all this time. What else have you kept from me?' 'Nothing,' he'd told her, pulling her to him. 'Nothing.'

He'd become accustomed to it – these people and their music in the midst of misery. It was different when first he'd moved to Kildare. And before that? Those years between Dublin, and London. Were his eyes closed, he wondered. Did he just fix on the road ahead whenever he travelled, not see the people? Perhaps it was that they did not stop before – in the early years, before their travel to the wilds of Canada and the Mississippi – never entered one of those cabins that dotted the roadsides, dark and damp, everything sallow with peat smoke. The first time, he'd thought it was a pig house, the doorway so low that though he ducked his head, it scraped along the low-hanging thatch. And inside, no pigs but a family, all barefoot except for the father. Where did they sleep, he wondered, before his eyes adjusted and he saw the stacked straw palliasses behind the door. No chimney at all in the place, so that the smoke seeping from a sullen heap of ashen turf in the centre was suspended under the reed roof. The children, five of them, stood staring first at Edward, who accepted the small stool near the door, and then at him, their narrow eyes unblinking. What did they see? His skin, yes – he was used to that look, but this stare was more than that. They were looking at his boots, his coat with its simple trim down the front, the buttons, unembossed but silver nonetheless, his white shirt, clean since the day before. He was other than them because of his clothes. He was different because they thought him rich.

Sometimes he dreamt of them. The children, the fiddler who played as night closed in. The smell of the cabins. Familiar and strange. The stink of misery.

'Tony.' Lady Pamela touched his arm. Her dark eyes were concerned. 'Are you well? Vous étiez ailleurs.'

'Oui, Madame.' He shook himself. 'Merci. I'm quite well.' He was sitting on the window seat. How long had he spent tugged by the past from this room, where Lucy and the butcher's daughters were sipping some punch from the table by the far corner? The men had left, probably for a quiet word with Edward in the hallway or the kitchen. Only O'Connor remained, causing a ripple of laughter when he joined the little group in the corner. Lucy was showing the two girls the tiny harp she had embroidered on her jacket.

'It's lovely.'

'Where will you wear it?'

Their voices were at once admiring and fearful. Pamela laughed. Tony watched O'Connor lean down and whisper something to Lucy. She shook her head and pulled away from him.

'La pauvre Lucy,' murmured Pamela. 'Dear Edward was quite harsh with her when he heard how late she sat up with Arthur last week, jusqu'au presque matin. He worries about her. What will Ogilvie say? So many worries about Ogilvie. Like a black crow, caw caw in his ear.'

She clapped her hands and crossed over to them. 'Please Lucy. Play something for us. Tony, can you bring her harp?'

Lucy was still protesting as he left the room, taking a candle from a sconce on the wall, and crossing the hall to the tiny parlour by the front door. He brushed against the cradle, empty now – it was sometimes used for baby Pammie to sleep in during the day – and lifted the candle a little higher, flickering light over a chair heaped with books and rolled-up maps, a stack of music sheets on the floor beside it. There. The harp, as expected, and the little stool. It was Lady Lucy's most recent passion. She declared herself descended from a line of poets and bards. She was good though, could pluck the sounds of trees and wild grass from those strings. He returned to the sitting room with the stool and harp and an armful of music sheets. Lucy riffled through them, agitated. 'Oh, but these are no good, not this one.'

O'Connor plucked one from the pile. 'This is my favourite. "Mabel Kelly". One of O'Carolan's.'

She looked as though she might refuse, but instead sat on the little stool in the centre of the room, the small gathering standing around expectantly. O'Connor drew up a chair. 'I'll hold your music since Tony forgot the stand.' Pamela smacked him lightly on the shoulder. Lucy began, fingers running over the strings, plucking notes from the harp like ripened seeds, and scattering them across the room.

The silence that followed was broken by O'Connor. 'Dear Lucy, 'twas my heartstrings you plucked with that.'

Lucy smiled. 'Thank you, Mr O'Connor but I thought only the new-strung harp of Erin interested you.'

'Now, now. No politics in here. Music and dance for the visitors.' O'Connor reached for another sheet of music and showed it to Lucy. 'How about "Farewell Killeavy" and someone might sing this new version, for Tony here.'

THE CAPTIVE NEGRO
Tune: 'Farewell Killeavy'

THE Negro with desponding heart,
And thoughts still stretched across the main,
Unceasing toil, his destined part,
While fierce the sun-beams scorch the plain.
Appear! Appear! Fair FREEDOM,
And set the captive Negro free,
With scourges whipt, till bleeding,
By th' enemies of Liberty.

When in some dungeon's solitude,
Denyed of light to cheer the day,
His soul by wrongs still unsubdu'd,
The Patriot wastes his life away.
Appear! Appear! Fair FREEDOM,
And set the captive Patriot free;
With scourges whipt, till bleeding,
By th' enemies of Liberty.

The Warrior first in FREEDOM's cause,
As champion of the human race,
Feels the rigour of despotic laws,
Won't purchase mercy with disgrace.
Appear! Appear! Fair FREEDOM,
And set the captive Warrior free:
With scourges whipt, till bleeding,
By th' enemies of Liberty.

When the victim of fanatic zeal,
Lifts up his eyes to Heaven, and sighs,
Fearless of contempt, or fire, or steel,
The tyrant's power his mind denies.
Appear! Appear! Fair FREEDOM,
And set the captive victim free:
With scourges whipt, till bleeding,
By th' enemies of Liberty.

The kitchen was cool compared to the sitting room. Edward and the two local men had been joined by Oliver Bond, that merchant gentleman from Dublin. Samuel Neilson was to have accompanied him and his arrest a few weeks before was a blow for all gathered, including Tony, and not just because he liked the man. He'd hoped to talk to Neilson about Equiano and his time in Belfast. Such a pity.

'Ah, Tony. Still keeping house for this man, I see. Someone needs to keep him in order.' Bond smiled in a distracted way before returning his attention to the papers in front of him. The other two men followed his lead, huddled, their hands hesitant, one pointing nervously at a column of figures, the other clasping his hands together at the table's edge as though he did not trust what they might do. Tony tidied up around them, removing empty glasses, offering food, more wine. He took his time, preparing a tray for the guests in the sitting room. Bottle of madeira, glasses. He checked them for blemishes again, polished them.

Edward spoke without even looking up. 'If I didn't know better, I'd think you were avoiding going back to the Ladies, just like Bran here.'

The dog opened his eyes at the sound of his name just as O'Connor entered the room.

'Either that or he's a spy.'

The butcher looked around at O'Connor, alarmed at the word. Spies were everywhere. Talk of them was everywhere. Which one of them had not felt the shadowy presence for himself? Edward knew with a certainty that his own letters came to him second hand, already subjected to the scrutiny of authorities at Dublin Castle or one of their men. The others remained impassive.

Tony carried on polishing. 'Just making sure all is as it should be. We're not running a tavern after all.'

O'Connor's laugh drilled into the company. The other men looked at him in bafflement.

'Maybe not a spy,' he said. 'But there's more to Tony than meets the eye.'

A day later and O'Connor and Edward were away to the West, checking on the numbers of men, on their loyalty, their ability to respond quickly to the French landing, and their leaders too, bolstering their flagging courage by showing their own. Tony did not travel with them. His presence was a hobble, limiting their movements, marking both men.

THE TRUE NARRATIVE

December 1796, and a ball at Castletown House; Lord Castlereagh visits; French fleet sighted off the South coast of Ireland.

The Castletown Ball was not a success. The two Ladies had dressed in the democratic fashion, short hair turned up at the sides, clusters of green ribbons and green ruffles about their dress. This despite having received word from Lady Louisa Conolly, Edward's aunt, advising against such displays. One of Conolly's carriages took them home early the following morning. Edward and Tony followed on horseback – slowly. The empty carriage passed them on the main street in Kildare, clipping back to Castletown again. Turning into the lane that led to the house, Edward remarked, 'I always have such a feeling of relief when I catch a glimpse of the trees ahead. Even now with no leaves, there's a kindness about them. A shelter.'

He turned his head up to the grey sky, breathed deeply. 'I'm to go North soon. With Arthur, though he'll go ahead of me. He tells me to let him handle the Northern Directory. The old-school United men. All those esteemed founders. And all those sober Presbyterians who are nervous of me and my aristocratic credentials.'

'And Mr O'Connor?' Tony asked.

'Oh, he is much more to their taste. Less suspicion of flamboyance.' He laughed. 'Though that just proves they don't really know the man. He says he'll stand for Antrim. Give him access to the people. He'll be in a position to speak out.'

'You're not sure about it?'

'O'Connor is a man who likes to speak. The problem is he may say too much. And now is not the time for him to draw attention to himself. He needs to ensure the North is ready for the French. Bring the Northern Directory along – what's left of them. They're nervous now and rightly so. Those arrests last month gutted them. Neilson and Russell, McCracken too. All facing charges of treason. Not that they'll get a trial, by the look of things. Left to rot in Kilmainham in Dublin.'

'I'm sorry to hear it. Especially about Neilson.'

'If Arthur is not careful, he'll be next.'

'And you?'

'Me? For now I'm safe. But once the French come and the whole keg blows, no one will be. Still, best to keep my eye on the prize and the means to that end. The Leinster Directory is strong. The people are strong. We should have the numbers when the time comes. Unlike the Presbyterians up North, the Catholic people here are much taken with the Fitzgerald name.'

'But you were concerned about the Catholics. Said they were reluctant to back the French involvement.'

'That's the remnants of the Catholic gentry. They're nervous they'd lose everything. But the people themselves, those who take up those pikes and ancient guns, what have they got to lose? They just hope to get something back.'

Edward shook his head.

'They will, won't they? I mean that's the point. Of freedom. Isn't it?' Tony looked at Edward's grim face. 'I assumed …'

'There are some in the leadership who harbour fears of the mob, as they call them. The same mob they expect to stand up to the British guns and their cavalry.' He shook his head. 'Who'd have thought that such a small country could have so many divisions. Christ, it's like trying to herd together wild boar and sheep with bears and chickens. And before you ask, I'm not assigning any group to any particular animals.'

Tony blew out his cheeks. Though he knew well enough that freedom was never absolute, it still came as a shock to hear it so contested, so easily compromised.

The horses clopped loudly on the gravel in front of the house and stopped by the three granite steps which led up to the door. On either side, a wicker cage stood, which once had contained a songbird each – a whim of Lady Pamela's when they moved down from Dublin. They sang for a short while until one of them died in the first frost of winter. Lady Pamela was upset, berating herself, and she released the other from his captivity. 'Vole, vole, petit oiseau!' she cried, clapping her hands. But he returned every morning to sit atop the cage, in silence. A few weeks after, Tony found the bird lying beside the cage, on fresh-fallen snow, its half-lidded eyes unseeing.

The cages remained empty on the top step, like they were waiting for something, or someone. A high-pitched wail from the house sawed through the air, on and on. Both men winced. 'Lady Lucy?' Tony wondered aloud.

'Why Tony, if you're not careful you'll lose your reputation as a man of gravity. I believe that is my dear baby Pammie.' The crying continued. Edward smiled wryly. 'Once more unto the breach.' He dismounted, and leaned his head against the saddle. 'Perhaps not. Do me a favour, Tony. Why don't you look after the two ladies and I'll take care of the horses.'

'Really? You'll take care of the horses?'

'Please. See if you can defuse Lucy's rage. You know she doesn't forgive lightly.'

The bags were scattered on the hallway tiles, inside the door. He picked up a coat that had been dropped across the stair post. Lady Pamela emerged from the doorway on the right, still in her American jacket and rabbit-trimmed hood. She looked tired.

'Ah, Monsieur Small. I cannot get warm. Is it possible to light the fire in my room? I'll rest there for the day, thank you Tony.'

In the sitting room, Lady Lucy was in a flurry of upset. 'The women are petty gossips and the men are cowards and dullards – except for Castlereagh. He's anything but a dullard and how I wish he were not married to Uncle Conolly's niece. There would be no reason our paths should cross. Instead, it seems he's always at Castletown, a snake in a pit, waiting to strike. Trying to charm information out of me about

Edward. His mouth smiles but his eyes, they …' She shuddered. 'I had to cross the floor to avoid him in case he mesmerised me.'

'Such fuss and blather,' Julia said as she carried a red-faced baby Pammie over her shoulder, up and down the stairs, trying to soothe her crying. 'As if there's not enough of it with a teething baby.'

Upstairs Lady Pamela sipped at the bone broth that he had brought. 'Poor little Pam,' she said. 'Has Julia tried oil of cloves? Is Lucy still upset? A pity. Je suis habitué a leurs mauvaises manières.'

Lady Lucy *was* still upset. Apparently, no amount of fan-flapping and foot-tapping could cover the vile and nasty things that were said. 'We were left standing alone,' she said. 'While even the plainest and dullest were up dancing.'

'What did she expect?' Julia rubbed the baby's gums with a cold cloth, and a dab of clove oil. 'Everyone's afraid. They're all barricading their houses, so why would they risk a dance with Lord Edward's wife and sister?'

The cook, Mrs Dowling, was plucking a chicken by the back door of the kitchen, and the wind was blowing feathers this way and that and all the while she muttered and grumbled about the 'stupid girl'.

'Who?' Tony asked as he scoured the pantry shelves, examining bottles, looking for elderberry wine.

'The scullery girl, that amadán, hasn't been here for three days. She's after courting a man and it turns out he's in the Yeomanry.'

Damn. Damn.

'How long?' he asked, thinking over their recent visitors and what she might have seen or heard or passed on.

'I don't know.' She ripped out feathers with casual ferocity. 'Didn't her brother discover them, and he a staunch United man. Can't say how the yeoman fared.'

She looked up from the plucked fowl on her lap. 'Don't you go worrying – but I expect His Lordship will have to know,' she sighed. Her hands were stained and sticky. Blood and feathers. She wiped them down her apron, slow and meticulous now. 'Her brother has spirited the girl away, and lucky for her. Though she says she told the man nothing, some others might have been less sympathetic to her.'

He'd added a small measure of brandy to the elderberry wine that he brought in for Lady Lucy. O'Connor was watching her with some amusement, from a supine position on the sopha, as she paced around the room. He had not attended Castletown. 'Never mind, Lucy. There'll be other dances, other outings.'

She snapped back at him. 'Of course. That's all I want. Someone to dance with.'

O'Connor snorted. 'I swear I'd have danced with you had I been there.'

'Easy to say when you were not invited. Not welcome.'

He clutched his chest, and Lucy's mouth tightened. 'Do you know that you dismiss everything I say? It might be funny sometimes but not now.' She took a glass from the tray as Tony placed it beside her. Took a long drink. O'Connor's face lost its mask of amusement, became serious. He gave his apologies, asked her to sit, so they could talk. 'Tell me about Castlereagh. What did he say?'

Across the hall, Edward was in the small parlour that served as an office, a sewing room, a music room and sometimes a nursery. He listened to the news about the maid without comment. Then murmured, 'That poor girl.'

The baby was asleep at last, her gums finally soothed. Julia took little Ettie with her for a walk to the village. Lady Pamela was in bed, reading perhaps or sleeping. Lady Lucy and O'Connor were talking quietly, for now. Edward returned to his sheets of paper, lined with columns and numbers. The newly plucked chicken was resting, dangling by its pale legs from a hook in the pantry. Mrs Dowling had gone home but would return in a few hours to prepare the supper. Tony went upstairs to the attic and settled himself under the window, book in hand. He'd been reading the same book, *Robinson Crusoe*, for over a month and was only halfway through. It wasn't just a question of time, or that the words were difficult. Edward said that it was archaic, seventy years old, but worth the effort.

'Did you know that "Master" was the first word Crusoe taught the native man?' Tony had asked him.

'No, I never noticed,' he had replied.

Shortly before Christmas, O'Connor departed for Belfast. Tony assisted with his luggage while Edward saw him off, walking the short distance to the Curragh coffee house where the coach had just arrived.

'Keep safe,' he urged his friend. 'If all goes well, the New Year should bring some fresh winds and fair seas to Galway.'

O'Connor laughed. 'I think you enjoy all this talking in code.'

'Not really,' Edward replied. 'It's just the way of things.'

'With luck, it won't be for much longer,' O'Connor muttered, 'I hope to God the people up North are ready. And that those arrests have not taken the heart out of them. It's a bad time to have the likes of Teeling under lock and key in Kilmainham. We could do with him to hold the Catholics in check.'

Tony looked over his shoulder as he handed the bags up to the coachman to secure on top. The men seemed to be talking loudly. Too loudly.

Edward tugged at O'Connor's coat sleeve. 'You know, Arthur they've had to endure a lot. So many displaced, arrested. No wonder they are wary. And now the Orangemen are armed, forcing families out of their homes—'

'Spare me Edward. If it weren't for the Orangemen, we wouldn't have got all those new recruits. Every time a new Orange Lodge is set up, the Catholics flock to swell the United Irish ranks.'

'Your cynicism can still astound me, Arthur. Good luck with hanging onto the reins of all those Northerners.'

Tony coughed. 'Speaking of reins, your coachman is looking impatient.'

O'Connor clambered inside, and pulled a rug about him. The only other passenger was an elderly man, fussing with a basket. Edward closed the door on the mismatched travellers, calling out. 'Have faith, Arthur! I know you're not short of courage.'

They walked back to the Lodge, to see a carriage waiting at the front steps; its gleaming burgundy paintwork and the crown atop the coat of arms did not bode well. 'What fresh torture is this?' Edward murmured to Tony. 'Let's slip around the back, the better to get our bearings.'

In the kitchen, Julia passed on the news of the Castlereaghs' visit with tight-lipped grimness. Unannounced and unexpected, she declared. They'd come to take their dear cousin Lucy to Castletown. She emphasised the word 'dear'.

'Lady Pamela is entertaining them at present. And she with no opportunity to dress for them.'

On occasion, Edward spoke with cautious admiration of the viscount, referring to him as coldly charming or icily clever, suggesting it were 'a pity he's not on our side'. Now he hissed through his teeth, 'Damn the man. Where's Lucy?'

Lucy was in her room according to Julia, dresses heaped on the bed. 'She doesn't want to go,' she told Edward. 'And to come without notice … She thinks they're trying to catch her out lest she have a chance to refuse.'

'He is a fox sniffing around the henhouse,' Tony said.

Edward was thoughtful. 'As long as she knows what he is after, she knows how to avoid telling him. I'll go up to her. Lucy was always good at theatricals. She can pretend. Be innocent. Come with me Tony, you can take her things down.'

'I don't know what to bring.' Lucy was agitated, opening and closing her travel box. 'I can't avoid him all the time. What if I say something in error?'

Edward sat beside her on the bed, and hugged her tight. In the low afternoon light, their hair gleamed an identical shade of copper. 'I trust you, dearest Lucia. And remember the watched can watch too.' She smiled tearfully, ran her hand over her face, and kissed him.

Edward looked over her head at Tony. 'We'll give her a few more minutes. Could you bring some whiskey to Lord Castlereagh while Lucy gets ready? Make sure it's Irish.'

'And I presume I should serve potato cakes with that?'

'Oh yes.' Lucy brightened up. 'And be sure to send on my harp to Castletown. I'll play some fine old Irish melodies for their entertainment.'

'Tony, Tony.' Lady Pamela was calling for him. He entered the sitting room to see Lord Castlereagh backed up against the bow window, and the wolfhound standing in a ripple of raised hair, muscle and erect tail. Here the winter sunlight made ash of Castlereaghs' hair, hollowed out his cheeks. Lady Pamela clicked at Bran but made little attempt to retrieve him, fluttering her hands. Tony caught her eye and she looked down, smiling slightly. The viscount remained still. 'It's strange,' he remarked through fixed lips. 'I usually have a way with dogs.'

'I'm sure you do, Sir.' He placed his hand on the dog's neck, felt the tension there, the low rumble from its throat. He let the moment last a little longer before he whispered, 'Come Bran,' and the dog dropped his hostile stance as quickly as he might have dropped a bone. Castlereagh smiled his thanks at Tony. 'A good hunting dog I'm certain, but hardly suitable for a Lady.'

'Nonsense, Robert.' Edward stood in the doorway, wearing a welcoming smile – and a green jacket and … not a green neckcloth as well? He shrugged when he saw Tony's expression. 'It was chilly,' he muttered in passing before urging Castlereagh to sit, that Tony would remove the threat. Bran followed Tony out of the room with his tail between his legs.

Lucy stayed at Castletown. Sent daily messages to Lady Pamela. How she had seen a particularly brazen fox, who just stared and was not easy to chase away. Tony rode over to Castletown daily, delivering Lady Pamela's short replies, and the occasional note from Edward. '*Foxes are not harmful in general but just in case, you should take a stick with you when you walk abroad. And remember not to get too close. Particularly if he should have rabies.*' Lucy wrote later that the fox had disappeared, and she was easier in her daily walks.

Tony didn't linger at Castletown, keen to avoid any questions from curious or devious servants. Nonetheless it was difficult to avoid the reports and rumours that scurried around that great house. They slipped along the warren of servants' corridors, carried from the drawing rooms, bedrooms and dining tables upstairs along with dirty plates, discarded clothes and overflowing chamber pots. In the servants' hall they were swapped for other stories gleaned from visits to town, from the man who delivered the post, from the coach driver who spent an afternoon waiting outside the Crown Tavern. The house itself was in constant movement, carriages arriving, visitors clambering out, luggage to be retrieved. And this despite Lady Louisa's precautions against any disaffected tenants: double locks on the doors; windows shuttered at night; armed guards within the house; patrolling groundsmen. Hunting parties came and went. Horses were led across the courtyard in the mornings and back in the afternoons, edgy and sweating, to be settled and brushed down. The Ladies' pleasures were more curtailed by the weather. Reading, recitals and painting – gentle scenes of Castletown, soft snowy fields and trees lined with white – in rooms stagnant with heat from fireplaces the size of a peasant's cabin.

Lucy became ill while at Castletown, and so her stay was prolonged. 'Do you think Lucy will find this amusing?' Lady Pamela was finishing a quick note for Tony to take to her. 'She has the jaundice and I have written to say I can no longer acknowledge her now that she is an Orange woman.' She laughed, not her usual light laugh but loudly, almost snorting at her joke. 'I hope she reads it aloud!'

But further rumours swelled in such an atmosphere, and there was little in them to amuse anyone. Rumours of terrible happenings. Of armed pike men attacking a local garrison. Of a local gentleman killed in his bed. Of the servants of poor old Mrs Harding, walking out one evening and deserting her entirely, leaving her at the mercy of who only knew what horrors. Of the shameful behaviour of a certain section of the Yeomen, who tore down cabins on the edge of Lucan village, and ran through several men suspected of belonging to the United Irishmen. Was it safe to go abroad? Would it ever be so? When would it end? Rumours and speculation. Tony carried them all back with him to the Lodge in Kildare, shared them with Edward, who nodded or laughed or rapped his fingers on the table.

He woke to Julia. Her hands on his face as she kissed him. 'Happy Christmas, Husband.' He pulled her body closer, pressing his lips to her neck, the soft flesh of her ear, the dark mole that she hated in daylight, and back to the hollow of her neck. She made a helpless sound, caressed his face, ran her hands over his shoulders, avoiding his scar with practised ease. His mouth lingered, tongue circling insistently, but his hands moved elsewhere, down the knuckles of her spine, in the small of her back, stroking her buttocks, slipping between her legs. He moved over her, tried to hold out, kissing her mouth again, her neck, but she shifted under him, opening up and all was lost.

Or won. He looked at her flushed face, her hair splayed around her like wet autumn ferns. He held her hand in his for a moment, linking his fingers through hers. Julia wriggled her fingers. 'Fear gorm,' she said.

'Mo chailín beag bán.'

She laughed. 'It sounds so funny on your tongue.' She tried to imitate him, pressing her chin into her neck to deepen her voice, and failed.

'So I cannot pass for an Irishman? Damn it.'

She pressed against him again. 'I have neither want nor need of an Irishman. Just you.'

'Speak some more Irish to me,' he said.

'Thug mo shúil áire dhuit, thug mo chroí taitneamh dhuit ...'

The words lapped against him, their meaning unclear, but he felt an unaccounted sadness. 'What is that?'

'It's a caoineadh, a lament. By a woman whose husband was shot. I've heard it sung.' Her voice wavered as she took up the notes, like the wind whistling through the gorse.

He brought little Ettie out to the stable. She laughed at the nickering sounds of the horses, and reached out with delight for their swishing manes. He couldn't shake off Julia's song. Everything sang of it. Mourned with it. The bare trees, the slate sky. The hens picking over yesterday's scraps on the dirty snow. The horses' ancient eyes. Outside it was still. No one else about yet. They had all the whiteness to themselves. The night's snowfall had covered all horse tracks, all footprints except their own, which followed them out of the courtyard and down the lane. Snow blunted the short branches of the apple trees. Ettie wriggled in his grasp and he placed some snow in her hands. A man on horseback turned abruptly into the lane, towards them. His face was meaty with cold and effort, gloved hands tight on the reins. The horse blew clouds of steamy breath.

'You're Lord Edward's man. Is he here?'

'No, Sir.' He always gave the same answer to strangers.

'No matter, perhaps he knows already. Word is travelling faster than the snow.'

'What is it?'

'It's the French. They've come. To the South, at Bantry Bay. The Militia are out, not just there, everywhere.' The man leaned out of the saddle, until he could feel the heat off him, the stink of him, and the horse. 'If your master is about, tell him to be careful.'

'What will happen?'

'Here?' The man's voice was hoarse. 'I don't know. Maybe your master will. Or maybe you'll have to wait. Wait and see.'

With that he wheeled the horse around, galloped off, throwing back clots of snow, to deliver his news elsewhere.

The True Narrative

December 1796, and Lord Edward is shocked to hear of the failed French Landing.

The Reader may wonder at such events and whether Lord Edward had any part in it, given all the calumny that has been spoken against him. I cannot silently suffer my Master to be so slandered. He had no knowledge of the plan, and was considerably distressed by it. He repudiated those involved. [38]

Edward left his Christmas dinner untouched yet would not give up the plate to Tony.

'Bantry? How did this happen? Why no word? Not a damn thing ready. And Bantry? That bastard Tone. Ignoring the people here, those who are expected to rise up. He always has to push harder. February. We talked of February. And it was to be Galway. How are we to organise any kind of support?' He paced as he talked. Lady Pamela attempted to calm him but he was not to be placated.

'Arthur's in Belfast awaiting news of the fleet setting sail. Yet there they are already in Bantry, trumpeting their presence off-shore. I tell you it's Tone. Can't you just see him with General Hoche, leading the fleet. No doubt kitted out in some uniform, to demonstrate his authority. This is nothing but a display of contempt for the rest of us.'

[38] This is excellent Tony. You are a clever weaver of Truth. LLF.

'Peut-être, qu'il a essayé d'envoyer un message,' Lady Pamela said.

'Perhaps,' Edward considered this for a moment. 'There are so many spies, perhaps it was intercepted.' He shook his head, turned to the fire and kicked at a spitting log. 'But if their plan were known, wouldn't the Navy have engaged them? No, I think Tone acted alone.'

'Perhaps …' Tony offered, 'perhaps they were unable to sail beyond Bantry to Galway? By all accounts the storm was ferocious.'

'Hmm. It's possible. Yes. But even so. Not yet January. And no word of it.' There was always tension when the name of Mr Theobald Wolfe Tone arose. And not just because he was a founding member of the United Irishmen. Edward had related how on their few meetings the man had brushed him off '… as though I'm some aristocratic mascot. Told me my face is stamped on all the jugs in the North as a "Man of the People" and sounded unamused by it.' Edward's slight became Tony's.

'Who can blame those Northerners, you've such a handsome face. Far prettier than Tone's from what I've heard.' Lady Pamela fiddled with the twist of fabric that decorated her hair, unravelling the ends and sending pearls scattering across the table. 'Merde!'

Tony gathered up most of them, placing them in a bowl. He took the cold tureens to the kitchen. Julia and Mrs Dowling busied themselves but their glances held questions which he could not answer.

By the time he returned to the dining room, Edward was once more seated, sipping some wine and resolving to go to Dublin. 'I can't stay here not knowing. Besides, this place is all eyes and ears.'

Tony resisted mentioning that Dublin was most likely worse, merely commenting that he himself had taken to saying nothing about anything to anyone.

'Plus ça change, Tony,' Edward responded, flicking a pearl across the table toward him. It ricocheted back off the carafe and hit Edward square in the chest.

They left Kildare at daybreak. Out into a bitter morning, the snow crunching underfoot, a dirty sky overhead. They travelled east, avoiding the main Dublin Road, taking the back lanes. Along the way, outside every cabin, every tavern, there was talk of sixty French ships all along the south coast. Of Cork having risen. But in Blessington, they were told only a handful of ships were still off the coast, the rest having been blown off-course. That the French had turned back. A storm in a teacup, Sir. Nothing to concern yourself with. As they headed north from Blessington, a detachment of soldiers approached.

Tony avoided looking at them, just murmured to his horse, watched his hooves churn the snow. Edward urged his mount forward, hailing them.

'Hey there.' The Captain rode up.

'We've just heard in that inn, tales of the French storming through the countryside. Are we in danger? My poor black is most anxious. He had a run in with the French in the Indies.'

Good God. Did he expect him to perform theatricals? Play the part of a buffoonish Mungo? He would not. He kept his face blank.

The Captain eyed him warily, then circled around Edward, looking him up and down. His horse snorted, and pawed the ground.

Tony tugged sharply at the reins to upset his own mount. 'We must be off, master. They're coming.'

'Your informant is mistaken.' The Captain's voice was sour with fatigue and contempt. The other soldiers were dirty and unshaven, their swords dull with rust or blood. 'Not a single French foot has landed on His Majesty's soil.'

'Just the same,' Edward cut in. 'My wife is unattended in Dublin. Are you travelling the Dublin road? I'd feel much safer in your company.'

The Captain sighed and turning to his Sergeant, instructed him to march on.

'You may follow behind if you wish.'

Tony took a deep breath as they set off.

'Oh they are coming!' Edward smirked. 'You did that so well, Tony.'

'Never again.'

'But that's how it's done. Sometimes you have to hide in the open.'

All very well for you, Tony thought.

The True Narrative

January 1797, and reflections on the French; A visit to Mr O'Connor in Belfast; Lord FitzGerald stays at Leinster House in Dublin; The Author encounters Mr Ogilvie.

The winter storms were relentless. Gales blew one day, snow fell the next – first the hills, then fields and houses. Mud cabins disappeared under a covering of white, their inhabitants forced to remain huddled together, eking out the last of their potatoes and milk. Further gales blew icy blasts across open country, freezing those out tending to frozen sheep. Two days after Christmas, at Great Yarmouth, unholy winds whipped up the water and drove twelve ships to the shore, disgorging their crew and cargo, thus providing the scavengers and wreckers with unexpected Christmas bounty. Off the coast of Cork, the French Fleet pushed forward and was blown back, off course. The landing parties could not be launched. The seas were too high, too wild, and when at last they settled enough to attempt it, a thick fog descended, obscuring land from sea and sea from land. It would never happen.

I accompanied my Lord Edward to Belfast, where he attended his dear friend Mr Arthur O'Connor, who was suffering from a debilitating relapsing fever which caused him to remain bedridden for almost a month. Mr O'Connor spent the time reading and writing; letters and political pamphlets. He endeavoured to draw Lord Edward into his plans. In particular he sought his opinion regarding an Address that he was composing to the County of Antrim (with the intention of publishing it in The Northern Star, and other newspapers besides).

I judged by Lord Edward's troubled countenance that the contents of the paper were of great concern to him. He had tried to persuade his friend to soften his position lest he risk being charged with treason. But he would not: 'I am willing to be taken up for my principles. I will not stand idly by while such calumny prevails.'

Lord Edward understood that he would not be swayed, neither by reason nor sentiment.[39]

Those domestic days in Kildare were over. Edward spent most of his time in Dublin and Lady Pamela would not be without him. They were a wandering household, staying sometimes in Leinster House, or a townhouse in St Stephen's Green and sometimes out at Frescati in Blackrock. Even that place, Edward's childhood home, was no longer the sanctuary it once had been, though they tried hard to keep up the pretence of normal life. Edward was always busy. Travelling. Trailing shadows in his wake. Watched. Always watched. There were soldiers everywhere. Who knew if they were regular army, or Militia or Yeomanry? The suspension of habeas corpus meant that anyone could be picked up, arrested and thrown in prison without trial. Those soldiers kept busy, setting alarm among the citizens, accosting the most innocent of workers, interrogating servants, filling the prisons – any action that might serve to restore control.

As he walked with Edward along Thomas Street in Dublin, it seemed the alarm raised by the French had not yet passed. Everyone was in a hurry, scuttling along the streets, head down, not stopping for news or conversation. A shoeblack called out to Edward but he shook his head at him. 'Another time.'

He patted his coat. 'Just wait until I show Lucy.' He meant the copy of O'Connor's address, secreted inside his shirt. 'I think at times she has doubted him. Not now.'

[39] I'm not certain about this passage; on the one hand it suggests Edward avoided involvement in Mr O'Connor's affairs, and yet it implicates O'Connor wholly. Is this necessary? LLF.

A small detachment of soldiers was standing at the corner by Digby's Coffee Shop. Tony hissed at Edward and they turned into a nearby courtyard, hurried across past a wagon loaded with casks. Two men were rolling barrels into a basement. One signalled to Edward, pointing to an entrance.

'Morning, Your Lordship.'

They rushed on, through the inn and out onto the Dog and Duck Yard.

'I don't know why we bother. They have no reason to take me up.'

Tony kept pace with Edward's springy walk. 'They don't need a reason. You heard what your brother had to say – and he got it directly from the Lord Lieutenant himself. "*Tell Edward to flee, he must leave the country. The case against him is very great.*"'

'I heard alright. You'd think he could have the decency to tell me himself. This way, Tony.'

A run of barnacled steps led down to the river, where a small wherry was moored, rocking on the incoming tide. Edward threw the boatman a coin and he in turn tipped the brim of his hat, making a sign with his hand.

'What have you got there in your hand?' Edward asked him, smiling.

'A green bough, Sir.'

'Where did it first grow?'

'In America.'

No need to say the rest. The man was one of their own, knew the catechism and understood the need to row quickly and say nothing. The river was busy as always, empty barges sweeping past heavily laden ones; smaller boats like their own, ferrying passengers up and down river. Seabirds swooped over the small fishing vessels, which pushed further upriver before docking by Merchant's Quay. Despite the strong incoming current, the oarsman worked with only an occasional grunt. The boat answered him with creaks and dipping oars, creaks and dripping oars. The river stank as always, with competing smells from the tanneries and maltsters upriver and effluent from the city houses. Edward closed his eyes for a moment.

'Do you remember skating here, that terrible winter when the river froze. Was that '83?'

'1784. First time I'd ever seen anything like it.'

'So long ago. Another life.' He pulled his collar up against the bite of evening air.

'One of several lives,' Tony said. The sky was daubed with a savage sunset, the clouds ribbed and reddened. 'I've been meaning to ask, that is, I would like …' He searched for words.

Edward opened one eye. 'Yes?'

'I would like to take the Oath.' He lowered his voice, though there was no sign that the boatman was anything other than deaf. 'The Oath of the United Irishmen.'

'But, Tony, you have nothing to prove. I know your loyalty.' His face looked bitten, by cold and anguish.

'It's not about proof or loyalty, but the name. My own decision to take the name.' For so long he'd wanted it, to be more than just on the edges. Hovering. Lord Edward's man. A black man. Always separate. 'It's more than just words you know, this equal and full representation. I would be equal. What am I in this country? Neither fish nor fowl. I want to choose this for myself, as you did. You say there are thousands of United Irishmen. If I should take the Oath then I would be one too.'

Edward looked closely at him. Did not smile or joke as he half expected. 'Very well. I'll swear you in myself.'

The rhythm of the oars changed as they drew near George's Quay, quiet as always compared with the chaos of ships and sloops jostling for inspection by the Custom House across the river. The boat rapped against the stone steps. The boatman gestured once more with his hand.

By the time they'd walked to Leinster House, with its long ranks of windows and grey blockwork, it was getting dark.

'Just as well,' Edward said. 'I might be able to get in without Brother William being aware of my presence.'

'Has he forbidden you from visiting?'

'Not in so many words. I think he just does not wish to know about it. I've become an embarrassment to him – more than that, I'm a liability. A thorn in the pillow of the finest family in Ireland.' The last said with a rueful smile. They slipped in around the back entrance, through the stables and along the servants' corridor. Past the kitchens, heading for the door leading to the stone stairwell.

'Mind you, he did oppose Martial Law in the House recently and has given me money, or rather the organisation. He does his best. Not everyone can afford to throw it all over. I forget sometimes that liberty and equality are just ideas for some people, and not necessarily worth pursuing at all costs.'

'And you, do you think it's worth it?'

Edward stopped and stared. 'How can you, of all people, ask that?'

'Where do you think you're going? I haven't had sight nor sound of you for two weeks and then you try to sneak past—'

It was Julia, standing in a doorway, her hands on her hips. She saw Edward. 'Oh. Begging your pardon. I didn't mean you, Milord. Just him.' She pointed at Tony.

Edward smiled at him. 'He's all yours Julia. Since you are here, is my little wife here also?'

'She is. And the baby too. I've just seen to them both.'

Edward leaned towards her. 'If I could detain you from Tony for just a moment longer …' Julia made a face. 'Could you go back up to her and ask her to meet me in Lucy's room. It's at the back of the house—'

'Lady Pamela is there already. She asked for those rooms. Said they'd be private, not wanting to be a nuisance to anyone, least of all your brother. The Duke I mean.'

'I know just what you mean. Thank you.' He turned into the stairwell and was gone.

Tony reached out a hand to Julia, surprised – and not for the first time – at how cool her hand was. Julia pulled away. 'I must see to Ettie now.'

There was another visitor in the house. Mr Ogilvie. He was dining with William – one of his least favourite stepchildren, according to Edward. Tony had heard this sort of talk for so many years that he paid no attention. Though he knew that no one could topple Edward.

Not with any amount of scandalous or seditious behaviour. He was his mother's Dearest Heart, Her Darling Eddie.

But it seemed Mr Ogilvie may have been losing patience. According to Julia, he'd already been to Castletown and Frescati in search of Edward.

'He's not at all pleased with the reports he's had of Lord Edward. Says the Duchess is stricken with headaches because of them.' Julia jabbed a poker at the cinders in the tiny fire of the servants' parlour. 'My God, the state of him. Wouldn't even sit down while talking to Lady Pamela. You know how he is with her. Eyes darting over her shoulder hoping someone more interesting, or tolerable will come through the door.'

'He has no hold over her,' Tony said. 'It annoys him immensely.' Ettie lay on his lap. She was asleep, eyelashes fanning, her mouth half open as she made soft sighing sounds.

'How did she find the journey in the carriage?' he asked, nodding down at the child.

'She stood on the seat for almost an hour, staring out the window, rocking about. I thought she'd never settle down. And now look at her.'

In the rooms upstairs, there was a display suggesting a parting of three years, not three weeks. Pamela was curled up on Edward's lap, her hands pressed to his face, kissing him loudly and exclaiming in between, 'Mon amour, mon fidèle.'

'Help me Tony. She has me trapped.' Edward was delighted. He was splayed out on the sopha. His neckcloth hung over the back and his shirt was wide open.

'I'm sorry to interrupt, but it seems Mr Ogilvie is here. Looking for you.'

Lady Pamela stopped kissing him. 'Everyone is looking for you. Are you being careful?'

'I think so. We do our best.' He took her hands in his. 'Tony, I'm not sure I want to see Ogilvie tonight. It's been a long day. Does he know I'm here?'

Lady Pamela pulled him to her. 'Since I did not know you were coming, how could he?'

Tony agreed. 'Unless one of the house servants has seen him. Or heard him.'

'I'll come back in the morning.' One final kiss for Pamela. 'Come to Frescati tomorrow. We'll take a holiday by the sea. Just ourselves. For a few days.'

She made a face. 'It's so cold and damp there.'

'I'll do Mother's trick. Get Mrs Henry to lie in the bed for the entire day. Air it for you.' He seized her round the waist and slid her off him onto the sopha. 'Ah Pamela, think of the snowdrops under the willows, and the crocuses pushing up, and the roses blooming—'

'Idiot. Roses? It will be snow blooming not roses … but I'll go. All of us will go. Lucy too if she is willing to miss the Castle ball.'

Ogilvie was in forbidding humour. He knew of Edward's visit. He forbade Lady Lucy to travel to Frescati. Insisted she was not well enough. He would not allow her to see Mr O'Connor, 'that dark and unwelcome influence', should he ever attempt to call. Lady Pamela determined to leave Leinster House without meeting Edward's stepfather, citing indisposition due the visit of her 'French Lady'. 'Be sure to tell him,' she told Julia. 'He is naturally wary of women in their monthlies.' Julia passed on the message, and reported his face puffing and creasing in response. Spirits were high as they packed up the Leinster House apartment to depart for Frescati, just ten or so miles away.

'I long to see the sea.' Lady Pamela said, knotting her bonnet under her chin. 'It always lifts my spirits.'

Julia looked doubtful. 'The sea is best viewed from inside,' she muttered, gathering up baby Pammie while Tony carried the bags and valise down to the great hall below, to await the carriage. Lady Pamela followed behind, tripping down the stairs, hatted and caped against the January weather. Before she reached the bottom, Mr Ogilvie appeared, stalking anxiously among the black marble columns, his heels clicking on the marble floor. 'Lady Edward, a moment of your time,' he said.

'Ah, Monsieur Ogilvie,' she said, fixing a button on her glove, 'Je suis désolé mais nous devons partir.'

'Please.'

She looked up at him, then over to where Tony was waiting by the door. 'Tony, is the carriage outside?'

'Yes Milady.'

'Lady Edward, please listen. You must persuade Edward to cease this path. It will only lead to more destruction, maybe even his own. Lord Castlereagh and Camden have let it be known that he should leave the country. A few years at most. That's all. Then this madness will have passed. You could go to America for a time. I beg you, think of your children. And his mother. You must know how the Duchess suffers through all of these rumours.'

'Ah, yes. We mothers must suffer,' she said. 'How is my son, my dear little Eddy? Six months since last I saw him. You must know that.' She moved away from him, and the footman opened one of the hall doors. But Ogilvie's words continued to fall like blows, relentless and heavy. 'Soon it will be too late to turn back.' A string of spittle appeared between his lips as he spoke to her departing back.

'Sir,' Tony moved between them. 'I will advise Lord Edward that you were enquiring after him.'

Ogilvie stopped then, his bristling head thrust forward, and jabbed his forefinger into Tony's shoulder. He smelt of desperation. 'You'd do better,' he hissed, and the spittle worked back and forth, 'to advise your mistress to release him from her Popish republican grasp.'

Tony stepped back from him and glanced over his shoulder, through the open door, where Lady Pamela had reached the carriage. She had not heard. The footman, standing ornate and still as any of the busts and sculptures that lined the hall, gave no sign of having heard either, but he knew what lay behind such a look of studied impassivity. He knew this sort of outburst would be sauce for their supper in the servants' hall by evening. 'Sir,' he began, 'I beg of you, please—'

Ogilvie's mouth opened, his jaw trembled but no words came and he pulled a large kerchief from his pocket and mopped his face. 'Go,' he said, waving Tony off with his free hand, 'Join them. But please look after them. Look after Edward. Please.'

The True Narrative

I beg leave to relate how I came to take the Oath. As the country's situation, and my Master's in particular, became more dangerous, my former slavery rose in fearful review to my mind. The Barbarities that occurred throughout the countryside recalled to my mind the misery, stripes and chains of former days. Once again I was visited with a sense of helplessness. Though I tried to turn to God, I could not understand how He could suffer such dreadful acts to take place. My concern was greatest on Lord Edward's account. During those days, my dark complexion rendered me a danger to him, for he could not travel quietly with me by his side. I was so much associated with him, and as clear a declaration of his Republican views as his short hair and his high collars. These other things he could disguise but not me. Another Master might have dispensed with my services, being faced with such a liability. But he was as no other; a man of high feeling, who reposed in me an unbounded confidence.

It was this confidence that hardened my determination to take the Oath. Besides, I had for a long time wanted to join that great assemblage of men who aspired to such noble sentiments as equal representation of all peoples. (Lord Edward went so far as to consider women among those who were worthy of suffrage.) These were men who took the words of Mr Paine and strove to make them flesh. Men

of Courage and Integrity. It is a great honour to have known such
men, and my Master foremost among them.

The more I saw of them and heard of them, the stronger my
desire to resemble them; to belong among them in such a way
that my hue was of little consequence; to imbibe their spirit and
imitate their selfless manners and actions. I believed that taking
the Oath would afford me the opportunity to become as them.
Not just a former slave, a poor black, but a true member of
a Brotherhood of Affection, bound by the same determination
and fortitude.

So it was that Lord Edward swore me in and I took the Oath
of the United Irishmen. Most who took the Oath did so in grubby
places, dark, hidden places: in cabins and caves, in bogs and barns, in
the half-light of candles and lanterns and shadowed moon. Some took
it in back rooms of shops, in offices, in cellars. As for me I stood in
front of the windows overlooking the green lawns of Frescati, with
the bright sea stretching into the distance. Lord Edward was solemn
before administering the Oath and, I fancy, somewhat tearful after. I
am certain that all who likewise were sworn in around the country felt
as I did in that moment, my heart squeezed tight as a fist, and then
bursting open, flooding light throughout my body. I want it known,
should anyone read this Narrative, that there in Frescati I became a
part of that Brotherhood. Even now the words I recited pluck some
chord within me. Even now I belong.

'In the awful presence of God, I, Anthony Small, do
voluntarily declare that I will persevere in endeavouring to
form a Brotherhood of Affection in Irishmen of every religious
persuasion, and that I will also persevere in endeavours to
obtain an equal, full and adequate representation of all the
People of Ireland. I do further declare that neither hopes,
fears, rewards or punishments shall ever induce me, directly
or indirectly to inform on, or give evidence against, any
member or members of this or similar societies for an act or

expression of theirs done or made collectively or individually in or out of this society, in pursuance of the spirit of this obligation.'

I defy my Reader not to be moved by these sentiments.[40]

---

[40] Ah, Tony. How could I forget? Brotherhood of Affection. Such words. You must know we cannot include this but my own heart was squeezed tight reading it, exactly as you said. It is good of you not to mention that I too took the Oath. Think how Mr Ogilvie would treat that information! I remember how fierce Edward became when he heard about it and outraged that Mr O'Connor himself should have sworn me in. Poor, Dear Edward. LLF.

THE TRUE NARRATIVE

February 1797, and news of O'Connor's arrest; The Ladies attempt to visit the prisoner at Dublin Castle; The Author meets with Jerry O'Leary.

The first day of spring, St Brigid's Day, and they were in Frescati, Edward's childhood home by the sea. Julia dispatched Tony to find some reeds. 'I must show Ettie how to fashion a cross. She'll only learn heathen ways in this household.' She caught his look. 'Now don't say it,' she laughed, head tilted and looking like a bright thrush in the early morning. He pulled her to him.

'Can I whisper it then?' He murmured into her hair. 'Pagan Julia.'

She pulled free of him, her hands against his chest. 'Don't you be mocking me. I've a great devotion to St Brigid.' Her lips pressed together, trying not to smile. Julia's religion was altogether different from Lady Pamela's, though both called themselves Catholic. Her Ladyship believed in sacraments and priests, and the power of incense and holy oils. Julia believed in the earth and the seasons and the unseen spirits that governed them, and dark spells or piseogs. And those who had passed away but who never quite left. These sentiments chimed within him, struck some lost, forgotten key within him, made Julia both a mystery to him and someone he recognised deep in his bones.

'Enough of that look.' But her hand lingered on his chest, and the brief stroke of her fingers softened her words before she gave him a gentle shove. 'Go on away, down by the stream. You'll get some reeds there. And make sure you pull them from down low, near the water. I need good long strands. I'll put it above her bed, for spring blessings.'

It was a bright, hard morning, the water dripping dark and cold as he pulled up handfuls of reeds. He heard the sound of hooves before he saw the horse approach; it was Edward, clattering up the rough bridleway. He must have taken the road from Dublin at a gallop for he and his mount were in a lather of sweat and agitation.

'It's O'Connor. Arthur,' he blurted as he swung from the saddle, and stood chest heaving, hands loose by his sides as though still disbelieving. 'He's been arrested. They were waiting for us on Frederick Street, outside the hotel.' He ran a hand through his hair. 'Made no effort to resist. Seemed to embrace it even.'

'But who?'

He shrugged. 'Militia. Or Castle men. Didn't even identify themselves. Said he'd be taken to the Castle first.' He seemed to notice Tony for the first time, the pile of reeds by feet. 'What—'

Tony waved his hand. 'Doesn't matter. Tell me what happened.'

Edward's foot nudged the reeds. 'Arthur told me to rest easy. You'd swear he was the Christ and I, Peter. Or Judas, the betrayer.' He beat his crop against his boots with increasing ferocity. 'And the arresting officer, the impudent bastard, looked me up and down, and told me that I might rest easy for now, but not for long. "You'll follow your friend soon enough. There's another list, for another day, and you're at the top of it."'

'But what list?' Tony asked.

'I'm not sure but I will find out,' he replied, voice hard. 'And soon.'

Edward conveyed the news to the two Ladies in the large drawing room overlooking the spartan flowerbeds. Lady Lucy, in defiance of Ogilvie's instructions, had travelled to Frescati as soon as he had left Leinster House.

The pale chalky walls reflected the morning sun, filling the room with light, making a lie of the misery which occupied them. Beyond the gardens, and the brave snowdrops, the sea glittered indifferently. Lucy had fits of weeping, tugging sodden handkerchiefs, remaining in her nightwear though the hour pushed past midday. Her words marked time, regular as the great clock that stood sentry by the wall. 'What will happen to him? Why did he have to risk it all with that Address?' She reached for the paper, reading aloud: '"...The suspension of the Habeas Corpus Bill ... has destroyed the bulwark of liberty by withholding the Trial by Jury ... which by proving their innocence must establish its guilt ... Too long her slaves, we must shew her we are resolved to be FREE!" As he is not.' She slumped in her chair.

Tony attempted to rouse the fire, which hissed but gave no heat. The kindling was damp, the January storms having blown the cover off the wood pile outside.

'Don't bother with the fire Tony. Nothing can warm us now.' She rubbed her hand over her eyes, reminding him of little Ettie.

'Perhaps Milady would care for a warming drink?'

He was rewarded with a brief flicker of a smile, a slight shake of the head.

Edward was quiet, thoughtful. 'There was something about that arresting officer. That look. I could swear he knew me. I don't mean he just knew of me but that we have crossed paths before. And he did not like what he saw.'

Lady Pamela was less distraught than Lucy. Arrests were nothing new to her. In Paris, she said, no one was safe from being taken up. Every day someone arrested. Someone you knew. 'Friends of my mother. We used to visit them, bring them food, money for the guards.' Less distraught perhaps, but somewhat bewildered. 'And now here too, comme la Révolution. What will become of us?'

Edward smiled at her, kissed her cheek. 'Come Ladies, you need a walk. Take in the sights of Dublin. It will cheer you up.'

'Nothing will cheer me,' Lucy said.

Pamela turned from him. 'It's just as I feared. Like Paris. And what of you? What will happen?'

Edward knelt beside her. 'I know. I'm sorry.' They wrapped their arms about each other in silence.

Tony made to leave, but Edward looked up. 'No Tony, please can you bring the Ladies to Town. I didn't really mean a walk or at least not

256 256 LAURA MCKENNA

a purposeless one. They may be able to persuade the prison Governor to admit them, to see Arthur. I'm afraid my presence would destroy any possibility of seeing him.'

Lady Pamela was up in an instant. 'Tony, send Julia up to me. And Lucy, wear your best dress.'

There were no soft hearts at the Castle. Nor eyes that could be tempted by a best dress. Not among the party of redcoats by the gates, nor the sergeant who escorted the Ladies to the Tower. There, the Officer-in-charge repeated what they had been told already. Mr O'Connor was permitted no visitors. On the orders of the Lord Chancellor. There was no more to be said on the matter. 'If you please, the sergeant will escort you back.' The sergeant, a barrel-chested man, red-faced to match his jacket, was more inclined to talk, as they skirted around a troop of soldiers drilling in the vast cobbled yard, and made towards the gate. 'He's in there, your Mr O'Connor.' He pointed to the grim Tower, then smiled at Lady Lucy.

'Just keep walking,' Tony urged. They reached the archway and the guard posts.

'So you're Lord Edward's man,' the sergeant said, his eyes sliding over him. 'You should warn him about the company he keeps. Newgate is fast filling up with his friends. And Kilmainham Gaol.'

Lady Pamela turned around. 'Lord Edward is my husband. Do not speak of him so.'

The man's face reddened even more. 'Ah, the pretty French spy.'

His breathing was laboured, but his expression was one of satisfaction. Lady Pamela looked stunned. Lucy pulled her by the arm. 'Say nothing to him.'

Outside the Castle, the afternoon sun dragged long shadows from the high walls. The lane by the Bermingham Tower, where the Ladies hoped to catch a glimpse of O'Connor, was foul with the stench of excrement. Traders' voices rasped out their wares. A large muddied pig shuffled around the legs of beggars and bootblacks, stalls and barrows. A soberly attired pamphleteer stood on a box, haranguing indifferent passers-by. Lady Lucy paid no heed to the motley assemblage but kept repeating the sergeant's words: A French spy. That he should be so discourteous. Shocking. So brazen. Lady Pamela was more sanguine.

'C'est comme Paris.' She shrugged and put her arm around Lucy, who was gazing up at the Tower. Not for the first time, Tony wondered about what she had seen and heard during the Revolution when she was caught in the eddying currents of Royalists, Republicans and Orléanists.

The small, barred windows of the Tower gave no hint of its illustrious occupants. He felt a hand on his shoulder, stiffened. A voice insinuated warmly against his ear.

'Well, Mr Tony Small, are you lost? Not the best place for sightseeing, and in such high company.' It was Jerry O'Leary, O'Connor's manservant, dressed as though out for a walk through a country estate, all boots and long coat and jaunty hat. He acknowledged Tony's examination with a little bow. 'I must look like a gentleman's gentleman. Else they'd never let me in there. Ludicrous sense of rank, those servile redcoats.'

'Not so respecting the Ladies,' Tony replied.

Jerry bowed briefly to them, and they appeared almost as delighted to see him as they would have his master. 'Your Ladyships. I can offer you a better view.' He pointed to a second-floor window of the Tower. 'Now watch,' he said, sticking a finger and thumb in his mouth. He gave two short whistles, then a long-drawn-out one. A figure appeared at the window.

'It's him, it's Arthur.' Lucy blew him kisses back and forth, waved her handkerchief, cried. O'Connor held his hand out through the bars, waving slowly. Lady Pamela asked Jerry if he was allowed to visit, to wait on his master. O'Leary nodded.

'Of course. Twice a day, and I can bring small items – food, books – but no letters. He is a particularly voracious reader of books you know.'

'Yes. Such a vital mind. He'll find incarceration so burdensome.' Lucy was still looking at O'Connor.

'He has a particular fondness for marginalia. Reads even the tiniest of notes in the margins. And ...' O'Leary paused as though to pluck a rabbit from his sleeve, '... has been known to make some of his own before returning the books.' O'Leary should really audition for the Crow Street Theatre, Tony thought, as Lucy turned around, smiling.

Lady Pamela insisted on walking back to Leinster House, urging her sister-in-law to forgo a chair despite the chill, and the eager attentions of several chairmen at the bottom of Dame Street. 'We'll borrow a transport from brother William's house to Frescati and so save the fare on both a chair and a hire carriage.' When they reached the entrance to Leinster House, she turned, a smile playing around her mouth. 'Dear Monsieur Small, I trust you'll agree that I am capable of curbing unnecessary extravagances. I have saved us … how much do you think?'

'Four shillings for the chair and at least eight for hire of a carriage.'

'What does it matter?' asked Lucy. 'Had I known we would be walking the streets of Dublin, I would have worn walking boots, not these.' She poked a soiled shoe out from her skirts. 'Imagine I thought my careful toilette might impress some ignorant sergeant at the Castle. I should have garnered more attention in green petticoats and green bonnet, albeit the wrong kind. He never even glanced at me.'

'Better not to be noticed by the likes of him,' Tony said before taking his leave of them. He hurried to meet Jerry O'Leary as had been arranged, unable, since his time in Hamburg, to resist the lure of a coffee-house. This one on Poolbeg Street was noisy, an air of unrestrained discourse about the place, in addition to the familiar murk of burnt coffee and pipe smoke. Such diversity of ages and faces. A few reading newspapers, the rest raucous in debate. Tightly packed groups, with hands gesturing, pointing, banging the table, and raised voices giving way to laughter. He managed to find O'Leary without drawing anything other than disinterested glances on himself. Not even from the darkly attired black man, sitting with a newspaper. He slowed down as he passed him, noticed his spectacles, the attention he was giving to the paper. He was certain the man knew he was there but chose neither to greet nor acknowledge him. So be it, he thought, moving on. He was greeted with O'Leary's usual sly half-smile but his words were warm.

'It's good to see you, Tony.' O'Leary looked closely at him. 'Was that a friend of yours you passed on the way in?' He looked in the direction of the man with the spectacles.

'Just because he's black doesn't mean I know him,' he replied, irritated. Should he know every black man in the city?

'Ah. Thought perhaps you might have met. He's Cooke's man. You know, the Undersecretary at the Castle.'

Cooke who had every informer and spy in Dublin reporting to him. Was that why O'Leary had suggested they meet here? Was it to test him? Tony pushed back his chair.

'Sit, sit. Don't make a scene.' O'Leary hissed, then drained his cup. 'I thought maybe you could strike up a friendship—'

'Jerry. I may not know who he is, but I'm quite sure he knows who I am. So it's beyond unlikely that—'

'Yes, yes. It was just a flittering idea. Forget it.' He shouted to the serving boy, who carried a large tray of cups. 'Two more here.'

O'Leary's equanimity regarding his master's imprisonment was disconcerting.

'Sure he'll weasel out of it. A few months at worst and they'll let him go. Meantime he can pen a few more heroic lines on the margins of his books.' His grey eyes were watchful. 'You do know he receives gifts from ladies other than Lady Lucy.'

'How would I?' Tony answered.

'You will at least have heard he keeps a mistress?'

'Who would tell me?' He responded, wondering if Jerry was testing him again, when of course he knew about Mr O'Connor. He'd even seen him with his little boy once, outside his newspaper offices in Dublin, though O'Connor never acknowledged him nor referred to the matter later. His own business, Tony thought, not mine.

Tony remained on edge, trying to navigate between Jerry's easy banter and his artful questions, never knowing how much Jerry knew or how much he could say. This is how it must be for Edward all the time, he thought. He must conduct two levels of conversation with his friends and acquaintances. Always on his guard while maintaining a façade of guilelessness.

The True Narrative

Spring 1797, Dublin and the Author has an unpleasant reminder of his past; Ill-treatment by the Town Major; A parting at the Pigeon House.

Two weeks later I was again on the road to Dublin, this time not to convey the Ladies but to return a horse to the stables behind Leinster House. I had frequent occasions to ride, almost always in the company of Lord Edward. Taking a horse out alone afforded me the opportunity to go at my own pace, to look about me and gratify any whim of foolishness or curiosity. I could slow down to examine a new windmill being built near the outskirts of the city. I could direct the horse off the road and along a quiet lane onto the long stretch of sand that ran beyond the marshes at Blackrock, for almost a mile. I could urge my mount forward, give him his head and let him gallop along through the shallow water. Not a soul in sight but some cockle pickers at a distance, bending to their task.

The wind blowing hard and sea spraying up in glittering sunshine, the power of the animal beneath me, my movements, my directions all of my own choosing – it felt like freedom. Freedom of the moment, awareness of being alive in the world without a thought of my place in it. Once again I felt the providential hand of God, that ever supplied my wants and provided Succour for my weary heart.[41]

---

[41] If I did not know better, I would think these were the words of Equiano himself. You are quite artful Tony! LLF.

I slowed the horse to a trot, and turned him back along country lanes whose edges gleamed yellow with wildflowers, before meeting the main road again, busy with footfall and carts, then on through the village of Ballsbridge – its bleaching green spread with linens like sacrificial offerings to the God of Spring, and all the attendant acrid smells from the calico print works – before I reached Maquay Bridge by the new Grand Canal Dock, whose waters churned with the movement of countless heavily laden barges. I paused a moment, to embrace the observation of such industry and commerce as was displayed there and to wonder at the Ingenuity of modern man who could bend rivers to his will. It was then that I heard the approach of another horse, and turned to see an officer riding down Canal Street toward me, followed on foot, by a hurrying party of redcoats. He blocked my egress from the bridge, awaiting his marching soldiers.

'A black man on a horse. It could only be Lord Edward's pet black. His Faithful Tony.' The last was uttered with such derision that I was struck dumb. Something about the man plucked a chord of memory within me but no more revealed itself. He was large of build, greying at the temples, possessed of an angular face and dominant nose. His eyes flicked over me with an unsettling mixture of excitement and contempt. A look I recognised from the Carolinas, and the Indies, though one I thought I should never see in Ireland.

'But should one such as you be free to ride about the city?' he asked, and his lips pressed together in distaste. 'Does the horse belong to you, or have you stolen it? Have you papers to prove who you are?'

'You have just told me who I am, Sir. And the horse belongs to the Duke of Leinster, who desires its return at the earliest hour.'

Though my words were delivered with a steady equanimity, I felt the stirrings of anger and alarm in my belly. This man knew me on my own account, and appeared thus to dislike me on my own account. There was something familiar about him though I could not recall where we might have met.

'If you'll excuse me Sir, I must get to Leinster House, lest the Duke should ask for his horse.'

The officer's lips twitched plumply, and his nostrils flared. 'I doubt it. He has more horses than he knows what to do with. Sergeant!' he called, and a soldier pressed forward. 'Search this man. He is an associate of more than one conspirator. He may be carrying seditious material, or concealed weapons. The rest of you men, ready at arms.' They moved as one, hands smacking off wood and metal. Alarmed, my horse stamped fretfully and I struggled to control him. 'Dismount, now!' The officer barked, waving his pistol at my chest.

I had no choice but to submit to the sergeant's search, and knowing he would find nothing of import, was certain my liberty would soon be restored. I let my body submit but kept my head high. The sergeant treated my person with grim indifference, as though he rummaged through a clothes chest. He turned out my pockets and saddle bag, throwing onto the road two shillings, a knife and a book.

The officer demanded to see the book, exclaiming that books were used to secrete information. 'What's this? "The Interesting Narrative of the Life of Olaudah Equiano, or Gustavus Vassa, the African." I've heard of him. He may well be the exception to your kind but you, I suspect, fit the rule.'

Strange how old habits – those carved in the marrow and hidden all these past years – can resurrect themselves in response to a tone of voice. I stopped myself from looking up, from watching, as the officer flicked the pages, knowing better than to let him see my anxiety.

'This is all?' He demanded of his sergeant.

'Yessir. There's nothing else.' This man's voice conveyed only disinterest. I raised my eyes again in hope of the book's return to me. A stupid mistake, to have shown such hope. How could I have forgotten the necessary outcome of such encounters: humiliation, insults and plunder without any hope of redress. The officer seized on it, tore all the pages out with meticulous care and scattered them to the ground, then pulled his horse in tight, causing him to stamp the pages into the dirt. A few escaped, fluttering over the bridge, to settle on the barges below. A slow-burning rage began to gather itself in my breast. My hands tightened into angry fists. I would drag him off his horse, see him trampled in the dirt. I would submit no longer. I was a free man.

And then God stayed my hand and instead directed my tongue to speak the words of Mr Equiano: 'I would sooner die like a free man than suffer myself to be scourged by the hands of ruffians and my blood drawn like a slave.'

The officer laughed harshly. 'You are mistaken if you think I want to kill you. For you are the one who paves the way and lights the path of the great Lord Edward. I will catch him out because of you. Besides,' and he looked down at me with an expression approaching anguish, 'how would it serve me to kill one who saved my life, though it gives me nothing but revulsion to think on it.' He pulled aside his neck stock to reveal four tiny pale scars, crescentic in shape, as though formed by fingernails. 'Marked forever by your hand,' he spat, taking his pistol and dealing me a sudden blow to the head.

I fell on my hands and knees, stupefied, hooves churning around me as he turned his mount, shouted orders at his men and cantered off up Canal Street. I lay there until roused by my horse, who snuffled about my face. It was a dejected man who trotted into the stable yard behind Leinster House. Was this God's way, I wondered? To raise my spirits earlier, give me a sense of freedom and self, only to dash such high feelings, and reduce me to wretchedness? I had no answer.[42]

Edward was in the study at Frescati, reading through his letters. Some still arrived by the conventional post – letters from his mother, from his aunts and Ogilvie – but all those showed signs of interference. The letters were refolded incorrectly, the seals cracked and carelessly waxed over.

'Ah, you're back,' he said, tossing a letter towards him. 'Smell this. Mutton grease.'There was a greasy stain on the corner.'Mother would never ...'He laughed but there was tightness in it. 'It seems my Aunt Louisa has been writing to Mother. Filling her head with tales of Arthur and prison visits, and Lucy's displays at the Castle ball. Of course she doesn't quite put it like that. She knows too well my post is not safe.'He reached for the

[42] Oh Tony, I didn't know of this incident. The vile Sirr. I was moved, almost to tears, by the ill-treatment you suffered at his hand. LLF.

offending letter again, read aloud a passage to Tony. "'… I am concerned for my Dear Lucy. I hear she has not been well, having been exposed to all manner of dangerous and capricious weather. I believe she has taken quite a fever, that continues unabated despite my urging her to take precautions. You and I know that such a fever is dangerous and unlikely to be cured by anything other than removal to London where I can look after her. Mr Ogilvie also feels very strongly on this matter.'"

'The fever being Mr O'Connor, I assume.'

Edward smiled briefly. 'Aunt Louisa will have heard from Castlereagh. A soft word in her ear. All couched with concern for the family. Though perhaps there is something in it.' He tossed the letter back on the desk, picked up a penknife and began pressing it into the leather top, making tiny nicks. He looked dishevelled as though he'd slept in his clothes last night. His shirt was crumpled, and he was unshaven.

'Were you out all night?' Tony asked.

'Almost.' He slumped back in the chair. The morning sun was harsh on his face and he closed his eyes against the glare.

'By the way. You were right about the arresting officer. You do know him. Major Sirr is the Sheriff. The same Sirr—'

'—from Gibraltar. Of course. His jug face was familiar, the one you saved. How did you find out?'

'I had an encounter with him near the canal this morning. He knew me immediately and couldn't seem to decide if he should shake my hand or shoot me. Instead he struck me with his pistol.'

Edward was on his feet. 'Damn. First Arthur and now you.' He shook his head. 'Are you alright? I see now, your eye … how did I not notice … all my prattling on … have you attended to it?'

'They patched me up in the kitchens at Leinster House. It's nothing.'

Silence sat with them for a few moments.

'I suppose he was never happy with either of us after that incident on the Rock, was he? Still I never thought …' He shook his head again, and banged the heel of his hand against his forehead.

'Just so you know, he believes I will betray you.'

Edward looked startled.

'By my presence. Something about paving the way and lighting your path. He has a point.'

'Please don't say you'll go elsewhere for a position. I need you. The number of people I can truly trust is dwindling by the day. Most are here in this house.' He knew Tony was going nowhere. 'Let's have a drink. Whiskey?' He poured two glasses without waiting for an answer. Tony sat, gulped back a good measure. It ran like fire down his throat, warming his belly.

Edward was talking, with his eyes closed. 'At night, I dream sometimes I'm on an island. A small one. The waves are taking it away bit by bit, getting closer to me every day as I scramble to stay dry. I wake thinking my feet are wet ...'

The room held on to another silence. Ten minutes passed, twenty.

Edward sighed. 'I think I'll do as Mother asks, bring Lucy to London. In the next month or so. I have someone to meet there.'

'And what will Lady Lucy think of this?'

'I don't know. It'll satisfy most parties, though not, I suspect, Lucy.' A pause. 'Tony. I want to ask you something.' Tony turned away from the view of the green lawn pierced by shafts of daffodils. Edward continued, 'You don't like Mr O'Connor.'

How to answer that. It wasn't even a question of liking. He could see why Edward was so attached to him. The man was clever and quick-witted, he spoke with great passion. He charmed the Ladies by seeming to reproach himself constantly. But there was something about him. It was not so much a question of trust or least it was not that he thought him a spy. There was a cold, hard centre in the man. A selfishness. But he could not give voice to it.

'I think ... the Duchess is right, it would be better for Lady Lucy to be away from Dublin.'

'Hah, you're a master of avoidance. I won't press you – I'm not sure I want to hear what you really think.'

Two Masters of Avoidance, he thought.

Edward sighed, then reached for the locked drawer in his desk.

'In case you were wondering about that other letter, the one last week, from America – and don't protest because I know you observe everything – I think I'd like you to see it.'

He remembered the letter alright, had seen the postmarks clearly stamped. Had noticed Edward's response to it, the tension as he broke the seal, and how he'd folded it away immediately without comment. But now Edward took it out and turned it over in his hands. 'I wasn't going to show you this. Felt too much like trying to salve my conscience. But now ...' He held it out to him. 'Read it. I'd prefer if you knew, even if I can't exactly say why.'

Tony took it. The seal was plain wax, no mark. He unfolded it slowly, noted the scrawling hand and the address. He looked at Edward, who turned away, putting on a coat with great deliberation. 'I'll leave it with you. I'm going for a walk with my two Pamelas, down to the sea.'

St Louis
December 1796

My Dear Sir,

I hope you will excuse the liberty I take in writing to you without a formal introduction. However I do so on behalf of a Miss Esther, whom I have reason to believe you may recall from your visit here in 1789.

Permit me to introduce myself. My name is Charles Brazeau, and I am a man of business in this thriving town of St Louis. I too can lay claim to an acquaintance with Miss Esther who is, I'm sure you'll agree, a rather remarkable negress. She wishes that I make known to you the existence of a certain child who shares the same name as yourself, Edward FitzGerald. He is some six years of age and a fine-looking boy if I am any judge of such matters.

Mr Jacques Clamorgan is of a mind to sell the boy. And Miss Esther thinks you may, as a matter of conscience, wish to provide monies to secure his release. She would like you to know that, thanks to the monies you sent from New Orleans, she finally persuaded Mr Clamorgan, only last year mind, to permit her to purchase her own freedom. By means of hard work and astute

business transactions, she reckons she will soon have
sufficient funds to buy her daughter.

The matter of the boy is more urgent and I am willing
to act as a broker on your behalf should you feel inclined to
proceed. Miss Esther believes that it is better that your name
does not appear on any transactions as, according to her, Mr
Clamorgan is a man with a great appetite for vengeance. She
says you will know the meaning of this.

And so to business. I have already acted in the capacity
of godfather to the boy (at the request of Mr Clamorgan)
and ensured he has been baptised into our church here in
St Louis. I would be honoured to oversee his continuing
religious instruction and his formal education.

As a gentleman, I am reluctant to broach the crass matter of
the costs but as I may not have further opportunity of contacting
you, I must be open with you on this matter. I estimate that the
sum of one hundred pounds would be sufficient to provide the
correct papers for the boy, and allow for his education over the
next four years. I can assure you that I will handle the specifics of
this matter with the utmost discretion.

I remain your humble servant,
Mr Charles Brazeau

Paid: The sum of £300, LEF

He had sent money from New Orleans almost seven years before. Never
said a word to me. Enough for Esther to buy her own freedom. And then
this news of a child. He didn't know whether to laugh or to swear. He saw
Edward from the window, watched as he walked with Lady Pamela, the
child on his shoulders clapping her little hands. They moved through the
long grass of the untended lawn, towards the mute sea beyond.

Tony folded the letter away, replaced it in the drawer and turned
the key again. He never spoke of it. There may have been a gesture of
acknowledgement, a look. Nothing else. But something changed with
the knowing of it.

He accompanied a silent brother and sister out to the Pigeon House to await the packet in Dublin Bay. They sat in the newly built hotel, drinking glasses of wine, while Lady Lucy refused the stew, refused to talk, stared through the rain-slashed window at the angry sea beyond. The dining room was packed with waiting passengers, sitting cramped together in damp clothes giving off smells of bodies, of dank wool, of greasy food. Tony thought of Julia, who was not happy that he was going to London. 'Leaving us again.' Her face a tight storm of fury. Like Lucy's. Lucy who got up, without a word to either of them and pushed through the inn and out the door.

'Tony, would you mind going after her? She won't speak to me or forgive me. Thinks I'm trying to separate her from Arthur.'

He sensed his eyebrows lifting involuntarily, and cursed himself. He used to be able to control his face, his expression, keep all his thoughts inside. The last few years, they'd been slipping out, proclaiming themselves on his face. He needed to remain on guard. Perhaps not with Julia, or even Edward, but with others …

'I know. You're right,' Edward shrugged. 'Lucy's right. But it's not for the reasons she thinks. At least not entirely. What's to be gained by her tainting herself with this association? She can't choose her brother but she can choose her husband, though she decries any such interest in Arthur.'

Lucy had wandered out along the Great South Wall. Rain swept in across the water, or perhaps it was spittle from the waves which beat and thrashed on the inner rocks. The wind had taken hold of her, sending her coat billowing and flapping wildly. Her hair had come loose – no sign of her hat – dark, coppery strands flying about her wet face. Her arms were wrapped around her. Was she crying? Should he intrude?

'Your Ladyship.' He stood beside her.

She remained silent, staring at the sea. He glanced at her profile, so like Edward's. Everything written on that face. The mutinous mouth, the stormy brow. She never felt the need to conceal her feelings. A freedom afforded by those with money. Or freedom itself. Though

Lucy did not have the look of one with such privilege. She was looking down at her hands.

'It's all wrong you know. They have it all wrong.'

'Milady?'

'It's not just Mr O'Connor. They treat me like a silly weak thing, that needs to be protected. Saved from myself. Mama, Mr O. Especially Mr O.' She kicked at a stone by her foot. 'I thought I was part of it. I want to be involved in it. It's been exciting.' Another stone went flying. 'And it's not just for diversion.' She turned to him. 'I believe in it. All of it. Ireland should have her own government, not be ruled by the damned English. And Mama should stop trying to change my mind. She encouraged all of us to think of ourselves as Irish. So what does she expect of me? To adopt the pretty parts, the music and poetry? But not this uncertain future?'

'They're concerned for you, Milady. Lest you should get too caught up. I think the Castle and their soldiers would not be averse to arresting a woman. Perhaps not even a Lady, if there's a war.'

She was crying. Crying and raging. Two seagulls settled on the wall and were mewling in concert with her.

'So Edward may do as he please, risk everything? I must go home and be dutiful? Why then does he trust me with some tasks? Like the delivery of a letter to his *friend* in London, to be passed on to Lady Pamela's cousin, Henriette, in Hamburg. Is that why he's sending me home? Making use of me? You know I have the letter sewn into the lining of this coat. Shall I show you?'

He put his hand up and she laughed. 'Of course I won't. Nor anyone else. I know what it contains, like many others I've passed on. The *green* silk scarf he mentions for dear Henriette's *arms*, that he always admired? I hope to God the spies do not read that one for they won't need a cipher to work it out. Edward could use a little more subtlety but he won't take advice from me.' She looked down at her feet, scuffed the ground. 'Still, why should he? That's only one letter among hundreds that he has sent. He works so hard. No. I don't blame him for my removal from Ireland.'

'I'm glad. It really is because they fear for you—'

'It's Ogilvie. The man who thinks a tutor's job is never done. Always interfering. Whispering in Mother's ear. Telling her what to do, what to write. Do you know what she wrote to me, before he last visited? She said I should hear all he has to say without interrupting him. That I should not be short or decisive or refuse plump to do as he advised.'

Tony coughed. 'If I may, I can't imagine anyone telling the Duchess what to do.'

'Oh, you know what I mean. She'd do anything to please her Dearest Mr Ogilvie. He's just afraid for the family name.'

Perhaps he was right to be. 'Please Milady, won't you come back inside. If you go home with a chill, the blame will be placed at Lord Edward's door.'

She picked up a large stone, fired it at the wall, at the two sea birds. They flapped and rose, legs dangling, while they squawked with indignation. Lucy turned to him.

'Well, we can't have dear Edward being blamed for that, I suppose. He has enough to carry.' She touched his arm for a moment. 'I'm glad he has you to look out for him.' She smiled wanly, and her hand still rested on his sleeve. 'Faithful Tony. That's what he used to call you. When he wrote from Canada. Did you know?'

Another of his names. 'Yes Milady, I knew.'

They walked back together towards the hotel only to find the besieged, would-be passengers spilling out, looking for carriages to take them back to the city. There would be no packet today. Those spring storms, so unexpected, would allow no boats in to Dublin Bay.

Edward had already secured a car, one of those odd jingles. He held the door open for Lucy. She said nothing but turned and kissed his cheek before she got in. Edward threw Tony a look, mouthing something silently.

They returned the following day; another uncomfortable hour or two spent awaiting the arrival of the boat. But on that occasion, Lucy was calm and less disposed to fight with Edward.

Sacred
To the Memory of
WILLIAM ORR
Who was offer'd up at Carrickfergus, on Saturday, the
14th of Oct. 1797
An awful Sacrifice to
IRISH FREEDOM
On the Altar of British Tyranny,
By the hands of Perjury,
Thro' the influence of Corruption
And the connivance of
PARTIAL JUSTICE!
O! Children ERIN! When ye forget him
His wrongs, his death, his cause,
The injured RIGHTS OF MAN;
Nor these revenge.—
May you be debarr'd THAT LIBERTY he
Sought, and forgotten in the Hist'ry of Nations;
Or, if remember'd,
Remember'd with disgust and execration,
Or nam'd with scorn and horror!
No, Irishmen! Let us bear him in steadfast
Memory;
Let his fate nerve the martial arm
To wreak the Wrong of ERIN
And assert her undoubted Claims —
Let ORR be the watch-word to LIBERTY

THE TRUE NARRATIVE

December 1797, and Lord Edward and Arthur O'Connor attend the Trial of Peter Finnerty.

Of course His Lordship was not merely accompanying his sister home to the safety of her family and England, but he had arranged a meeting to take place somewhere outside London. A private meeting with a man called J—. A sort of intermediary. Some might call him a spy. For the French.

On his return, he spent much of the summer supporting friends who had the misfortune to come before the courts charged with involvement with the outlawed United Irish. He secured the release of his Dear Friend, Mr Arthur O'Connor, by paying a large sum of money for his bail – some of which he had secured against his estate at Kilrush with a view to providing for his family.[43] Lord Edward was most affected by the trial and execution of William Orr. Though he had never met him, the names of all those Northern men (Mr N—n, and Mr R—l among them) – held in prison without trial for over a year – were known to everyone with an interest in the Rights of Man. That Mr Orr should have been convicted when so many others were eventually released, led my Master to believe it was the man's very insignificance, his genteel Presbyterian background and moral character, that was his undoing.

[43] Tony, this must end. LLF.

It was judicial murder of a good man. In court Mr Orr addressed the Judge – who later wept (what manner of tears) when passing the dreadful sentence – and his words were oft repeated by Lord Edward.

'If to have loved my country, to have known its wrongs, to have felt the injuries of the persecuted Catholics, and to have united with them and all other religious Persuasions ... if these be felonies, then I am a felon, but not otherwise.'

Lord Edward kept a memorial card about his person though the discovery of such was cause enough to be taken up. His days of attending balls, or any of the pleasurable entertainments available to the ruling classes, were largely over. His most public outings took place in the courts in Dublin or at the country Assizes where he made a point of making visible his support for his fellows who had suffered arrest. Before Christmas he and Arthur O'Connor listened to the futile defence arguments of that great orator and lawyer, Mr Philpot Curran, at the trial of the printer of The Press. That paper, Mr O'Connor's own, had published all manner of letters and poems relating to the execution of Mr Orr, to the dismay of the Lord Lieutenant. But it was the young printer, a Mr Peter Finnerty, who bore the burden of responsibility for printing seditious and libellous material, and was duly sentenced to imprisonment, with a spell in the pillory first as a public humiliation.

'Tony, bring Ogilvie's walking stick.'

'A stick? Damn it Edward, at least bring a sword.' O'Connor had already belted his in place. 'There'll likely be a riot in there.'

'All the more reason not to carry a sword.' Edward was firm. 'You should remove yours. You're not all that well acquainted with its use. Besides the stick is for Tony, so he can come to our aid. Isn't that so, Tony?'

'Yes Milord.'

O'Connor muttered under his breath, tossed the sword aside.

They clattered out of Frescati's courtyard and on to the Dublin road. The new year was almost upon them, and the day was cold, the sea reflecting the weight of cloud above. There was little conversation. O'Connor was in foul humour. Tony tried to read him. The thought of Finnerty on the pillory outside Newgate, no doubt. Did he feel guilt?

Had he thought there would be no repercussions for printing such things in his paper? The matter was wholly O'Connor's doing – he had Finnerty registered as owner, despite it being entirely his own, and for what purpose other than to avoid being held responsible?

'That poor bastard.' O'Connor voiced Tony's thought exactly but with such vehemence that his horse was alarmed and pulled forward.

'Easy Arthur,' Edward called after him. 'There's little to be gained by giving way to anger.'

'I should have left it in my name. It shouldn't be him in Newgate.'

'You'll be there soon enough again if you keep this up.'

The city had spilled out on to the streets. Tony, having stabled the horses, pressed past the darkly dressed men who normally sat totting up columns of numbers in Dublin's money houses and merchant institutions; past bootblacks and butchers, ironmongers and chandlers who seemed to have left their places of work still wearing aprons and bearing the tools of their trade. There were women too. A surprise. Some of them gentlewomen, by the cut of their dress. The mood was good-humoured enough. What were they doing there? Was it to jeer the man or protest at his treatment? The closer they got to Green Street and the grey bulk of Newgate, the quieter the crowd became.

Tony saw some familiar faces from Edward's circle, McNevin with Oliver and Mrs Bond, all deep in conversation. Bond waved at him and pointed to Edward.

The pillory was mounted on a large wooden stage opposite the Sessions House encircled by a guard of soldiers from the Armagh Militia. Tony pushed forward and reached Edward just as Finnerty was led up the steps. The crowd responded with roars and curses. Tony was still unclear if the target of abuse was Finnerty or the soldiers.

'Stay with me,' Edward hissed to Tony and he approached one of the men at the foot of the steps. The soldier raised his gun, bayonet pointing.

'Let me pass, I wish to stand with my friend.'

'Stay back with the rest of the rabble or you'll feel the sharp end of this.' The soldier's hands shook, the rifle wavering. His greasy face reddened. A stone landed at his feet, flung from deep in the crowd. The other privates turned their weapons on Edward and O'Connor. Tony gripped the stick with both hands. O'Connor reached for where his sword should have been.

'Edward be damned,' he hissed.

On the platform Sheriff Paisley quickly read out the order of the Court and Finnerty was bound in the pillory. The crowd booed and shouted. Edward held out his hands, palms upward, to the soldier.

'I will join my friend.'

The redcoat jabbed his bayonet, shouting. 'Get back, all of you. You have it coming.' He lunged at Edward but Tony stepped in front, slamming the walking stick down on the rifle with a sharp clunking sound. O'Connor tugged Edward back. The soldier turned on Tony, his face meaty with sweat and anger.

'You black bastard.'

He struck Tony in the chest with the butt of the rifle, and he fell into the press of the crowd. The other soldiers scuffled forward. The crowd seemed to hold their breath.

'Put down your weapons. Who is the Officer in command here?' The Sheriff shouted down from the platform, before descending the steps, pressing his bulk between the soldiers, addressing an officer.

'Sir, ensure these men do not act without orders.' He looked at Edward and O'Connor. 'Let these two pass.'

A cheer went up from the crowd.

'And their man too.'

In a low voice he addressed the officer, a fresh-faced boy. 'Get control of these men unless you want a riot.'

The Guard stepped aside and the small party climbed the steps and stood beside Finnerty, locked into the pillory. He was a slight man, dark-haired and pale of face. Already his hands were purple. His voice shook a little as he shouted out.

'My friends, you see how cheerfully I can suffer; I can suffer anything provided it promotes the liberty of my country.'

The crowd cheered and whooped. The Sheriff turned on him. 'Not another word or I'll give that Officer free rein.'

The crowd fell silent again. Some walked away, the promise of a spectacle seemingly over. The party at the pillory spoke in conversational tones. Finnerty related how he'd been threatened with torture to reveal the identity of the author of the 'damnable seditious letter'.

'Two days before the alderman and his men. Called me every sort of name. Teague, fucking papist bastard, straw man for the United Irish traitors. Wasn't difficult to say nothing.'

O'Connor had turned pale. Edward muttered to Finnerty, 'You are a true patriot.'

The Sheriff frowned. 'You'll have to leave if there's any more talk like that.'

A cold wind funnelled down Green Street, disrupting a line of pigeons who were looking down on the proceedings from the session house gutter. They flapped awkwardly, trying to find balance. Finnerty twisted his wrists, the skin now raw and red.

'Gentlemen,' he spoke quietly. 'You really shouldn't have come. I thought there was going to be slaughter there, and 'twould take all the attention from me. But I'm glad of your company.'

He attempted to laugh. O'Connor reached out a hand to him but faltered, ruffling the man's hair instead. 'We are humbled by yours,' he said.

Tony eyed O'Connor. He appeared genuinely distressed. People could still surprise him.

He handed O'Connor a flask of rum. 'Sir, shall I or would you …?'

O'Connor seized it. 'Certainly I will. Thanks Tony.' He held it to Finnerty's mouth. 'I hope it's strong,' he said grimly. Liquid dribbled from the man's lips.

The sky darkened and a wintry drizzle descended, driving off the more elegant of the crowd. A few persisted. An elderly man, formally dressed in a wig and dress coat, harangued not Finnerty but Edward, calling him a traitor to his class and country. His words were cheered by a small party who stood with him. Edward didn't respond.

Tony found it difficult to stand beside Finnerty, to witness his discomfort. At last as darkness threatened to envelop them, and the drizzle turned to snow, the Sheriff gave the signal. Finnerty was removed and marched back into Newgate to serve his two years.

'Hopefully I'll emerge to a brighter dawn,' he said. 'Isn't that what I'm supposed to say?'

His companions made no reply.

In the back hallway at Frescati the gentlemen removed their boots, leaving them in slushy puddles, staining the patterned oilcloth on the floor. Snow clung to their coats, which Tony carried into the kitchen to dry. When he returned the men were padding along in stockinged feet to the study and he joined them there. The fire was burning, the room almost warm. Edward dug his hands into his waistcoat and removed two small pistols.

O'Connor turned from the cabinet where he was pouring out whiskey. 'You were carrying those all the time? And you told me not to take my sword?'

'A sword is little use against an armed guard. One thrust and they'd have shot you down. But these …' He tested them in his hands. 'These could be quite effective.' He handed them to Tony. 'You know where to put them.'

'Damn you, Edward. You talk caution but prepare for battle.'

'Better than the other way round.'

Tony replaced the pistols in the dark velvet compartment at the base of Edward's writing box. He clicked the letters' shelf in place on top and closed over the lid. O'Connor sat in front of the fire, stretching his soiled, stockinged feet to the flames. 'You know I put *The Press* back in my name at the start of Finnerty's trial. May even see the circulation increase. Who knows?'

THE TRUE NARRATIVE

March 1798, Dublin and some account of Lord Edward's business and the happenings of the time; Mr O'Connor is arrested again; The Author is wary of his Master's visitor; Arrests at Mr Bond's house; The Author warns Lord Edward that the Town Major has come to Leinster House with a warrant for his arrest.

The first two months of 1798 were marked more by Edward's absence than by his presence. He was in Belfast, Kildare, Wexford, Kilkenny, everywhere. I endeavoured to keep busy, to bring about some minor repairs and improvements at Frescati but though it may seem harsh to say so, it was a household of women and children and I was rarely needed.

It is possible for a servant to be privy to the most intimate details of his Master's life but not always the most important. This became increasingly true of me. As the weeks went by, I saw little of Edward and knew even less about his associates. This not knowing felt dangerous, left me feeling anxious for my Master, and prey to unnamed fears and suspicions.

On his brief visits to his family, Edward was edgy, talked at length and couldn't sleep. Or he was morose, refusing food and only able to sleep. His face was gaunt with the strain of travel, of meetings, of organising and training of men, of manufacturing weapons. The Rebellion could not be put off. The Rebellion must be put off to wait for the French. So many opinions, divisions and indecisions. The hidden armies of the United Irish must wait, couldn't wait. Everyone was on a knife edge.

'And not even O'Connor to rally me. He's still in London. Being entertained by Sheridan and his set.' Edward had received word from Lucy. 'Listen to this "... so wonderful to have Dear Mr O'Connor with us. I am pleased to say that with all of our lively conversation and entertainments, we have banished the melancholy cast of his face, and he says he is finding it very difficult to drag himself away from our company. We only wish you could join us. Please say you will and bring dearest Pamela ..." She wishes I could join them!' He threw the letter on the floor.

'You know Tony, I'm not sure if this is code or not. I actually believe Arthur is enjoying himself while we ... I am saddle-sore and throat-sore and my head aches. And what of the French? What is going on?'[44]

Is there a moment that proves to be the beginning? The beginning of the end? The tipping point. There was certainly a month, if not a moment. March. And word came of O'Connor's arrest at Margate, trying to take a boat to France. It was terrible news.

'As bad as it gets,' Edward said. A hanging offence. Caught red-handed, and with Edward's cipher in his possession. 'How could he be so careless?'

Tony had no answer. What could he say either to the news that O'Connor was being held in the Tower of London? 'Your friend too, his man O'Leary,' Edward added.

Word blew across the Irish sea from every source: newspapers, pamphlets and friends. Edward's cousin Fox sent on a message of his visit to O'Connor in the Tower where he found him in an anxious and melancholy state.

Strangely, this report served to brace Edward's flagging spirits. More secret meetings followed, usually at night, at Frescati, where the narrow rear bridleway became muddied, while the main entrance was untouched by hoof fall. They came in small groups of two or three. Tony knew most of them by name, had met them many times over

---

[44] What is going on indeed? You must stop Tony. Who are you writing this for? And you must use his proper title when you write my brother's name. Remember this Narrative is for posterity. We shall all be judged by its contents. LLF.

the previous few years. Fine men all. They repaired to the study, often closeted there for hours amid smoke and wine and uneaten plates of cold meat. Tony's orders were always the same. To prepare the room and the refreshments and go back and wait on Lady Pamela. 'Both of you must be able to say in truth that you were not in attendance and you witnessed nothing. Whatever happens, Lady Pamela must not be tainted by this.'

Fine men indeed. For the most part. Not all.

Mr Thomas Reynolds, of Kilkea Castle arrived unannounced one evening in March. He stood in the drizzling rain, looking as dejected as his mount, no longer parading his green jacket, nor his jovial bluster. He forbore to hand over his soiled, wet coat. He would stay just a minute; no need to stable his horse either. Tony watched him, saw how his eyes looked past him, how he flinched at Edward's warm greeting and prattled when Edward enquired about the purpose of his visit.

'Oh social, social, I came on a whim,' Tony heard him say. His clasped hands, his tight mouth, his rigid frame in the fireside chair belied his words.

'Not the best evening for it, Thomas,' Edward observed, handing him a brandy. The visitor looked up, his brow furrowed as if to discern his meaning.

'Rain,' Edward explained. 'You may leave us, Tony.'

He left, but a feeling of unease did not.

He found occasion to walk past the study door several times but heard nothing. No laughter, which usually marked even the most tense meetings with the members of the Directorate. Eventually the man left, ignoring Tony as he held the door for him. He looked more dejected than when he'd arrived, his shoulders slumped and a tremor in his hands as he stuffed some papers in his pockets, fumbled for the reins of his horse.

'Safe journey, Mr Reynolds,' Tony said.

Afterwards he returned to the study, unable to quell the worm of unease that had grown in him. Edward was flicking through a heap of papers. Tony gestured at them. 'Are those from Mr Reynolds?'

They were not. The meeting had improved Edward's spirits much as they had drained his visitor's. 'I took advantage of the poor man,' he said. 'He came on a social call and has left as a member of the Leinster Provincial.'

'He didn't look happy.'

'He underestimates his abilities.'

'There's something about him … you should be careful.'

'If I am any more careful, I will never leave this house again.'

'You didn't give him anything, did you?'

'Nothing he doesn't already know. It's just spelt out now in black and white for him to convince the members that we can't wait for France. I've asked him to deliver the count for Kildare. Ten thousand men ready to answer the call.'

'Still, I can't help but—'

'Tony, I cannot be everywhere and speak with everyone. Others must play a part.'

They moved back to Leinster House once martial law was declared. Edward couldn't suffer others to take risks that he would not. That huge house was empty save for their tiny household and a few servants. They saw nothing of the Fitzgerald family, or the Conollys who were barricaded into their country estate at Castletown terrified of their tenants, of Defenders, of the United Irish and even of the Yeomanry who might at any time seize the very weapons they needed for protection. Dublin itself was taut with fear and terror. The soldiers or Militia, whatever they were, needed no trial, no justice but their own. And they dispensed it wherever they wished. A man strung up to a triangle of posts, whipped. A cat-of-nine-tails. Another, hanged from Sackville Bridge when he refused to give up the names of his fellow United men. Got to the point of creeping about the shadows, lest you might be stopped. Might even suffer the pitchcap just on a mere suspicion. Tony had smelt it himself one evening, off in the distance. Burning skin and hair. And heard the screams. Everyone seemed to be suspect. White skin was no protection in Dublin.

In his sleep, Julia said, Tony twitched and jerked like a man dangling from a noose.

On a bright morning in the middle of March, a young lad staggered up Stable Lane and collapsed in the courtyard, where Tony had just finished tending to Edward's horse. The boy's lungs were creaking for want of air. 'Ran all the way from Bridge Street,' he gasped. 'The Town Major, redcoats, marched 'em all out and ... away to the Castle.'

'Who?' he asked, alarmed, for Edward had departed earlier, on foot as usual, leaving no word of his destination.

''Twas Mr Bond's house,' the boy stuttered.

'Ssh.' Tony brought him to the kitchen, down to the cold store, saw to some milk for him, and closed the door behind them.

Oliver Bond's house on Bridge Street. Where the United men met. The leaders of the Leinster Directorate including – 'Did you see Lord Edward?'

No he did not, he was not among them. 'But the rest walked out under guard ... heads high ... and the crowd shouting and roaring ...' The boy could not stop. His voice gasped and stuttered.

Where was Edward?

For the next three hours they waited: Tony, Julia and Lady Pamela gathered in the upper apartment, not knowing who would come first, Edward or soldiers. They were a shipwrecked crew huddled in an open boat, at the mercy of the vagaries of the seas. Leinster House, despite its vastness, was a flimsy, empty place that offered no protection; its huge windows were unshuttered, gaping dull-eyed at the surrounding streets; no bars held the main door and only a small winter household was in occupation.

Once again he was useless. Everything happening at a distance. Beyond burning some letters on Lady Pamela's insistence and hiding some maps belonging to Edward, he could do nothing. Nothing but wait. Always waiting. Wondering if he should go and find Edward, warn him or whether, as the bastard Sirr had said, that risked drawing soldiers to him. From the kitchens below to the servants' quarters above, there was hardly a sound beyond the shifting hiss of the fire and Lady Pamela's tired weeping as she lay, large with child, in a heap of blankets on the sopha. Little Pammie played on the floor beside her, stirring a spoon in an empty bowl and then holding it up for her mother's attention. Lady Pamela patted her head.

'I cannot rest. I cannot eat. My mouth is filled with worry.' Lady Pamela waved her hands as though banishing a spirit. 'Take her from me, Julia.'

Julia lifted the child, who wailed, 'Maman, Maman.'

'Ma petite. Ma bebé. I must have her back with me.' The arms were outstretched, and pleading. Julia sighed and placed Pammie back beside her mother on the sopha.

'Perhaps a little draught might help Milady to rest.'

Lady Pamela looked up sharply. 'Tu es stupide, Julia?'

He heard Julia's sharp intake of breath, and watched as she returned stiffly to the chair behind the sopha. Tony turned his attention back to the window. No sign of him. But then he was unlikely to march up to the front door. He'd have heard about the warrant for his arrest.

The silence stretched. Who would come for him? Militia? Soldiers? Major Sirr?

Lady Pamela raised her head from the sopha, looked across at him. He shook his head.

'Perhaps you should go, cherchez pour ...' She stopped. She had heard it too. The scuffing of boots. No mistaking the sound. And not one man. They'd sent a party around the rear entrance as well. He could see them in his mind's eye, darting across the courtyard. And then there was no need to imagine them. Through the window he saw soldiers hurrying through the large gateway at the front, across the gravel to the steps below.

'They're here.'

All was quiet inside. Not a breath exhaled. Even the child on the floor was still, though her eyes widened as she looked from her mother to Julia. And there, the knocking, loud and repeated.

Lady Pamela struggled to sit upright. 'Julia, aide moi.'

She clutched at Julia's hand. She was helpless, her belly large, despite being months from her time.

'Find him, Tony.' Perhaps not so helpless after all. 'He must not come to us. Tell him to stay away no matter what he hears.'

The soldiers were inside. Urgent voices, boots clicking and slapping across the marble floor, up the stairs. He slipped out the concealed panelled door into the back hall, running now, his breath on a leash. The grey walls tunnelled ahead, on and on. Down the twisting back stairs, ricocheting off each turn, into the wide open passage below, heading for the wooden door at the end. Blood drumming in his ears. No one stepped out to block his path but every shadow was a hidden tracker, the softest sound a rifle cocked. A hot sweet smell as he pushed through to the stables. The horses were uneasy, their ears flicking, hooves shifting on the straw. He slowed just in time. Two soldiers stood at the entrance. Back into the shadows. He slipped the latch on one stall, then the next. One more. Picking up a broom, he murmured an apology to the horse in the first stall and lashed the coarse brush across the animal's flank. The horse shrieked and reared, setting the others in motion. One darted from the stall to the entrance, just as the two soldiers turned into the stables to investigate the disturbance. The three horses were oblivious in their haste to exit, knocking them aside, hooves trampling the fallen men. He slipped out as the pair were still reeling and bloodied on the ground.

Once more he was back on the streets, trying to be inconspicuous. He cursed his position: to be Crusoe among the islanders, to stand out so when all he wanted was to hide, to see and not be seen. It was a frosty, cloudless day, and the March sun a cold white eye, interrogating his every movement. Surprisingly he was not stopped. No one seemed to notice him. He slowed down, walked with purpose, his mind sharpened. Where would Edward hide out? He wouldn't risk going to the homes of any of the Executive. Too dangerous, besides most were probably under arrest. Where would he go? Where was the safest place? Suddenly he knew; the safest place would be the last place he'd find Edward. He doubled back, trying not to run, veered into the grounds of a church, out the other side, across, down Johnson's Court, forcing himself to slow down again. To be just a servant about his business among other busy people. Not making eye contact. Not seeing a man stagger out of an eating house until he went smack into him and a hail of curses descended until Tony pulled back and recognised him.

'Mr Reynolds, your pardon Sir.' The man eyed him warily. He looked even more dishevelled than the last time Tony had seen him at Frescati.

'Mr Reynolds. I wonder if you might have chanced upon Lord Edward? I am—'

The man pulled back. 'How should I know anything about him. I don't know his business nor anyone's for that matter. Who are you to question me? Why would you think to ask me?' He was sweating, breathing heavily and reeked of wine or port. His neck stock was loose and stained. 'You'd be better off minding your mistress. These are dangerous times.'

Tony swore under his breath as he turned from Reynolds. A waste of time. On again.

Down the narrow alley that ran behind the terrace of large houses, he looked for the back entrance into Lord Charles's apartment. Edward's brother took rooms in Dublin for the parliamentary season, in one of the houses on Kildare Street. It was on the opposite side of the street to Leinster House, where Sheriff Oliver Carleton was most likely already questioning Lady Pamela with a restrained politeness while his men searched her rooms. Had they managed to burn everything that might have been incriminating? He hoped they wouldn't search the servants' rooms and find the maps. A barrow man trundled past, paying no heed to him, and a groom looked him over with a dismissive eye, but no soldiers. He entered the house through the basement kitchen, up the narrow stone steps at the rear, and tried the door to the upper apartments. It was unlocked. All was quiet inside. No voices, no sound of movement. The sitting room was empty – no sign that anyone had been there – but the door to the bedroom was ajar. He peered into a darkened room. The shutters were half-closed and the light fragmented, so he had no chance to see anything before he felt the barrel of a pistol at the side of his head.

'Christ, Edward, it's me.'

The gun was snatched away.

'What the hell? I was so close to pulling the trigger.' Tony's eyes adjusted to the figure standing in front of him. Edward's hand had fallen to his side. 'I just saw Carleton's men. They're there now, with Pamela. I didn't know whether I should rush over or whether that would make it worse for them.' He banged the pistol against his forehead.

'No, you'd be giving yourself up to them and it will make no difference. They will still search the house, still question her. She sent me to find you, to tell you not to come back.'

But Edward stuffed the pistol in his waistband and pulled the shutters open, the better to see onto the street below. Tony pulled him away from the window.

'You'll be seen.'

'I must go over there.'

'You'll put them all in more danger if you do.'

He cursed at this, and began pacing.

'Carleton won't harm her.' He spoke more to himself than to Tony as he straightened his clothing, and poured water at the washstand, splashing some on his face. 'Though if he does …' He wiped his hands on the cloth and flung it back into the basin.

'There will be patrols everywhere looking for you. Where will you go?'

Edward gave a dry laugh. 'I'd best get out of Dublin at least for the next week or so. Can you get word to Aungier Street, to Doctor Kennedy? He can arrange something for me.' Voices outside, from the street below. Was that boots ringing on the frost-hardened street? 'You know the code? In case you're challenged?'

'Has it changed?'

'I hope not,' Edward replied. 'Who is left to change it? I'm one of the last of the Executive left. And Arthur is in prison. Makes me Commander-in-Chief. For my sins.' He laughed harshly. 'Typical Arthur, attempting to get to France at such a time. Thinking he could spur them on. And now?'

Now they waited. More waiting, listening for the sound of the departing soldiers, for the clink of metal, the grumble of voices to fade up Kildare Street. Sitting on the floor under one of the windows, they waited for the treacherous sun to slip west and release the shadows of the evening. Edward swung his watch back and forth, then let the chain pool in his hand.

'Tony, I must ask. Have you ever thought what you might do if, by some divine intervention, this increasingly hopeless Rebellion ever succeeds? Or even if it fails and you must ... no, let's say it succeeds, and you and your family can do anything you want, where would you go? What would you do?'

'You mean if I no longer work for you.' His voice was flat. 'Sometimes I imagine myself back in Hamburg, setting up an ink business, but that probably wouldn't work, not with Julia and Harriet. Besides you cannot recreate the past so easily. So Dublin perhaps, or London. Or maybe I should become an Irish farmer. Keep a cow, and a horse. A spread of fields. And the house must measure up of course. Julia would demand nothing less than two good rooms downstairs, and three bedrooms upstairs. Oh and all the outside buildings you'd expect.'

Edward laughed. 'A gentleman farmer then. And the third bedroom? You plan to have another small Small?'

'Plan? If one comes ... but actually in this fanciful vision I keep it for your visits, for you and Lady Pamela. When you can tear yourself away from the business of government.'

Edward looked stricken, sad. 'Can you really imagine this, my friend?' He looked down at his watch. The room was growing dark.

'Yes,' he answered. 'Certainly. And you must too, otherwise—'

'Let's not think of otherwise.'

Edward wrote, one note for Lady Pamela, several for the remaining members of the Executive. Tony placed them in his pocket, felt the press of them, just like the ones he used to carry.

'Don't think of delivering those. Just get them to Doctor Kennedy and let him look after them. And Tony ...' He looked at him, trying to smile, and he looked so much like his young son. 'Don't get caught. Please.'

THE TRUE NARRATIVE

April 1798, Dublin and Edward in disguise; A baby is born.

Some things are beyond reason. Some urges cannot be silenced. Edward used to say I was too cautious but then he was a man of impulse. As when he came to see Lady Pamela on the very day that the Proclamation was issued, calling for his arrest, urging the public to turn him in, offering a reward of immense proportions. But he could go no longer without setting his eyes on her. It was his nature. Such passions he had.

He'd been on the run, in hiding for over a month. Rumours abounded and spread, faster than fever. He was in France. He'd departed in a post-chaise for Belfast, smuggled out by his brother, Charles. He was aboard ship, bound for America. He'd run away to the Quakers in Cork. He was training recruits in Galway. He was trying to secure O'Connor's release. He was seen in broad daylight, brazen as a boot boy, strolling through Marlborough Gardens. But not us, we never saw him.

We were in Denzille Street at the time, in that mean house that Her Ladyship was persuaded to take. The Family found her presence in Leinster House an embarrassment, and she in turn found it too large, too open and unsafe. She refused to leave Dublin, thinking Edward might need her, might visit her. We were a small household then and with her lady's maid having been let go, there was but Julia, myself and a girl to help in the kitchen. And the errand boy whom Lady Sarah, Edward's aunt, noted with a sniff on the one occasion that she chose to visit. 'So many of you and she with such a small purse.' She being Lady Pamela, at the time larger than a loaded barge, as my Julia was quick to point out. Lady Sarah didn't like that but Julia persisted, adding that she hoped there would be money to provide for a doctor or nurse when her time came. 'When Lord Edward's child shall be born.' Of course, of course everything would be arranged. There was no question of that. Edward's aunt would see to the matter. Lady Pamela sat by the fire, not taking any interest, as though the two were discussing the birthing of a litter of street kittens. But other days she had more energy, as when she sent me to Frescati to find the folder containing Edward's property deeds, and other legal papers. I had raised with her the matter of the outstanding rents at the FitzGeralds' estate in Kilrush. Immediately she realised the urgency. She would write to the land agent. 'We must also get the leases back, and quickly, or we will have no money when ... bien sûr vous comprenez.'

I understood. She was making ready.

That night in April. I was in the back yard, throwing the remains of our supper to some street dogs, when I noticed the gate that led to the back lane was ajar. I pressed it shut, peering into the blackness as I did so. And then a voice, one of those voices you might hear around Smithfield or at the back of Green Street, coarse and lewd, calling from behind the wooden storehouse. 'Any food, Blackie?' A rustle of skirts and a slim cloaked figure appeared. It was difficult to make out her features with only the candlelight from the kitchen glowing behind her. I demanded that she leave the way she came, saying that she had no business here. And she turned then, so that I could ascertain her profile. 'Very well,' I said, though my breath was caught in the cage of my chest, 'come in for some leftovers, but nothing else. Her Ladyship would not see any woman turned away for want of food.'

My voice rang false to my ears. A click of boots followed me to the kitchen entrance and I took care to snuff the candles inside. 'For God's sake keep the hood up,' I urged. 'There are watchers everywhere.'

He slumped on a bench. 'It has taken me hours to get here, even in this disguise. How is she? Is she abed?'

I led him through the basement and up the front stairs, into the sitting room where Lady Pamela sat with Julia, their heads bent over their sewing, and two candles sputtering on the low table between them.

'A visitor, Milady.' I took pleasure in the formality of the announcement. Julia rose in protest.

'This is no hour for ...'

Edward rushed forward and fell at Pamela's side, pressing his head against her knees and she cradled him as she would her children, kissing his head, murmuring, 'Je savais, je croyais,' her hands fluttering over his hair, turning his face up to hers. We left them.

He stayed for three hours, perhaps five. I waited below in the kitchen, hung a linen over the back window, kept the fire going till night pushed towards dawn. When he finally left her, his face was shadowed. Tired. Thinner. He thanked me for staying. For Julia. 'I won't ask if you've been paid,' he muttered. He thanked me again, promised he would see it right, when it was all over. 'Not long now,' he said, his voice flat. 'It's better you don't know. Just in case.' His voice drifted away. In the silence, the stale smells of the household were oppressive. I could see them in my mind's eye; islands of fat floating on top of yesterday's mutton stew; washing hung in front of the fire hissing sourly; the milk turning in the jug, splitting, cream rising, rising ...

'Dear God Tony, have you brandy or something to see me off?'

I prepared some whey and sherry. He gulped it back.

'Must you,' I began. 'Can't you get away? To France?'

He rubbed his hand over his face, looking so tired. 'Don't you think I'd love to? Part of me would pay a small fortune to be rowed down the Liffey and off out to a waiting ship. I have so many doubts. About the leadership, the prospect of ever getting enough men to fight, let alone trained men. And there's the constant threat of betrayal. Someone among those close to me will turn. It's a certainty. And you could go mad trying to think who.'

'So why not go, if it's all pointless? Lady Pamela could follow you over. You don't have to go through with it.'

He poured himself another glass, ignoring the dish of whey this time, played with it, holding it up to the firelight before sipping it slowly.

'I'm trapped in it now. So many others depending on me.' He shook his head. Drained his glass. 'No. If I don't set in motion, pull all the divisions together, get the timings right ... you've no idea how difficult it is. The wild Catholic peasants pulling one way, the men from the North set on another. And even here in Dublin where the rebel army is supposed to rise as one at a signal, take the Castle, the barracks – even here there's dissent.'

He had never spoken so freely before and now he'd started he couldn't stop. 'We called them divisions you know, the different branches of the United Irish. The word has proven prophetic. Each division, Leinster, Ulster, all of them, wants to do things their own way. And if they do—' He caught the candle flame between finger and thumb – 'It'll sputter out. And we must succeed. I must. I picked the wrong side once before, not again.'

'America?'

'Of course. I won't be found wanting this time.'

I begged him to assign a task to me. Anything. His only response was that I should continue to care for his wife; Julia and myself were the only ones he could depend on to put her interests first.

'And she won't leave the country though I have begged her to go to her mother in Paris for her lying-in. We are all caught in the same trap now.' He sighed for a moment then straightened up, dropped a quick curtsey. 'Do I make a fine lady?' But his face was sadder than ever I had seen it. 'I know one thing you could do now. Have you a scissors?'

I cut his hair, kept back locks and wrapped them in butter paper; for Mother, for Lucy and for Pam he'd said. 'I couldn't ask her to do it herself.' I kept my feelings tight in my chest as he bent his head, and the scissors crunched and his hair fell to the ground around my feet. I coughed but it brought no relief.

'Remember Paris,' he said. 'When you liberated me from my queue.' He flicked the imaginary queue at the back of his head.

'At your request. You wanted the coiffure à la Titus I believe.'

'All things Republican.' He smiled and looked like the boy he was when we first met. I began to speak, but he interrupted me. 'And you remarked that I could hardly justify the expense of a manservant anymore, with no hair or wigs to attend to.'

I smiled at the recollection, put the scissors back in its linen wrap.

'I wanted to say to you, it's something that has come to me recently, that I understand now, how you were when we first met.'

I told him I was unsure what he meant.

'I mean your closed face. The way you kept your feelings inside. Or maybe they were trapped there. These last few weeks, I've found myself watching, checking, trying not to show anything of the suspicion and fear I have for ... Christ, almost everything. And everyone. It's exhausting.'

'It is,' I said. 'You're doing well, Edward. So well.'

'I hope Tony,' he began, 'that your life has been—'

A noise at the back door. A pot overturned. A muttered curse. Edward drew a pistol from deep in his skirts, crossed the floor to the door in the time it took me to snuff the lantern. I rushed to the fireside, grabbed the poker. A fist on the door. Two raps. A pause. Three slow knocks. 'Bloody hell,' muttered Edward, opening the door, revealing the silhouettes of two figures, one of whom seemed a giant in proportions. 'Tony, meet my bodyguards.'

The smaller one spoke. 'Milord we must leave. It'll be bright soon and that disguise won't fool anyone by daylight.'

'Really? I am getting no credit today. Is there anyone about?'

'Only Sirr's miserable man, Cahill, huddling on the doorstop opposite on Denzille Street. And asleep the last time we looked. No one out the back. I beg you, come now.'

He clapped me on my shoulder, hesitated, as though he might speak, then shook his head. He left down the back yard, skirts swishing, the giant trailing after him. The sickle moon had disappeared, and a pale band of light was visible in the gaps between the buildings opposite. Nearly morning. I closed the door, returned to the kitchen.

'He's gone then.' It was Julia. 'Thanks be to God. She's been trying to keep quiet. Not let on.'

'Who?'

'Her Ladyship. The babe is coming. The fright of it I expect, seeing him. But she couldn't say. Afraid it would detain him.' She threw some wood on the fire, then stood back, hands on her hips. 'Can't find the damn poker.'

I retrieved the poker from the doorway, and still she was talking, the words pouring forth. 'The pains are bad and the poor creature has been biting it back so as not to alarm him. She prayed he would leave. I prayed you'd get rid of him.'

'Julia, you must go back up to attend her.'

'Give me patience,' she hissed. 'Do something useful, instead of sitting about yapping like a lapdog. Prepare her a hot draught and then send to Lady Moira for help. She promised a nurse for her confinement. Go yourself or write a note for that boy if ever he comes.' All the while she spat out her instructions to me, she was fixing a pot of water, taking down a jar from a shelf, spooning out some powders into a small pan, disappearing briefly into the narrow passage behind the fireplace, returning with armloads of linen. The kitchen was transformed from a place of shadows and whispers to one of flames and banging – spoons, pots, the grate, lids, doors.

A busy woman, my Julia. The errand boy arrived in time to deliver the message to Lady Moira. The sitting nurse came. The clock in the drawing room contrived to sound out the passing hours in rude gongs that became louder and more alarming as the day pressed on. It was almost nightfall before Her Ladyship was delivered of a daughter. She was a tiny scrap, according to Julia. 'God willing she'll survive. Seems to have no interest in suckling. And Her Ladyship's most terribly weak.'

Indeed the linens bore testament to her sufferings that day. Lady Pamela could scarce lift her head from the pillows to look at her new baby. Old Lady Moira came to visit and brought with her something of the outside to the close, overheated world of Denzille Street. She procured a wet nurse for Lady Pamela who promptly succumbed to fits of weeping at the thoughts of her child at another's breast, and so she was paid off.

These events took place in April for I can remember the child's birth, one of the last things of which I am certain. Lucy she was named, for Edward's sister, who once was such a close companion to

Lady Pamela. But the child was never to be hers for she was taken from Lady Pamela some two months later and given to Edward's other unmarried sister Sophia. But that was after. Before, there was such horror, such sadness and my memories of that time are so confused, I'm not sure I shall be able to give a correct account.

THE TRUE NARRATIVE

*May 1798, Dublin and Mr Ogilvie visits Lady Pamela; An account
of the Author's increasing trepidation.*

The Reader may find it somewhat unusual that a servant should have been
so closely involved in Lady Pamela's daily affairs. But the truth is that
she had no one else — with the exception of that noble Lady Moira who
steered through all the troubled water to offer whatever assistance was in
her power. But for the most part, it was Julia and I who passed those
long days in Denzille Street with Lady Pamela. It was Julia who took
possession of the occasional treasured notes from Edward, or the cursory
missives informing Lady Pamela that all was well. Julia walked out every
second day, visiting the market stalls from Clarendon, through Glib and as
far as Thomas Street. Somewhere along the route a note would be placed
in her basket among the vegetables and bread. In the same way, letters
from Lady Pamela were passed over along with money. No hint in those
lines of any weakening of resolve as May began to bloom.

I can't ever forget those days. Within the household the hours
passed slowly, in commonplace grubwork and domestic tasks. There
were three children in the household and the pending mayhem outside
the walls of Denzille must never reach their ears. Where once I had
travelled freely across the country, now I was curtailed, like a slave
without a pass. I could scarcely leave the house by daylight for fear
of being taken up by the Militia. On one occasion I made the short
journey as far as Eades Vintners off Dame Street, and my shadow grew

ever longer behind me as not one but two men trailed in my wake. Nor could Lady Pamela leave, being so lately after her confinement. We were all trapped in different ways.

I hope the Reader will not think I trespass overmuch on His sympathies by declaring that those days of waiting and hiding weighed heavy on me. I was bound by my loyalty to Lady Pamela to stay close and watch for her, as well as to my own family. But a greater loyalty tugged at my heart like a rope, and that was to see Edward with my own eyes and assure myself of his wellbeing. Once the Proclamation was passed and the city walls were pasted with notices offering £1,000 for information leading to my Master's capture, I was sick with fear for what must happen to him. Dublin was a fearful place, and I found the only people I could trust were those within our household – though the errand boy's pale face and narrow eyes suggested some sort of mischief for me. I became oversensitive to faces, reading into them desires and intentions of a most treacherous nature. The slack-jawed scavenger clearing the ash trap was a Castle man for certain. The shawled woman, who delivered bread to the back door, asking after 'the childers' and enquiring for Her Ladyship in an ingratiating manner, was a paid informer, I was almost certain. I refused to answer her. The chairmen carrying their passengers past our door – did they? Yes – they definitely paused to study our comings and goings. Even the sun was complicit. As May days unfolded, and it dallied ever longer each evening like an unwelcome guest, there was less darkness about to cast its kindly shadows over Edward as he was moved from one safe house to another.

Mr Ogilvie glanced at the infant Lucy, craning his neck into her cradle. A bony heron about to snatch a fish.

'The child looks well enough, considering.' His words snapped at Her Ladyship, small bites but so many. She must get word to Edward. Order him to leave. Had she no influence? Did she not care for her children's future? She should leave. She was putting him in danger. If she left the country, he too would go. Time was running out.

Tony stayed with her during this visit at her insistence. Ogilvie's head jerked and bobbed with each cutting remark he delivered, causing his wig to slip slightly. He could have seemed comical. He was not. It was her fault, he told her, she had led him this way with her revolutionary fancies. 'By his conduct, he has blasted the most promising hopes of his youth.'

Instead of crying, she just smiled at him and sighed. 'Ah, Monsieur Ogilvie. You do it so well. Always love and disesteem together. My poor Edward.'

He looked first at Tony, raising his fringed brows. A questioning look, as if he needed her words translated. He unknotted his long fingers and tapped them off his knees.

'What do you mean by such a statement?'

But she stood suddenly, like a fever had gripped her. Still pale from her lying-in, her dark hair hanging loose about her shoulders, she stood over him.

'You knew him as a boy. You still treat him as a boy. You think his mind is ...' She waved her hand, trying to grasp the word, muttering in French. 'A garden. Your garden. You want to plant it with your ideas. Watch it grow. You think now I put weeds in it.' She shook her head. 'He has his own thoughts. Not yours. Not mine. But you,' she pointed at him, 'you are always at the edge of his mind, a snake hissing doubts.'

He protested. 'My dear Lady Pamela. Please. I beg of you to be ruled by me in this matter, however disagreeable it may be to you in other respects. You must tell him to flee, or divulge to me his hiding place that I may persuade him.' He looked as though he would stand but she remained in front of him. He told her he loved Lord Edward as his own son, more—

She turned from him, muttered the word love under her breath. The baby stirred and she reached into the cradle for her. Mr Ogilvie sat on the edge of his seat. Lady Pamela paced up and down with the child over one shoulder. Tony said nothing; there was nothing to say. Into that stifled silence, Julia brought tea, clattering the tray on the table, apologising crisply for the absence of any sugar to accompany it.

'Seeing as the household cannot afford such luxuries.'

Mr Ogilvie frowned and Lady Pamela continued her pacing.

Once more, rumour began to cast its web about. The Rising was planned for June. No, it was to happen before the week's end. The

Executive had been infiltrated by Castle spies; the Rising was called off. Lady Pamela must flee to Hamburg. We were to pack our belongings and take the Saturday packet to Holyhead. Like spiders scuttling along silken strings, the news and false news reached us daily, spinning us into a state of anxiety and fear. Perhaps I should not say 'us' and confess that of all the household, it was I who was most affected. Lady Pamela maintained a front of savoir-faire that would have done credit to the most accomplished actress. She entertained her occasional visitors with great courtesy, albeit without her customary lively charm. She gave all her attention to her children, lavishing them with affection. When I admitted to some surprise at her manner, Julia snapped at me, calling me a fool – did I not see that she was in fear that these may be her last days with her children? Hadn't little Eddy already been removed from her, she cried. I tried to reason with her, that Edward and Lady Pamela had entrusted the young boy to the care of the Duchess. The only difference is in how you phrase it, was Julia's response. By the time this is over, Lady Pamela will be fortunate to have any child; let alone a husband. Oh Lord help me when she said this. I think that until that moment, though I lived in dread, it was still a vague and nameless dread. But as Julia stood before me wringing her hands, I feared the worst for Edward.

Lady Pamela applied to Lord Castlereagh for passports, in case she might need to travel. She finally accepted an invitation from Lady Moira to stay at her Dublin house. Lady Moira was the most worthy of all the titled Ladies I ever had the honour to meet. Though of advancing years, she moved with lively grace, was blessed with a facility for confidences, and unwavering in her friendship for Lady Pamela in a city that had turned its back on her.

May was warm. Clear-skied. Trees pushed out bright sticky leaves, thick candles of blooms. Weeds crowded the back yard, around the ash pit. The stink from the Cork Street tanneries choked the house on Denzille Street. Lies and rumours and tales of savagery scurried in its wake. Word came at last from Lord Edward, urging Lady Pamela to pay a visit to her cousin Henriette Matthiessen in Hamburg, to get passports together so they might leave in a hurry.

'Soon. They must give the signal for the Rising soon.' Lady Pamela paced the small sitting room, in the half light. 'He would not send such explicit word. They must have set the date. What shall I do?' She glanced out the window. Her dark eyes were shadowed, her face hollowed. It struck him how she had taken the brunt of carrying on. Living under the hostile gaze of the Castle and many of her set. Refusing the offer of a wet nurse for her new baby, saying she could not trust an outsider even if she could bear to pass the child over.

Edward at least was hiding among sympathetic fellows.

'I hate to apply to Castlereagh for passports. He will rejoice that I must, be … sous une obligation envers lui. But what choice do I have?'

It was true. She had so little choice. No choice at all.

Moments before Lady Moira's carriage arrived, a man called to the door with a letter for Lady Pamela. The messenger had the look and manner of a Castle man. No need for him to wait for a response, he said, Her Ladyship's instructions were contained within. He peered into the hallway, taking in the trunk and the bags set beside the door. 'Just as well she's readying herself,' he said. 'You will all be gone from here by the week's end.'

Tony took the letter to Lady Pamela's room but dreaded handing it to her. The activity of packing, the visit to Moira House, had done much to raise her spirits. This note from the Castle would be a blow. She was wrapping a small bundle of papers and letters in one of the baby's swaddling sheets.

'I'll place it under her mattress, to keep them safe until we reach Lady Moira's,' she declared with an air of satisfaction.

'A good idea,' he said. 'But I'm afraid you have a letter, from the Castle.'

'You mean Castlereagh. I recognise his hand.' She broke the seal and ran her eyes over it. 'Quel homme méchant. He has given me a week to quit the country.'

Lady Pamela was silent as the carriage creaked past Trinity College. She did not look out, showed no interest in the geese strutting across the bowling green, nor at the sight of a ragged child swinging his bare legs from the plinth of King William's statue on College Green. Looked like he'd be trampled under the hooves of the dead monarch's mighty horse.

The letter remained crushed in her hand. He wondered what thoughts lay behind her unseeing eyes. Not enough that she should be expelled, but she must collect the passports in person – *so we may confirm your identity*. No one spoke. The baby slept in Julia's arms. The carriage halted briefly on Dame Street. A group of young boys jumped up at a cluster of notices pasted to the walls of the old Shakespeare Gallery, attempting to tear them down. He leaned towards the window. Could just discern the wording on the remaining scraps.

> Whereas we have received information upon oath, that Edward FitzGerald ...
> ... guilty of high treason ... to justice ... a reward of one thousand pounds ... persons who shall discover the said Lord Ed ...
> ... apprehended and committed to prison.
> ... charge and command all justices of the ... His Majesty's loving subjects, to use their utmost diligence ...
> 11th day of May 1798.

A sound escaped him. A barely suppressed expletive. Lady Pamela followed his gaze, pressed forward, her wrap slipping from her shoulders. Saw some of it at least before the horse was urged on and the carriage lurched forward. 'Milady, I'm sorry ...'

She shook her head, pressed her fist and the crushed letter to her mouth and said nothing.

Moira House was ensconced behind the shelter of a high stone wall, set back from the grubby traffic of the quays and the Liffey; an island of sorts on Usher's Island. Once inside those walls, Lady Pamela was safe from prying eyes, spying eyes. She gave voice to her fury and anguish.

'So now they offer money for him. Like he is meat at the market. Mon pauvre Ed.'

Lady Moira, unruffled as a summer partridge, directed them upstairs, but Lady Pamela continued to talk.

'It is like Paris, la Terreur. And Castlereagh would humiliate me, attack Edward.' Lady Moira tucked her arm around her and steered her into a bright room overlooking the rear garden.

'There, my dear Lady Pamela, take a seat and I will send for something to revive you.' She spoke briefly to the footman outside the door, while Julia settled the children on a large sopha. 'I will let your servants look after you for now and perhaps you will take tea with me later? Can you spare Mr Small before that for a few moments?'

He was shown to her neat sitting room, almost masculine in its array of prints and books. She turned from her writing desk. 'Come in, Mr Small. Thank you.'

Her lace-capped head cocked to one side as she spoke, and she looked directly at him, with keen eyes. 'I understand there have been occasional visitors to Lady Edward, some unwelcome?'

He nodded. She smiled briefly to convey her understanding of the unsaid. 'But no family have offered to stay with her? Apart from Lady Lucy, but as Dear Pamela has wisely observed, it is no place for an unattached young woman.'

'Lord Edward would also be opposed to her return, if he were asked. He is most protective of his sister,' he said, thinking of his concern for her and the rumours she attracted.

'Being possessed of a political opinion is probably the worst possible indiscretion for her reputation. A single woman may get away with all manner of flirtations in her dealings with young men, but a heartfelt political view is not to be tolerated. I, on the other hand, being of a certain age and with a list of titles to my name, may do as I please.' She rose briskly from her chair.

'We must look after Lady Pamela for if we do not, then who will?' Her voice trailed away briefly. 'She needs rest, her infant being so small. But more than anything, she needs respite from rumours and unpleasant news. I know I may rely upon your discretion.'

'Of course, Your Ladyship.'

'I wish there was some way to bring an end to this. Lord Edward would not …?'

What did she mean? That Edward might give himself up, slip out of the country, call off the Rising? He'd thought she knew him better than that. He started to speak, to protest. 'I'm sorry, but I do not think I could presume to know all that is in Lord Edward's heart. Nor of his affairs as they now stand.'

Her lips pressed together briefly in a glimmer of a smile and she shook her head. 'Unfair of me to ask you but I'm glad I did if only to have heard your response. I am particularly fond of him you see. He is possessed of a unique charm, a purity of intention.' She looked down at her hands and turned them over as though she might find something there. Behind her he could see through the window, a glimpse of a small sloop passing downriver, its white sail puffing and lulling in the fickle breeze. Lady Moira glanced over her shoulder at it and sighed.

'Would you travel with your mistress? I could arrange for someone to accompany her. I intend no disrespect to you, but sometimes, a person of …' she paused, as if searching for the right words. 'A person of some authority can open doors and cross borders that might otherwise be closed to a smaller, more intimate group.'

'I understand. My authority, as you put it, is too easily called into question. But I promised Lord Edward I would remain with her. If that means seeing her safely abroad, to London or even to her cousin in Hamburg, so be it.'

He thought of Julia, how she would feel on leaving Ireland, could hardly imagine her in the strange, busy world of Hamburg knowing how much she dreaded change. But he'd given a promise. Almost an oath really. And if good fortune prevailed then perhaps Edward would come for Lady Pamela in time. When all this was over. And perhaps he and Julia and Ettie might stay. He could return to Herr Höcker. Become his assistant. And Julia would have settled in Hamburg by then. Perhaps, perhaps.

'Your fidelity does you great credit,' Lady Moira was saying. 'Well then, I suggest you and Mrs Small return to Denzille Street in the morning, to begin preparations for your mistress's departure.'

Julia would sleep in the dressing room alongside Lady Pamela's bedroom while Tony was given a room in the attic. After he had eaten in the servants' hall – the usual mix of easy chatter, sympathetic enquiry regarding his master, covert glances and avoidance – he followed a young lad up the stone steps, up and up, to the second-last floor, where it became a rough wooden staircase, and was finally shown to his allotted room. It was as expected. Small, no fireplace, no furniture other than two narrow beds, the other thankfully unoccupied. And it was warm. Those attic rooms soaked up the heat of the day.

The window overlooked the garden. The sky was a fury of livid clouds and a throbbing evening sun. From that height he could see the walls of the Marshalsea Prison in the distance across a stretch of open hillocked ground. Dung heaps. So many. Such a view for such a grand house – dung heaps and a prison.

He wondered where Edward was now. Hopefully out of the county, safe with sympathetic hosts, but given his recent message to Lady Pamela, this seemed unlikely. What would happen? When? Would it be like the war in America? Battles with soldiers pitched against each other? Were the Irish prepared for such fighting? Or would it be a worsening of the daily horrors, of burnings, reprisals, hangings? And where would he be in all of it, and Julia? Looking on, as now? Not knowing. Wondering. Not doing. Not doing anything. The futility of it.

He slammed the heel of his palm against the window frame, driving a splinter deep under the skin. A sharp stab of pain. A rush of blood. Again he drove his hand on the rough wood. Another dart of … not pain, but animation, alertness. He pulled the splinter free, glanced once more out the window, at the last of the evening's sun playing on the apple blossom, the large marble fountain in the centre of the garden glowing gold, and the glinting movement of bayonet tips beyond the rear wall. Several, up and down, then stopping, on the other side of a garden door.

Odd. Something not right.

Down the stairs, into the servants' hall, along the low passage to the laundry, ignoring the sideways look of the maidservant who was scrubbing out a large basin, and out into the garden. His boots grated on the stones so he took to the grass, hugging the long shadows of the westerly wall, and skirting along the rear wall to stand where he'd last seen movement. The light had all but surrendered to night. All that was left seeped from the back windows of the house, flimsy flickers of lamps and candlelight. Somewhere a church bell sounded out the hour, eight dull tolls. He pressed his back against the garden door, willed his heart, his breath, to silence and listened. Heard the scrape of metal on wood on the other side, a hissed voice. 'If it takes all night … steady.' A shuffling sound, a soft clinking, a stifled cough, then nothing. Or maybe just the sound of breathing, heavy and irregular. He took a step to the side, hearing the bend of grass beneath his feet, the spring of it as he lifted his foot again, and again, back towards the light of the house.

A certainty gripped him beyond reasoning. Those men on the other side of the wall, with their bayonets at the ready, were there for Edward. It was a trap. But how? Did he know Lady Pamela was here? Would he really risk visiting her? He knew the answer. But no, he couldn't have known she would be here. Something else then, some other reason why he might be on the move, and these soldiers knew of his expected movements. Someone had betrayed him. He knew this. Without proof. And yet he was certain. There was no one he could ask without arousing interest, and then it might be too late. His mind's eye travelled ahead of him, drawing on his memory of the streets here, the road they had taken earlier today.

The Moira carriage was sheltered in the covered passage to the side of the house. Two storm lanterns lit the way to the small stable area and the horses; four bays, clearly coach horses, and one in the last stall, a mare. He saddled her quickly, more by feel than sight, and took a long stable coat and hat from a hook near the carriage. On impulse, he glanced inside the coach and felt around in the dim interior. His fingers patted the seats, the floor, touched silk. Lady Pamela's shawl. He wrapped it round his neck and pulled it up to cover his nose.

The darkness outside was welcome; his odd clothing, hat and covered face would draw little attention, though the river was alive yet with wind-borne voices, the plash of oars and the sway of lanterns, near and far. He would circle the waiting soldiers. Passing the remaining narrow houses that fronted the quays, the skin on his neck prickled. Was someone watching him? His attention was snagged by a figure at an upper window. He slowed to look up, saw a dark form silhouetted against a low flicker of candlelight in the room behind. A man standing absolutely still, looking out into the darkness, onto the black pull of the Liffey. Though it was unlikely the man could see him, Tony pulled his hat brim a little lower and gently urged the horse forward again. He turned up Watling Street, giving his mount a long rein, so her drooping neck and slow walk would give the air of having journeyed long. A brief glance left, down the lane that ran behind Moira House. Five, six soldiers perhaps, at the corner, pressed against the wall. He ambled on up the street. No sign of him. He kicked the mare now, past the yards and warehouses, the onslaught of rank smells proclaiming them as skinners, curriers, and tanneries, nudging memories of – not now. Press on. Towards Thomas Street. People walking, groups of two and three, but none that looked like Edward. A strange rhythmic creaking, the vast arms of a windmill, turning slowly. Thomas Street was busy despite the hour. No way of telling where Edward was, safely hidden in any one of these buildings or on the move, like so many others making their way home after a day's work at any number of factories, or great houses or distilleries. The tide of humans flowed out from the city as he trotted back towards its centre. Stupid to think he might just chance upon him. Stupid.

He veered back again, down a narrow road leading to the river. Back towards the soldiers. If anything were to happen they would be at the centre of it. He'd wait as they waited. Watch as they watched. The lane behind Moira House was suspended in darkness and smells of apple blossom, hops, and dung. At the far end, the dull glow from the shebeen on Watling Street conjured up the dark shapes huddled against the wall. The horse asked no questions of him but stood silent as night. Minutes thickened like spilt blood. Distant sounds of the river belonged to another time.

The mare's ears flickered. A movement in the distance, a vague gleam of metal against the blackness. The soldiers were moving. He dug his heels in. Down the lane, through the darkness towards the shadowy, flickering movements, the horse's hooves thudded on the dry ground: thud, clump. More shapes moving now, sounds of a scuffle up ahead, a clash of metal.

His was a winged horse gaining, gaining on them. A sabre moon cleaved the dark heavens. Men and soldiers at a standoff. He saw them and kept on, into the heart of the uniformed men. His was a war horse, rearing up, toppling one man, two perhaps. Backing up, then forward again, snorting, hooves ringing against metal. Shouts and further scuffles.

'Get him off the horse,' a voice bawled, amid the chaos. From the corner of his eye, a soldier raising a gun. But his blood surged as the gun exploded, and the air whooshed past him, a smell of powder, and singeing. Stinging pain in his arm. It's nothing. Wrench the reins, drag the horse around. The soldiers' quarry running up Watling Street, becoming shadow. Is he among them? No point following.

Behind, the soldiers were gathering themselves. One lying on the ground, groaning. Clink of metal. Slap of hands on wood. 'Get him,' the voice bellowed again, harsh and urgent. And familiar. As was the angry jut of lip, his chin. Four crescent-shaped scars flashed across his mind's eye. He turned, at one with the horse. Aimed directly at Major Sirr. Toppled him to the ground. Whack of hoof against his cheekbone. Hands grappled with the bridle. Soldiers swearing. Bastard. Pull him off. Sweat and spittle. The butt of a rifle against his thigh as he wheeled away.

The clouds closed over once again, dimming the moonlight as the walls and gates of the lane sped by, and the bullets behind him punctured nothing more than the empty darkness. He reached the corner and turned in a clatter of hooves and shifting dirt, and a whoop rose from his chest. His thighs were damp with sweat, the air around him cloaked with noisy exhalations and the pump, thrump of a beating heart. Just a short distance away, the river was writhing against the banks, surging against the stone quays, the steps, shouldering the little boats aside. Until the next tide, and shift of water. He gathered himself. Must get back before they catch up with him.

'What's happened?' A voice hissed from a darkened entrance opposite him. 'The gunfire?'

'I don't know,' he muttered, walking the horse on past the doorway. 'Probably trying to arrest someone. I didn't stay to find out.'

A movement, a figure separated from the rest. 'Tony?'

He leaned out from the saddle, peered into shadows. A hand grabbed the bridle. Edward.

'You weren't with the other party?'

'No, we had two. Hoping to trick them, if necessary. Did they get away?'

'Yes. Up Watling. You should go.'

The other two men came forward. 'Now.'

Edward rocked on his heels. 'How did you come to be here?'

Did he suspect him? 'I saw the soldiers ... on the lane. I thought of you ... that you might know ... Lady Pamela is in Moira House.' His voice was rough, the words forced out between jagged breaths. 'That it was a trap.'

'Tony.' He grabbed the reins. 'I never meant you ...'

His chest was tight. 'But it does mean someone has given you up.'

'Your Lordship, we must go.' A woman's voice? The taller figure put a hand on Edward's arm but he shook it off.

'Just now. The rifle fire? Who—'

'I charged at the soldiers. At Major Sirr. For God's sake, go.'

'Just tell me. Pamela. The baby.'

'Lady Moira is looking after her. She'll leave within days.'

Edward leaned against the horse, murmured something. Thank God? The mare shifted uneasily. The darkness threatening. Edward reached for Tony's arm then pulled away. 'Tell Pamela I—'

His words went with him as he ran. Three figures, coats flapping, merged with the darkness of the hill ahead.

The True Narrative

19th May 1798, Dublin and the Author learns of Edward's arrest;
He embarks on a painful journey.

What a person knows and what he writes may not be the same. Even if I had been there when Edward was arrested, I could not have seen everything, I could not know everything. Each story has a different teller whose eyes will seek different things, whose ears will, by habit, pick up voices and words familiar to them and whose opinions will guide their retelling. My account that I put before you is my retelling of the story of a witness, and even hers was garnished by the words of a gathered crowd. My own remembering is likely tainted by the great burden of feeling, and by what I read and heard afterwards. But it is the best I can do – it is all I can do. I was not a witness.

Lady Pamela was still at Moira House, Julia and I having returned to the hired house in Denzille Street. Ettie was suffering an earache, the tending of which distracted us from thoughts of Edward, and the trap of informers and spies. Julia eventually put her to bed. It was well after nightfall when a rap came to the back door. Two raps and a pause. And my own heart beat to the same dread pattern. I was off the settle, lantern in hand before the first of the three spaced knocks, pulling the bolts by the last. A young woman, loose-haired, plainly dressed, stood there, gasping for air, shivering despite the warm night. 'Come in,' I urged and she stepped inside. 'He's been taken up,' she rasped. 'There was a struggle, a knife, gunshot.' She was not certain, but thought Lord Edward and at least one other was wounded. I begged her to sit, to catch her breath, and was calm in the way people can be when the worst happens.

'Were you there?' I asked her. She told us what she knew, and what she was told by the crowd who gathered outside the house on Thomas Street. The official story, the names of those involved, may be familiar to many Readers, having attained a widespread notoriety in the papers of the day. But I will write the account as it was told to me.

'You know what happened. Last night. How he was almost taken then.'

The realisation had been slow. It was her. 'You were there. The girl with Edward by the lane.'

'Yes. I often travelled with him. For his disguise. But after what happened we couldn't bring him on to Mr Magan's house as arranged, nor back to my father's, for someone knew of our plans and there was no time, no time to think of what to do. So we took him to a man who had sheltered him before. Murphy, just along from my house. And we left him, thinking him safe, or almost so. I cannot think who betrayed us. So few knew of it.'

She stopped, her eyes staring straight ahead as though the dreadful scene were playing out before her eyes.

'There was blood, such blood.'

She had not witnessed the struggle, just the aftermath, when the troop of soldiers dragged him from the house, oh such blood on the flagstones outside, and a crowd gathered and the soldiers shouting, get back, and Major Sirr ordered a chair to be brought, for Lord Edward was sinking to his knees though they tried to hold him upright and she saw his shirt was stained with blood, and his face pale, and the crowd moved in closer, she along with them, a loud grumbling and shouting, and it seemed the soldiers were much in fear for their lives, for they fired shots in the air and Lord Edward tried to speak, told the crowd to go back, said this was not the time, not the day.

'He lifted his drooping head then, and though his complexion was waxy and pallid, and his hair matted, his eyes glittered and his voice was strong when he urged the crowd. "Be assured, it's coming soon. You will know the day, and the hour. We will rise up, soon.'"

The girl wept aloud at this. Julia rushed into the room and adjudged the situation in an instant, pulling a bottle from a dresser and placing three glasses on the table. While I poured the wine, Julia put an arm about the girl, urging her to drink. She gulped it back and her pale face flushed as she repeated Edward's words.

"'It's coming soon,' he said, but Major Sirr struck him across the face and he slumped between his two captors. An old woman spat at the feet of the Major. He called for his men. "Take that, bitch," he ordered and the crowd grew restive again as the woman was hustled away. "Anyone else who raises a hand to His Majesty's men will be shot.'"

Many drifted away. She remained, saw a bloodied officer carried from the house.

'And all the while, Lord Edward appeared insensible, whether from the ball in his chest or the Major's blow to his head.'

I recalled the blow I had suffered at the hands of the Major the year before.

The girl continued as though entranced, compelled to finish her tale. She told of the chair that finally arrived for Edward, the two chairmen refusing, at first, to take him, for they didn't want the blood of some rebel on the bench inside, nor bloody marks on the leather outside. The Major was saved the necessity of ordering them at gunpoint for a voice called out, "That's Lord Edward, may the Lord have mercy on him, he's not fit to stand.'"

It took four men to carry him and wedge him in the chair. The soldiers surrounded him as the chairmen took him away. To the Castle, by all accounts.

'I thought to inform Lady Edward. Will you tell her? I must go. I must check on my father though he too is most likely imprisoned by now.' She pulled her shawl about her and only then did I recognise 'the ingratiating bread woman who used to call. She acknowledged my recognition and told me that Edward had sent her to find out how his family were, though he complained that, 'Tony wouldn't grant a sip of water to a man dying of thirst.' And I recalled dismissing her from the doorstop without answering her queries about the children.

She guessed my thoughts. 'He always endeavoured to be cheerful and courteous and grateful. I pray to God his wounds are not serious and his friends will secure his release.'

I was strangely cheered by this. And the news that, while he was captured and wounded, he was still alive. I was now the man looking for any sip of water.

I shall not write her name down in Lady Lucy's Narrative. She's sure to strike it out. But I must write it here, in my private musings. Mary Moore. She risked everything to look after Edward at her father's house on Thomas Street. In her distress, and her telling of Edward's arrest, she let slip another name. Francis Magan. It was to his house, just down from Moira House, that Edward was being moved, while the soldiers waited for him. Someone knew he was coming. And I had a sudden memory of a figure at a window. Unmoving. Seemingly gazing at darkness.

'I cannot think who betrayed us.' She repeated this over and over, her still-damp hair curtaining her face. 'I cannot think. So few knew of it. My father, certainly. And Magan. Yes Magan. But surely not.' She never made any accusations but I thought I saw an understanding in her eyes as though she'd reached some conclusion.

I will put neither name in the Narrative for it may yet cause harm to Miss Moore, and a chill feeling in the guts is no proof against any man, Magan or otherwise.

The names of the wounded soldiers became common to all in the days after Edward's arrest and committal to Newgate.

Captain Ryan, who was stabbed in the chest by Edward during his struggle to escape, and whose injuries proved fatal.

Major Swan, who suffered a minor stab wound.

Major Sirr, he who fired the shot, who planted the ball in my Master.

He was moved from the Castle to Newgate Gaol. No one could see him. Not Lady Pamela, though she begged to share his prison cell with him, to tend to him. Nor his aunt Lady Louisa though she sought the highest authority, including that of her kinsman Lord Castlereagh.

Lady Pamela gave me some jewellery. 'From my mother, from when I lived in Paris – it must have some value. Get what you can for it.' I was relieved to have a task. I could not rest at the house. How could I remain within those walls knowing that Edward was imprisoned, knowing he had been shot, not knowing how he fared? I tried a pawn shop on Kennedy's Lane. The woman there recognised the jewellery as French, and turned her assessing eye on me. Recognised me too. Told me I'd have trouble getting a fair price as everyone believed Lord Edward's wife was the cause of his downfall. I made to remove the pieces from her grasp.

'That's just what people will say to suit themselves. Tell me how the branch of liberty grows and I'll give you what their worth is to your Master.'

I stared. This woman too had been sworn in. I answered without comment but the slightest of smirks let me know she'd observed my surprise. We were all deceivers and spies but at least this one was on the side of Edward.

And so I found myself at the prison again. Three days in a row, I'd paced around the walls, joining the queue of the desperate hoping to gain admission to see their husbands, sons or friends but before I even reached the top of the huddled mass, I was turned away. This time though I had money. I pressed the turnkey for admittance, pressed a coin in his hand, a half guinea, but he looked frightened, glancing about lest anyone should see what had passed.

'Only person that gets to see your Lord Edward is the surgeon.' I told him I too had some skill in remedies and if only I were allowed in I could bring some relief to my Master's wounds. The man's face changed, his eyes seemed to close down like shutters on a window.

'No one gets in,' he said. As he turned away he muttered, 'and no one tends to his wounds.'

'What do you mean?' I asked. 'What of the surgeon?'

'Looks at him. Looks at the wound. Does nothing but replace the bandage. That's all I can say.'

All around me people heaved and pressed, shouting out names. The heat was oppressive in the cramped anteroom. A woman in a stained dress, reeking of lye and grease, pushed against me, hissing at me to move aside, as she slid a large dripping pie across the counter. The guard took it carefully and motioned her towards the door.

'Not you, Sir,' he told me, not without regret. 'Get yourself home.' Outside the gaol entrance, the sun continued to shine. The scaffold platform was happily empty.

A voice in my head. Failed, you have failed.

A voice calling my name. Tony. Hissing my name. Tony.

On the other side of the street, pressed into a doorway, was a stocky figure, with greying hair, and loose jowls, dressed in the sober black garments of a clergyman. But not a clergyman; for he appeared ill at ease in the garb. It was Mr N——, who had himself been released from Kilmainham Gaol only a few months before. His appearance bore the marks of it. He questioned me closely. Had I heard anything? Had I seen him? Was there any news of his health? Did the guards seem sympathetic? How many soldiers guarding the inner walls?

I could scarcely believe he would contemplate a rescue but nonetheless, I told him all I knew, of the guard changes, the times, those who had seemed at least other than pleased about Edward's imprisonment. There were men in place, Mr N—— said. 'Men who are waiting for orders. When the signal comes tomorrow.' I was gladdened by the prospect, and the sight of Mr N——, but not without doubt.

Mr Neilson was captured the same evening, beaten black and blue, his eyes so swollen he could not see. He was placed, not in Newgate – as perhaps had been his intention all along, to be close to Edward – but in Broadstone instead. There was no rescue, just as there was no surgeon attending unless you count a butcher who was prepared to watch a man suffer agonies, endure suppuration and lockjaw and refrain from operating, from removing the ball that festered in his chest. Only his lawyer was allowed in and only to make a will.

The day after Neilson's arrest, on the twenty-third day, the Rising began.

I was part of that Brotherhood of United Irishmen but I did nothing.

We were to be swept from the country, like the leavings from a slaughter house. We were not to see Edward, not I, nor Lady Pamela nor any of the Family. We were to leave him to suffer alone, within the grim walls of Newgate Prison.

Seventeen years. We were together for seventeen years. Though he was my Master, I knew him like a Brother.

He was my Brother. Yes.

One day is all we had to pack up, being told to take only the essentials, that all else would be forwarded in time. I tried to make good Edward's correspondence, bring it with us lest any should be lost or fall into the wrong hands.

Lady Pamela and Julia worked through the night, burning letters, stitching others, especially those from her cousin Henriette in Hamburg, into their clothing and quilting papers into the baby's coverlet.

We were escorted to the boat in Dun Leary by Edward's aunts, Lady Louisa and Lady Sarah, and advised to make our way as quickly and as quietly as possible. Many society Ladies, especially those associated with the Government, were also aboard the packet, fleeing the erupting chaos in Dublin. Lady Pamela had an awkward meeting with Lady Castlereagh, the latter not personally disposed to dislike her but politically compelled to shun her.

She fluttered her hand at Lady Pamela, a low tentative signal, as she turned from her on the deck, to join her fellow elegant refugees.

From Holyhead onward, all along the route, in coach houses and inns, we followed in the path of other refugees, landowners and wealthy merchants, fleeing the Rebellion in Ireland. The news of Edward's arrest greeted us afresh at each stop, different versions, sometimes spoken of with spite or glee but more often with a restrained sympathy. Lady Pamela's baby was stricken with fever, and veered between a state of agitated distress, crying without solace for miles and miles as the carriage jogged over the bumpy road before succumbing to a pale drowsy state that caused great alarm in all who saw her.

We arrived at the Duchess's house in London, a house thronged with all of Edward's old friends who had congregated there to bemoan his situation — and do nothing for him — to find a muted welcome for Lady Pamela and her small party of children and servants. Only Lady Lucy sought her out, embracing her with affection and sharing her distress for a short time. She mentioned her relief at Arthur O'Connor's acquittal in Kent and the pity of the death sentence passed on his travelling companion, Father Coigly. Then she rejoined the Duchess and the gabble of visitors, leaving Lady Pamela to sit apart. I knew their names, his friends of old: Charles Fox, Richard Sheridan, Sir Francis Burdett. Rich men. Men of influence. Men who pleaded with Pitt, the Prince of Wales, the King himself. But men who could do nothing.

THE TRUE NARRATIVE

4th June 1798, London and the Author experiences Death vicariously.

I felt how he died though I was not there. There are things you can feel, without knowing. So it was. Not a dream for I was not asleep but with Lady Pamela, in the same room in London's Harley Street where I'd first met the Duchess some sixteen years before. The same carpet on the floor, the prison of vines and those horned figures, faces fat with malevolence. The sun gave way to nightfall. Lady Pamela sat by the window with her back to me gazing out the darkening window in silence. Just the two of us sitting in silence. And the clock. The clock stood guard, gazing down as minutes spread like mould on bloated hours.

The house was empty, Edward's old friends departed. Mr Ogilvie, the Duchess and Lady Lucy were on their way to Holyhead, hoping to catch a boat to take them to Dublin and on to Edward's prison bedside.

So we sat, Lady Pamela refusing to eat, refusing to go to bed. 'This is my Gethsemane,' she said. 'Je ne donnerai ni sommeil à mes yeux, ni assoupissement à mes paupières.' Ah, she knew also. Not long. Not much longer. I could not leave her. As the hour approached midnight, one of the few remaining candles snuffed out. Lady Pamela's grip tightened on the arms of her chair and she glanced behind at me. Nothing said. Back to our thoughts, his thoughts.

The tangle of flickering vines on the floor tightened. Into the silence the clock hammered out midnight. The blow struck me in my right shoulder, my old scar alight with gunpowder. A fierce burning spread to my neck and jaw. My tongue was huge, swollen. I could not cry out. My body was seized by a convulsion, and I toppled to the floor.

A tightening spread across my chest. Held there and slowly released. The breath fading slowly, a small downy feather falling slowly, swaying, just out of reach.

There's a place between the world of the living and the dead where one might briefly meet another for a last time. I stayed there until Lady Pamela roused me.

'He's gone, isn't he?' Lady Pamela knew. She held a glass to my lips.

Neither of us cried. Not then.

My Beloved Edward. He was the brightest star in the firmament. When he died a light was snuffed in the very soul of me. Lucy FitzGerald

IV

ENDINGS

Miss Harriet Pamela Small, Mrs Wellington, Mrs Marquis, Mrs Hattie, Mrs Bloom, Harriet, Miss Harriet Pamela Small, Fat Harriet Pamela Small, Harriet Pamela Fricker, Hattie Fricker, Sable Songbird, Black Swan, Hattie, Mrs

Mr Anthony Small, Unknown, Rather Citizen, Rather Irishman, United Irishman, Mr Tony Small, Tony Small, Unfortunate black, Poor Tony, Faithful Freeman, Poor black, Faithful Tony, Manservant

We was expecting the Surgeon Heavisides that day in 1804 when *The Visit* happened. Springtime it were and I know that for Ma had placed a jug of daffodils beside Baaba's bed. But instead of that fat gander Heavisides, there stood Lady Lucy on the step of our house in Air Street. No gleaming footman this time, just her in a beautiful coat and beautiful hat, what was got up with flowers and feathers to the side.

Her Ladyship seemed to have an outline that were different to us common people. In the narrow hallway of our house on Air Street, I looked up at her and thought that she shimmered. Sounds fanciful now and maybe it were just down to the way in which the tiny snatch of daylight fell through the narrow half circle above the door, or the fabric of her gown, but she seemed to glow round her edges, like someone not quite real, belonging to a different world.

Ma didn't see the shimmer. She spoke to her in a tight voice, like someone had sewn up her mouth at the edges. Same way she spoke anytime a packet or letter came from Her Ladyship too. Her lips would pleat together like a little pocket purse.

I see that mouth most days now, when I catch a glimpse of myself in the piece of looking glass nailed above my wash stand. Before I have a chance to rearrange my face. I may have my Baaba's nose – to which I am finally accustomed – and his hair, still dark and full when not pulled back tight at my neck, and some taint of his complexion – though lighter I hope, having spent years applying everything from lemon juice to almond emulsions to Beetham's Pomade – but my mouth is my mother's even if were not always so.

But I've done it again. Like one of them dripping honeycombs what they sell in the market, my head is full of sticky holes. And I have wandered off from where I started and the story I wanted to tell. Of Lady Lucy's visit. I were a little fledgling then, forever darting my head from the nest looking about me, listening. Oh yes, always listening. Even so, I cannot say for certain how much of what plays out in my head, I were actually privy to. Maybe Ma told me some after. And I must confess that my imagination can always fill in what's missing. I do hold with a little colour in a story.

I like to imagine Sir Thomas Foley's carriage easing down Piccadilly; and inside Lady Lucy, his wife of two years, travelling alone, looking out as the carriage turned onto Air Street. Was she surprised at how respectable the street appeared. What would the passers-by – the cloaked woman with the heavy basket, the young gentleman in the muddy boots, the button-maker sisters – have made of her should they even have caught a glimpse. Simco, the bookseller, were most likely hopeful when the carriage halted opposite his shop. I expect he were sorely disappointed to see her clamber down the steps and the footman knocking on the door of number ten. I imagine that long moment of pause while the Lady waited to be admitted – no doubt becoming aware of eyes peeking at her – but I fancy she just stared straight ahead at the door. And then it were opened by a little girl, who truth be told were a tad affrighted by the Lady even though she recognised her from months before, but she held the door wider just the same, to allow her in. And the Lady looked down with a lovely smile and said thank you Ettie.

That girl were me. How old was I. I'd say seven or eight though Baaba never mentions my exact birth date in his Narrative. But I remind myself that he were a sick man at that time, trying so very hard to scramble to the end of his History. And all the time Lady Lucy were driving him on. Yes Tony. No Tony. This won't do, Tony. More Tony. Less Tony. No more, Tony.

I stood between her and Ma in the hallway. Looking from Ma's soiled apron to Lady Lucy in her pale blue coat. Pelisse, that's what Ma called it later. At the time though she just pinned her hands tightly in the cord of her apron in front of her like she was afraid they'd do something without her say so. They were raw-looking, like two skinned rabbits.

He is doing his very best, Milady. Ma spoke in her tight voice. The one she used to keep from saying too much. He's not been all that well, you know.

Lady Lucy was sad. Her face said so, the way it tilted, and her eyes became kind. She murmured something in a soft voice, too soft for me to catch.

But you don't know what it costs him to write, Ma said. Even sitting up leaves him breathless. Come, see him for yourself, why don't you.

I darted into Baaba's room ahead of them, as Ma asked if she could relieve her of her coat.

Baaba, it's the Lady come to see you.

He must have heard all the commotion in the hall for he were already pulling himself upright in the bed, and that always led to coughing, loud as the scraping of a burnt pot. Sometimes too there were blood, spitty blots, but not then. By the time Lady Lucy rustled through his doorway – still in her hat and coat, all wrong for the room with its soft pretty colour and ruffles – his chest had settled a bit.

He spoke quietly. Your Ladyship. Please. You should not come close.

Her face lit with alarm, and she looked about her but Ma paid her no heed and pulled over the chair what Baaba usually sat on for his writing, the one under the desk by the window. The beautiful desk of patterned wood, what I loved so much. But the chair I think were ordinary enough. Perhaps too ordinary compared with what she were used to, for she hesitated until Ma urged her to sit and to make herself comfortable. I sat on the edge of Baaba's bed.

Your daughter is lovely, Julia. She looks like her father of course, but I think she has your eyes.

I were pleased with this, and smiled at her but Ma just lifted her eyebrows. She were never one to be swayed by soft remarks.

You'll remember she was named for Lady Pamela.

But is she not Ettie? The Lady looked round at Ma.

Harriet Pamela. Ma's voice were firm again.

Ah. That was … good of you.

Baaba was looking at Ma, his face creased with all the thinking he were doing.

No, Your Ladyship, he said, we were honoured that she should have her name.

Ma smiled at that. A nod and a smile.

Lady Lucy seemed more comfortable too. She said as how Lady Pamela were fortunate to have had Ma and Baaba when she decided to leave England.

Decided. Ma repeated the word and started to mutter under her breath, something about little choice in the matter, but Lady Lucy must not have heard for she turned to Baaba instead and placed her delicate hand on his arm.

Tony, I am sorry you have had this ague. I trust you are feeling better.

Yes, indeed Milady. Much improved. Baaba's smile were most reassuring. I shall be up and about in no time.

I knew that weren't so. Ma's hands began twisting again and her mouth flattened into a thin line. Will you take some refreshment? she asked.

The Lady started to shake her head.

It's tea you'll have, or chocolate. I knew that tone of Ma's. I could not have said no to that voice.

Tea would be perfect. Lady Lucy glanced over her shoulder at Ma as she left, marching like a soldier. Baaba smiled at her.

I am sorry if my visit has caught you off guard.

Baaba coughed, and the Lady pulled back, busying herself with a brocade bag that hung from her wrist.

I have brought some of your money. Ten guineas.

He coughed again, and grappled with a kerchief. Oh no, I thought. Don't let there be blood. Red on white. That'll frighten the Lady.

Baaba, I whispered.

Tony, the Lady said. You really must not trouble yourself with writing while you're unwell.

Thank you, Milady.

No one spoke for a moment.

In the distance I could hear Ma in the kitchen, banging the pots or spoons or perhaps it was a tray that she slapped down. I wondered if I should go and help her, but couldn't leave, couldn't take my eyes off the Lady.

She looked about the room and her feelings tripped back and forth across her face and I could guess what she thought, how the place appeared to her. The narrow bedstead and its patchwork cover – though that were Ma's work, nothing to be ashamed of. Bare wood floors, none of your fancy Turkey rugs, not there, in Air Street. I saw her glance at the scratched rosewood table sitting so snug under the tiny bow window and she rose from her seat to look at the shuddering street traffic outside. She ran a gloved finger over the inkstand (a present from Lady Pamela), and picked up Baaba's quill, before dropping it back in the pot where it tilted and turned for a time. A single sheet of paper, sitting in the centre of the table, snagged her wandering attention. Baaba struggled to see what she were doing, so I told him how she were looking at one of his inked papers. He sank back again at that.

And then she moved away from the window to the cosy fireplace, her back to us. She leaned towards one of the pictures hanging there. Not the strange painting of wobbly houses in Hamburg that Baaba loved. It were the small oval portrait of Lord Edward. She stopped and stared at it and she hissed. Yes, she hissed. Not something I made up nor ever forgot.

I never knew … How did it come to be in your possession? Without asking, she plucked it from the wall, her fingers tracing over the image of her brother's face.

Lady Pamela gave it away … to you?

I were quite frightened by her, more so when she turned and held it out to Baaba. Her face were like a child's, boiling with fury, her gaping mouth scarcely able to form the words.

Had … had she so little regard for him by then. Had she lost all sense of herself, of him … How could she. How—

The door opened, interrupting her temper. It were Ma. I were most relieved to see her. Baaba didn't seem to know what to say to the Lady, nor how to calm her down. But Ma … she just said, Excuse me, Milady, in her firmest voice, the one she used for the old fishmonger, Mr Kennet, when he tried to slip her last week's catch. And firm as anything she put the tray down on top of Baaba's writing. Then spoke low and very clear. It were thrilling. She told the Lady how the miniature was indeed a gift from Lady Pamela.

She commissioned a copy especially for Mr Small on our departure from Hamburg. When she could no longer afford to keep us on. Even so, she were most generous, knowing how much it would mean to him, to have the miniature copied for him after he had served poor Lord Edward for so long and so faithfully.

Ma's hands were planted on her hips. She kept her voice low.

You'll excuse me for saying this but it's a terrible thing to hear you talk of Lady Pamela so – that you might think she would part with her only memento of her Dear Husband, whom she spoke of always as the only true love of her soul.

Julia, please. I'm sure Lady Lucy meant nothing – Baaba coughed loudly.

Ma curled her lip. Oh really? She meant nothing? She turned back to Lady Lucy who were looking ever so flustered. Do you know, that when Lady Pamela sent His Lordship's picture to the miniaturist to be copied, she wept all that day, and fretted for the following week lest something should happen to it. Excepting that week, there wasn't a day went by when she did not look at his portrait. Not one day all the while we lived in Hamburg. Not even after she married that man, Pitcairn.

And then Ma were crying, great blubby tears falling down her face. And that set me off. Ma, please don't cry.

But Ma were still at sixes and sevens over Lady Lucy. Couldn't stop at that point.

How can you say she had no regard for him? Is that why you hardly wrote to her, rarely answered her letters—

Julia, enough. You must stop. Baaba's voice were scratchy but it worked. Lady Lucy flopped down in the little chair, and began to cry, but hers were a dainty sniffy kind of tears. Ma sank on to the edge of the bed, shaking, one hand plucking the coverlet. Baaba laid his hand over hers, squeezing gently. The other arm were wrapped tight about me, and I buried my head in his chest. Such comfort in the warmth and beat of it.

After a time, Lady Lucy stopped her crying. The room were so quiet I could hear the wheezing calls of the oyster woman outside on the street. And the sound of Mr Simco, dragging his book barrows back into his shop opposite. I knew the hour were late then.

Forgive me, Lady Lucy said, and her lovely eyes were creased with sadness. The miniature lay idly in her hands.

Baaba asked Ma if he could have his tea. She got up, brushed down her apron and busied herself with the tray while the Lady leaned forward to my father.

I did not mean to imply that you should not have had a picture – perhaps the family should have thought of that at the time.

A short hmm came from Ma but she did not speak.

Baaba spoke instead, and his voice carried all the might of his stories' endings. She loved him dearly, Milady. You must not doubt it.

I expect you're right. Perhaps I thought too much about my own misery when he died.

She rustled up from her chair, moving slow like she were sleep walking and replaced the miniature on the nail.

And then they had their tea party. Lady Lucy removed her hat. Ma were a bit clattery with the cups so she asked me to hand the tea cup to Her Ladyship who also accepted a plate of plum cake. I tried out another little dip of a curtsey. I were getting better at it.

Thank you Ettie. Harriet, she said with her Lady smile. I remember you when you began to walk, out in the stables in Kildare. You used to hold a few strands of hay up to the horses. They were such …

She searched for something. She were missing a word. We all waited for her to find it. But instead of a word she said how those days in Kildare still shone in her mind. I think I have never been happier, she said. Nor ever will.

But Your Ladyship is not long married? Ma poured some more tea for Baaba.

Lady Lucy smiled again. But it were a sad smile. I think it is a different kind of happiness I share with my dear husband. What I mean is that in Kildare there was excitement, and adventure, and … passion.

She stopped, flustered once more.

What's passion, I asked.

Ma and Baaba didn't answer. Then Lady Lucy rolled her eyes. Oh heavens I cannot seem to say the right thing. I felt useful, involved in something more than balls and visits to galleries. I loved the intrigue. I especially loved defying all their expectations. And none more so than Mr Ogilvie's. He did not approve of my Nationalist ways. I think that every time I went to Castletown with Pamela, dressed in the democratic way – you remember Julia, our hair short, all those green cockades – I secretly hoped that the outrage we caused would get back to Ogilvie. Give him pause for thought. Cut through all his complacent certainty.

She laughed. And Ma as well before she said, you two never did see eye to eye.

Are you not reconciled then, Baaba asked her.

Oh yes. My marriage to Sir Thomas set all his fears to rest. My dear stepfather must have heaved a great sigh of relief to have me off his hands. And I suspect my mother felt the same, though she would never say so. I think I gave her much cause for concern.

Ma whispered to me to gather up the cups and put them carefully on the tray. No one spoke as I did this so it seemed to me I were making a fearsome racket. And then more noise outside, the lamplighter dragging his ladder to the post. A long, ragged scraping sound. I listened to his footsteps, heavy on each rung, and waited for the light to bloom again in the dark outside. Some spilled into the room, making it softer.

Ma were talking now, saying something about the Kildare days, how they was so happy for her too. All that talk of happiness made everyone sad and quiet.

What was it like after, in Hamburg. Lady Lucy asked.

Ma spoke in a slow voice. Sad. Lonely. Always the worry about money.

And Lady Pamela ...

It's her I'm talking about. Ma looked like one of them terrier dogs, with its back up. Started speaking ever so quick. Sure she'd nothing. And only Pammie left to her. Not enough that the Duchess should take their boy, Eddy, but to make her part with little Lucy as well, and her sick with grief, why I—

But the children are better off where they are, with my mother and sister. They have everything—

Yes, yes. But she could have cared for all of them if Lord Edward's family had seen fit to provide what was right and proper for his widow. You cut her off. Sure didn't Hamburg suit you all just fine, far away, out of sight and nothing but dribs and drabs of monies coming from—

Baaba coughed, like the sound of wet cloths slapped against the stone sink.

And all of them was saying sorry, sorry, though Baaba only managed to gasp the words. This time though there was blood, spoiling the white of his sheet, and staining the edge of the quilt, as Ma pressed a rag around his mouth. Lady Lucy stood up, speaking in a worried rush.

I'm sorry Tony, Julia. I've kept you too long. She looked about her as though wishing her carriage would appear in the room.

But just so you know, it wasn't true about us not writing. We wrote. But then when she married Mr Pitcairn ... and so soon after Edward ... I thought she'd found a new life with a new husband. That she'd left us and all that happened behind. But not the children, I knew how desperate she was ...

Ma said she could stop now. That there'd been more than enough said and Lady Lucy, said yes, yes, she really must leave.

Ma and she moved to the doorway. No, no, you must not apologise, Ma said, like she meant it.

I probably deserved your tirade. Lady Lucy tucked her shimmery blue arm under Ma's grey woollen one and leaned in to her, like they was the best of friends. Her blue eyes were round and shining, her voice soft again.

I found it a relief to be able to talk of him and those days with you who were there, who knew him so well. I think I'd forgotten how they were together. How Pamela doted on him.

She turned to wave back to Baaba and spoke loudly so he might hear her.

Do you know that Lady Pamela wrote to us about your return to England, to ask for help with your passports. And she mentioned that Julia might seek work as a Femme de Chambre.

Ma cocked her head to one side, like one of them starling birds what strut about the yards after the hens' scraps. Yes. Why not. I did the work of three Lady's maids.

Perhaps it's as well you didn't, for she also mentioned that she thought you would be unsuited for the role with anyone other than her. On account of ... your impertinence. I'd forgotten what it was like with you – until now.

Baaba's chest began to heave. There'll be blood again I thought, pressing a clean cloth into his hand. But no. Laughter, which turned to another coughing fit. Ma did not look pleased.

Impertinent. Then you won't be surprised that I ask you now for the monies owing to Mr Small.

Ma counted the ten guineas back into the cloth purse that Lady Lucy had left with her. It were pretty, patterned with roses. Ma pulled it tight and slid it into her apron pocket, and stroked it as she might stroke a dog. Or sometimes my hair. She followed Lady Lucy outside onto the street. I watched from Baaba's window which I'd opened, just a crack. It were shadowy dark out there, but the Lady stood under the glow of the lamp and turned to Ma and bent her head close to say something. I only heard some of it.

... the wrong time for such a Narrative, Mr Ogilvie has said as much. There'd be little interest in such a book what with the war going on with France ... talk of rebels and revolutions most ill-judged ... You do understand Julia ... Julia.

Ma's chin dropped down. She never spoke, just folded her arms across her chest. She did not look up to see the coachman drop the steps and open the door, just stood there head down. I heard the click of hooves, the clink clank of harness and buckles, the creak of Her Ladyship's boots on steps, the door snapping shut, click, whip and off they went in a rumble and clip. Away.

Ma were so quiet as she washed the plates and cups. She didn't even splash the water nor bang them on the counter. I thought it best to stay quiet too, and knew better than to mention Lady Lucy. But Ma it were who said the name first. Said how Lady Lucy did not want any more of Baaba's writing. That he should stop. That's why she'd come but seeing how poorly Mr Small was, she'd thought it best to say nothing. Better that I should tell him. Better for all if Mr Small simply stopped.

So, says Ma, flapping her damp cloth about, rubbing first the counter then the potato pail then wiping some crumbs from my mouth, while I tried to pull away. So, off she sails in her carriage, leaving me to do her dirty work and tell my poor Tony.

When will you Ma, I whispered. When will you tell him.

I won't. I can't. Her voice had shrunk. And nor shall you, mind. Perhaps I'll tell him not to bother himself over all the writing. But not that they don't want it. Sure how could I tell him that.

After *The Visit*, Baaba's writing got smaller and smaller. I saw how his pen struggled to stay on the page, how the ink began to run in places, as did his thoughts. Not long after, Ma were begging him, to please, please stop. He called me to him, asked me to take up his pen. I were eager to do things for him, a dutiful girl. (Thank God I did not grow to be a dutiful woman. Such women end up with nothing.) I sat on the little chair what Baaba himself had made when he were well. I sat neatly, and quietly for a time at least, with the paper resting upon a box on my lap, the pen set in my hand, a pot of ink by my feet, waiting to capture the words, to pin them with my nib. Being so young I could not tell what to set down and what to leave out. I expect I missed some of what were said as my hand were not the swiftest and I so wanted to get the words right. Poor Baaba had to interrupt himself to spell out letters for me. So there are but six or so pages for all the hours I spent with him, and the meaning is not always clear to me. Looking at them words now, all jumbled and out of place, I feel sad. Seems to me that's the way most of us go, the end of our lives unravelling like a bolt of ragged cloth.

These be the last words of Mr Anthony Small of Number 10, Air Street as recorded by his daughter Harriet Small this day: 6th April 1804.

My Name is Tony. I am not Tony. The name was not given to me but I made it mine. Good girl Ettie. Always so good. Look after your mother. I did not always look after those I loved. Tried. With you. With Edward. Saved him. Pulled him from a heap of bodies. Never forget the sounds of after. Men moaning, crying out. Smell of blood like rotten meat, and flies. So loud, in my ears. A thousand heartbeats, sawing, sawing. Sorry Ettie. Keep writing. Saved one though I wanted only to run. And hide. Keep hiding. Dig a hole so deep I might find only darkness.

In my mind is darkness. My brother. Yes Ettie. My name is Tony. My real name was left where green rivers open wide and the sun drops in the ocean ...

You smell that? Fish drying. I see them, hanging in the sun, silver winking, flies clustering. Clustered on Edward too.

Got Edward instead of my brother.

You don't worry 'bout it, Ettie. Is a story.

Once there were three. And they was close like a family but not. Two boys and a girl. Had no family. And they were in darkness. There are places Ettie and men ... so cruel. Take you from family and family from you. And mothers are taken from the dark place when they grow cold. Smells I cannot describe. Put down the word. Hell. My mother taken up to the light, to a square of light. But not gentle. They were rough with her. And I left in the dark. A dark that never stayed still, heaved up and down. Was never quiet, but a moaning dark, a slapping dark.

No. I don't know my father. Just the word. Baaba. And a smell of grass or leaves. Or earth. That's all.

My brother and Minda.

Was love.

Was just the two. And me. I also loved.

Her face was a bird in flight. Glossy winged.

Her laugh was water running on stones.

She was love.

Yes like you. Like your Ma. Before your Ma.

Day came we knew this was the now. Minda she can't wait no longer, else it be too late. She so full now. My brother's child. Couldn't stay when there was a chance. Others had gone. Bingham's plantation. Carson's place. Word travelled down those tracks like cool breezes. Seemed almost easy. So we was told. Thought we could just leave. Early. Birds still quiet, hunkered in the night. Got to the river. Planned to follow it east. The British were east. Watch for the silver rising. Staining the water, hard and cold. Then go.

We moved quiet. Loudest thing was within us. Beating breathing. Even my eyelids, blinking, snapping open. Minda was slow. Her belly was large. Kept stopping to hold herself. Not her fault, nor anyone's. What's that noise dogs make? Not barking. Not quite. Heard it. Distant. Like in a dream before waking. Not sure. Keep going. Closer. No question.

Funny. Wasn't even the old Master, nor his dogs. Just plain misfortune. One of those raggedy Militia bands. Hunting for food, or redcoats or runaways.

Cross the river. My brother says. Take Minda.

My brother so strong.

Through the swamp. I'll continue this side he says.

Let them come to me. Cross further on.

Lose them. Meet further upriver.

So, we cross.

Water has weight. Good as chains.

Minda slow, her belly large.

Every step heavy. Water drags like chains.

Hot. Air thick. So slow.

A sound.

Horses' hooves in water.

We crouch. Me. Minda.

The ground sucking beneath. Minda panting.

A shout. Who?

My brother shouts, Run.

My brother says, take Minda.

Swamp lifts with hidden birds. An explosion of birds.

Flapping. Screeching.

My brother's voice. Run.

And he's running towards us, through open water.

Unchained by the weight of it. Running.

The water parting for him ahead of the horse.

Ahead of the man sitting astride the horse, his sabre rising.

Bright shining movement.

A sword shining in sunlight.

Run.

I spring.

Running on water, flying across the water.

My hands will drag him down.

Set the horseman in my sights.

My finger steady on the trigger.

Draw the bowstring taut. Smell the musk of feathers.

My arrow will fell him.

Unleash arrows, bullets, myself.

Did I?

So many times. Over and over. Thought of it, dreamt it.

Saw him, arms wide.

Saw Minda beside me, panting.

Saw time hauled in slow as an anchor, hand over hand.

But each time ends the same

My brother's arms are raised. The sword above is raised.

He is the Christ, pierced by the sword.

The water, the foul water, mixing red.

Churned by the stomp and rearing of the horse.

The air is lashed by the horse's shrieks.

By the horseman's grunts, by my brother's silent fall.

The water cleansed by his blood.

My hands stained by his blood.

Rest of it washed down river rusting the stones for a time, then gone.

Cold.

My bones are cold. What month now? April? You sure? There's no sun.

Just fire. Julia kindled it. Kindled me with love.

My Julia. Put this down on that paper while I can still hold the memory. I first saw her when she came to look after Edward. Baby Eddy. Yes another one. Her first day. Standing by the fireplace. Like a cornered fox. Her father not long dead. Would not sit down.

Does she understand me? Lady Pamela asked.

But Edward, he smiled at her, led her to the chair.

Said, You are most welcome among us. Fáilte. Julia.

Julia. Summer and winter. Pale and fiery. Small and strong.

Filled with the passion of a thousand wrongs. Raging at her mother's passing in childbirth. Despising the Militia who killed her father. Hating the word slave. Don't speak of it. I will close my ears to such talk. No man can make a beast of another.

She loved him first though. Edward.

The way everyone did. He was a flame to every moth.

I had to work harder than he, do more than smile at her and lead her to a chair.

What was I saying? Your Ma? Her hair the colour of cedar.

She was an arrow. Smooth, straight and deadly sharp. Her words could kill me.

But she have her softness too. Her feathers. I used to beg her. Show me your feathers Julia. Your downy ...

No Ettie. Not tears. Just the fire is smoking. Let me rest. Come back later.

When the river turn red Minda grew weak.

She tell me to leave.

Leave this swamp. Leave me.

I want to leave this sticky gnawing heat.

You must come, now.

She's heavy. She wants to stay. Cannot leave him.

He's gone.

The blade opened him and the water found him.

Washed his heart out. The river has taken him.

Her face is closed. The wings have folded. Come. They may be back.

Still her face closed, her lips pressed tight. Hands across her belly.

I cannot leave her. My arm is around her, pulling her through brackish water. Her skirts sodden, heavy with water. On. Keeping on. Through the folding of wings, settling of leaves, stilling, stilling. Slipping sun spilling blood on muddied pools. Minda's breathing louder. Gasping through her teeth held tight. Just as we clear the swamp, she cries out.

I think of dogs, guns, running, the water rusting red. My heart pierced. Wet, sweat. Blood running on Minda's legs, staining the wooden beads she wears on her ankle. She as good as shackled to me. I to her. The blade of the moon hovers. Seems it will cleave us.

Wanted to be my brother. Not the one who hid. Wanted to be my brother, who gave Minda her babe, who drew the dogs and men on himself to save Minda. And me. Who gave himself to the sword. No saving him.

I saved Edward. Would have died without. Did that right. First time anyway. Couldn't save him twice. Kept from him. The grey walls, foul smells. Felt it. The pain in his shoulder. The rage of it. His darkness.

Alone is a cold dark place.

No square of light above. It's the dark woods, it's distant barking. A putrid smell. Your body betraying you. It's a woman who refuses to scream.

Face a ropey knot.

Hands between her legs.

Cannot come here. Cannot come now.

Teeth clamped, no cry.

No nurse. Just an ignorant boy.

But can't keep the babe inside. Comes with the dawn.

Frightening, slick with blood and life.

Slippery with life. Sucked it from Minda.

A desperate grappling thing.

Grappling for her mother's breast. Desperate to suckle.

And Minda refusing, refusing.

To recognise, to name, to feed.

Her face turned from me. The babe's hand at her breast. A girl. She would not give her a name. If she had a name, she'd need love and she scarce had even milk for her. If she died and had no name then maybe she never lived. She had no tears for her. Nor for him.

I was not him. Not my brother. I was his shadow in the daylight. Couldn't do nothing. The shelter collapsed, the fire gave no heat at night. The berries were bitter to her, the butchered cottontail too bloody, the journey cakes were dirt in her mouth. I was not him. We was shadows both. Saw no one and no one saw us. Sometimes a house. A fence. Kept moving but slow as shadows. She trailed after me, the babe bound to her. She not bound to me. Day I came back to her resting place, holding a quail by its leather legs, thinking this I will roast and she will taste it. Her face will open as she licks her fingers. The sun was near full high then.

And she was gone.

Baby gone.

Just a scatter of beads on the ground. The string torn. Useless.

I searched. Circled like a hawk. More like a rabid dog. This way, that. Calling her name. Fearing to call.

Hissing it.

Minda. Minda.

Breeze took the name from me.

Took her from me. Left me in shadow.

No, stay. Dear Ettie. What's that? A moth? Perhaps.

Not a shadow then. I was a moth. Moving at night. Hiding. Folding into shadows.

Couldn't help but see her. Back there in Carolina. Everywhere. She was everywhere. Saw her often, a figure running among trees, a crouched animal, a wattle bush at dusk. And I feared finding her. Dreaded her dead eyes. Heard the baby too, its fierce cry in the night, the lonely keening of nameless creatures. Long after too, in London, I'd see someone, a woman with a certain walk, a way about her that showed she knew herself, and my breath would leave me, that moment between the turning of her head and the meeting of eyes; not her, not her eyes and my body filling again with air.

Good girl Ettie. Should have written Lady Lucy's story for me. I was stupid with words. Didn't see how they could be used. Say this, mean that. Leave in, leave out.

You know she asks me once, do I think O'Connor loves her. I want to say can't you read his face. Can't you see his eyes move over you but they don't see you. Don't stay with you. You just something for now. He has no later. But I say I'm sorry Milady. I can't tell. Some people just listen to words and don't read faces. I could read them sideways. Never looked straight on. You can tell a lot by seeing sideways.

Lady Lucy must have learned though that what you hear isn't always true. She wanted her own story. Wanted Edward to be a fool. A soft-hearted fool. A dupe for unprincipled friends. Not a soldier who had killed in battle. Nor a major who had led men in Canada. Nor a man who spoke against the Government in parliament – though they rounded on him he would not back down. He could not back down. Not with all the planning. Meetings in Paris, Hamburg, London. Not with all the travels around the country, to groups of men arming themselves, pikes and guns. Urging them on. He would never back down. The most loyal of men. He would not leave a brother to die in the river. He would not have run but would have risen from his hiding place and shouted take me. He would not have lost his brother's wife. He gave up his name. Called himself Citoyen. He never tried to be anyone but himself. His loyalty was a pistol in his enemies' hands.

A good man. A brother. Said I was his brother. Always said I saved him. Faithful Tony. Said he loved me. Could say things like that. Not me. Though I learned to say it to Julia. To your mother. Not enough. Call her. Must tell her.

So ends the last words of Mr Anthony Small. As writ by Ettie Small.

Did he talk like that. It don't seem familiar. I thought he spoke as he wrote. But time makes mysteries of those who once was close to us and liars of those we hardly knew. And he were near his end then.

I remember Surgeon Heavisides's last visit to Baaba. Tried to bleed him again. Had the lid off the jar in a quick swipe. Baaba said no. But he already had his fat fingers in the jar, and took out an oily handful.

Ma said, did you not hear my husband. No more of those.

The doctor were flustered by Ma's tone. He sucked in air. Said as how there were little else to be done and he shook them leeches back into the jar. He told Baaba he could visit his rooms on the next occasion. Only half a florin, he said but I saw that the hand he laid on Baaba's shoulder were gentle. So were his voice when he said he was sorry to Ma.

I expect he were also a little shamefaced, as well he might be. The fat camphor-stinking gander.

We sat with him as his life began to slip away, though I had no understanding that he would go, and even less understanding of the torments of his mind. Ma tried to quieten him down when words fluttered from his mouth. She told me I must stop scribing else all them words, words, words would drain the life out of him. But Baaba said no, Julia, no, let the girl be. Let her write these words while you are beside me to hear them. You Julia, my wife. You saved me, not Edward. Yours are the only eyes I could look at since …

Ma cried saying he must stop his nonsense but Baaba begged her to look at him. So she wiped her eyes with her sleeve, smoothed back her hair from her face, knelt beside him and took his hands in hers and they held each other's gaze in a way what pains my heart all these years later.

Suaimhneas. Save your breath, please, she did say. Don't torment yourself so. And she dipped a cloth in water, and passed it gently over his lips then rubbed a balm of rosemary and mint on his chest.

I listened to his whispers, which did not sound like his voice, but seemed to come from some far-off place. Or maybe it was the moth in his throat. Back then I had no sense of the world nor of his journey through it. The only names that echo with me now, all these years on, are Edward, Pamela and Lucy. They were my bedtime tales of Lords and Ladies. I fancied I knew them but the truth is I didn't. They was just a mirror to my own imaginings.

When he died, Ma searched for the amulet Baaba used to wear around his neck. Said he'd worn it always during his travels with Lord Edward but that it came from his life before ever he met His Lordship. Baaba took it off some time after meeting Ma. He said how Ma had cast her own spell on him and he no longer needed it. But then he died and Ma were so exercised, searching and searching, saying he must have his amulet for his journey to the other side. I thought it must be something valuable but it were nothing more than a worn leather purse, the size of a small cracknel, on a length of leather cord. Ma found it hanging in his workshop, behind the door. I wanted to undo the stitching, and see what were all sewn up inside but Ma smacked my hand away. Said no. He will take it with him as it is and as it was. Still she let me hold it for a bit, and I sniffed it first, thinking I could smell Baaba, then pressed it between my fingers hoping to guess what were inside. I felt something alright, small and hard and round. May have been a stone, or a shell or even a bead. Who knows.

The parish offered to take him to the plot at the side of St James. Ma said he were Mr Anthony Small and he would be buried in a grave all to himself, not sharing with every whore and pauper in the place. It were Surgeon Heavisides who suggested it. St Mary's of Wimbledon. I expect he were familiar with many churchyards if he lost patients as easy as he lost my father.

Before we left our house on Air Street, Ma packed up all of Baaba's writings and letters and asked Mr Simco to send a note to Manchester Square. A man came, said he were footman to Lady Lucy and he took away the bundle of papers. And Simco took us in. For a time. Ma worked and worked. Ma were that good with a needle. She'd been a mantua maker back before Baaba got ill with the consumption. After he passed, we didn't have time nor money for nothing beautiful. Even Ma's sewing, even that were plain and without colour. No silks, no brocades, no damask. I missed them, the patterns on those brocades, the places they took me in my imagination. I wove stories in my head while tracing the leaves and flowers and running my fingers over the stitching, in threads of brightest blue and yellow, that became fantastic birds from the lands of Africa. But the stories in my head stopped when Baaba passed, when we moved. When Ma stopped taking in silks. Just common cottons, and coarse linsey woolsey. And all of it in greys and browns and dirty white. Ma tried to teach me sewing but I hated it. Everything were darker after Baaba passed. Our candles was tallow stubs or mean rushlights; the cloth were dull and rough; our rooms was narrower, the windows smaller – only four panes of glass in each – and we was at the back of the building overlooking the coachmaker's yard behind with all its noise and clatter and dust, such dust as coated the windows and made it impossible to see more than shadows beyond.

A letter came from Lady Lucy. Simco gave it to Ma. Held it out to her like a gift, his pale bready face almost smiling. Shall I read it to you Mrs Small. It would be my pleasure. I expect that he thought as we did, that the family would finally send on what were owed to Baaba. That even though he had passed, they would do honour to his memory, and the right thing by Ma. I cannot recall exactly what the note contained, except that she were sorry to hear of Mrs Small's loss and wanted us to know that Mr Small was fondly remembered by the family for the devoted service he had shown to their dearest Lord Edward. And that Mrs Small should send the bills and receipts for the funeral to Mr Ogilvie. The rest ... I did not keep the words with me, only the memory of Ma's face as she listened. How it seemed to lose its shape, like an apple on the turn. And Simco's eyes, dark as raisins, lifting from the letter, and resting on Ma's face, and his voice just a murmur saying sorry. I cried though I didn't know why I were crying, just that Baaba were dead and something else were wrong. Ma never cried. I see now she were brave though, not cold.

I never asked Mr Panizzi at the British Library to show me where that terrible Island is, the one what's named for the Devil. My own imagination serves me well enough. Too well. I've heard tales of wild black people there who'd spear a man as soon as look at him. But that could just be a story.

My son Ed, he got seven years on that Island. I said already how I saw him, boarding the *Augusta Jessie*. Chained to the man in front and the one behind. The sad aching smell of him. My son. He almost made it to the end of his term. So I was told long after. But he couldn't make it easy for himself. Spent a lot of his time in chains doing hard labour. Perhaps he tried to escape. And when his freedom was almost in sight, only three months off, he drowned. In Port Arthur. How – I don't know nor ever will. Don't know how he lived those seven years. Just got word from a man who knew a man who'd made it back from there. And he hadn't much to tell me apart from the sad facts of it. He drowned.

I basted him with questions but all he could say was how that's all this other fellow had told him. Made it worse somehow, knowing something, but not enough. Leaves too much for the imagination. And mine creeps up on me in the night, along with that cursed ditty, in the time between the deepest dark and the spill of dawn. I always hate that time. Seems there's just enough waking in the dim light to make all of my fears real and terrifying. I feel the blankets smother me, the weight of the water above me, blocking my nose, my mouth, a bubble, bubble in my ears, and cold like a hard slap on a tiny slippery body surging and eddying in the filthy Thames among bottles and rags and slick busy rats; and the water churns above me, as a strange man runs, dragging bloody water after him, his arms stretched wide as he splashes into the muddy river; and now he floats the same man but not the same, this one's smaller, familiar, his brown eyes open to the heathen sky, to countless unknown stars, his face turning on a wave, his mouth is open, gushing water, gushing words, no Ma don't let them take me, and my throat is gulping hard, hands pushing against the water, reaching, heaving and the blankets tumble to the floor. I never reach him.

I returned to Mr Butler's rooms in Borough. So pleased were he to see me, that he fussed and cleared some papers from a chair and begged me to sit, sit, while he rang his little bell, and called for tea. I don't mind saying I enjoyed his attention.

I was getting a little worried when I had not heard from you, Mrs Small.

I drank the tea, talked what I call soup talk – being light, and having no substance – about my lodgings and being busy and so forth.

And your father's papers? Mr Butler also wanted to get to the main course. What is your opinion of them now you have finished?

I told him straight up, how I were excited, saddened, horrified and angry. And more besides. Even mentioned *Uncle Tom's Cabin*. Do you know it, I asked.

I've not yet had the opportunity to read it but I shall make it my business to do so. Tell me, is your anger still directed against Lady Lucy. I do hope it is not the case.

I told him that I could see her side of things but still ...

He seized on this chink with delight, proceeded to tell me how he'd handled her charitable affairs for many years.

Donations for Famine Relief in Ireland. She never forgot the Irish peasants, he sniffed. Large sums, he insisted. You know, despite what she asked your father to do, I think she really did believe in the same cause as her brother. It was just difficult for her after he died. No one in the family wanted to hear a word of Ireland, or rebellion, especially from a Lady. I think she was rather lonely.

I didn't like that word lonely. It lurked somewhere in my own body, that word did. It's a cold word and one not easily shifted. I shivered then and crossed my arms about me. Mr Butler asked if I'd taken ill.

No, no. Thank you, Mr Butler. Go on.

There are some extra papers here, that she wanted you to have. She instructed me to keep them until you had read your father's papers first. Why not read them at home?

Lady Lucy has left me some of her own papers. Perhaps she thought it might explain something. I'm not sure if it does but it makes me wonder about her.

London, June 1798

An Address to Irishmen and Countrymen

It is Edward FitzGerald's sister who addresses you; it is a woman, but that woman is his sister; she would therefore die for you as he did ... He was a Paddy and no more; he desired no other title than this ... Yes this is the moment, the precious moment which must either stamp with infamy the name of Irishmen and denote you for ever wretched, enslaved to the power of England, or raise the Paddies to the consequences which they deserve and which England shall no longer withhold, to happiness, freedom, glory. These are but names as yet to you, my countrymen. As yet you are strangers to the reality with the power in your hands to realise them. One noble struggle and you will gain, you will enjoy them forever.

Your devoted Countrywoman,
Lucy FitzGerald

Boyle Farm
June 1798

Dear Lucy,

You will not publish this Address. You will not. You will destroy the original draft. If not you will be visiting sedition and scandal upon yourself and ignominy upon this family. You have taken the licentious examples of uncultivated savages as your models in defiance of religion, morality and sentiment. I urge you to be ruled by me in this respect, no matter how it may provoke you. I urge you to consider your mother. Am I also to understand you have sent a letter to Mr Paine and addressed him as Citizen? You will cease these communications.

I have learned that you are easily seduced by false passions but now I hope to make you ashamed of your imprudence. You will observe proper mourning and desist from any public expressions or appearances. You will once more be a dutiful daughter and sister.

Your stepfather,
Mr William Ogilvie

He wishes me silent as my brother's grave.

Fort George, Scotland
20th June, 1802

My Dear Lucy,

We have just received word that we are to be pardoned and released.
A strange pardon. One that says we are banished from Ireland and
England. A transport, the *Ariadne*, will take me and my fellow prisoners
to Hamburg. Thus I may see Lady Pamela there, but will be deprived
of the opportunity to visit you or your dear mother in London. Forgive
the tiny scrap of paper, it is all I possess. I will give it to Jerry O'Leary
who attends on me faithfully still, even in this Godforsaken place. He
tells me Tony is back in London and in some distress. Perhaps you
were not aware of it.

It cheered me to hear you are better. What you say of grief
is true. One does get used to the loss of happiness, though the
melancholy comfort you refer to – that nothing so bad can happen
again – is a poor one indeed. I hope you will find something or
someone to fill the void left by Edward.

Believe me your most affectionate friend,
Arthur O'Connor

I tried to help him. How could Arthur have thought otherwise? I hoped Arthur might fill the void. How foolish. He offered not so much as a word to suggest he would try to return. Nothing. I married Sir Thomas the following month. LLF.

17th June, 1858
A journey to Ireland. Maybe.

I asked Mr Butler to return to the matter of the deeds. Seems my Baaba had been promised a place called the Mill Lands in Kildare. Lord Edward had writ it, not in the will what he scrawled in the prison, but long before. But after all the sadness of His Death, and the snatching of His Estates by the Evil Government, and what with Mr Ogilvie passing and no one being quite sure and people forgetting who was due what, in the way they do, well I suppose it's hardly surprising there were no one keeping track of a promise to a servant. Mr Butler has a way with speeches what can almost make you see the words, spelt out all big and bold, and make you believe his words to be the truth.

I'm sad for Ma now, how she sent that package of Baaba's papers in hope, thinking there'd be something of value in it. That it might bring some money in. But Mr Butler says it were unfortunate timing. With the French Wars carrying on and on, there would have been little appetite for a story about an escaped slave whose master instigated a revolution. He allowed himself a little heehaw at that, before returning to the matter of the parcel of land. Wanted to know how I wished to proceed.

What with all my attention being on Baaba's Narrative, I had given little thought to it.

If I may, that is, if I were to suggest anything at this point, then it would be to consider the matter of ... he paused.

Yes, I urged him on.

The matter of your husband.

I look forward to my visits to Tooley Street. I love the dark of them, the wooden walls, the books, the mess of papers and folders stacked on shelves, his gas lanterns. I like to watch him write. He tilts his head to one side, and his baldy patch gleams as he dips his pen so carefully, tapping it on the side of the well before leaning down to the paper and writing my name. Makes the hairs on my neck stand to hear my name being scratched across the sheet. To think of owning them lands that he puts down on the paper.

He's a cautious man, Mr Butler. Reminded me that though my husband deserted me all them years ago, he too was entitled, legally not morally mind, to those lands. But – he held his hand up to stop my tirade – but it doesn't have to be so. Turns out the Government have just passed a Bill, to make it possible for a woman of business and property, such as myself, and one who has been deserted for so long, also such as myself, to stop another, such as a deserter husband, from trying to get his hands on that to which he has no right. Such as my Lodging House.

So I too will be cautious. Mr Butler will apply to Her Majesty's Court for an Order for Protection of Property. My property. And he tells me I shall be one of the first to make such an application under the new law. Times are changing, he says, and he sounds happy about it.

When the Court sees fit to grant the Order, I may consider applying for a divorce, though Mr Butler advises against this.

It's costly and you may have to appear in court.

So what, I said. I'd be glad to.

But if you don't mind my saying, you've been there before, in – he coughed – vexatious circumstances. And there's the matter of your hue. It may be marked against you. Your husband being an Englishman, he might find the judge sympathetic.

My hue. I'm sorry to hear this, that a judge might take against me on account of it. But I'm not surprised. People presume all sorts, don't they, based on what they see, and all the mean little notions what they hold tight to themselves. Mr Butler says it's the way of the world, but at least I can keep my property. That's progress, he says.

Even so, I'll not use the name Fricker ever again. It's like that brand what Baaba had on his chest. It does not belong to me but ensured I belonged to him, for a time. I will sign myself Harriet Pamela Small even if Mr Butler says it's not entirely legal.

I may take a boat to Ireland, and a coach to Kildare. Or the canal what Baaba mentioned in his Narrative. To the townland of Kilrush and the Mill Lands.

The thought of crossing all that water makes my sleep uneasy.

I'll ask Mr Butler for his advice. And perhaps I might take it. Or perhaps not.

Author's Note

I first encountered the story of Tony Small in Stella Tillyard's 1997 biography of Lord Edward Fitzgerald, *Citizen Lord*. Unlike previous accounts, she highlighted the importance of Tony in Fitzgerald's life, and I became fascinated by him, his life of travel and his time in Ireland. Curiosity became a quest to discover more about Tony, or Mr Anthony Small, as he is listed in the record of wills in Dublin – the last of many iterations of his name. There is no account of his origins or any record of him prior to his rescue of Fitzgerald from the battlefield at Eutaw Springs in 1781. He was a much-travelled man, likely adept in languages, and such an important part of Fitzgerald's life that he is mentioned in the wider family correspondence. He was careful with money, literate, and there is evidence he exchanged letters with Jerry O'Leary, manservant of Arthur O'Connor. He was married to the Fitzgeralds' Irish nursemaid, Julia, and they had two children of their own, clearly named for their employers and friends: Edward, born in Dublin, and Harriet Pamela. When he left the employ of Fitzgerald's widow, Pamela, in Hamburg, Tony set up a business in London and Julia advertised as lady's maid or dressmaker. He also had some entitlement to money from the Fitzgerald family as shown in his letter written in 1803 (National Library of Ireland), when he expressed his fears for his family on account of his illness. Yet he could still afford to engage Surgeon Heavisides, Surgeon Extraordinary to King George III, to attend to him. Tony died in 1804, aged about forty. His children forged their own lives in London; Edward became a customs locker at the bonded warehouses on the Thames and Harriet Pamela, showing both the necessary financial means and gumption, was one of the first women to apply under the new Protection of Property Act in 1859.

Readers who may wish to explore further could start with Tillyard's biography *Citizen Lord, Edward Fitzgerald, 1763–1798*. My novel also refers to *The Interesting Narrative of the Life of Olaudah Equiano, or Gustavus Vassa, The African*, published in 1789, which is widely available online. Though by no means the first, this was one of the most important slave narratives of the 1700s, and Equiano, writer, abolitionist and radical, was a prominent figure in late eighteenth-century London. He also spent much of 1791 in Ireland promoting his book and releasing another edition in Dublin. My article published in *History Ireland*, Vol 28 No. 6 in 2020, 'Every Man is Exactly What He Makes Himself', expands on the life of Tony Small and his family. Further reading on Ireland's relationship with slavery can be found in Nini Rodger's comprehensive book from 2007, *Ireland, Slavery and Anti-Slavery: 1612–1865*.

Throughout the process of research and writing, the characters of this novel stayed with me, inserting themselves onto the page, sometimes loudly as in the case of Harriet, or quietly insistent like Tony himself. I felt a duty of care towards them, to represent them as truthfully as I could, being mindful of the many ethical considerations of fictionalising real people. But research and facts are only part of the story. There are always gaps and in the gaps lie the unknowable of mystery and possibility. This, then, is my own glimpse of the unknowable.

Acknowledgements

Over the years of writing this book I have had wonderful support in many forms. Early on I had the good fortune to meet Eibhear Walshe and Claire Connolly when I approached University College Cork with a proposal for a novel on the life of Tony Small as part of a doctorate in Creative Writing. Thank you both for your early support, and to Eibhear particularly for his supervision and to Clíona Ó Gallchoir and Lee Jenkins for their interest and direction. I am grateful for the award of funding for my doctorate and for having the opportunity to present some of my research on Tony Small at other academic institutions in Ireland and the UK, thereby broadening the knowledge base of black lives in late eighteenth-century Ireland.

Writing may be a solitary pursuit but beyond the time spent on the page, writing has opened up a whole group of writer friends to me, who have been, well, such good friends. I offer sincere thanks to the wonderful Mary Morrissy for her considered reading of the novel and her incisive comments and suggestions. To my two fellow novelists, Fiona Whyte and Madeleine D'Arcy, our novel peer group has been such a source of encouragement as well as endless cups of coffee – thank you. I also wish to thank Mary Reynolds, Mairead Rooney and Sarah Ridout for their reading and commentary when this novel was at an early stage and for their friendship going back to our MA days at UCD. To the fabulous Crawford Writing Group – Anne O'Leary, Eileen O'Sullivan, Lourdes Mackey, Brenda O'Driscoll and Sinead Slattery – thank you. I am so fortunate to have such great friends in Waterfall and in the book club; thank you all for the kindness, interest and the fun we have – discussing books has never been such a lively affair. Beyond the world of books I am indebted to Jennifer Wiltshire, who epitomises the word 'friend' and has always been so.

I am very grateful to Aoife K. Walsh at New Island Books for her interest in this novel and for just 'getting' it, and to the rest of the team at New Island, Caoimhe Fox, Mariel Deegan and Stephen Reid, whom I've only seen onscreen so far. Thanks for that COVID! And also to my agent Faith O'Grady, thank you – the Irish Writers Centre Novel Fair happily brought us all together. Many thanks to Susan McKeever for her steadying editorial hand – it was needed!

I'd like to acknowledge Cork County Council for their bursary, allowing me to attend the Tyrone Guthrie Centre for two weeks. That time out was so important in the writing of this novel. To the staff at the following libraries, archives and record offices, many of whom helped in person as well as online, thank you. In Cork, Boole Library at UCC; in Dublin, the National Library of Ireland (specifically for permission to use a portion of Lady Lucy Fitzgerald's actual Address to the Irish people), Marsh's Library, National Archives of Ireland, the Registry of Deeds, Trinity College Library; in the U.S., the National Museum of African American History and Culture (now that was an unforgettable experience!), St Louis County Library; and in the UK, the National Archives, Kew. I'd like to also acknowledge a text, which contains the song that Arthur O'Connor asks Lady Lucy to play and sing in the novel. It was published in 1795 by James Porter, with the wonderfully self-explanatory title *Paddy's resource: Being a select collection of original and modern patriotic songs, toasts and sentiments, compiled for the use of the people of Ireland*. It's a gem!

Finally my family. They have been so patient and encouraging of my writing and research all these years – even when I cried on finding a photo of Tony Small's granddaughter. This book is in some way a realisation of the efforts of my wonderful parents who from a young age pointed each of their children toward the local library and encouraged my early scribblings. My father is sadly missed but my inspirational mother is still my chief unofficial promoter and my siblings (and great friends), Hugh, Ciara, Dione, Rachel and Maria, have all been tapped in some way for their wide-ranging expertise and experience. And warning! There'll be more of that to come. For my lovely children, Oisín, Liadan, Fionnúir and Tighernán, this novel has taken up a lot of our shared years, and I couldn't have spent them in better company. Luckily they're all adults now and have also been called upon for assistance, opinions artistic and otherwise. Finally to my husband Íomhar, who has been so supportive of my writing in so many ways – all my love.